THE CONFRONTATION

Silver, after watching for a moment, stepped over toward her.

"Listen!" she said firmly. "He's my father just as much as yours. *He was my father first.* We're sisters you know. We can't help that—"

Athalie whirled on her with blazing eyes.

"We're not *sisters!*" She stamped her foot. "I'll never call you my sister. You've no business here! Now I'll give you one day to get out and stay out, and if you don't do it, I'll make *hell* for you . . ."

She lit a cigarette insolently and flung the lighted match full into the face of the other girl, turning with another whirl, and marching down the garden path with her cigarette atilt in her contemptuous red lips . . .

Grace
Livingston
Hill

Tomorrow About
This Time

BANTAM BOOKS · TORONTO · NEW YORK · LONDON

TOMORROW ABOUT THIS TIME
A Bantam Book / published by arrangement with
J. B. Lippincott Company

PRINTING HISTORY
Lippincott edition published in 1923
Bantam edition / June 1978

ISBN 0-553-11762-9

Published simultaneously in the United States and Canada

Chapter I

THE letter lay on the top of the pile of mail on the old mahogany desk, a square envelope of thick parchment with high, dashing handwriting and faint, subtle fragrance.

The man saw it the instant he entered the room. It gave him a sick dull thrust like an unexpected blow in the solar plexus. He had come back to the home of his childhood after hard years to rest, and here was this!

It was from his former wife, Lilla, and no word from her in all the twelve years since their divorce had ever brought anything but disgust and annoyance.

He half turned toward the door with an impulse of retreat, but thought better of it and stalked over to the desk, tearing open the envelope roughly as if to have the worst over quickly. It began abruptly, as Lilla would. He could see the white jewelled fingers flying across the page, the half flippant fling of the pen. Somehow the very tilt of the letters as she had formed them contrived to give the taunting inflection of her voice as he read.

"Well, Pat, the time is up, and as the court decreed I am sending you your daughter. I hope you haven't forgotten, for it would be rather awkward for the poor thing. I'm going to be married in a few days now and wouldn't know what to do with her. She's fourteen and has your stubbornness, but she's not so bad if you let her have her own way in everything. Don't worry, she's the kind that marries young, and she'll probably take herself off your hands soon. I wish you well of your task.—Lilla."

He sat back in the old mahogany chair and steadied his arms on the chair-arms. The paper was shaking in

1

his fingers. Something inside of him began to tremble. He had a feeling that it was his soul that was shaking. Like quicksilver along his veins the weakness ran, like quicksands his strength slid away from beneath his groping feet. He had not known that a man in his prime could be so puny, so helpless. Why, all the little particles of his flesh were quivering! His lips were trembling like an old person's. He was as a frail ship tossed in the trough of great waves. He could not right himself nor get any hold on his self-control. He could not seem to think what it all meant. He tried to read it over again and found the words dancing before his eyes with strange, grotesque amusement at his horror, like the look in Lilla's eyes when she knew she had hit one hard in a sensitive spot.

"His daughter!"

He had not seen her since she was two years old, and had taken very little notice of her then. His mind had been too much filled with horror and disappointment to notice the well-suppressed infant who spent her days in a nursery at the top of the house when she was not out in the park with her nurse. A memory of ribbons and frills, pink-and-whiteness, and a stolid stare from a pair of alien eyes that were all too much like Lilla's to make any appeal to his fatherhood, that was his child, all he could recall of her. Even her name, he remembered bitterly, had been a matter of contention. *Athalie*, the name of a heathen queen! That had been her mother's whim. She said it was euphonious. Athalie Greeves! And she had enjoyed his horror and distaste. And now this child with the heathen name was coming home to him!

He had looked on her as an infant still. He had not realized in the big sharp experiences of the life he was living that the years were flying. It could not be fourteen! He had heard the judge's decree that the child was to remain with her mother until she reached the age of fourteen years, and was then to pass to the guardianship of her father, but he had thought he would not be living when that came to pass. He had felt that his life was over. He had only to work hard enough and fill every moment with something absorbing, and he would wear out early. But here he was, a young man yet, with honors upon him, and new vistas opening up in his intellectual life in spite of the blighted years behind him; and here was this child of his folly, suddenly grown up and flung upon him, as if his mistakes would not let him go, but were determined to drag him back and claim him for their own!

He bowed his head upon his arms and groaned aloud.

Patterson Greeves, brilliant scholar, noted bacteriologist, honored in France for his feats of bravery and his noted discoveries along the line of his chosen profession, which had made it possible to save many lives during the war; late of Siberia where he had spent the time after the signing of the armistice doing reconstruction work and making more noteworthy discoveries in science; had at last come back to his childhood's home after many years, hoping to find the rest and quiet he needed in which to write the book for which the scientific world was clamoring, and this had met him on the very doorstep as it were and flung him back into the horror of the tragedy of his younger days.

In his senior year of college, Patterson Greeves had fallen in love with Alice Jarvis, the lovely daughter of the Presbyterian minister in the little college town where he had spent the years of his collegiate work.

Eagerly putting aside the protests of her father and mother, for he was very much in love, and obtaining his failing uncle's reluctant consent, he had married Alice as soon as he was graduated, and accepted a flattering offer to teach biology in his Alma Mater.

They lived with his wife's mother and father, because that was the condition on which the consent for the marriage had been given, for Alice was barely eighteen.

A wonderful, holy, happy time it was, during which heaven seemed to come down to earth and surround them, and the faith of his childhood appeared to be fulfilled through this ideal kind of living, with an exalted belief in all things eternal.

Then had fallen the blow!

Sweet Alice, exquisite, perfect in all he had ever dreamed a wife could be, without a moment's warning, slipped away into the Eternal, leaving a tiny flower of a child behind, but leaving his world dark—forever dark—without hope or God—so he felt.

He had been too stunned to take hold of life, but the sudden death of his uncle, Standish Silver, who had been more than a father to him, called him to action, and he was forced to go back to his childhood's home at Silver Sands to settle up the estate, which had all been left to him.

While he was still at Silver Sands his father-in-law had written to ask if he would let them adopt the little girl as their own in place of the daughter whom they had lost. Of course he would always be welcomed as a son, but the grandfather felt he could not risk letting his wife keep the child and grow to love it tenderly, if there were danger of its being torn away from them in three or four years and put under the care of a stepmother. The letter had been very gentle, but very firm, quite sensible and convincing. The young father accepted the offer without a protest. In his stunned condition he did not care. He had scarcely got to know his child. He shrank from the little morsel of humanity because she seemed to his shocked senses to have been the cause of her mother's death. It was like pressing a sore wound and opening it afresh. Also he loved his wife's father and mother tenderly, and felt that in a measure it was due them that he should make up in every way he could for the daughter they had lost.

So he gave his consent and the papers were signed.

Business matters held him longer than he had expected, but for a time he fully expected to return to his father-in-law's house. A chance call, however, to a much better position in the East, which would make it possible for him to pursue interesting studies in Columbia University and fill his thoughts to the fuller exclusion of his pain, finally swayed him. He accepted the new life somewhat indifferently, almost stolidly, and went his way out of the life of his little child of whom he could not bear even to hear much.

From time to time he had sent generous gifts of money, but he had never gone back, because as the years passed he shrank even more from the scene where he had been so happy.

He had absorbed himself in his studies fiercely until his health began to suffer, and then some of his old college friends who lived in New York got hold of him and insisted that he should go out with them. Before he realized it, he was plunged into a gay, reckless company of people who appeared to be living for the moment and having a great time out of it. It seemed to satisfy something fierce in him that had been roused by the death of Alice and he found himself going more and more with them. For one thing, he found common ground among them in that they had cast aside the old beliefs in holy things. It gave him a sort of fierce pleasure to feel that he had identified himself with those who defied God and the Bible and went their wilful way. He could not forgive God, if there were a God, for having taken away his wife, and he wanted to pay Him back by unbelief.

They were brilliant men and women, many of those with whom he had come to companion, and they kept his heart busy with their lightness and mirth, so that gradually his sorrow wore away and he was able to shut the door upon it and take up a kind of contentment in life.

And then he met Lilla!

From the first his judgment had not approved of her. From the first she seemed a desecration to Alice, and he stayed away deliberately from many places where he knew she was to be. But Lilla was a strong personality, as clever in her way as he, and she found that she could use Patterson Greeves to climb to social realms from which her own reckless acts had shut her out. Moreover, Patterson Greeves was attractive, with his scholarly face, his fine physique, his brilliant wit, flashing through a premature sternness that only served to make him the more distinguished. When

Lilla found that he not only belonged to a fine old family dating back to Revolutionary times, but had a goodly fortune in his own right, she literally laid aside every weight, and for a time, almost "the sin which doth so easily beset," and wove a net for his unsuspecting feet.

Then, all unaware, the lonely, weary, rebellious man walked into the pleasant net. He read with her for hours at a time, and found himself enjoying her quaint comments, her quick wit, her little tendernesses. He suddenly realized that his first prejudice had vanished, and he was really enjoying himself in her society.

Lilla was clever. She knew her man from the start. She played to his weaknesses, she fostered his fancies, and she finally broke down one day and told him her troubles. Then somehow he found himself comforting her. From that day on matters moved rapidly. Lilla managed to make him think he was really in love with her. He wondered if perhaps after all the sun were going to shine again for him; and he put the past under lock and key and began to smile again.

He and Lilla were married soon, and set up an establishment in New York, but almost from the start he began to be undeceived. The evenings of reading together suddenly began to openly bore her. Lilla had no notion of settling down to a domestic life. Her husband was only one of many on whom she lavished her smiles, and as soon as she had him safely she began to show her true nature, selfish, untrue, disloyal, mercenary, ambitious.

The revelation did not come all at once. Even after their child was born he still had hope of winning her to a simpler, more possible manner of life. But he found that the child was in her eyes only a hindrance to her ambitions and that he was not even that; and when Lilla filled his house with men and women of another world than his, whose tastes and ways were utterly distasteful to him, he began to absent himself more and more from home. This had been made possible by the growing demand for his services as lecturer and adviser in the world of science. So it came about that whenever he received an invitation of this sort he accepted it, until sometimes he would be away lecturing in universities for weeks at a time, or touring the West.

The little Athalie had never meant anything to him but a reproach. Somehow her round blank stare had always sent his thoughts back to the first little one whom he had given away; and he felt a reproach in spite of the fact that he always reasoned it out within himself that he had done well in so doing.

So, at war with himself, he had grown more and more morose, living to himself whenever he was at home; scarcely ever even a figurehead in his own house at the functions which his wife delighted to give to her own gay set. As he grew to understand the true character of his second wife his mind reverted to his old bitterness against a God—if there were a God—who had thrust this hard fate upon him.

So, bitterly and haughtily, he had lifted his proud head and taken the blows of life without comfort. And now he had come home.

He had arrived in the late afternoon, and found the town of Silver Sands much as he left it years ago. There was a new thrifty little stucco station in place of the grimy one of clapboards of the old days, but the old barns and blacksmith-shop were there just as he left them, a trifle more weather-beaten and dilapidated, but doing a thriving business in automobile-tires and truck-repairs.

The old stone church where as a child he went to Sunday-school, and sat beside Aunt Lavinia in the dim pew afterwards, with Uncle Standish next the aisle, and squirmed or slept through a long service, looked just the same, save that the ivy on the tower grew thicker and higher. The graveyard sloping down the hill behind, the Baptist church across the corner— red brick with aspen-trees in front and chalk-marks where the children played hopscotch during the week on the brick walk up to the steps, were unchanged. A little farther on he could see the red brick school-house where he went to school glimmering through the trees, and the old bare playground where he used

to play baseball. There he had somehow bluffed his
way into high school and finally prepared for college.
He had heard rumors of a new high school up in the
new part of town, but the old part where he had lived
his young life seemed almost unchanged.

He had gone into the old house expecting to find
the chill of the long-closed place about it, but the
door had swung open, and the old servitor, Joe Quinn,
with his wife Molly, the cook, had stood smiling at
the end of the hall a little wrinkled and gray, rounder
as to form, more bent; and there in the parlor door
quite ceremoniously had stood Anne Truesdale, an
English woman whom his Aunt Lavinia had be-
friended when her husband died, and who had been
housekeeper since his aunt's death. Her hair was
white and she had lost her rosy cheeks, but her eyes
were bright and her thin form as erect as ever in its
black silk and thin white cuffs and collar. She put out
a ceremonious hand to welcome the boy she used to
chide, with a deference to his years and station that
showed her reverence for him.

"Well, Master Pat," she said, using the old name he
had not heard for years, "So yer come again. Welcome home! It's right glad we are to see ye!"

For the moment it almost seemed as if he were a
boy again coming home for vacation.

He went up to his room and found it unchanged
with the years. He spent a happy moment glancing
over the old pictures of high-school teams that were
framed on his walls. Then he came down to the
dining-room and sat at the wide table alone eating a
supper as like to those of his childhood as the same
cook could make it: stewed chicken with little bis-
cuits, currant jelly from the bushes in the garden,
prune jam and cherry delight from the trees he had
helped to plant, mashed potatoes as smooth as cream,
peas that were incredibly sweet, little white onions
smothered in cream, cherry pie that would melt in
your mouth for flakiness, and coffee like ambrosia.

Shades of the starving Russians! Was he dreaming?
Where was Siberia? Had the war ever been? Was he
perhaps a boy again?

But no! Those empty places across the table! That ivy-covered church down the street surrounded by its white gravestones showing in the dusk! A world of horror in France between! Other gravestones too, and an empty sinful world! Ah! No, he was not a boy again!

He opened the door of the dear old library half expecting to see the kindly face of his Uncle Standish sitting at the desk, and instead, there was the letter!

He had come home for rest and peace, and this had met him! He seemed to hear Lilla's mocking laugh ringing clearly through the distant halls as if her spirit had lingered to watch over her letter and enjoy its reception. It was like Lilla to prepare the setting of a musical comedy for anything she had to do. Why couldn't she have written to ask him what he wanted her to do about the child?

His anger rose. Lilla should not make a laughing-stock of him in any such way. He glanced at the date of the letter and angrily reached for the telephone:

"Give me Western Union!" he demanded sternly, and dictated his telegram crisply:

"On no account send the child here. Will make immediate arrangements for her elsewhere. Letter follows by first mail.   P.S.G."

He hung up the receiver with a click of relief as if he had thus averted some terrible calamity, and sank wearily back in his chair, beads of perspiration standing out on his forehead. It was almost as if he had had a personal encounter with Lilla. Any crossing of swords between them had always left him with a sense of defeat.

He tried to rally and busy himself with the other letters. Two from his publishers demanding copy at once, an invitation from an exclusive scientific society to speak before their next national convention, a call from a western college to occupy the chair of sciences, a proposition from a lecture bureau to place his name on their list in a course of brilliant speakers. He threw them down aimlessly and took up the last letter without glancing at the address. They all seemed so trivial. What was fame to an empty life?

Then he brought back his wandering gaze and read:

"Dear Father:—"

He started. Not for several years had he read a letter beginning that way. Athalie had never written to him. He had not expected it. She was Lilla's child.

But this was from Alice's child. The writing was so exactly like her girl-mother's that it gave his heart a wrench to look at it. She had not written him since he had married Lilla. Well, it had not mattered. She did not belong to him—never had. He had given her away. He had always felt her childish little letters full of stilted gratitude for the gifts he sent were merely perfunctory. Why should she care for him? She could not remember him. He had been rather relieved than otherwise because he had a troubled feeling that they entailed more than a mere check at Christmas and birthdays. And now after several years' silence she had written again! Strange that both his children should have been suddenly thrust upon his notice on this same day! He read on:

"I suppose you received the word I sent while you were abroad that Grandfather died of influenza last November right in the midst of his work. Grandmother has been slipping away ever since, though she tried to rally for my sake. But two weeks ago she left me, and now I am alone. I sent a letter to your foreign address, but I saw in the papers today that you had landed and were going to Silver Sands, and a great longing has come over me to see my father once before I go to work. I am not going to be a burden to you. Grandfather had saved enough to keep me comfortably even if I did nothing, but I have, also secured a good position with a very good salary for a beginner, and I shall be able to care for myself, I think, without at present touching the money that was left me.

"Grandmother said something a few days before she died that has given me courage to write this letter. I have always felt, and especially since you married again, that you did not want me or you would not have given me to Grandmother, and of course I don't want to intrude upon you, although I've always been very proud of you and have read everything I could find in the papers about you. But one day two weeks ago Grandmother said: 'Silver,'—they always called me Silver, you know, because they wanted to keep the Alice for Mother,—'Silver' I've been thinking that perhaps your father might need you now. After I'm gone perhaps you better go and see.'"

"So, father, I'm coming! I hope you won't mind—"

Patterson Greeves suddenly dropped the letter and buried his face in his hands with a groan which was half anguish, half anger, at a Fate which had suddenly decided to make him a puppet in the comedy of life. He was like one under mortal anguish. He kicked the heavy desk-chair savagely back from under him, and strode to the window like a caged animal. Staring out with unseeing eyes at the calm dusk of the evening sky across the meadow, he tried to realize that this was really himself, Patterson Greeves, to whom all this incredible thing was happening. Horrible! Impossible!

He sensed that somewhere back in his soul was a large engulfing contempt for himself. This was no attitude, of course, for a father to have toward his children. But then they had never really been his children in the strict sense of the word, and nothing had ever been right in his life. Why should *he* try to be? It was all God's fault, if there were a God—taking Alice away! None of these unnatural things would ever have happened if Alice had lived! And now God was trying to force him back to the blackness of his ruined life again after he had in a measure gained a certain hard kind of peace.

He flung his head up defiantly toward the evening sky, as if he would vow that God should make nothing from him by treating him so. He was master of his fate no matter how "charged with punishment the scroll." God! To dare to be a God and yet to treat him so!

Chapter II

The old Silver place stood back from the street just far enough for privacy and not far enough to seem exclusive.

The General Silver who built it in Revolutionary times had been a democratic soul, and his sons who had followed him were of like mind. The last grandson, Standish Silver, now sleeping in the quiet churchyard just below the bend of the hill, was the friend and counsellor of every one in the village, his home alike the rendezvous and refuge of all classes. Perhaps it was the habit of the house through the long years that had given it that genial attitude, wide-spread and welcoming as it stood among its trees and old-fashioned shrubs, with the same dignity and gentleness of bearing it had worn in the days when its owners were living within, as if it had a character to maintain in the name of the family, though all its immediate members were gone.

There were many newer houses in Silver Sands that boasted modern architecture, and in their ornate and pretentious decorations made claim to be the finest houses in town, but still the old Silver place held its own with dignity and gentle grace, as if it had no need for pretension. Like a strong, handsome old man of high birth, it lifted its distinguished head among all the others of the place. There was something classic about its simple lines, its lofty columns reaching to the roof, its ample windows with wide drawn snowy curtains giving of old a glimpse of companionable firelight blazing on a generous hearth. It had a home-like, friendly look that drew the eye of a visitor as home draws the soul. It had always been kept in perfect repair, and the well-made bricks of which it was built had been painted every year a clear

12

cream-white, always white with myrtle-green blinds, so that old age had only mellowed it and made the color a part of the material. It had the air of well-preserved age, like an old, old person with beautiful white hair who still cared to keep himself fine and distinguished.

About its feet the myrtle crept, with blue starry blossoms in summer; and lush beds of lilies-of-the-valley, generation after generation of them, clustering, occupied the spaces between the front walk and the end verandas, giving forth their delicate fragrance even as far as the dusty street. A tall wall of old lilacs made a background behind the verandas at each end. A gnarled wistaria draped a pergola at one end while a rich blooming trumpet vine flared at the other, miraculously preserved from the devastation of painters each year. A row of rare peonies bordered the walk down to the box hedge in front, and the grass was fine and velvety, broken here and there by maples, a couple of lacy hemlock-trees, and the soft blending plumes of the smoke-bush. In the back yard there were roses and honeysuckle, snowballs and bridal-wreath, bittersweet vines, mountain-ash trees, and a quaint corner with walks and borders, where sweet-williams, Johnny-jump-ups, canterbury-bells, and phlox still held sway, with heliotrope, mignonette, and clove-pinks cloying the air with their sweetness, and in their midst an old-fashioned sun-dial marking the marching of the quiet hours. Almost hidden in the rose-vines was a rustic arbor of retreat, where one might go to read, and be undisturbed save by the birds who dared to nest above it and sing their lullabies unafraid. One would scarcely have dreamed that there was left a spot so sweet, so quaint, so true and peaceful in this twentieth century rushing world.

Across the road a meadow stretched far down to misty vapors rising from the little stream, whose sand, of a peculiar fine and white variety, suitable for use in manufacturing fine grades of sandpaper, had given to the Silver family its prosperity, and helped to give a name to the place started by the first old family— "Silver Sands."

The meadow was rimmed with trees, and here and there a group broke the smoothness of its green, but for the most part the view was kept open, down across its rippling smoothness of close-cropped grass in summer, or glistening whiteness of deeplaid snow in winter, open down to the gleaming "river" as they sometimes dignified the little stream. And one looked back to the owners of that strip of land with gratitude that they had done this thing for the house and for all who should sojourn therein, to give this wide stretch of beauty untouched, with room for souls who had vision to grow.

Down beyond the meadow, off to the right, camouflaged now and again by a casual tree, or a cropping of rocks, huddled the heterogeneous group of buildings which had come to be known as Frogtown. It was really originally called "the Flats" of Silver Sands, but since the factories had gone up, the ironfoundry, the glass-works, the silk-mill, and like mushrooms, a swarm of little "overnight houses" filled with a motley foreign and colored population, it had somehow grown into the name of Frogtown, and one felt that if the original Silver who had held the land, and planned the view across the long misty meadow, could have looked ahead far enough he would have planted a row of tall elms or maples like a wall to shut *in* his view as well as out. For Frogtown in winter lifted stark, grim chimneys of red brick, and belched forth volumes of soft black smoke, which, when it got into the picture, was enough to spoil any view.

But in summer the kindly trees had spread more and more to shut out the ugliness of the dirty little tenements and stark red chimneys, and the tall grass reached up and blended the town till one could almost forget it was there. Especially at evening could one look out from the windows of the dignified old Silver mansion and see the river winding smoothly like a silver ribbon just beyond the stretch of misty green without a thought of dirty laborers, blazing furnaces, flaring pots of molten glass and metal. It

was like a vision of Peaceful Valley in its still natural
beauty.

But it was most mysterious just after the sun had
set, and the "trailing clouds of glory" left behind were
lying in lovely tatters across a field of jade, above the
pearly shadows where the river pulsed in dusk, and a
single star pricked out like a living thing and winked
to show the night alive.

For the last fifteen years, since the death of Standish Silver, few had looked at this particular view
from the angle of the Silver house for the reason that
there had seldom during that period been any one
occupying the house except the three old servants,
who lived in the back part, and went "front" only to
clean and air it. They cared little for views. For this
reason it was all the more wonderful that the house
had kept its atmosphere of home, and its air of alert
friendliness, its miracle of distinction from all other
houses of the town that sat upon it with a kind of
pride.

But on this night, after all the years, the old house
seemed to smile with content as the evening settled
down upon it, and nestled among its shrubbery with
an air of satisfaction. Back in the inner rooms soft
lights began to glow under quiet shades, and there
seemed a warmth and life about the place as if it had
wakened because the owner had come home.

As Patterson Greeves stood at the window surrounded by this sweetness of the night, this peace of
home, his raging soul could not but feel the calm of
it all, the balm, the beauty. The sweet air stole in
upon his troubled senses and his soul cried out for
comfort. Why couldn't they have left him in peace to
get what inspiration there was in this quiet old spot
for the hard work that he had before him?

The spell of the meadow came upon him, the mist
stealing up from the river in wreaths till he felt the
blue eyes of the violets from their hiding-places as if
they were greeting him, sensed the folded wings of a
butterfly poised for the night on a dandelion, began
to gather up and single out and identify all the deli-

cate smells and sounds and stirrings in the meadow
that he used to know so long ago. Even without going
he could seem to know where a big flat stone could be
lifted up to show the scurrying sawbugs surprised
from early sleep. His anger began to slip from him, his
bitterness of soul to be forgotten. A desire stirred in
him to steal out and find the particular tree-toad that
was chirping above his mates, and watch him do it.
He drank in the night with its clear jade sky, littered
with tatters of pink and gold. He answered the wink
of the single star, his old friend from boyhood—and
then he remembered!

Out there was the meadow and the mist and the
silver sand in the starlight, but off down the street
in the quiet churchyard were two graves! Out the
other way was a dead schoolhouse where other boys
played ball and bluffed their way through lessons. He
was not a boy. He had no part nor lot in this old
village life. He had been a fool to come. His life was
dead. He had thought he could come to this old
refuge for inspiration to write a book that would add
to the world's store of wisdom and then pass on—out
—Where? How different it all was from what he had
dreamed in those happy boy days!

Even the old church with its faith in God, in love,
in humanity and life, in death and resurrection! What
were they now but dead fallacies? Poor Aunt Lavinia
with her beautiful trust! How hard she strove to teach
him lies! Poor Uncle Standish, clean, kind, loving, severe, but fatherly and Christian—always *Christian!*
How far he had gone from all that now! It seemed as
different, the life he had been living since Alice died,
as a wind-swept, arid desert of sand in the pitch-dark
would be from this living, dusky, mysterious, pulsing
meadow under the quiet evening sky. And yet—!
Well, he *believed* in the meadow of course because
he *knew* it, had lived with the bugs and butterflies
and bits of growing things. If he had only read about
it or been taught of it he might perhaps think the
earth all arid. He had a passing wish that he might
again believe in the old faith that seemed to his

world-weary heart like an old couch whereon one might lie at peace and really rest. But of course that was out of the question. He had eaten of the tree of knowledge and he could not go back into Eden. Poor credulous Uncle Standish, poor Aunt Lavinia! Strong and fine and good, but woefully ignorant and gullible! How little they knew of life! How pleasant to have been like them! And yet, they stagnated in the old town, walking in grooves their forebears had carved for them, even thinking the thoughts that had been taught them. That was not life.

Well, why not? He had seen life. And what had it given him? Dust and ashes! A bitter taste! Responsibilities that galled! Hindrances and disappointments! Two daughters whom he did not know! An empty heart and a jaded soul! Ah! Why live?

Into the midst of his bitter thoughts a crimson stain flared into the luminous gray of the evening sky as if it had been spilled by an impish hand, and almost simultaneously out from the old bell-tower in the public square there rang a clang that had never in the years gone by failed to bring his entire forces to instant attention. The red flared higher, and down behind the tall chimneys beside the silver beach, a little modern siren set up a shriek that almost drowned out the hurried imperious clang of the firebell. Another instant and the cry went up from young throats down the street, where the voices of play had echoed but a second ago, and following upon the sound came the gong of the fire-engine, the pulsing of the engine-motor, the shouts of men, the chime of boys' voices, hurried, excited, dying away in a breath as the hastily formed procession tore away and was lost in the distance, leaving the tree-toads to heal over the rent air.

It took Patterson Greeves but an instant to come to life and answer that call that clanged on after the firemen had gone on their way. He stayed not for hat nor coat. He flung open the front door, swung wide the white gate, made one step of the road, and vaulted the fence into the meadow. Down through the dear old mysterious meadow he bounded, finding the way as if he were a boy again, his eye on the crimson flare in the sky. Once he struck his foot against a boulder and fell full length, his head swimming, stars vibrating before his eyes, and for an instant he lay still, feeling the cool of the close-cropped grass in his face, the faint mingle of violet and mint wafted gently like an enchantment over him, and an impulse to lie still seized him, to give up the mad race and just stay here quietly. Then the siren screeched out again and his senses whirled into line. Footsteps were coming thud, thud across the sod. He struggled half up and a strong young arm braced against him and set him on his feet:

"C'mon!" breathed the boy tersely. "It's *some fire!*"

"What is it?" puffed the scientist, endeavoring to keep pace with the lithe young bounds.

"Pickle factory!" murmured the youth, taking a little stream with a single leap. "There goes the hook 'n ladder! We'll beat 'em to it. Job Trotter cert'nly takes his time. I'll bet a hat the minister was running the engine. He certainly can make that little old engine hump herself! Here we are! Down this alley an' turn to yer right—!"

They came suddenly upon the great spectacle of leaping flames ascending to heaven, making the golden markings of the late-departed sun seem dim and far away as if one drew near to the edge of the pit.

The crude framework of the hastily built factory was already writhing in its death-throes. The firemen stood out against the brightness like shining black beetles in their wet rubber coats and helmets. The faces of the crowd lit up fearfully with rugged, tense lines and deep shadows. Even the children seemed old and sad in the lurid light. One little toddler fell down and was almost crushed beneath the feet of the crowd as a detachment of firemen turned with their hose to run to another spot farther up the street where fire had just broken out. The air was dense with shouts and curses. Women screamed and men hurried out of the ramshackle houses bearing bits of furniture. Just a fire. Just an ordinary fire. Thousands of them happening all over the land every day. Nothing in it at all compared to the terror of the war. Yet there was a tang in the air, a stir in the pulses, that made him thrill like a boy to the excitement of it. He wondered at himself as he dived to pick up the fallen child and found his young companion had been more agile. The baby was restored to her mother before her first outcry had fully left her lips.

"Good work, Blink!" commended a fireman with face blackened beyond recognition, and a form draped in dripping mackintosh.

"That's the minister!" breathed the boy in Patterson Greeves' ear, and darted off to pounce upon a young bully who was struggling with his baby sister for possession of some household treasures.

Then, as quickly as it had arisen, the fire was gone; the homeless families parcelled out among their neighbors; the bits of furniture safely disposed of for the night, and the fire company getting ready to depart.

"Ain't you goin' to drive her back?" the boy asked of the tall figure standing beside him.

Patterson Greeves warmed to the voice that replied:

"No, son, I'm going back across the fields with you if you don't mind. I want to get quiet under the stars before I sleep, after all this crash."

They tramped it together, the three, and there was an air of congeniality from the start as of long friendship. The boy was quiet and grave as if bringing his intelligence up to the honored standard of his friend, and the new man was accepted as naturally as the grass they walked upon or a new star in the sky. There was no introduction. They just began. They were talking about the rotten condition of the homes that had just burned and the rottener condition of the men's minds who were the workers in the industries in Frogtown. The minister said it was the natural outcome of conditions after the war, and it was going to be worse before it was better, but it was going to be better before a fatal climax came, and the scientist put in a word about conditions on the other side.

When they had crossed the final fence and stood in the village street once more Patterson Greeves waved his hand toward the house and said:

"You're coming in for a cup of coffee with me," and his tone included the boy cordially.

They went in quite as naturally as if they had been doing it often and the minister as he laid aside his rubber coat and helmet remarked with a genial smile:

"I thought it must be you when I first sighted you at the Flats. They told me you were coming home. I'm glad I lost no time in making your acquaintance!"

Blink stuffed his old grimy cap in his hip pocket and glowed with pride as he watched the two men shake hands with the real hearty handclasp that betokens liking on both sides.

The old servants joyfully responded to the call for coffee, and speedily brought a fine old silver tray with delicate Sèvres cups, and rare silver service, plates of hastily made sandwiches—pink with wafer-thin slices of sweetbriar ham, more plates of delicate filled cookies, crumby with nuts and raisins. Blink ate and ate again and gloried in the feast, basking in the geniality of the two men, his special particular "finds" in the way of companions. "Gee! It was great!" He wouldn't mind a fire every night!

The coffee-cups were empty and the two men were deep in a discussion of industrial conditions in foreign lands when suddenly, with sharp insistence the telephone-bell rang out and startled into the conversation. With a frown of annoyance Patterson Greeves finished his sentence and turned to take down the receiver.

"Western Union. Telegram for Patterson Greeves!" the words smote across his consciousness and jerked him back into his own troubled life. "Yes?" he breathed sharply.

"Too late! Athalie already on her way. She should reach you tomorrow morning."

Signed "Lilla."

It seemed to him as he hung up the receiver, a dazed, baffled look upon his face, that he could hear Lilla's mocking laughter ringing out somewhere in the distance. Again she had outwitted him!

Chapter III

Having diligently enquired what time the night express from the East reached the near-by city, and finding that it was scheduled to arrive fifteen minutes after the early morning train left for Silver Sands, and that there was not another local train that could bring his unwelcome daughter before eleven o'clock, Patterson Greeves ate his carefully prepared breakfast with a degree of comfort and lingered over his morning paper.

He had in a long-distance call for the principal of a well-known and exclusive girls' school in New England, and he was quite prepared to take the child there at once without even bringing her to the house. He had already secured by telephone the service of an automobile to convey them at once back to the city, that she might be placed on the first train possible for Boston. It remained but to arrange the preliminaries with the principal, who was well known to him. He anticipated no difficulty in entering his daughter even though it was late in the spring, for he knew that it was likely that a personally conducted tour of some sort, or a summer camp, could possibly be arranged through this school. These plans were the result of a night of vigil. So he read his paper at ease with himself and the world. For the moment he had forgotten the possible advent of his elder daughter.

His breakfast finished, he adjourned to the library to await the long-distance call. The scattered mail on the desk at once recalled Silver and her suggestion that she would like to visit him. He frowned and sat down at the desk, drawing pen and paper toward him. That must be stopped at once. He had not time nor desire to break the strangeness between them at present. In fact his very soul shrank from seeing Alice's child, the more so since he had become so aware of Lilla's child's approach.

He wrote a kind if somewhat brusque note to Silver saying that she had better defer her visit to some indefinite period for the present, as he was suddenly called away on business—his half intention to take Athalie to her school served as excuse for that statement to his dulled conscience—and that he was deeply immersed in important literary work in which he could not be disturbed. It sounded well as he read it over and he felt decidedly pleased with himself for having worded it so tactfully. He resolved to send it by special delivery to make sure that it reached her before she started. And by the way—what was it she said about taking a position? Of course that must not be allowed. He was fully able and willing to support her. And she could not be too old to go to school. He would arrange for that—not in the school where Athalie was to be, however! Perhaps she herself would have a preference. He would ask her. He reached his hand for her letter, which lay on the top of the pile where he had dropped it the night before, for both Molly and Anne had been well trained by the former master that the papers on that desk were sacred and never to be touched.

As he drew the letter toward him and his eyes fell again upon those unaccustomed words: "Dear Father," something sad and sweet like a forgotten thrill of tenderness went through him, and the face of his beautiful young wife came up before his vision as it had not come now in years.

But before he could read further, or even realize that he had not finished reading the letter the day before, the telephone rang out sharply in the prolonged titillation that proclaims a long-distance call, and he dropped the paper and reached for the receiver.

It was the distant school, and the principal for whom they had been searching; but she did not fall in with Patterson Greeves' plans with readiness, as he had expected, although she at once recognized him.

Instead, her voice was anxious and distraught and she vetoed his arrangements emphatically. An epidemic of measles had broken out in the school in most virulent form. The school was under strict quarantine, and it was even doubtful, as it was now so late in the spring, whether they would open again until fall. They could not possibly accept his daughter under the circumstances.

In the midst of his dismay there came an excited tapping at the door, following certain disturbing sounds of commotion in the hall, which had not yet been fully analyzed in his consciousness, but which rushed in now to his perturbed mind as if they had been penned up while he telephoned and lost none of their annoying element by the fact that they were but memories.

He called "Come in," and Anne Truesdale in her immaculate morning alpaca and stiff white apron and cuffs stood before him, a bright spot of color in her already rosy cheeks, and a look of indignant excitement in her dignified blue eyes.

"If you please, Master Pat—" she began hurriedly, with a furtive glance over her shoulder, "there's a strange young woman at the front door—"

"Hello! Daddy Pat!" blared out a hoydenish young voice insolently, and the young woman, who had stayed not on the order of her going, appeared behind the horrified back of the housekeeper.

For Athalie Greeves, never at a loss for a way to carry out her designs and get all the fun there was going, had not waited decorously at the city station for the train which should have brought her to Silver Sands, but had called from his early morning slumbers a one-time lover of her mother whose address she looked up in the telephone book, and made him bring her out in his automobile. In his luxurious car he was even now disappearing cityward having an innate conviction that he and her father would not be congenial.

Patterson Greeves swung around sharply, his hand still on the telephone, his mind a startled blank, and stared.

Anne Truesdale stiffened into indignant reproof, her hands clasped tightly at her white-aproned waist, her chin drawn in like a balky horse, her nostrils spread in almost a snort, as the youngest daughter of the house sauntered nonchalantly into the dignified old library and cast a quick, appraising glance about, levelling her gaze on her father with a half-indifferent impudence.

"Bring my luggage right in here, Quinn! Didn't you say your name was Quinn?" she ordered imperiously. "I want to show dad some things I've brought. Bring them in *here* I said! Didn't you hear me?"

The old servitor hovered anxiously in the offing, a pallor in his humble, intelligent face, a troubled eye on his master's form in the dim shadow of the book-lined room. He turned a deprecatory glance on Anne Truesdale, as he entered with two bags, a shiny suitcase, a hat-box, a tennis-racket, and a bag of golf-sticks, looking for an unobtrusive corner in which to deposit them and thereby stop the noisy young tongue which seemed to him to be committing irretrievable indignities to the very atmosphere of the beloved old house.

"Take them out, Joe," said Anne Truesdale in her quiet voice of command.

"No, you *shan't* take them out!" screamed Athalie, stamping her heavy young foot indignantly. "I want them here! Put them right down there! *She* has nothing to say about it!"

Joe vibrated from the library to the hall and back again uncertainly and looked pitifully toward his master.

"Put the things in the hall, Joe, and then go out and shut the door!" ordered the master with something in his controlled voice that caused his daughter to look at him with surprise. Joe obeyed, Anne Truesdale thankfully melted away, and Patterson Greeves found himself in the library alone with his child.

Athalie faced him with storm in her face.

"I think you are a perfectly horrid old thing!" she declared hysterically with a look in her eyes that at once reminded him of her mother. "I said I wanted those things in here and *I'm going to have them!* I guess they are *my* things, aren't they?" She faced him a second defiantly and then opened the door swiftly, thereby causing a scuttling sound in the back hall near the kitchen entrance. Vehemently she recovered her property, banging each piece down with unnecessary force and slamming the door shut with a comical grimace of triumph toward the departed servants.

"Now, we're ready to talk!" she declared, with suddenly returning good humor, as she dropped to the edge of a large leather chair and faced her father again.

Patterson Greeves was terribly shaken and furiously angry, yet he realized fully that he had the worst of the argument with this child as he had nearly always had with her mother, and he felt the utter futility of attempting further discipline until he had a better grasp of the situation. As he sat in his uncle's comfortable leather chair, entrenched as it were in this fine old dignified castle, it seemed absurd that a mere child could rout him, could so put his courage to flight and torment his quiet world. He turned his attention upon her as he might have turned it upon some new specimen of viper that had crossed his path and become annoying; and once having looked, he stared and studied her again.

There was no denying that Athalie Greeves was pretty so far as the modern world counts prettiness. Some of the girls in her set called her "simply stunning," and the young men with whom she was contemporary called her a "winner." She was fair and fat and fourteen with handsome teeth and large, bold, dark eyes. But the lips around the teeth were too red, and the lashes around the eyes overladen, I might almost have said *beaded*. Her fairness had been accentuated to the point of ghastliness, with a hectic point in each cheek which gave her the appearance of an amateur pastel portrait.

She wore a cloth suit of bright tan, absurdly short and narrow for her size. A dashing little jade-green suède hat beaded in black and white sat jauntily on a bushy head of bobbed and extraordinarily electrified black hair, and whatever kind of eyebrows she had possessed had been effectually plucked and obliterated, their substitutes being so finely pencilled and so far up under the overshadowing hat-brim as to be practically out of the running. She wore flesh-colored silk stockings and tall, unbuckled, flapping galoshes with astrakhan tops, out of which her plump silken ankles rose sturdily. Her father sat and stared at her for a full minute. No biological specimen had ever so startled or puzzled him. Was this then his child? His and Lilla's? How unexpected! How impossible! How terrible!

It wasn't as if she were just Lilla, made young again, pretty and wily and sly, with a delicate feminine charm and an underlying falseness. That was what he had expected. That was what he was prepared for. That he could have borne. But this creature was gross—coarse—openly brazen, almost as if she had reverted to primeval type, and yet—vile thought! he could see all the worst traits of himself stamped upon that plump, painted young face.

Athalie gave a self-conscious tilt to her head and enquired in a preening voice:

"Well, how do you like me?"

The man started, an unconscious moan coming to his lips, and dropped his head into his hands; then swung himself up angrily and strode back and forth across the far end of the room, glaring at her as he walked and making no reply. It was obvious that he was forcing himself to study her in detail, and as his eyes dropped to her feet he paused in front of her and enquired harshly:

"Haven't you any—any *hosiery?*"

Perhaps the good attendant angels smothered a hysterical laugh, but Athalie, quite wrought upon in her nerves by this time and not a little hurt, stretched out a plump silken limb indignantly.

"I should like to know what fault you have to find with my stockings?" she blazed angrily. "They cost four dollars and a half a pair and are imported, with hand-embroidered clocks—"

He looked down at the smooth silk ankles helplessly.

"You are too stout to wear things like that!" he said coldly, and let his glance travel up again to her face. "How did they let you get so stout anyway? It can't be natural at your age!"

The full painted lips trembled for an instant and real red flared under the powder of the cheek, then she gave her head a haughty toss.

"You aren't very polite, are you? Lilla said I'd find you that way, but I thought maybe you had changed since she saw you. She told me—"

"You needn't trouble to mention anything that your mother said about me. I shouldn't care to hear it," he said coldly.

"Well, Lilla's my mother, if I have come to live with you, and I shall mention what I like. You can't stop me!"

There was defiance in the tone and in her glance that swept remindingly toward the pile of luggage at her feet, and he veered away from another encounter.

"Do you always call your mother by her first name? It doesn't sound very respectful."

"Oh, bother respect! Why should I respect her? Certainly, I call her Lilla! I had it in mind to call you Pat too, if I liked you well enough, but if you keep on like this I'll call you Old Greeves! So there! Oh, heck! This isn't beginning very well—" she pouted, "Let's start over again. Here Pat, let's sit down and be real friendly. Have a cigarette?" and she held forth a gay little gold case with a delightfully friendly woman-of-the-world air, much as her mother might have done. As she stood thus poised with the golden bauble held in her exquisitely manicured rose-leaf hands she seemed the epitome of all that was insolent and sensual to her horrified and disgusted father. He felt like striking her down. He wanted to curse her mother for allowing her to grow up into this, but most of all he felt a loathing for himself that he had made himself responsible for this abnormal specimen of womanhood. Scarcely more than a child and yet wearing the charm of the serpent with ease.

Then suddenly the shades of all the Silvers looking down upon him from the painted canvasses on the wall, the sweetly highborn gentlewomen and gentlemen of strong, fine character, seemed to rise in audience on the scene and bring him back to the things he had been taught and had always deep down in his heart believed, no matter how far he had wandered from their practice. And here was this child, scarcely turned toward womanhood, daring to offer her father a cigarette, daring to strike a match pertly and light one for herself; here in this old Silver house, where grandmothers of four generations had been *ladies*, and where dear Aunt Lavinia had taught him his golden texts every Sunday morning—taught him about purity and righteousness. Oh! it was all her sweet, blind innocence—her ignorance of the world, of course, yet sweet and wonderful. And to have this child—*his child* transgressing the old order in her playful, brazen way! It was too terrible! His child! Flesh of his flesh!

"Athalie!"

"Oh, don't you *smoke*? I thought all real *men* smoked. Lilla said"—she pursed her lips and lifted her cigarette prettily.

"Athalie!" he thundered, "Never mind what your mother said! Don't you dare to smoke in this house! Don't you ever let me see you—"

"Oh, very well! Shall I go outside? Perhaps you'll take a little walk down the street with me—"

The child was roused. There were sparks in her dark eyes. She looked very much like the old Lilla he knew so well. This was not the way to handle her. He was bungling everything. What should he do? He must establish his authority. The court had handed her over to his charge. What a mistake! He should have had her when she was young if he was ever to hope to do anything with her. But he must do *something*. He reached out a sudden hand and took possession of the cigarette and case before the surprised girl had time to protest.

"Those are not fit things for a young girl to have," he said sternly. "While you are under my protection it must not happen again. Do you understand?"

She pouted.

"You wouldn't talk!"

"I can't talk to you while you look like that," he said with a note of desperation in his voice, "Go upstairs and wash your face. And haven't you got some less outlandish clothes? You look like a circus child. I'm ashamed to look at you!"

He stepped to the wall and rang a bell while Athalie, after staring at him in utter dismay burst into sudden and appalling tears. Almost simultaneously Anne Truesdale appeared at the door with a white, frightened face looking from one to the other. Patterson Greeves registered a distinct wish that a portion of the floor might open and swallow him forever, but he endeavored to face the situation like a Silver and a master in his own house.

"This is my daughter Athalie, Mrs. Truesdale, and she wishes to wash her face and change her apparel. Will you kindly show her to a room and see that her bags are brought up and that she has everything she needs? I did not expect her to arrive so soon or I would have given you warning. It was my intention to keep her in school—"

"Oh-h-h-h!" moaned Athalie into a scrap of a green and black bordered handkerchief—"O—hhhhh!"

Anne Truesdale looked at the plump tailored shoulders as she might have looked at a stray cat whom she was told to put out of the room, and then rose to the occasion. She slid a firm but polite arm around the reluctant guest and drew her from the room, and Patterson Greeves shut the library door and dropped with a groan into his chair, burying his face in his hands and wishing he had never been born. Somehow the sight of his daughter weeping, with her foolish frizzled hair and her fat, flesh-colored silk legs in their flapping galoshes, being led away by "Trudie," as he always used to call the housekeeper, made him

suddenly recognize her species. She was a flapper!
The most despicable thing known to girlhood, according to his bred and inherited standards. The thing
that all the newspapers and magazines held in scorn
and dread; the thing that all noted people were writing about and trying to eradicate; the thing they were
afraid of and bowed to and let be; and his child was
a *flapper!*

Just as after long and careful study a new specimen
would at last unexpectedly reveal some trait by which
he could place it, so now his child had shown forth
her true character.

It was terrible enough to acknowledge; it was easy
enough to understand how it had come about; but the
thing to consider was, what was he going to do about
it? How could he do anything? It was too late! And
God thought men would believe in Him when He let
things like this happen! Somehow all his bitterness of
the years seemed to have focussed on this one morning. All that he called in scorn the "outraged faith of
his childhood" seemed to rise and protest against his
fate, proving that he still had some faith lurking in
his soul, else how could he blame a God who did not
exist?

He rose and paced his study back and forth, dashing his rumpled hair from his forehead, glaring about
on the familiar old room that had always spoken to
him of things righteous and orderly, as if in some way
it too, with God, were to blame for what had befallen
him. He had taken perhaps three turns back and forth
in his wrath and perplexity when he was aware that
a light tapping on the door had been going on for
perhaps several seconds. He swung to the door and
jerked it angrily open. Had that girl concluded her
toilet so soon, before he had thought what to do
about her? Well, he would tell her exactly what she
was, what a disgrace to a fine old family; what a—
mistake—what a—!

In the hall stood Anne Truesdale with deprecatory
air, her fingers working nervously with the corner of
her apron, which she held as if to keep her balance.
Her beloved Master Pat had turned into an inscrut-

able old ogre whom she loved, but scarcely dared to brave. She felt assured, in view of the modern young specimen upstairs, that he had reason to be in this mood, and she but adored and feared him the more, after the old-fashioned feminine way, that he had it in him to storm around in this fashion; but she was frightened to death to have to deal with him while it lasted. Behind her, smiling quite assured, and splendid to look upon this morning with the soot washed from his face, and his big body attired fittingly, stood the minister, a book in his hand and a look of pleasant anticipation in his face.

Then Patterson Greeves remembered as in a dream of something far past that he had invited the minister to take a hike with him this morning and afterwards lunch with him. The boy Blink was to have gone along. How fair and innocent the prospect compared to what had now befallen him! He looked as one who was about to tear his hair, so helpless and tragic his eyes.

Chapter IV

"Oh! It's you!" There was at least a wistfulness in his tone.

"Good morning!" said the minister. "Am I—? Perhaps our plans are not convenient for you this morning—?"

"Oh!" said Patterson Greeves stupidly, as if he had just remembered.

"You look done out, man! Is anything the matter? Can I help? If not, sha'n't I just leave this book I promised and run along till another time?"

"No. Come in!" said Patterson Greeves with a desperate look in his face. "You're a minister! It's your business to help people in trouble. I'm in the deuce of a mess and no mistake. You can't help me out. Nobody can. But it would afford me some satisfaction to ask you how the devil you can go around preaching the love of God when He allows such Satanic curses to fall on men?"

Bannard gave him a quick, keen glance, and set his clean-shaven lips in a firm line as he threw his hat on the hall console and stepped inside the door.

Anne Truesdale retreated hastily to the pantry and paused to wipe a frightened tear from her white cheek. The other servants must not suspect what had befallen the master. Was this then the secret of the sadness of his face, that he had forsaken the faith of his fathers and taken to cursing and swearing. It made her shiver even yet to remember how familiarly he had spoken of the devil. Dear old Mr. Standish Silver! It was well he was not present to be grieved! And little pretty Miss Lavinia! If she had heard her darling's voice talking that way about her heavenly Father it would have killed her outright! Just have killed her outright! Oh, it was sad times, and the world a growing weary instead of bright. And she so glad but the day before that Master Pat was coming home! Poor Master Pat! She must order waffles for lunch. He was always so fond of them. She must do all in her power to win him back to right living. It must have been that awful war! They said some of the officers were that careless! And of course he'd been a long time away from home. Poor Master Pat! She must pray for him humbly. There was no one else left to do it. That was what Miss Lavinia would have done, crept to her old padded wing-chair and knelt long with the shades drawn. So she always did when Master Pat was a boy and did wrong. There was the time when he told his first lie. How she minded that day. Miss Lavinia ate nothing for a whole four and twenty hours, just fasted and prayed.

She too would fast, and would go to Miss Lavinia's room and the old wing-chair, and draw the shades and lock the door, and pray for the master! Perhaps if she fasted, humble though she was, her prayer might be heard and answered. She would ask for the sake of Miss Lavinia and his uncle Silver. They had always stood well with Heaven. They must be beloved of the Lord. It would be terrible to have their nephew come out an unbeliever in these days of unbelief. The family must not be disgraced. But she must not let the servants know that she was fasting. They must not find that aught was amiss with the master. Surely the Lord would hear and all might yet be well in spite of the awful young woman that had arrived, apparently to remain.

So she scuttled away to Miss Lavinia's sunny south bedroom and locked the door.

Downstairs Patterson Greeves gave his guest a chair and began to pour out invectives against God.

Bannard listened a moment, head up, a startled, searching, almost pitying look in his eyes, then he arose with an air of decision.

"Look here, Greeves, you can't expect me to sit quietly and listen while you abuse my best Friend! I can't do it!" and he turned sharply toward the door.

Patterson Greeves stared at his guest with surprise and a growing sanity and apology in his eyes.

"I beg your pardon," he said brusquely. "I suppose God must be that to you or you wouldn't be in the business you are. I hadn't realized that there was anybody with an education left on earth that still felt that way, but you look like an honest man. Sit down and tell me how on earth you reconcile this hell we live in with a loving and kindly Supreme Being."

"You don't look as if you were in the mood for a discussion on theology to do you any good now," answered the younger man quietly. "I would rather wait until another time for a talk like that. Is there anything I can do for you, friend, or would you rather I got out of your way just now?"

"No, stay if you don't mind my ravings. I have an idea you'd be a pretty good friend to have and I've been hard hit. The fact is, I suppose I've been a good deal of a fool! I married again. A woman who was utterly selfish and unprincipled. We've been divorced for years. Now suddenly our daughter is thrust back upon me, a decree of the court I'd utterly forgotten! She arrived without warning and she's the most impossible specimen of young womanhood I've ever come across—! If a loving God could ever—! What are you smiling about man? It's no joke I'm telling you—!".

"I was thinking how much you remind me of a man I have been reading about in the Bible. Jehoram is his name. Ever make his acquaintance?"

"Not especially," answered Greeves coldly, with evident annoyance at the digression. "He was one of those old Israelitish kings, wasn't he?"

"Yes, a king, but he blamed God for the results of his own action."

"Mm! Yes. I see! But how am I to blame for having a daughter like that? Didn't God make her what she is? Why couldn't she have been the right kind of a girl? How was I to blame for that?"

"You married a woman whom you described as utterly selfish and unprincipled, didn't you? You left the child in her keeping during these first formative years. What else could you expect but that she would be brought up in a way displeasing to yourself?"

The scientist took three impatient turns up and down the room before he attempted to answer.

"Man! How could I know? Such a thing wasn't in my thoughts—! I insist it was a dastardly thing to wreak vengeance on me in this way. No, you can't convince me. This thing came from your God—if there is such a being. I've been watching and waiting through the years for a turn in my luck to prove that the God I'd been taught loved me had any thought toward me. But this is too much. Why should I wait any longer? I *know!* God, if there is a God, is a God of hate rather than love."

"Jehoram's exact words," said the minister. " 'This evil is of the Lord. Why should I wait for the Lord any longer?' "

"Exactly!" said Greeves. "Don't you see? Jehoram was a wise man. I respect him."

"But he found he was mistaken, you know. Wait till 'tomorrow about this time' and perhaps you too will find it out. God's purposes always work out—"

Patterson Greeves wheeled and looked sharply at his visitor. "What do you mean, 'tomorrow about this time'?"

"Go read the story of Jehoram and you'll understand. The city was in a state of siege. The people were starving; crazed by hunger, were eating their own children, and appealing to the king to settle their demoniacal quarrels. The king was blaming God for it all, and suddenly the prophet appeared and told him that 'tomorrow about this time' there would be plenty to eat and cheap enough for everybody. How do you know but tomorrow about this time God may have relief and joy all planned and on the way?"

Greeves turned away impatiently and began his angry pacing of the room again.

"Oh, that's the kind of idealism you were prating about last night with your dreams that God was working out His purposes for the laboring classes and all that bosh! Excuse me, but I don't believe any such rot any more for the classes or the nations than I do for the individual. Take myself for instance. If I don't send off a letter I just wrote to stop it, by tomorrow about this time I may have a worse mess on my hands than I have now. I tell you your God has it in for me! I didn't tell you I had another daughter, did I? Well, I have, and she's taken it into her head to come here also. Here! Read this letter!"

He caught up Silver's letter and thrust it into the young man's hand. The minister glanced at the clear handwriting, caught the words "Dear Father," and pressed it back upon Greeves.

"I oughtn't to read this!" he said earnestly.

"Yes! Read!" commanded the older man. "I want you to know the situation. Then perhaps you'll understand my position. I'd like to have one person in the town who understands."

Bannard glanced through the lines with apology and deference in his eyes.

"This is no letter to be ashamed of!" he exclaimed as he read. "This girl had a good mother, I'm sure! Or a good grandmother, anyway!"

Greeves stopped suddenly by the window, staring out with unseeing eyes, and his voice was husky with feeling when he spoke, after an instant of silence.

"She had the best grandmother in the world I think —but—her *mother* was *wonderful!*" There was reverence and heart-break in the tones.

"Ah!" said the minister earnestly. "Then she will be like her mother!"

"I *could not bear it*—if she were like her mother!" breathed the man at the window with a voice almost like a sob, and flung himself away from the light, pacing excitedly back to the shadowed end of the room.

"But you say you have written her not to come?" interrupted the minister suddenly, glancing thoughtfully at the missive in his hand. "Why did you do that? I should think from the letter she might be a great help. Why not let her come?"

The father wheeled sharply again, kicking a corner of the rug that almost tripped him as if it had personality and were interfering with his transit.

"Let her come! Let her come here and meet that other girl? Not on any account. I—*could not bear it!*"

Again that tortured wistfulness in his voice like a half sob.

The minister watched him curiously with a sorrowful glance at the letter in his hand.

"I don't quite see—*how you can bear not to!*" he said slowly. "After reading that appeal for your love—!"

"Appeal? What appeal? I don't know what you mean?"

He caught the letter hurriedly and dashed himself into his desk chair with a deep sigh, beginning to read with hurried, feverish eyes.

"Man! I didn't read all this before! I was so upset! And then the other girl came!"

There was silence for an instant while he read. Then his eyes lifted with a look of almost fear in them.

"Man alive!" he gasped, "she's coming this morning! My letter will be too late!" He caught up the envelope he had so recently addressed and looked at it savagely as if somehow it were to blame. "Too late!" He flung it angrily on the floor, where it slid under the edge of the desk and lay. The tortured man jerked himself out of his chair again and began his walk up and down.

"What shall I do? You're a minister. You ought to know. She's on her way now. She'll be here in a few minutes and I can't have her. She mustn't meet that other girl! I can't have Alice's child see her! What would you do? Oh, why did God let all this situation come about?" He wheeled impatiently and stamped off again.

"I'll have to get the other one off to school somewhere, I suppose. You wouldn't be willing to meet that train and say I was called away, would you? Get her to go to a hotel in the city somewhere and wait? I could hire an automobile and take Athalie away. Perhaps there's a school near her old home. Wait! I know a woman on the Hudson—I wonder—'Give me long distance, central'." He caught up the phone and began to tap the floor with his foot, glancing anxiously toward the clock that was giving a warning whirr preparatory to striking. "What time does that train get in, Bannard? Have you a time-table?"

Bannard glanced at the clock.

"Why! You haven't much time," he said in a startled tone. "It gets here at eleven ten. Would you like my car?" He stepped to the window, glanced out, gave a long, low musical whistle, and in a moment Blink appeared, darting up the front walk warily, with eyes on the front window.

The minister leaned out of the window and called:

"Blink, can you get my car here from the garage in five minutes? I want to meet that train."

Blink murmured a nonchalant "Sure!" and was gone. The minister turned back to the frantic father, who was foaming angrily at the telephone-operator and demanding better service.

"Mr. Greeves," he said placing his hand on the other's arm affectionately, "my car will be here in a moment. I think you had better take it and meet your daughter. It will be embarrassing for her to have to meet a stranger—"

Patterson Greeves shook his head angrily.

"No, no! I can't meet her! I can't help it! She'll have to be embarrassed then. She got up the whole trouble by coming, didn't she? Well, she'll have to take the consequences. I have to stay here and get this other one off somewhere. I'll send her back to her mother if I can't do anything else! I won't be tormented this way. I know. You're thinking this is no way for a father to act, but I'm not a father! I've never had the privileges of a father and I don't intend to begin now. If my wife had lived it would have been different—! But she had to be taken away—! 'Central! Central! Can't you give me long distance?'"

He set the instrument jiggling snappily, and down the long flight of polished mahogany stairs heavy, reluctant footsteps could be heard approaching.

Patterson Greeves hung up the receiver with a click and wheeled about in his chair with an ashen look, listening.

"She's coming now!" he exclaimed nervously. "I'll

have to do something. Bannard, if you'd just take that car of yours and go meet that train, I'll be everlastingly obliged to you. If you don't want to do it, let her get here the best way she can. It will give us that much more time. I've got to do something with Athalie at once—!" He arose and went anxiously toward the door, opening it a crack and listening. The steps came on, slowly, and yet more slowly. The minister pitied his new friend from the bottom of his heart, and yet there was a humorous side to the situation. To think of a man of this one's attainments and standing being afraid of a mere girl, afraid of two girls! His own children! It was a simple matter, of course, to meet a train and tell the girl her father had been occupied for the time. The car slid briskly up to the curb in the street on time to the dot, and the minister turned pleasantly and picked up his hat.

"I'll go. Certainly. What do you wish me to say to her?"

"Oh! Nothing. Anything! You'll have to bring her here I suppose! Make it as long a trip as possible, won't you? I'll try to clear the coast somehow—!" He glanced down at the huddled baggage of his younger daughter with a troubled frown." There's a carriage here—The servants will—Well, I'll see what can be done. You better go quickly please!" He looked nervously toward the door, and Bannard opened it and hurried out to his car, Athalie entering almost as he left, her eyes upon the departing visitor.

"Who was that stunning-looking man, dad? Why didn't you introduce me? You could just as well as not, and I don't want to waste any time getting to know people. It's horribly dull in a new place till you know everybody."

Chapter V

ATHALIE entered with nonchalance and no sign of the recent tears. Her face had perhaps been washed and a portion of her complexion removed, but she still had a vivid look and her hair was more startling than ever, now that her rakish hat was removed. It stood out in a fluffy puff-ball like a dandelion gone to seed, and gave her an amazing appearance. Her father stared at her with a fascinated horror and was speechless.

She had changed her travelling frock for an accordion-pleated affair of soft jade-green silk with an expansive neck-line and sleeves that were slit several times from wrist to shoulder and swung jauntily in festoon-like serpentine curves around and among her plump pink arms. She had compromised on a pair of black chiffon-silk stockings with open work clocking and black satin sandals with glittering little rhinestone clasps. A platinum wristwatch and a glitter of jewels attended every movement of her plump pink hands with their pointed sea-shell fingertips, and a long string of carved ivory beads swung downward from her neck and mingled with the clutter of a clattering, noisy little girdle. No wonder he stared. And she had done all that amazing toilet while he was talking with the minister.

He stared, and her dimples began to come with reminder of her mother in the old luring way, filling him with pain and anger and a worse than helplessness. Her mother's face was not so fat as hers, but the dimples went and came with such familiar play!

"Dad, you needn't think you can keep me shut up away from things," she said archly. "I'm going to know all your men friends and be real chummy with them. The men always like me. I'm like Lilla in that!

They bring me stacks of presents and slews of chocolates. I've got a lot of going-away boxes in my trunks. Some of them are jimdandies. This watch is a present from Bobs. You know who Bobs is, don't you? Bobs Farrell. He was dead gone on Lilla. He gave me this watch on my last birthday. It's platinum and diamond. Isn't it great? He brought me out in his car this morning or I would have had to wait two hours. When I found out what time this little old train started, I just called up his apartment and he came right down and got me and took me up to his place for breakfast. He has the darlingest apartments all by himself with a Japanese man to wait on him, and the most adorable cooking! And he's going to have a theatre party for me some night with a dinner afterward at his apartment. Won't that be simply great? I'm to ask any two girls from school I like, and he will get the men. And by the way, Daddy, I've invited a house-party for the first week in June. You don't mind, do you? There are ten of the girls in my class and I've promised them the time of their life. The fellows won't be here only at the week-end. They have to be back at prep. Monday morning. Their old school doesn't close for two weeks after ours."

His most amazing child had rattled on without let-up thus far, and this was the first period he had been able to grasp. He hastened to avail himself of it, meanwhile glancing nervously at the clock.

"School! Yes. School! May I ask why you are not in school yourself?"

"Oh!" she wreathed the dimples coquettishly around her lips, "why! didn't you know I had been fired!" She dimpled charmingly as though it were something to be proud about. "I suppose Lilla didn't tell you because she was afraid you'd be shocked, but you might as well know all about it at the start. It saves misunderstandings. You see, we had a pajama party!"

"A pajama party!" cried the horrified father.

"O now, daddy Pat! You needn't pull a long face and make out you never did such things. You know you had gay times when you went to school, and you

can't be young but once. There isn't anything so terrible in a pajama party! You see the whole trouble
was I got caught out on the fire-escape in mine and all
the rest got away, so I had to be fired, but it was fun.
I don't care. I'd be fired over again just to see how
Guzzy Foster, that's the math. prof., looked when that
ice and salt went down his back. You see it was this
way. One of the girls had a dandy box from home,
and she happened to tell one of the boys from the military prep. that she had it, and he coaxed to get some
of the things. So May Beth told him if he and some of
his friends would come under the fire-escape at exactly midnight she'd drop down a box of cake for them.
Well, everything went all right till the party was almost over and the girls had eaten all they could stuff,
and they had the box for the boys all packed and I
was to go out and throw it down to them because
May Beth had an awful cold and her pajamas were
just thin crêpe de Chine and she was all of a shiver
anyway from eating so much cold ice cream. So I said
I didn't mind even if it was cold. I thought it would be
fun, and I went out with the box and whistled softly
for the boys and they answered once, and then, it was
all very still. It was moonlight and I could see them
lined up among the bushes on the campus. I swung
the box over the railing and whispered, "Here she
comes," and just as I did it I somehow caught my toe
in the burlap that came off the ice-cream freezer—I
had on Tillie Irvin's pink satin mules with forget-me-
nots on them, and she was sore as a boil at me about
that too—and then before I know what was happening, I somehow hit the ice-cream freezer and knocked
it over, and *slosh!* out went all the sloppy ice and salt
water through the iron grating of the fire-escape, and
I looked down and there was Guzzy Foster—he and
his wife have their apartment right under my room,
and we thought they were away for the week-end,
that's why we chose my room for the party—he was
just inside his window with his head stuck out of an
old red bath robe looking up—the old ferret. He was
always snooping round to stop any fun that was going
—and he caught the whole stream of icy salt water

full in his face and down his old mathematical back, and I hope he gets pneumonia from it. He's the limit! Well, I heard him gasp and splutter, and draw in his head, and I heard the boys snicker down in the bushes and scatter out to the street—they got the cake all right. I called one of 'em up on the phone at the station before I left and found out—and I just danced up and down in those pink satin mules with the forget-me-nots and howled for a minute, it was so funny. And then all of a sudden I realized it had got very still behind me and I looked in the window and the lights were out. There wasn't a sound of a girl to be heard, and down the hall I could hear hard steps that sounded like Mrs. Foster, so I tried to get in the window, but it was fastened! Babe Heath did that because she thought if the window was locked they wouldn't think to look out. But there was I in thin china-silk pajamas and the wind blowing up from the river like ice! It was grand skating the next day, so you may know it was pretty fierce! But I stuck it out till she found me, and they fired me so quick Lilla didn't have a chance to come and see what was the matter. They just sent me home that night in charge of Guzzy Foster himself. His name's Augustus Charles, but we call him Guzzy and I had a horrid, horrid time, so it's up to you to be good to me!"

Patterson Greeves gasped, and grasped the arms of the big chair into which he had dropped as Athalie entered, looking at his child in abject helplessness.

The distant sound of an approaching train stirred him to nervous action once more.

"I certainly cannot approve of your outrageous conduct," he began, in a tone such as he might have used in his classroom. "It was inexcusable, impossible, indecent—! I cannot think how a girl could bring herself to so demean herself. And the first thing you must do will be to write a humble acknowledgment and apology to the principal of the institution and promise that for the future your conduct shall be irreproachable. I will see at once about your reinstatement, and I cannot countenance in future any disregard of the rules of the school or of the rules of good breeding."

But the girl broke in with a boisterous laugh:

"What's that you say? Me go back to that school? Well, I guess anyhow not. *Not on your life, I don't!* You couldn't *drag* me within sight of the old dump. I'm done with it forever, and I'll tell the world *I'm glad!* Why? Don't you like me? Doesn't this dress suit you any better? I've got some stunners in my trunks. When do you think they will bring them out from the city? Can't we get a car and go after them? I'm just dying to show you some of my things, and the big portrait of Lilla she had taken for the General—!"

Greeves arose, white and angry.

"Get on your things at once!" he almost shouted. "We are going back to your school. It is impossible for you to stay here. I am a very busy man. I have important work to do." He glanced wildly at his watch, and then gave a quick look out of the window as he strode to the bell and touched it, flinging open the hall door and looking up the stairs.

"But I am not going back to school!" declared Athalie with a black look. "I'm going to stay right here! I won't be the least trouble in the world. I'll have my friends, and you can have yours. I'll go my way, and you can go yours. That's the way Lilla and I always did. Only, Daddy Pat, have we got to have that old limb of a housekeeper around? I hate her! I couldn't get on with her a day. I'm sure I'd shock her. She's a pie-faced hypocrite and you'd better fire her. I'll run the house. I know how! Daddy Pat—may I call you *Pat?*"

"*No!*" thundered the scientist. "You may not. You may say 'Father' if it's necessary to call me anything!" He glared at her. "And you may go to your room at once and stay there until I send for you!" he added suddenly, as he glanced once more out of the window and saw an automobile draw up before the door. Then both of them became aware that Anne Truesdale stood in the open door, her face as white as her starched apron, a look of consternation upon her meek face and her hands clasped nervously at her belt.

Chapter VI

IT had not occurred to the minister until he came within sight of the station and heard the whistle of the approaching train, that he had come on a most embarrassing errand.

It had appeared to him as he talked with her father and read her letter that the girl he was about to escort to her home might be anywhere between twelve and fifteen years old. His information concerning Patterson Greeves' history had been vague and incomplete. He looked to be a young man for all this experience, and the minister had jumped to the conclusion that both girls were quite young.

But when the train drew up at the station and the only stranger who got out proved to be a lovely young woman dressed with quiet but exquisite taste and with an air of sweet sophistication, he became suddenly aware that the errand he had come upon was one of an exceedingly delicate nature and he wished with all his soul he had not undertaken it.

She carried a small suitcase in her hand and walked with an air of knowing exactly where she was going. She paused only an instant to glance about her and then went straight to the station waiting-room and checked her suitcase. She did it with so much apparent forethought as if she had been there before and knew exactly what she had to do, that the young man hesitated and looked about for a possible other arrival who might be the girl he came to meet. But the train snorted and puffed its way slowly into motion and started on, and no other passengers appeared. As she turned away from the checking desk he came hesitantly upon her and their eyes met.

She was slight and small with a well formed head poised alertly, and delicate features that gave one the sense of being moulded and used by a spirit alive to more than the things of this earth. The impression was so strong that he hesitated, with hat lifted in the very act of introducing himself, to look again with startled directness into a face that was so exactly a counterpart of what he had dreamed a girl some day might be that he had the feeling of having been thrust with appalling unreadiness into her presence to whom he would have willed to come with his soul newly shriven.

She had violet eyes with a frank clear glance, hair that curled naturally and frilled about her face catching the sunbeams, lips that curved sweetly but firmly, and the complexion of a wild rose newly washed in dew. She looked like a spirit flower that yet was entirely able to take care of herself on earth.

"Is this—" he hesitated and remembered that he did not know her name—finishing lamely "Mr. Greeves' daughter?"

She lifted her eyes, with a quick searching look and smiled:

"You are not—You could not be—my father."

Bannard smiled.

"No, I have not that honor. Your father is—" he hesitated again. Why hadn't he thought up some excuse for the father who was not there? It seemed inexcusable now that he saw the daughter, not to meet such a daughter! "Your father is—importantly engaged! He has but just arrived himself!"

He felt he was doing better.

"He only had opportunity to read your letter a few minutes ago, and it was impossible for him to get to the train. He asked me to meet you—"

She smiled with a rich warm welcome for her father's friend and he felt a glow of comfort.

"My name is Bannard," he finished, "I hope we're to be friends also." He put out his hand and she took it graciously and thanked him.

He piloted her to his car and helped her in, then hesitated:

"Your baggage? Didn't I see you check a suitcase? Wouldn't you like me to get it?"

A soft rose bloomed out in the girl's cheeks and the fringes drooped deeply over her cheeks for an instant, then she lifted steady eyes and said:

"No. I believe not, thank you. I'm not sure until I see—my father—whether I shall remain or go on to New York this afternoon."

He found himself strangely disturbed over this state of things. He wanted to assure her that of course she must not go on anywhere. This was the place that needed her. But of course he could say nothing. He might not even tell her that her father was in trouble. He had not been given permission to do anything but convey her to her home and that by as long a route as possible.

"We're going by a round-about way," he explained as he headed his car for a detour quite away from the old Silver Place. "There's a bad bit of road they are repairing—" he was thankful that he had happened to notice the men at work on his way down and therefore could truthfully give an explanation to this clear-eyed maiden who it seemed to him must be able to read his embarrassment through the very serge of his coat.

"Shall we pass the old Presbyterian church?" she asked eagerly leaning forward and looking about as though it were a spot she knew well by heart but had never seen with her eyes.

"Why, yes, we can," he responded eagerly, "Are you especially interested in that?" and he looked down with a smile and then a wonder at the light in her eyes.

"It is where my father went to church," she answered, as if conning things she had learned well—"and there is a cemetery where my relatives are buried. I was interested to see it."

He drove the car down a smooth ribbon of a road that curved about with wooded land on one hand and mellow fields of rippling green on the other, with a glimpse off at the right of the Silver River and Frogtown factories smothered in pale budding willows against a turquoise sky.

"It is beautiful here, isn't it?" The girl's eyes glowed. She drew in long breaths of the spring air. There were violets at the side of the road and it came to him how like her eyes they were.

They crossed a stone bridge and headed more directly toward the river and she exclaimed over the bright winding ribbon of water. Just because he had promised to make the time long, because he liked to see the wild rose color in the round cheeks glow when she opened her eyes wide at the view, he slowed down the car and investigated some minute squeek in the mechanism. Not that it was important. Not that he did anything about it. Just a pleasant little delay. It seemed to him he was experiencing a charmed privilege which was slipping by all too fleetly, and which he would grasp as it went. It might not ever come his way again.

On their way again they wound around the clump of beeches and came into the main street of Silver Sands all shining in the morning sunlight with serene houses on either hand in long stretches of green, and new gardens in geometrical lines behind the houses flanked by regiments of bean poles. A wide straw hat sheltered a lady picking strawberries in the patch of luxuriant vines. The breath of the day was sweet with growing things. The people walked crisply down the pleasant maple shaded pavements as though the going were enjoyment. The anvil rang out with silver sound from the blacksmith-shop as they passed. People began to hail the minister with glad lighting of eyes, and he was kept busy lifting his hat and waving his hand cheerily. Even the boys in the street gave him a greeting and then curiously half-jealous eyes turned to study his companion as they swept on their way.

"They all know you," the girl commented. "I'm sure you must live in Silver Sands."

"I do," he responded. "It is a good place to live. My particular corner is just down that next street, the white house with the rose trellis over the door. I board with a blessed old lady whom everybody calls Aunt Katie Barnes. She nearly turns herself out of house and home trying to find new ways of making me comfortable. It is a very friendly community. They take one in heart and soul."

She flashed him an appreciative glance and asked thoughtfully:

"Have you known my father long?"

"Well, not so very long—" the minister answered—"that is—you know he has only recently returned—but we are wonderfully good friends considering the short time. I—you—" he hesitated. There was something he wanted to tell her for her reassurance, to answer the question in her eyes which he felt sure she was too loyal to her father to ask, but his lips were sealed. And after all what was there to say even if they had not been? What reassurance had he himself that the man he had left raving at Fate in the old library would give any sort of an adequate welcome to this pearl of a girl? He felt as if he wanted to tell her that if her father wasn't glad to see her he would take him by the neck and shake him till he was. But one couldn't tell a strange girl things like that about her father.

"This is the Presbyterian church we are coming to now, the one on the left. The main part was built in sixteen hundred and seventeen. Hasn't it nobly simple lines? The stones have weathered to as fine a color as any cathedral in the old world. I love to see it against the sky with the sunset behind it. That spire is a thing of beauty don't you think? And those doves in the belfry are a continual delight. Do you know Aldrich's bit of a verse, 'And on the belfry sits a dove with purple ripples on her neck?' There goes one now swooping down to the pavement. Did you see the silver flash on her wing? And now we're coming to the part of the cemetery where your ancestors are buried. See that big gray granite column? No, the plain one just beyond. That is the old Silver lot. All the Silvers are lying there. Your grandfather and great-grandfather and their wives in that centre plot, and those side plots are for the sons and their wives and children. It was a peculiar arrangement and forethought of the first Silver settler and carried out by each succeeding one in turn. There, those two gray stones are for Standish Silver and his sister Lavinia, the last of the family who bore the Silver name."

"Aunt Lavinia and Uncle Standish. I have their pictures," said the girl softly as if doing homage to their memory. "They brought up my father."

She lifted shy friendly eyes:

"Silver is my name, too. It's a queer name for a girl isn't it? But I like it. I like to think I'm a Silver too."

"It is a beautiful name," said the young man, doing homage with his eyes.

"They were a wonderful people from all I hear. I would like to have known them."

And now all too soon they were at the Silver door and he was helping her out of the car.

He found his heart, pounding strangely with anticipation for the girl at his side. How would she be received? He felt as if he must stay by her till he was sure, although delicacy dictated that he disappear as soon as his errand was done.

Blink with nonchalant foresight was idly flipping pebbles at a toad in the meadow from his perch on the fence, his back to the road. At his feet, attentive to each motion, apparently approving and aiding and abetting the game barked a big yellow collie. The dog bounded jealously across the road at sight of the car and precipitated himself upon the minister with a wag and a glad grin of recognition, then gave a friendly snuff to the girl's hands, looked up and smiled a dog greeting with open cordiality.

"What a dear dog!" exclaimed the girl. "What a beauty!" She was bending over him with the enthusiasm of a true dog lover and Blink sauntered idly over and leaned against the car pleased at her demonstration, eyeing her furtively, appraisingly. "May I introduce his master Barry Lincoln, otherwise 'Blink' to his intimate friends?" said Bannard.

The girl lifted frank, friendly eyes to Blink's embarrassed ones and liked him at once. She put out her hand warmly and grasped his rough shy one as she might have done to an older man, and the boy's heart warmed toward her.

"What a very interesting name!" she said gaily, "If I stay here long I am sure I shall try to qualify to use it. Is the dog's name Link?"

The boy grinned.

"He's Buddie," he admitted shyly.

"Well, Buddie, I hope I meet you again," she said, with another flash of warmth in her eyes for the boy whose own were now filled with open admiration. She passed into the white gate and Blink looked after her with a new stirring in his heart, call it loyalty if you like, Blink had no idea what it was. He lifted his glance to the minister's smile and found the same thing in his friend's eyes, and an unspoken covenant flashed between them to protect her if ever she needed their protection. Blink would have expressed it in words, "She's a good scout." Blink and the dog stood by the car, Buddie wagging his plume of a tail vigorously, and watched the man and the girl go up the flower-bordered walk to the big mullioned door.

From inside the library Patterson Greeves watched the two figures arrive.

Joe Quinn watched from the shelter of the smoke bush close to the lilac hedge where he was digging about the tulip beds, and Molly the cook, having seen the car from her pantry window, had hurried up to the front hall window on pretext of looking for the housekeeper, and was gazing down curiously on the two, wondering what next was coming to the old house.

At the extreme dark end of the back hall Anne Truesdale, in hiding, could glimpse the minister's hat through the side lights of the hall door, and a snatch now and then of the lady's feather, and she stood with hand involuntarily on her heart, waiting, not daring to come forth till "that huzzy" as she thought of Athalie, had gone upstairs. But Athalie, one foot on the lower step, had turned back to look at her irate father, perfectly aware that he was disturbed by the sight of something out of the window, and herself caught a glimpse of the minister returning. Ah! So that was why she was being sent upstairs! A good looking young man and she bundled away! This was no part of Miss Athalie's plan of life, so she whirled about on the lowest step and waited also.

Then the fine old knocker reverberated through the long silent house, Patterson Greeves retreated hastily in panic to his library and Anne Truesdale, chained to duty by an inexorable conscience, was forced to come forth and open the door.

The stage was set and the actors came on as the door was timidly opened by Anne.

Chapter VII

ATHALIE GREEVES came noiselessly forward to the library door, a look of expectancy on her round pink face, a cat-and-cream expression about her lips. As noiselessly Patterson Greeves forced himself to step to the doorway again, a heavy frown upon his brow, a look of extreme suffering, one would almost have said dread, in his eyes. Anne with frightened eyes peered bravely round the door, and the two on the wide flagging stones of the porch waited, the girl with wistful eager, yet courageous eyes, ready for either love or renunciation, whichever the indications showed; the minister hovering tall above her, a look almost of defiance on his strong face, an air of championship and protection about him.

Nobody spoke for the first instant which seemed almost like an eternity. The two girls saw each other first, for Patterson Greeves stood within the library door.

The girl on the steps was gowned in a blue-gray tweed suit, well fitted and tailored and a trim little soft blue straw toque with a sharp black wing piquantly stabbing the folds of the straw. Her hair was golden in the sunlight, and as she stood seemed like a halo round her face. The light of the morning was in her eyes as she peered into the shadows of the hall, then suddenly grayed with chill and reserve as she met the eyes of the other girl.

Athalie's plump face grew suddenly hard, her lips drooped, her eyes glared, her head went slightly forward with a look of stealth and jealousy and her hand went instinctively out to catch the doorframe. Her whole form seemed to crouch with a catlike motion, and green lights danced in her eyes, though they might have been reflected from her dress. The minister lifted amazed eyes and saw her. He put out an involuntary hand of protection toward the girl by his side.

Then Patterson Greeves stepped into the hall sternly, his back to Athalie and came toward the door. He looked and stopped short, his hands suddenly stretched out and then drawn back to his eyes with a quick hysterical motion as if he would brush a fantasm from his vision:

"Alice!" came from his lips in a low broken tone of agony, as if the torture and mistakes of the years were summed up in the words.

During that instant while he stood with his fingers pressing his eyes Athalie began stealthily to step back and across the hall to the wide arched doorway of the stately old parlor that ran the depth of the house on the other side of the hall from the library. Her eyes wide and round were fixed on her father. An instant later there was only left the swaying of the old silk cord tassel that held the heavy maroon curtains of the doorway.

Then the girl on the doorstep came to vivid life and stepped up quickly toward her father with eager light in her face.

"Father!" She said the word with a world of reverence and stored up love, tender caressing sound, so genuine, so wistful, it could not fail to reach the heart of any man who was not utterly dead to his fatherhood. They were clasping hands now, looking earnestly, eagerly into one another's eyes.

Anne Truesdale, behind the door, averting her loyal gaze, the minister with anxious attitude upon the doorstep, the alien daughter behind the heavy portière, one eye applied to a loop-hole close to the doorframe, were breathless witnesses of the moment. Then Patterson Greeves drew his daughter within the library door with the one word "Come," and closed the door behind them. The minister came to himself, murmuring that he would return or telephone later, and took his departure. Anne Truesdale closed the front door, and with an anxious glance as she tiptoed by the library door, vanished up the stairs. A soft stirring at the end of the back hall where Molly listened, a cautiously closed latch, and all was still.

Athalie in the big dim parlor held her breath, listening, peered cautiously, and then drew back and gazed about her with a leisurely air.

The room was wide and very long, with windows heavily curtained in the old-fashioned stately way. The ceilings high, the walls hung with dim old portraits in heavy gilt frames. The floor was covered with heavy velvet carpet, rich and thick in scrolls and roses, bright with care, though the years had passed many times over it. The furniture was rare and old and comfortable, and would have graced many a finer mansion. One or two chairs done in fine hand-made tapestry softly faded with the years, tables and cabinets that had come down from the masters in wood work. A rosewood piano of a make some thirty years back, whose name was still dignified and honored. Athalie stood and gazed about, half contemptuously. The chairs, yes—but the carpet! How funny! She would have to see that it was taken up at once and a hardwood floor—of *course*—this would be a grand room for a dance. She gave an experimental whirl on a cautious toe. Those curtains were gloomy! She slid a sleek hand into a well camouflaged silken pocket and brought forth chocolates wherewith she had fortified herself. Her mouth comfortingly filled with the creamy velvet of Dutch creams she started on a tour of inspection, pausing first before an ancestral portrait hanging above a curiously carved sofa with hand-wrought tapestry upholstery. The picture frame, tarnished with the years, seemed like an open doorway to the past. From it looked forth a woman plain of face, smooth of hair, with a carved high back comb towering above her sleek head, and bearing a bird on her finger. The eyes were so expressionless and the face so sombre that it was impossible not to connect it with a monotonous existence. A woman satisfied with a pet bird! Athalie paused and took in the thought. A lift of her well-rounded shoulders, a contemptuous smile, that was her reaction to the woman of long ago. She meant little to the girl modern in all her thoughts and feel-

ings. There was hardly a shadow of conception of
that sheltered, sweet, strong life that had given much
to the world in her passing. The girl passed to the
portrait of the man in military uniform hanging between the two long front windows and her jaws
paused in their slow rhythmic manipulation of the
chocolates to study him a moment. This must be old
General Silver. Her mother had told her about him.
Not much, only that he had been something—made
some great mark in the Civil War, or was it the war
before that? Athalie's ideas of history were most
vague. She knew only that it was very long ago if one
might judge by the old-fashioned hair-cut, the high
collar, the strange war trappings, not in the least like
a modern soldier. He had bushy eyebrows, from beneath which his piercing eyes looked over her head
straight out to some far seen enemy, keen, cutting,
stern—the girl shuddered. There had been that look in
the eye of this new-found father of hers, not at all
fatherly, not "dadish" as she expressed it to herself,
purely official. He was like his ancestor, she decided,
as she stood and watched the picture. Disappointing.
Quite as Lilla had said he would be. Hard as adamant.
Flint in his eye. No yielding to coaxing. No weakness
anywhere that one could probe. Was the bird lady
his wife or daughter? She looked back and studied
the first portrait critically, deciding she must have
been his wife. No wonder she looked as if she had
dragged out a drab existence! And yet—she looked
back to the soldier's face. There was a fascination
about him somewhere. What was it? The moulding of
the firm lips? The arch of the heavy brow? The curve
of the wavy hair, brushed fiercely forward from either
side of the head and focussing over the forehead in a
high standing brush? Well—somehow that made you
long to conquer, to draw a smile to those stern lips, a
soft light to the eyes—it must have been that something that made Lilla marry her father. It couldn't
have all been money nor station for Athalie had heard
her mother tell many times of other lovers, far famed
and wealthy. There was something about her father
she had come to conquer, and she hardened her own

wilful lips in determination and passed on to the next wall opposite the bird lady.

A stately dame with soft white hair and a cap looked forth from the next frame with a smile, more human than the others, the girl felt; her stiff black silk seemed almost to rustle from its frame with dignity and kindliness, and the painted hands held primly a wide, gracious fan of rare old lace. And by its side hung the portrait of her husband apparently, a fine old gentleman with silvered hair, high stock, and courtly manner, fitting mate for the dear old lady, both portraits so lifelike that Athalie paused almost abashed for an instant as if someone unexpectedly had entered the room. It gave her a feeling of unaccustomed awe, these strong, painted personalities all about her, past history caught and imprisoned on the canvas for another age to know intimately. They looked down at her with kindly gracious eyes and she turned away awkwardly, uncomfortable, and swept the room with another glance.

On the back wall Uncle Standish Silver in more modern business garb, and his sister Lavinia, in her Sunday best silk, long sleeved, high necked, fastened with a great cameo at the throat, and pretty crimped hair drawn back and up from her ears in a knot on top of her shapely head, were too modern to excite her curiosity, too old-fashioned to hold her interest. Her eyes wandered to the frame opposite the side window, half in shadow of the heavy curtain, a picture of a young man, a mere boy he was. She walked the length of the room eagerly to inspect it and stopped in admiration. A boy a little older than herself, and looking strangely like herself, only slim and tall, and with eyes—yes with eyes like the soldier—and—yes—*eyes like her father's!* It must be her father when he was a boy!

She stood a long time looking at it with mingled feelings, admiring, jealous, determined, studying him as he had been when almost her age. She felt if she knew him then, she would be more able to understand and influence him now. Finally, with a sigh of impatience she turned and was about to slip out of the

room when she suddenly saw for the first time—how
had it escaped her?—the portrait of a young and
beautiful woman, fresh, vivid, smiling, from a great
oval frame over the white marble mantel. The eyes
were wonderful, large, loving, innocent, deeply intelligent and with a look of life about them that made
the girl uneasy. Those eyes seemed suddenly to have
been watching her all the time, to have followed her
around the room, to be searching her down to the
depths of her mean, selfish little soul. They were
maddening eyes to a girl like Athalie. They belied
every purpose of her life, every standard and ideal
dear to her soul, every act of which she was conscious.
They were like an angel's eyes come down to earth
for judgment.

Slowly, with gathering storm in her own dark eyes,
she approached, and the two eyes seemed to meet.
Who was this young girl dressed in misty white like a
bride, fashioned not so long ago either? And was that
a veil on her head? And orange blossoms—a spray?
What bride of recent years had a right there, in the
centre of the great room, the place of honor? It must
be—! It *was* her father's first wife! Here in the house
where she had come to live! Watching her with
searching angel-eyes like that! Clean eyes that made
her conscious of herself! Assured eyes that claimed
their right to be there!

And who was it she resembled? Where had she seen
that face before, those true clear eyes?

It suddenly flashed over her and she trembled from
head to foot with rage and ground her teeth in quick
fury. *That girl out on the doorstep!* Was that the girl
of the portrait? Or had her father married another
wife, a young girl like that? Had he *dared,* and not
let them know? Could he do that? Or—stay! There
had been a child. Lilla had always said that it died
—but perhaps!

Suddenly Athalie, in a burst of rage, took a long
step toward the portrait, a spring up, and spat forth a
great mouthful of well masticated sticky chocolate
straight into the lovely painted face, covering eyes
and nose and smiling lips, and dripping in ugly brown

courses down cheeks and chin. The girl surveyed her work of desecration with satisfaction and a lifted chin and stuck out tongue as any naughty child of three might have done. Then lifting her hands in a hateful defiant gesture she darted from the room and went lightly upstairs.

In a moment more after rummaging in her suitcase, she stole forth with a large framed photograph hidden in the folds of her skirt, and slipped down to the parlor again, going straight to the mantel and putting her picture directly under the picture of the girl bride.

It was a recent picture of Lilla taken in exceedingly gauzy negligee, one of the expensive affairs of velvet and chiffon and fur she loved to don, an intimate picture not meant for public gaze, a bold-eyed, challenging, still beautiful woman, with amazing hair falling over bare shoulders and down upon the silk pillows of her chaise longue, on which she was half reclining. It was framed in an exquisite silver frame and intended for Athalie to show her former husband that he might see how lovely she still remained in spite of his indifference.

Athalie stood back and surveyed with jealous eye the picture smiling defiantly forth beneath the defaced one, made another grimace of hate and flew up the stairs again to her room, leaving her mother's picture to hold its own with the other portraits of the family.

Chapter VIII

WITHIN the quiet library the father and daughter were coming to their own. The alienation of the years like a great wall of ice was slowly melting between them and they were groping for phantom ends of heart ties broken long ago.

He had seated his daughter in one chair and drawn another opposite her. He was unnerved with the events of the night and morning. He seemed to find it hard to control his faculties and adjust himself to the present circumstances. He hardly seemed to hear her voice or the words she was speaking. It was his dead wife's voice that he heard. And there was no reproach in it, but it rebuked him. It rebuked him so that he could scarcely speak.

"I have wanted to see you so long—father—I have wanted to know—!" she was saying.

He groaned as he dropped his head for an instant and put his hands up to his eyes:

"You—are—*Alice!*" he said hoarsely.

She smiled. That smile he had loved so well! Was ever man tortured like this man? To have the dead come back in such perfection, yet in another body— and with another soul? "His daughter! His *daughter!*" he tried to say to himself, yet it was as babbling. He could not get its meaning. This was Alice come to rebuke him. Alice as when he first knew her.

"They always have called me Silver," she said wistfully. "Grandmother couldn't quite bear to call me Alice. But—I shall be glad to have you call me what you like—"

He looked at her as in a dream. He could not think what to say to her. He wanted to reach out and touch that lock of hair that was drooping over her ear, the one with the sunbeam netted in it, it was brushing against her cheek, that cheek rounded with the same contour as his lost Alice.

What a fool he had been not to know Alice would leave him her image in her child. How he had given it away, this dear growing vision of the lost one! Given it away without a thought, actually been glad to be rid of the responsibility! And now he had lost it! Lost the right! It was like giving light to a blind man, bread to a dead man, to give her to him now. He could never get in touch with her after these years. He had carved out his life in a different line, a line where she did not fit. He could never learn to speak her language, nor teach her his. He would not have her learn his. He shuddered at the thought. He could only look at her and watch her as she talked, scarcely hearing anything she said.

Afterward some of her sentences came back, stored up by his subconscious mind perhaps; details of her life, where she had been at school, how she had occupied her time, sweet incidents of the last years of those she loved. He understood enough to be rebuked again, seeing how he had failed in what might have been a pleasant duty toward the beloved of his beloved.

"You are not—*angry*—with me for coming?" she asked at last lifting her eyes anxiously to his silent staring face.

A swift contortion as of sudden pain darted over his face. It seemed as if he might be trying to smile in unaccustomed lines. It hurt him that she should ask such a thing. He had not thought that would hurt! It hurt him that he could not answer her with the right cordial words! What were the right words? Why could he not get hold of them? What a complex thing this life was anyway that one could go on for years according to a certain plan and standard, and then suddenly be confronted by unsuspected emotions which upset the whole universe! He became aware that she was still awaiting an answer, with sorrow gathering in those dear blue eyes.

"Angry? Oh, no! Why should I be angry?" he found himself saying in a cold distant tone. It was as if he were dead trying to call to the living, so strange and far away his own voice seemed to him.

A slow flush rose in her cheeks and her troubled eyes searched his face for sign of welcome.

He struggled once more for words:

"I am glad you have come." The words had not been formed in his intention. He found to his wonder that they were nevertheless true.

"I wish you had come before!"

"But you were not here!"

"Of course!" he said foolishly. "Then I wish I had come sooner. I wish I had never gone—from you!"

"Oh, father, do you really? How many times I have wished that!" The blue eyes were full of wistful eagerness now. It had meant a great deal to her! Why had it? Was that her mother looking at him through her eyes? Was he going stark staring crazy? It was Alice's look. Alice was looking through those eyes of her daughter's as one might look through a window!

He was not gazing at the girl now, only at Alice looking through her eyes. Alice was trying to signal to him, to make him understand something. What was that the lips so like hers were saying?

"When I was a little, little child grandmother used to tell me all about you, how you first came to see mother—" Ah! she called her *"Mother"!*—"How you looked, how you used to sing, and play football and baseball—how handsome you were—"

Ah! He had lost the thread for a moment and now she was speaking of her first little baby thoughts of him, how grandmother had taught her lisping lips to pray "Dod bess favver!" Suddenly the thought of rosy baby fingers about his neck—where had he seen rosy baby fingers? Not Lilla's baby! That had seemed too much a part of Lilla to be pleasant to him. He had never made much or seen much of Lilla's baby. He shuddered at the thought of that other girl upstairs. How should he tell this girl about her?

"I used to wonder how it would be to have a father, a *young* father, like other children, to carry me upstairs at night—grandfather was dear, but you know he had that accident—oh, didn't you know about that? I was only two years old when it happened. He was knocked down by a heavy truck in trying to cross the city street on his way to Presbytery. He was always lame after that and had to be very careful about lifting. I used to so long to be lifted up and carried in strong arms—!"

The man wondered at the exquisite thrill that came to him. After all these years of dreary living, his heart burnt out to ashes, that the thought of a little child, *his* little child being carried in his arms should so stir him! The thought of a rosy cheek cuddling in his neck, moist lips dropping furtive kisses, soft breath coming and going against his cheek, golden curls spreading on his shoulder— she would have had golden curls he knew by the curl of the sunshine in the tendrils about her forehead. His baby! *Alice's* baby! Alice's gift to him to comfort him through the lonely years! And *he had let her go!* Was that what the eyes had been trying to signal him? It was as if Alice stood there behind the windows of her daughter's eyes and held out her baby to him with a smile; and suddenly he understood and reached out the arms of his heart to gather her to his life. Fool that he had been that he had not known it sooner, before the mistakes of his life had thickened about him and unfitted him for caring for her! Suddenly he dropped his face into his hands again and groaned.

"Father! Dear father! What is it? Did I hurt you somehow?"

"Too late! Too late!" he moaned. "What a fool I have been!"

And there somehow he told her all that she needed to know of the years that had separated them, broken sentences, more reserves than words, tender silences. The grafting process had begun in that which had been so long severed.

When Anne Truesdale, after long lingering and listening to the low murmur of voices, finally brought herself to tap on the door and announce lunch, their faces were like the clear shining after rain.

"Come in, Anne!" His voice was more like himself than it had been since his arrival. Anne entered bravely, suppressing her own excitement.

"I'm afraid, Anne, we've been upsetting all your arrangements," he began penitently as he used to do when as a boy he took all the cookies in the cooky jar to feed a hungry horde of boys.

"Don't speak of it, Master Pat. Yer not to apologize to me. This is yer own house. I and the rest are but here to do yer bidding. It is the pleasure of us all to have things as you'll be wanting them."

The woman held her hands tightly clasped at her waist and made a low courtesy of respect. The master's face softened with affection.

"Thank you, Trudie," he said, using the old childhood name. Then turning toward the girl he said:

"Trudie, this is Alice's child! My daughter—Silver! Silver—Alice!"

He turned quickly away, his voice husky with feeling, but wheeled as suddenly back again:

"Could she have Aunt Lavinia's room? I'd like to have her there—!"

Anne gave the girl one swift sifting glance and rendered instant homage:

"Indeed she could, Master Pat," she said heartily, satisfaction in her eyes, "and right pleased would Miss Lavinia be to have such a successor. Shall I show the way at once? Lunch is putting on the table."

"Why, I'll only be a moment," said the girl beginning to remove her gloves. "How beautiful to have Aunt Lavinia's room!"

Anne Truesdale stepped back as Silver advanced to the stairs and spoke in a guarded voice:

"And what about the young Miss upstairs? Must I speak to her to come down?"

The man looked as though she had struck him, and the light of shining went suddenly out of his eyes:

"Oh, why! Yes—I suppose you'll have to—tell her to come down please!" he finished with an attempt at ease, and bracing himself made one of his quick turns and went and stood staring out of the long narrow window that framed the front doorway.

Silver had paused, glancing back, and caught the low words, felt the pain in his voice and the sudden dashing of his spirit. It seemed that a cloud must have just passed over the sun. "The young Miss upstairs!" That would be the flapper-looking child she saw when she first entered. Who was she? What right had she here in her father's house?

But Anne Truesdale's black silk was rustling close behind and she mounted the stairs looking with eager eyes around, nor saw the glitter of an evil black eye at the keyhole as she passed down the upper hall.

"This was Miss Silver's room," said Anne swinging wide the panelled mahogany door, and revealing quaint rare furniture, rich faded carpet, a glimpse of a pineapple carved fourposter, and the depths of a flowered wing-chair by the window, with a little sewing table drawn up and even a work basket with a bit of white linen tidily folded atop.

Anne bustled about, setting straight a chair, patting a pillow, and smoothing a dent out of the wing-chair cushion where she had but just been kneeling. Then she slipped away down the hall and tapped at a door nearer the head of the stairs on the other side.

Silver took off her hat, ran her fingers through her hair, washed her face and hands in the great blue and white china bowl, dried them on a fine linen towel fragrant with rose leaves and exquisitely wrought with a great S at one end. Then she fluffed up her hair a bit more, gave a glance into the mirror, and another lingering one about the sweet old room and went quickly downstairs arriving just in time to hear Anne's low murmured:

"She says she'll not come down. She's not feeling so good," and to vision her father's relief at the message.

At the head of the stairs, Athalie with velvet tread had crept to the railing to listen, and peer over from the shadows of the upper hall as they went to the old stately dining-room, father and daughter, for their first meal together. As they disappeared and the heavy door closed silently behind them the girl leaned far over the baluster and made an ugly face ending in a hiss. Then as stealthily as she had come she crept back to her room, closed the door, locked it, rummaged among her luggage for a five pound box of chocolates and a novel and established herself amid pillows on the foot of the big old bed.

Anne Truesdale came up presently with a laden tray of good things, but Athalie with her face smothered in the pillow and her chocolates and book hid out of sight declined any sustenance. Whereupon Anne, pausing thoughtfully in the hall, finally scuttled down the dark narrow back stairs and whisked the tray out of sight, deciding that the master should not know of this hunger strike yet.

After lunch Silver and her father went back to the library for a time, and their low voices in steady cheerful conversation were not soothing to the other daughter's nerves. She tiptoed to the open window to see if she could hear any words, but found she could not on account of a family of sparrows who were nesting in the honeysuckle below and seemed to have been retained for the purpose of chattering.

About half past two Silver and her father went out together down the street. Athalie watched them from the shelter of the window curtain frowning and noting the amicable footing on which they seemed to be.

They went to the station and reclaimed the girl's suitcase. On the way back they stopped at the old church and walked slowly through the graveyard, the father pointing out the names on the white stones, of those who would be of interest to her among her unknown kin, the girl's face kindling with tender emotions as she read the records mossy with age.

While they were gone the village expressman arrived with four immense trunks and three wooden boxes. Athalie arose with alacrity from her couch of pain and superintended their installment in the house.

"You can bring the two wardrobe trunks right in here and unpack them at once," she informed Anne Truesdale haughtily. "I shall need more closet room. I think I'll take that room across the hall. You might put the other two trunks and the boxes there till we get them unpacked. I shall probably use that for my boudoir."

"That is the spare bedroom," said Anne coldly but firmly. "There's a trunk room in the attic where your trunks can be stored." Athalie gave her a withering look, but such looks had no effect on Anne. She went her way and called the faithful servitor. He managed an extra hand from the street, to help the expressman, and Athalie's mammoth trunks were carried slowly up the stairs. Nothing so huge in the way of a trunk had ever entered that house before, and Anne stood aghast as the first one hove in sight and cast a quick and calculating eye toward the attic stairs. But when she saw how heavy they all were she changed her mind. They should go no farther until they were unpacked. So the first was placed in the back hall for further consideration, while the remaining three proved to be so enormous that Anne demanded the key and down in the wide old front hall Athalie's frivolous possessions were brought to light and carried up in the abashed and indignant arms of the three old-fashioned servants, who looked upon the trifles of lingerie with averted gaze and felt that the daring evening frocks of scarlet and silver and turquoise were little short of blasphemies. They hastened them up to the oblivion of the second floor before the master should return, and Anne stood for a full minute gazing out of the hall window across the sunny meadow and pondering whether she ought not perhaps to have left them all down on the back porch where the boxes had been remanded, until the return of the master. Such doings! And a young girl who ought to be in leading strings yet. Four trunks! What would Miss Lavinia have said!

Athalie meanwhile was rummaging among her brilliant raiment, pulling out this and that, deciding what she would wear next after she had sufficiently cowed that hard-hearted father of hers, and finally burrowed her way among silks and organdies to her chocolates and her pillow again, deciding not to put anything away until that objectionable "Anne" person came to do her bidding. She felt she must make it understood from the start that she would be waited upon. Anne wasn't much like her mother's maid, but such as she was she must be reduced to obedience. Perhaps she could coax her father to let her have a French maid all her own, a young girl about her own age. That would be rather fun.

Chapter IX

WHILE Athalie was thus engaged her father and Silver were wandering through the quiet graveyard, talking of the past. The man found himself telling his child about his own boyhood, his aunt, his uncle, the old minister, the long sweet services in the quaint old church. There was no bitterness in his voice now as he spoke of the religion of those who had brought him up. Something softening had come upon him. He hardly understood himself.

And then suddenly they had come upon the young minister, stooping over a little new made grave, working with some violet plants in full bloom, planting them in the mellow soil until the little mound became a lovely couch.

They did not see him until they were almost upon him, and then he rose quickly, his hands covered with earth, his hat on the back of his head, his dark hair curling in little moist waves about his white forehead, and a light of welcome in his face:

"I'm just fixing up this place a bit before the mother comes," he explained. "It looked so desolate and bare, and this was her only child!" He stooped again and pressed the earth firmly about the violets, with strong capable fingers, arranging the plants as he talked till the whole little mound was one mass of lovely bloom. Then he rose, dusted the earth away from his hands and strolled along with them.

"Would you like a glimpse of the old church?" he flashed a smile at Silver.

"Oh, I would!" she exclaimed eagerly, "grandmother used to tell me stories of my father's home, all she knew, and she always told about the old church. Mother was here—once—wasn't she?" She looked up shyly at her father who was walking absentmindedly, sadly beside the young people, his hands clasped behind him as if his thoughts were far in the past. He started as she asked the question, and a pain seemed to stab into his eyes as of one who is suddenly brought to view something long lost and very dear:

"Yes, yes! Your mother was here! On our wedding trip! We went to church. We sat in the old pew. She wore a little white hat with white flowers on it, and a thin blue dress—!" It was as if he were musing over a beloved picture. The minister and the girl exchanged swift understanding glances.

"We will go in," said the young man, "I have the key."

He unlocked the old oaken door and the sunshine poured behind them into the ancient hall, lighting up the well-kept red ingrain carpet and meeting the sunshine that poured down from a stained glass window above in curious blended dancing colors like the pattern of some well-remembered hymn sacred to many services held within those holy courts.

Patterson Greeves walked beside the young Alice as he had walked beside her mother up those stairs to the assembly room above, so many years ago, and saw again in imagination the eager friends of his youth leaning over the grained oak railing to get the first glimpse of the bride. Felt again the swell of pride in the girl he had chosen, remembered the look of pleasure in the eyes of his Uncle Standish as he met them at the head of the stairs and escorted them down the aisle to the pew, and Alice's smile as she looked up at him. Ah! That he had thought was to be the beginning of life! And only one short year it lasted! They all turned to bitterness and night! Fool that he had been that he had thought anything so heavenly could have lasted on this earth! That he had believed there existed a God who cared for him and planned for him! Ah! Well—! Bitterness!

The blood rolled over his frame in a sickly, prickly, smothering wave, and he mopped his brow with his handkerchief, and wondered why he had let himself in for this sort of thing after all these years? Why had he come down to the old church so full of memories?

Then he lifted his eyes to his girl who stood in the open doorway of the assembly room now, framed in all her girlish beauty against the background of the rich coloring of the church, its jeweled windows casting rich fantastic lights in a rainbow flood of beauty, glancing away from the cluster of gilt organ pipes, glinting the gold fringe of the pulpit Bible bookmark, focussing on the blood red of the bright old carpet, and beating it into a tessellated aisle of precious gems, mellowing the age worn woodwork of the square high pews, and the carvings of the pulpit and red plush pulpit chairs. There was something in the look of his girl as she stood there against that background with all the heritage of her grandfather's and grandmother's religion behind her that took away the pain again, and made him watch her breathlessly, and trace out every likeness to the mother who was gone, made him glad that she had come in spite of all the pain. Even glad of the pain, if it brought this vision.

The minister was explaining about the organ. "Not a wonderful organ, and a bit old, but one of the good old makes, and with two or three beautiful stops." Did she play? She did. He was sure she did. Wouldn't she try the organ?

"Her mother could play! Oh, she could play!"

Greeves had spoken without intending, but the other two gave no sign that they had seen the emotion in his face.

"Yes, I know," the girl said quietly. "I studied with her teacher for two years. He was an old man but he was wonderful. After he died grandfather sent me away to study for awhile."

They lingered nearly an hour in the church, the girl drawing sweet harmonies from the old yellow keys, the minister lingering near, calling for this and that favorite, while Greeves sat long in the old family pew and read without seeing them the old familiar texts twined among the fresco, "THE LORD IS IN HIS HOLY TEMPLE. LET ALL THE EARTH KEEP SILENCE BEFORE HIM." Even now after the years it sounded a certain note of awe in his soul, an echo of the old days when God was real and life a rare vista before him. There were the same old windows. He used to count the medallions in the border when the sermon was unusually long. There was the shepherd and the lambs, and the first verse of the twenty-third psalm. There was the storm one, purple clouds driven hard across an iron sky, trees and shrubs bowing before it, and the inscription, "FOR IN THE TIME OF TROUBLE HE SHALL HIDE ME IN HIS PAVILLION. IN THE SECRET OF HIS TABERNACLE SHALL HE HIDE ME."

How firmly he used to believe in that when he was a child! How truly he expected to take refuge in that tabernacle if any storm overtook him! And how far he was now from any refuge. What a farce it had been! Beautiful while it lasted. But a farce! He drew himself up with a shudder of disgust at it all and the tones of the organ caught him as Silver's fingers trailed over the keys while she talked in low tones with the minister:

> "Nearer my God to Thee,
> Nearer to Thee—"

It had been Aunt Lavinia's favorite, and it stung its way into his soul in spite of his intention otherwise. He could hear her singing it, twilights in the nursery when she held him on her lap, his earliest remembrance, while her eyes watched the evening sky grow red and gray and deepen into starry blue, and the look about her mouth told him even in his baby days that there was something sad back somewhere in her life, something that she might have given up, possibly for him.

"Nearer my God to Thee, E'en though it be a cross—"

He could hear the gentle murmur of her timid voice in that very pew as he had sat beside her many years. Ah! The tears stung into his eyes unaccountably after all these years. And he? His song had been:

> "Farther my God from Thee,
> Farther from Thee—!"

How Aunt Lavinia would have agonized in prayer before her deep old wing-chair if she could have known! He had seen her kneeling once thus, in her decorous high-necked long-sleeved night dress with the little tatted ruffles round her throat and wrists, her eyes closed, her gentle face illuminated with a wistful joy that had awed him, her lips murmuring softly words of pleading for him:

"O God, bless our little Pat. Make him grow up a good man, loving God more than all else in life! Make him sorry for his sins! Make him love righteousness and hate wrong—"

The words were indelibly graven on his soul. He had not thought of them in years but they were there just as sharply discernible as when that day he stole into her room to ask some trivial request for the next day's pleasure, and came upon her unaware, and stood breathless as in the presence of the Most High, stealing away on tiptoe not to disturb her, lying wakeful in his bed till far into the night—! Ah! He turned sharply toward the two and his voice jarred a discord as he spoke to break the spell of solemnity.

"Come home with us and take dinner! Bannard!"

He had not intended to give that invitation. It had been the farthest from his thoughts but a moment before, his tongue had spoken without leave. But now that it was given he found ease in the thought of a guest. Why not? He liked the young man. A guest more or less made little difference in the strange make up of his sudden family. Perhaps it might even help out the embarrassing situation. But he was not prepared for the quick lighting of the young man's face.

"That would be great!" he responded, "But—" and his eyes sought the girl's face for the flicker of a glance. "Are you quite sure you want—guests this first evening?"

"Oh, yes, come along!" said Greeves impatiently, half sorry now he had asked him, yet determined not to go back on his invitation. And Silver's eyes gave him pleasant impersonal welcome.

"I'll be there at five o'clock," he said looking at his

watch, "I must meet the little mother out in the cemetery first, and there's an old man who is dying—I must drop in there a few moments. I think I can make it by five. Will that be too soon? There's something I've been wanting to talk over with you ever since I knew you were coming. Will you have a few minutes to spare?"

"Make it by five and we'll have tea in the garden. Silver-Alice can you make tea?" His tone was a shy attempt at playfulness but it brought a great light into the girl's eyes as she turned a sparkling face:

"Oh, surely!"

"Then make it five. I acquired a foreign habit of drinking tea in the afternoon while I was over there. We'll have plenty of time for a talk then. We dine at seven." Then suddenly it occurred to him that he had another daughter awaiting him and that the prospect was anything but pleasant, so with an almost brusque manner he took a hasty leave. Turning back at the very door he said to the minister: "Oh, by the way. What has become of that young person, Blink, I think you called him? We had an engagement with him this morning, hadn't we? I had completely forgotten it. Do you know where I could find him to make my apologies?"

"He is washing my car at present," laughed the minister, "I shall see him before long and can carry your message. You needn't worry about Blink. He is very wise for his years."

"Well, suppose you tell him to drop in to dinner at seven. Tell him we'll talk over bait after dinner."

Terrence Bannard's eyes registered appreciation.

"Thank you," said he, "I doubt if he'll come. He's shy and proud among ladies, but he'll appreciate the invitation."

"Oh, that's all right!" said the older man not in the least realizing that he was getting a party of proportions on his hands, but determined to discharge his obligations to the young friend of the evening before. "Tell him to come. I liked him."

They were gone down the maple-shaded street, and the minister stood for an instant in the doorway watching the graceful girl as she walked beside her father, with a look in his eyes which would have brought the spy glasses of his congregation to play upon him if any had been there to tell the tale.

Meanwhile, Athalie, never long content at a time, grew restless under her story, and wriggling out from the finery on the bed stole to the door and listened. All was quiet belowstairs save a distant subdued kitchen sound somewhere off toward the back. That impudent housekeeper was away about her business. Now was Athalie's time to pry.

Removing her shoes and substituting blue satin mules she stole cautiously down the hall, and tried her father's door, the front room on the same side of the hall with her own, but separated by deep closets, one belonging to her room, the other to his.

She stood curiously staring about. It was a boy's room, with college photographs and pennants, football groups, and Lacrosse sticks, being its chief adornings. Only a Gladstone bag fitted with toilet articles, and a locked suitcase gave evidence of the entrance of the owner after the years of absence. Patterson Greeves had been too weary and too perturbed to unpack or make any changes since his arrival the night before. Athalie made very sure that there was nothing among his belongings to give any clue to his present character. She went stealthily from bag to suitcase, even opened bureau drawers, but no picture, or letter or anything was brought to light that might be of possible interest, though she conducted her search with the manner and wisdom of a young detective.

Coming out she closed the door again and stole across the hall to the room that had been Aunt Lavinia's.

Her eyes took in the details sharply, the old-fashioned neatness and comfort, and quiet beauty of the room, and the fact that the other girl had been taken there rather than herself, the front room, the best room in the house, with the big sunny windows to the street and at the side! Jealousy filled her heart and her full petulant lips came out in ugly lines. She walked quickly to the bed, snatched Silver's hat and gloves and flung them across the room behind a chair. She took up her handbag and went through it carefully, ruthlessly, tearing in half and restoring to its silken pocket a small photograph of a woman, the woman whose portrait was downstairs she felt sure. Then she went over to the closet and flung wide the door. After a moment's survey of two or three shrouded dresses of ancient fashion that hung there she gathered them up and flung them on a chair. Then she went back to her own room and selected an armful of her gayest garments and returning began to hang them on the hooks.

All at once she became aware that someone was near, and turning, her arms still half full of finery, she found herself facing Silver.

Not in the least abashed she looked her up and down contemptuously a full second before either spoke. Then Athalie spoke:

"Well! Who are *you?*" she asked rudely.

"I beg your pardon," said Silver hesitating on the threshold, "am I intruding? Have I made a mistake? I was told this was my room—"

"Well, it *isn't,*" said Athalie roughly, "I'm going to take it myself! I don't like the room that old frump gave me so I'm moving over here. You can have my room when I get out if you're going to stay over night. I'm Athalie Greeves, and this is my father's house, so *what I say goes!*"

Silver stood quite still for an instant, the smile frozen on her lips, her eyes taking in the details of this impossible sister, her ears trying to refuse the evidence of the sounds they had heard. Something seemed to flicker and go out in her face, a stricken look flitted over it, succeeded by a sweet dignity and a lifting of her chin that in another might have amounted to haughtiness. Then she said quietly:

"I see. Well, I will not trouble you."

She walked over to the other side of the bed, recovered her hat and gloves, took up her handbag, and went out and down the stairs. Athalie did not stop to notice where she went nor care. She went on arrang-

ing her garments on the hooks, an ugly expression on
her heavy young brow.

Silver passed quietly downstairs and found an
unobtrusive resting place for hat and gloves on the
console in the depth of the wide hall, and then went
on to the now open door that gave to a wide bricked
terrace with the garden just below, reached by mossy
brick steps set in the sod, and edged by crocuses and
daffodils. Beyond, a flare of color and the perfume of
hyacinths and tulips lured the senses, and the subtle
breath of lilies-of-the-valley stole from out the deep
green border of the terrace. Silver stood for a moment
looking out and trying to quiet the excited beating of
her heart from the encounter. Trying to think what
she ought to do. Wondering why her father had said
nothing about this strange inmate of the house. Wondering why she had forgotten to ask him who the
girl was she had seen on the stairs when she arrived.
Thinking that in all likelihood the attitude of this
other girl would make even a visit to her father impossible, and grieving at the thought.

Already Molly and Anne Truesdale were bustling
about, setting out a leaved table on the terrace,
spreading it with fine old embroidered linen and delicate cups of other days, quaint heavy silver, plates of
delectable cookies, and squares of spicy gingerbread.
The pleasant garden and the bright show of flowers,
the coming guest and the air of happiness seemed not
to belong to her. She felt a sudden loneliness, as if
she were intruding, abashed in the presence of the
things she could enjoy, appalled by the fact of this
other girl in the house. The story then had been true
that they had heard, that there had been a child by
her father's second marriage. And she must have
lived instead of dying as rumor had brought to them.
Her father had never written a word about either
birth or death to her grandfather and grandmother.
She wondered again why? Her loyal heart refused to
admit that her father had been wrong. He was her
father. Perhaps there was some excuse. Perhaps there
was some explanation.

Sudden tears came at this juncture and threatened
to overflow. In a panic she withdrew into the shadows
of the hall lest the servants should see her, and almost
ran into her father's arms as he came down toward
the door to see if his orders had been understood. He
passed a loving arm around her, gently, as if he were
almost afraid to touch her, almost shyly, she thought,
and he whispered very low:

"I'm glad you've come—Silver-Alice!"

Then Anne bustled in to ask some question and
Silver slipped back to the library for a moment searching for her handkerchief, and so got control of herself. She came back to walk down the terrace with
her father and see the places where he used to play
as a child, and hear all about the old fountain and
the fairy tales he used to make up about it. Walking
thus she almost forgot the sister upstairs who was so
ungracious, almost forgot that sometime she would
have to speak about her if her father did not speak
first.

There was a cloud on her father's brow. She noticed
it first as they paused beside the sun-dial and she
traced the line of clear-cut shadow half between the
four and five of the quaint old figures. A sun-dial.
How delightful! It was like digging up antiquities.
Her heart leaped to the poetry of it. Then she looked
up and saw the shadow on the stern sad face above
her. Something was troubling him. What was it? Her
presence here? Perhaps he knew how distasteful it
was to the girl upstairs, and he did not know what to
do. Perhaps it was best for her not to stay at all—perhaps—!

She put out a wistful hand and touched his sleeve:
"Father!"

"Yes," he said as if answering the thought of her
heart. "There is something I must tell you, child.
Come over to the old arbor and let us sit down. It is—
unpleasant."

"Is it about—Athalie, father?" she asked as she
turned to follow him.

He stopped and looked at her astonished.

"How did you know? Had any one sent you word she was coming?" with quick suspicion in his voice. Lilla was quite capable of preparing such a setting for the advent of her daughter. She seemed to have a sort of demoniacal insight into what would be exquisite torture for him. But Silver shook her head.

"Oh, no. But I saw her standing on the stairs behind you when I arrived, and again upstairs just now. She was moving her things into the room where I had laid off my hat. She asked me who I was. I am almost sure she does not like my coming. I think— father—*dear*, it isn't quite convenient for you to have me visit you just now. I believe it would be better if I went back tonight and perhaps came again later, in a few years when she is older, or away on a visit or something. I would not like to make you trouble. And it has been wonderful to see you and to talk with you for even this short time. I shall never feel quite alone in the world again now that I know I have a father—*such* a father!"

"Stop!" His voice was choked with consternation, anger, something else that sounded almost like humility! Strange to see that expression sitting unaccustomedly on Patterson Greeves' haughty features.

"Don't say any more things like that, Silver," he said brokenly, "I can't bear them. It is bad enough to have got in such a mess. Bad enough to have a daughter like that! Bad enough to have her come here unannounced—she came only a few minutes before you did—without having you reproach me by flying up and leaving. You *cannot* leave me now, my child! You must stay by and help me. *I need you!*"

"Oh, father, dear!" She put out a loving hand to his arm again and he drew her within his embrace and down the path toward the summer house.

It was so that Athalie saw them as coming to the window of her own room, her arms full of more finery, she stood and gazed. Suddenly she dropped her armful, and great jealous tears of rage welled into her large bold eyes. From her handsome full lips a smothered sound almost like a roar of some enraged young animal came and was quickly suppressed. For a moment she watched then she turned about and began to search wildly among the confusion of clothing on bed and chairs, and to hastily array herself in other attire.

Chapter X

ABOUT this time also, Blink, having received the invitation by word of mouth from the minister, and not having declared himself either way about accepting it, repaired to the meadow lot opposite the Silver place and proceeded to fill a large tin can with the choicest bait the town afforded from a private and secret source underneath some old rotting logs which had long furnished him with better angles than any other boy was able to produce. He was not yet sure whether he would go to the party, but he would at least be ready with an offering should the fates, when the time arrived, seem propitious.

Sooner than he had expected the can was filled, and he lay back on the sweet smelling turf of the meadow and gazed up at the blue of the sky, watching the tiny, lazy, gauzy clouds that floated slowly, drifting like thistle down whither it happened. It was easy to feel he was floating on one of them drifting too. He often did that. It was his way of reading poetry. He read a great deal of living poetry at that stage of his existence.

Lying so with a clump of blue violets close to his hand, and the tinkle of a cow bell not far away he could drift and think of a great many things that an ordinary boy in the everyday of life wouldn't consider profitable for one of his standing.

Out of the tail of his eye he saw the minister, presently, going in the white gate between the hedges. He thought of the little grave covered with violets, and the young mother, a social outcast, with her new sorrow and bewilderment in her face. No one had told him about it. It was one of those things that Blink always knew. By and by he would slip back to the cemetery and water those flowers. It wouldn't be nec-

essary for the minister to bother with that. The flowers would just grow all right and he could let them off
his mind. Blink knew how to relieve him at odd little
phases of the way. The minister was a good scout. If
Silas Pettigrew made any more of those pharisaical
remarks about the minister letting handsome young
women of the street go to some "mother in Israel"
when they were in trouble he would see that he
found a way to tell Silas where to get off. Silas wasn't
such a saint anyway if he *was* an elder in the church!
There was that time when he bought Widow Emmet's
house for twenty-five hundred dollars and then discovered the very next day that the railroad would buy
it at twelve thousand to complete their new franchise,
and he never let the widow in on the deal! Old cotton
mouth! Thinking he could put one over on the town,
and get the minister in Dutch with the old tabbies,
just because that poor girl—when everybody knew
young Sil Pettigrew—but *there!*

He watched with satisfaction as the great door
opened with a glimpse of Anne in black silk and
sheer collar. He too might be thus received later in
the evening if he so chose. He reflected that "the girl"
would be there. It seemed a pleasing circumstance.
She liked dogs. She was all right.

Then suddenly his attention was attracted to a motion, a shadow, what was it moving at an upper
side window of the house. Someone was climbing out
to the pergola below, a boy it looked like, heavily
built with a shock of football hair, knee trousers, and
a strange belted kind of jacket.

He sat up stealthily, leaning on one elbow, his
young face growing grave as he watched. Now who
the deuce could that be? Not a burglar, this time of
afternoon, sun still up? Still. That wasn't any town
figure, none of the boys' shoulders that shape, nor
hair. It might be a disguise but—how pink the face
looked, like a Chinese painting on a fan!

Without taking his eyes from the object of his attention he made ready to take a hasty departure. One
hand went out and secured the can of bait. His mind

turned over the available hiding places where he might store it safely. How clumsy that guy was! Wasn't much of a climber. What in time was he doing up there in that house anyway?

Slowly the figure crept to the front of the pergola, glanced cautiously around, peeked back and over the vines as if watching some one, and then dropped heavily down among the myrtle beds. A moment more and he saw it rise, jamb a curious looking mushroom hat down over the shock of hair, and come out the gate to the street, with furtive glances back toward the house. The whole attitude of the person showed secrecy and stealth. Once outside the gate it turned toward the direction of the stores and walked rapidly with a free stride despite its stocky build.

Blink arose from his bed of green and lost no time in following. The can of bait was deposited in the hollow of a tree a rod from the street, and Blink was over the fence and making good time in a trice. The stranger was still in sight, had passed the first cross street and was almost to the drug store. Blink fell into a lope and made the garage diagonally across from the drug store just as the figure paused, one foot on the step, one hand on the latch and looked up and down the street. He had a full view of her face. Good night! It was a *girl!* A girl in knickers! They passed through the town sometimes, girls like that, out on walks with men Sundays and holidays, but there were none indigenous to the soil of Silver Sands. It was *not done!* And look at her face! Ye gods. Fell in the flour barrel! Painted like an image! Good night! Did a girl think she was nice looking that way he would like to know? And coming from the Silver house! How was it possible? Blink did not use the word "incongruous" in common parlance but it was the way he felt. For one awful second he experienced deep and horrible disappointment. "The girl." She liked dogs but she was like that! Then instantly the thing was impossible. No, she hadn't been a fat thing like that. She wasn't the same one. But who was she? Some interloper? How did she get there without

his knowing? Did the family know? What did she
have to do with them? Oughtn't something to be
done about it?

Since he had been able to walk alone Blink had
been a self-constituted member of the police force of
Silver Sands. He belonged to a clan who seldom
said what they meant, seldom talked but in parables,
and kept their eyes open. Many a wrong had been
righted and a petty criminal saved through their
ministrations to become a worthy citizen after due
chastisement and discipline. They reserved the right
to use their own judgment, and on occasion had been
known to evade the law for their own wise and
worthy reasons, to save an underlying principle which
in their opinion would be lost if the law had its course.
The strangest part of it all was that the outcome
usually would seem to warrant the venture, and occasionally the Chief of Police himself had been
known to wink at some open break on the part of the
boy because he had come to have utter faith in his
working principle. Blink had been known to search
out the criminal and the facts in some mystery more
than once where others had failed to get a clue, and
the Chief always felt it well to keep in with Blink.
He took him with him now and again when a raid on
some lawbreaker was imminent. He had faith in
Blink's intuition.

Blink himself had unerring faith in his own judgment. It was to him like a clear magnifying glass that
had been given him at birth, which showed up Truth,
and he couldn't see why other people didn't exercise
the same faculty. They all must have the same thing
if they only used it.

Athalie seeing nothing else down the principal business street more attractive than the drug store,
opened the door and went in. Blink leaned up against
the show window of the garage in front of a great
pasteboard model of a new kind of tire, looked idly
up and down the street and saw every move the
strange girl made.

She looked about the store with that curious appraising glance she gave to everything the first time of

seeing, and then turned into one of the two telephone booths that huddled by the corner window, close to the entrance door. She took the front one facing the door and seemed to be looking through the book for a number. When she had taken down the receiver, Blink, without seeming to have been looking that way, sauntered thoughtfully across the street and entered the drug store most casually, taking one full impersonal look at the girl's face as he passed. No, it was not *the* girl. He had been pretty sure before, but he was glad to *know*.

And this one was pretty enough, if she hadn't been so ghastly painted, and such funny eyebrows, almost as if she wanted you to see she hadn't them in the right place. She had big brilliant white teeth, with those vivid red lips like the clown in the circus, and she had a hard bold look in her eyes. When he entered she was talking and laughing boisterously. She could be heard all over the store, if there had been anyone around to hear but stupid Sam Hutchins the "soda" clerk.

Blink stalked over to the counter and threw down a nickel for a package of life savers, and then as if he had had no other purpose in entering he sauntered straight to the other telephone booth and shut himself in to a careful inspection of the W's in the telephone directory. Not that he wanted anyone with a name beginning with W. It was just the first page he happened to open.

Clear and distinct came the voice from the booth ahead:

"Now *Bobs!* You don't mean you didn't know my voice! Well, I'll say that's a slam! I'm off you for life! Oh! Really? Awwww—Bobbbbs! Now, that's awfully *darling* of you!"

Blink was disgusted. Just one of these foolish Janes. He had heard them talk before, only why did they want to dress like a man, and why should one of them climb out of a second story window in the Silver house? He slammed the book shut and called up the captain of a neighboring baseball team in the next township. He was disgusted with himself for caring.

He would listen no more. It was likely some queer visitor. But one thing was settled. He was not going to the Silver house that night. Not with so many girls about. He couldn't stand girls!

"Is that you, kid? Oh, isn't he? Well, call him won't you? I'll wait. This is Blink. *I* said it."

"Boom!" came the girl's voice into his waiting. "Well, you've got to come and get me, Bobs. You said you would if I sent for you. I'm having a horrid time. No, I haven't been down to meals. I didn't have any success at all. If it hadn't been for your five pounder I'd have starved. Yes, been on a hunger strike. But honestly, Bobs, it's no use. I simply can't stick it out! I shall expire. Can't you come down this evening and take me a ride? No, he'd never find it out. I've retired to my room with a sick headache, see? He expected to hear nothing more from me till morning. I've shocked him so hard he would be glad if he never had to see me any more. I'll make him sit up and take notice yet. I promised Lilla I would and I mean to keep my word. But Bobs, you've simply got to stand by or I sha'n't survive. Aw, come on, Bobs! I've found a way to get in the window. We can stay as late as we like. Nobody will ever find it out. I can shin up the pergola. Oh, sure! I useta do it in gym. . . . Aw, *why* Bobs? . . . . I think you're *too mean*—! . . . . Well, then, how about t'morra? . . . . You won't stand me up? . . . . Well, if you do all right for you! . . . . Where will I meet you? . . . . Why I'm down at the drug store now. Couldn't you come here? . . . . Aw why? . . . . I don't see. What do I care for these country simps! Let 'em tell dad! I'll have the fun first, won't I? Leave it to me. I'll get away with it . . . . What is it you're afraid of, you poor fish? Your reputation? Well I like that! I didn't know you had any! . . . . All right, Bobs. I'll come. Where do you say it is? Walk over the bridge at the other end of the village? . . Yes . . . . Woods? On the right hand side? . . . . I didn't get that. Oh, you want me to walk in a little way from the road out of sight? . . . . I see. Yes, Sure. All right, I'll be there, Bobs. Four o'clock sharp! But don't you be late or fail me. If you do I'll never speak to you

again, Bobs. And I'll tell Lilla how mean you were.
No. I'll tell her you said she was getting *old*. That'll
get her goat! Then she won't speak to you either! . . . .
All right, Bobs. I'll be there!"

The receiver hung up with a click and the girl
adjourned to the soda water counter where she tried
various compounds and chatted affably with Sam
Hutchins in a lofty patronizing tone, telling him how
to prepare the special concoctions they used to get at
school. She made out quite a respectable lunch, what
with the sponge cake they kept in a glass showcase,
and several chocolate ice cream sundaes. Certainly
enough to keep the breath of life in her plump well
cared for body until the next morning, and then she
took her leave and stalked on down the street to the
end of the village and crossed the bridge. Blink went
across to the garage, borrowed a motor cycle, and
took a breezy turn that way himself. He felt that this
young adventuress needed a chaperone. She came
from the house of a man he liked and loyalty to his
friends, even his very new friends, was one of Blink's
specialties. He felt instinctively that Patterson Greeves
would not like a guest of his whoever she might be to
be sailing through the open country side alone in such
a garb at the hour when the workmen from the quarry
half a mile below the town would be coming home.

So he chortled noisily by her on his wheezy steed
and sailed on down the road, arranging to have something the matter with the cycle about the time she
turned off the road toward the woods, which made it
necessary for him to dismount and get down in the
road to examine into it.

Athalie did not stay in the woods very long. Nature unadorned never had much attraction for her.
She entered a narrow winding path, followed it to a
log a few rods within the thick grove, and sat down.
But solitude never appealed to Athalie, and after a
moment's reconnoitering she came back to the road
again and pursued a monotonous way to the village.

"Fat thing!" reflected Blink contemptuously jogging
along behind at a sickly pace for one of his ambitions. Whenever he came too near he had to stop and

examine his engine again, but in course of time the
two arrived in the neighborhood of the drug store.
Athalie went in, purchased some salted almonds and
went on to her father's house. Blink returned his motor
cycle, and took a back way to the meadow, arriving
in plenty of time to watch the lady mount the pergola
and enter her window once more.

The incident finished, Blink sat for some minutes
turning it over in his mind, decided there was something here that needed further investigation, and
that he must accept the invitation to the house and
see what he might see, although he could not bring
himself to go through the agony of a dinner with *girls*.
To this end he picked himself up from the ground,
retrieved his can of bait and took the shortest cut to
his home, where he began a thorough search for a
clean shirt and its accompaniments.

Athalie, having regained the stronghold of her room
was about to return to her task of moving her clothes
to the front room closet when suddenly the sound of a
tinkling spoon against a thin china cup, and a ripple of soft laughter, with an undertone of heavier
gaiety sent her flying to her window.

For an instant her face took on the wild look of a
young savage as she gazed down at the pretty tea
table set out on the terrace below, the plate of thin
bread and butter, so tempting to her bonbon-jaded
appetite, the orange marmalade like drops of amber,
the dainty dish of sugar cookies, thin and attractive in
clover leaf form. The whiff of orange pekoe wafted
up as Silver passed her father his cup. Tea on the
terrace and she not even told! And there was that
stunning looking man again! Who was he? Did that
other girl think she would take possession of him too
as well as her father, and the house, and the best
room, and everything? Well, they would find out! She
was going down at once. She would show that stuck
up girl—!

Athalie turned from the window after a moment
more and began to fly around with catlike tread,
dropping off garments and sliding into others, searching wildly amid the mass of finery for the thing she

wanted. It was a coral crêpe she finally chose, with a
low cut bodice of silver cloth, and startling touches of
black velvet fastened with jewelled buckles.

She worked frantically over her complexion and
brushed out her permanent waves until they looked
like an electric sign. A platinum chain like a breath
of air about her plump white neck held a single jewel
like a drop of dew. In her ears were long jet earrings,
giving her a more brazen expression than ever. Her
large pink arms were guiltless of sleeves as she stood
before the mirror, turning this way and that on the
high heels of her little silver slippers into which her
plump feet seemed to be fairly forced. She was well
pleased with herself. Probably this wasn't exactly the
right kind of costume according to social rules, for that
early hour in the day, but at least it was effective, and
that was all she really cared. She felt that she could
afford to be a law unto herself.

As she took her final glimpse and tiptoed toward
the door she seemed like some great gay bird with a
large part of its gaudy plumage plucked away. The
floating coral and silver were inadequate. "Naked"
was what Anne Truesdale expressed it to herself as
she stood in frozen horror behind the pantry door
with a plate of fresh cookies and watched the bright
apparition move out of the door to the terrace and
stand a moment, "the very devil of a smile on her
lips" as Tom who was watching behind the lilacs
afterwards told his wife Molly.

Then Patterson Greeves with his cup half way to
his lips, and a look of comfort and relaxation on his
brow, suddenly looked up and stared. They all looked
up and saw her. Athalie came forward, her eyes fixed
straight upon the minister, her most coaxing spoiled-
baby look on her pink over-fed face.

Chapter XI

IF a cavern had opened beneath his feet revealing dead men's bones Patterson Greeves could not have been more shaken. He was white with consternation as he faced his astounding daughter and trembled.

"I hope you haven't eaten everything up," she said airily, coming forward, "I'm simply dying of starvation. Why don't you introduce me, dad?"

She stood facing the young man, her bare pink shoulders turned toward her step-sister utterly ignoring her, her whole forward young personality flaunting itself at Man in the concrete, this man in particular, the kind of an appeal that a woman of her mother's sort always used with a good man to disarm his disapproval. Greeves recognized instantly Lilla's arts and ways with himself, and pain and rage shot through his heart. Why had he not understood it then? Why had he let himself be fooled? Would this young man be inveigled? He glanced anxiously toward his guest and saw that the minister's eyes were meeting Silver's in a quick look of understanding as if the two had joined forces to protect him against the humiliation his daughter was bringing upon him. Ah! so might the memory of Silver's mother have protected him if he had not been too sore and bitter to let it! Fool! Fool! Was he destined to go always from this time seeing nothing but his folly, his everlasting folly that was bringing with it retribution now? Athalie, his daughter, seemed to him an embodiment of his own sins, come back after years to torment him. Was this what hell meant? The old-fashioned hell that nobody believed in any more?

He was still standing, shaken and trembling, his cup in his hand, but nobody was paying any attention to him. He gradually realized this and was glad.

They were trying to help him. Silver had poured a cup of tea and held it out to her sister, but Athalie ignored it, as if it were a ghost she did not see, and reaching out poured another for herself.

"Isn't there any lemon?" she asked looking the table over. "Quinn, bring some lemon. I never take cream. Why don't you pass the cakes, Mr. Man?" She was addressing the minister with a pert freedom that made Silver turn her eyes away in pain for her father's embarrassment. But the young man handed the plate of cookies with a gentle impersonal dignity that seemed to take the edge from the girl's audacity and put her down in the class of a child who knew no better than to take the centre of publicity.

"Gracious but you're a grouch!" commented Athalie gaily, looking straight into his eyes with her bold black ones, "won't you smile any more just because we haven't been introduced? You must excuse dad, he seems to be—"

But just then her father stepped forward haughtily and took the cup from the girl's hand.

"Athalie, you are not properly dressed to be out here. Go upstairs and put on—a—a—*sweater* or something," he ended helplessly. "It is chilly—"

But the girl burst forth in a ripple of hoydenish laughter.

"A sweater with an evening dress! Oh, dad! You certainly have been out of the world. Don't worry about me. I'm never cold. I'll take another cake, Quinn."

Patterson Greeves' face hardened into a set helpless look. He was one whom men had always obeyed. This embryo woman defied him openly and something somewhere in his moral armor was so weak that he could not meet her and conquer her. His lips shut sternly and his voice was like icicles.

"Then I will go farther and say that your dress is unseemly and out of taste. What may have seemed to you fitting among girls of your school is not in keeping with our quiet homelife in this village. We do nor wear evening dress on ordinary days and you will oblige me by finishing your tea in your room and then changing into something less flimsy, that has sleeves and a—a—*neck* to it. Something more—*adequate*. Let me introduce to you your—" he hesitated— "my eldest daughter, Silver. She is older than you are. She will be able to advise you about your wearing apparel. I commend you to her friendship. She is— ah—your sister, of course, you know."

Silver knew instantly that her father had touched the wrong chord. Athalie's impudent chin went up, her eyebrows, what there was left of them went up, her full cupid's bow of an upper lip went up, and the sharp red corners were drawn quickly and contemptuously down in a smirk of hate. She did not look at Silver. She did not acknowledge the introduction. Her big black eyes were fixed on her father who had already turned his back having manlike cast his burden thus upon womankind, and was moving off toward the door with a relieved note in his voice.

"Come, Bannard, let's go into the library and have our talk. It grows chilly out here already. The spring sun has not much warmth yet."

"Thanks! I don't need any advice from anyone about my clothes! I generally wear what I like!" Athalie hurled after him, her shoulders lifted irately. But he was already inside the door and did not choose to hear further defiance. He hurried toward the library door and drew chairs in front of the fireplace where a fire was already laid.

"Sit here, Bannard. I'm sorry and ashamed that you should have seen my family under these trying circumstances. What would you do with a girl like that? What are young people coming to? Wasn't I right in saying she was impossible?"

Out on the terrace Athalie whirled so that her back was turned to Silver. So she stood facing the glow of hyacinths and tulips, herself a flaring tulip of them all, and drank her tea in leisurely manner, helped herself to more cake, and another cup of tea, and utterly ignored the presence of the other girl.

Silver, after watching her a moment stepped over toward her.

"Listen!" she said firmly, "you might as well cut

that out. It's just as hard for me as it is for you. He's my father just as much as yours, you know. *He was my father first!* We're sisters, you know. We can't help that—!"

Athalie whirled on her with her eyes blazing.

"We're not *sisters!*" she stamped her foot. "I'll never call you my sister. You've no business here! I know all about *you!* My father *gave you away*, and you're *adopted!* You're the same as dead! You have no right to turn up and spoil my life! And you needn't think you can get his money away either. I'm his natural heir! The court—"

"Stop!" cried Silver suddenly white with anger. "As if *money* had anything to do with it!"

"Shut up!" flashed Athalie, "I'll say what I please. And you needn't pretend you're so awfully saintly. I know your kind, you mealy mouthed hypocrite! You can't put one over on me. You're in for the money as well as anybody. Now I'll give you one day to get out and stay out, and if you don't do it I'll make *hell* for you, do you understand? And I know how to do it when I try! You're not going to stick around here and spoil my plans! And if you go and tell dad *you'll be sorry*, that's all I've got to say!"

She jerked the little gold case out of a silken hiding place among her draperies, lighted a cigarette insolently, and flung the lighted match full into the face of the other girl turning with another whirl, and marching down the garden path with her cigarette atilt in her contemptuous red lips, her gaudy draperies looking as out of place in the quiet garden among the spring blossoms as a painted lily in the woods.

Silver started back from the flaring match just in time to escape the flame, gazed in consternation for an instant after the plump arrogant figure of the other girl and then throwing her head back she sent a clear ringing laugh after her sister. Athalie paused in her majestic progress to turn and stare angrily but Silver was gone into the house.

Anne Truesdale slipped a ready arm about her as she entered the shadow of the hall.

"Yer not to mind, my sweetie, what a huzzy like

that says. She'll not be here long, I'm thinking. The master was telephoning the morn' something about a school for her. He'll be soon sending her kiting, the little upstart."

"Oh, thank you, Mrs. Truesdale," quivered Silver, "I'm sorry you had to overhear this disgraceful conversation. I thought I could get her to see things in a different way, but I see it was very unwise to speak at all. She wasn't in the right mood—"

"I doubt if she has any right moods, my dearie. She's a little sinner, that girl is. I've read about 'em in the newspaper. Look at her now, puffing away like a man, the impertinent chit. Disgracing her father and his respectable house! The sooner she gets out of this respectable town the better for all concerned. Her mother must be one of the devil's own to bring up a girl like that. Now come upstairs, my dearie and I'll help you to dress and fix yer hair. Yer trunks haven't come yet, but that doesn't matter, the master doesn't care for things to be formal—"

"Oh, but Mrs. Truesdale—"

"Call me Anne, Miss Silver, I like it better. It's what yer father always calls me."

"Oh, Anne, I thank you, but I must get ready and go away. Couldn't you help me to go at once before my father hears anything about it? It would only distress him to know the reason. You could just tell him that I felt that I must go for the present, and that perhaps some day I will come back if he wants me—or he can come to see me. I didn't really intend staying when I came. I have a position and I ought to begin my work right away this week. Can you find out how soon there is a train back to the city, and help me to get away quietly before she comes in? I haven't anything to pack. My suitcase hasn't been opened yet—"

"Indeed no, my dearie!" said Anne firmly. "I'll no help ye to any such fool doings. Yer not to go away at all. And my master would half kill me if he found me a party to any such thing. Besides, can't ye see he needs ye just now? He's beside hisself with grief and shame over yonder fat young bully. Do ye think it's a

joke fer a man to come back from a far land and find
a thing like that is child o' his? You'll stay right
where ye are, my sweet lady, and help that distracted
father o' yours back into sanity. Besides, he's got company, and he's depending on you to help entertain
him this night. He told me to open the old piano
and light a fire in the drawing room. He's looking forward to hearing ye sing I'm thinking, and yer not to
disappoint him. He's been a much disappointed man
already, and it's not good fer him."

She drew Silver up the stairs to the bedroom
where she had first taken her, and then gazed around
with a growing fury in her strong old face.

"The young *viper!*" she exclaimed under her breath,
"I'll teach her to upset orders! The master's orders
too!"

Before Silver could stop her she had seized an armful of silks and lingerie from the bed where Athalie
had deposited them in her last trip, and rushed
across the hall, throwing them in a heap on the floor of
the room she had given Athalie, and was back for another.

"But you mustn't!" cried Silver, "it will only make
her angrier. Let her have the room she wants. I don't
care where I am put. If I stay at all, one room will
do as well as another."

"Indeed no!" said Anne with fire in her eye, "do
you think I'm going to have the sacred room of the
dear mistress profaned by a little devil like her? The
master would in no wise allow her to enter here. He
considers his aunt's room as a holy place, and it shows
where he feels you belong that he gave orders you
should be put in here. Now, my dear, you just sit
down while I empty this closet in a trice, and then
I'll help you unpack your suitcase."

"But Anne, I'm sure Athalie will lay this to me. She
came in while I was up here and told me she wanted
this room and I could go into the other one."

"Did she indeed! The limb of Satan! Well, I'll see
that she understands you had nothing to do with it.
I'm still housekeeper here, I hope, and the master
is still master! I'm not thinking he'll take her impu-

dence long." She seized another armful ruthlessly and marched them across the hall, and in a brief space of time the closet was again cleared.

"And look at the dear lady's best black silk!" she crooned suddenly discovering the garments that Athalie had flung from their hooks to the floor, "it's a desecration, it certainly is! If Miss Lavinia had lived to see the day that a huzzy like that that flaunts her nakedness before the gentlemen and tried to drag her womanhood in the dust by smoking the vile cigarettes like a man—!"

Anne drew her breath in a sob of grief and humiliation.

"I'm thinking she's what they call in the newspapers a 'flopper'! And I never thought when I read about their like that we'd be having a real live flopper here in this blessed house the day! Aw! It's a sorry day in the old house that's always been that respectable!"

All the time she was babbling away in her intense voice her fingers were flying, making the room right once more. She straightened the cover of the little sewing table that had been twisted awry, pulled the winged chair back to its place, picked up a wisp of malines that had floated under the bed, and even produced a duster and wiped down the walls and shelves of the closet, shaking as it were the very dust from the alien garments out of the sacred chamber.

Silver stood at the front window looking out across the field with troubled eyes, trying to think out the horrible situation. She was convinced that she ought not to have come, that she had followed her heart rather than her good judgment, and probably a bit selfishly and determinedly too, coming thus unannounced. She had wanted to forestall any attempt on the part of her father to refuse to see her. She had wanted him so, and now see!

It took no very great stretch of imagination for her to realize that this other girl was in greater need of a father than she herself, Oh much greater! No matter how fatherless or lonely she would be she would never be tempted to go in a wrong path or do anything to disgrace the family. She had been too well grounded in the things of righteousness for that. She was established. But this other girl was all too apparently self-willed, lawless, ungoverned, like a wild little craft set sail upon a stormy sea without a rudder, and liable to wreck not only herself but any others that happened in her path.

Silver was accustomed to look on life in this way; to think of what would be good for others as well as herself. Her conscience had been well trained and was in good working order. If she became convinced that she ought to go no argument would keep her there. She had a duty toward life to perform and her highest aim was to perform it aright. She was as utterly different from the other daughter as two human souls could well be. And how could there ever be harmony in such an ill assorted household?

Into the midst of her thoughts came a summons from her father. Would she come down to the library and talk something over with himself and his guest as soon as she was ready for dinner?

Anne nodded approval. That settled it. She must hurry and get ready. Had she another dress, or did she wish just to wear her suit.

Silver realized that this was no time to parley when her father had a guest, hastily shook out of her suitcase a little silk crêpe dress that fell about her like the soft shadows of evening, the color of twilight with gleams of silver in the fastenings that reminded one of the afterglow in the sunset sky, and set off her delicate complexion and the gold of her hair, making her eyes starry. The little cloud of worry on her brow only brought out the sweet thoughtfulness and made her more like her mother, as she entered the library a few minutes later. Her father could scarcely take his eyes from her face. The wonder of it that Alice's face and form had come back in the person of her child! The sorrow of it that he had not had the patience to wait for this and enjoy the privilege of seeing it grow! The selfishness of himself!

Bannard had a work down among the foreigners of Frogtown. He had a plan for a school for them that they might learn English and be fitted to take out citizen's papers. He wanted a class in cooking and sewing for the mothers, and meetings where they might learn American ways, and how to care for their children and make their homes sanitary and attractive. He wanted a meeting place for them and some men and women with tact and love of humanity to come down and help him. He had been waiting for Professor Greeves to arrive feeling that he would be the very one to help him get the educational department started. There was a small room over a grocery they could have for the present. It was lighted with lamps and heated by a small box stove, but warm weather was coming, they could even meet out of doors somewhere down by the river.

"Why not build a hall, a gymnasium or something of the sort, with accommodation for all the different classes? It oughtn't to cost much. It wouldn't have to be elaborate. I'll look after the financial part. I'd be glad to give something to a work like that."

"Oh, father! Can you do that?" Silver's eyes were large with wonder and joy. Money had not been in overabundance in the little parsonage where the Jarvises lived. Greeves looked sharply, keenly at his daughter. Was it possible that there had been any lack in her life that money might have supplied? He had sent presents now and then, a hundred dollars or so. Why had it never occurred to him to send more? His own child never having a real part in his abundant worldly possessions. He began to see more and more how wrong he had been to separate himself from her. And yet, how sweet and unspoiled she was! That other one, Athalie, had had an abundant income stipulated by the court, and see what she had become! Perhaps it had been better for Silver to have been brought up without riches. That was the way her dear mother had been reared. Ah! but it all shut him out of her life, and he had had the right to be in it and had thrown it away! Well! he would make up for it now all he could, but he could not go back and gather from the years the precious experiences that were gone forever.

They talked until the silver-tongued gong sounded through the house for dinner, and then, still quite absorbed in their theme they went out to the dining room, forgetting that there was aught in the world save beautiful plans for the uplifting of others. And there, like an arrogant young goddess stood Athalie, still in her silver and coral undress as she had been in the garden, with only the addition of a wide coral colored ribbon, the kind her girl friends called a "headache band" drawn firmly over her forehead from the little sketchy uplifted eyebrows, to the crown of her head, the ends concealed in some mysterious way under the shock of outlandish hair somewhere in the neighborhood of where her ears ought to be. She had arrived unbidden on the scene the moment the dinner gong sounded and stood like an apparition, belligerent and sullen behind a chair at the foot of the table, eyeing her father defiantly.

There had been a pleased smile on his face as he entered, his hand just touching Silver's arm caressingly, but when he saw her he stopped short and a stern angry look came into his eyes. It was not a baffled look as Athalie had counted upon. She felt that he had weakened during that scene on the terrace, and she could dare anything, but she saw a light in his eyes that boded no good for the one who disobeyed his orders. His eyes gave one full glance at the bare arms and neck, the low tight silver bodice with its straps of tiny coral roses, the flimsy draperies, and his lips set sternly, then he looked away and ignored her presence. This was not the time for further demonstration. He was a gentleman. He would deal with her later. Yet all through the meal as he spoke to the others his voice was harsh, restrained. They could see that he was very angry. His attitude perhaps awed the girl, or else she was very hungry, for she said not a word except to demand second helpings of everything from the servants. For the rest she maintained a sullen silence, her eyes on her plate, only now and then raising them in a blank stare of amazement at Bannard when he spoke of his church and his work with earnest enthusiasm. She had never met any one like him before. Also, she was angry that he ignored her so utterly, giving his entire attention to Silver and her father.

Everyone was glad when the meal was concluded. It had been a particularly trying time to Silver. And as they rose from the table the master of the house said almost sternly:

"Now we will go into the drawing room and have some music." His eyes dwelt on Silver lovingly, but something in the tone told Athalie that she was excluded from the company. As he stepped back to let the ladies pass through the door Bannard caught a look of hate on the face of Athalie that almost startled him in one so young. Yet she did not slip away as he had supposed she would after the snub she had received at the table. She followed, slowly, almost stealthily toward the heavy crimson curtains of the wide doorway, as if she had some evil intent in her going.

Old Joe had built a fire in the fireplace and the flames flickered and leaped rosily on the white marble mantel, making shadows and fitful lights on the high ceiling as they entered, and giving a look to the life-like paintings on the wall as if the owners were there awaiting them. They stepped within and Greeves touched the switch and flooded the room with electric light. Old Standish Silver had been a progressive man and the house had been wired as soon as electricity for lighting had come to Silver Sands. It flared up garishly now and brought the sleeping portraits to life, and instinctively all eyes were raised to the painting over the mantel, where special lights had been placed to show it to advantage.

Joe Quinn had been mending the fire and was just backing away, Anne Truesdale was hovering uneasily beside the curtain, wondering how she could extract the fly from the ointment. The minister and Silver stood within the doorway at one side, with Athalie still defiant just behind them, when Patterson Greeves stepped within and looked up. They all looked up, and breath was suspended. For there rose the lovely face of Alice Jarvis within her gilded frame, smeared and disfigured with chocolate, covering the sweet lips, dripping down the curve of cheek and chin grotesquely! And there below with bold sensuous challenge, exulted the pictured eyes of Lilla!

Chapter XII

THERE was a tense moment during which all eyes were fastened with a horrible fascination on the desecrated picture. Then Patterson Greeves' army-officer voice rang out like cut steel.

"Who perpetrated that?"

His face had grown so white that it frightened Silver to look at him. Athalie instinctively withdrew to the shelter of the portière. He stood looking around on the group, slowly from one face to another, beginning with old Joe, who had halted midway to the door and was ashy under his weather tanned skin, answering back his master's severe gaze with grave frightened eyes.

"I dunno, sir. I ain't seen it, sir, before, sir! It was that dark when I come in to light the fire I didn't look up, sir!"

The look passed on, steadily, unflinchingly, recognizing the sympathy in the eyes of Bannard and Silver only by a quiver of the set upper lip. He read the face of Anne Truesdale like a book. It said in every quiver of indignant lip and fiery eye that she was not to blame, though she could tell him where to search for the culprit, and only awaited a word from him to turn the tide of retribution as it certainly ought to be turned. So his eyes came to rest upon the daring, unsorry face of his younger daughter, peering out eerily as if relishing the dénouement of her escapade.

No one dared turn and look at her. It would seem that look of her father's must have scorched her soul, so full it was of outraged pride and love and sanctity. She must have learned from it at once how deep her arrow had gone in his soul, how much he had cared for that woman in the golden frame. How impossible it had been for him ever to care for her own mother like that. How really futile in the light of that look her mission in the house had become. Yet part spirit of his spirit, she dared him back with a glance as steady, as haughty, even while she trembled visibly at what she had invoked. It was as though she had been the embodiment of all his mistakes and sins come to mock him. So their eyes clashed, and the man with one final thrust of judgment and condemnation in the flash of his eye, turned back once more to the profaned picture.

It was then for the first time that he saw the portrait beneath it, set out in the clear detail of perfect photography, as beautiful yet sensuous, as dauntless, as abandoned in every line of supple body and smiling face as the daughter whose hand had placed her there.

A low exclamation of horror burst from his lips and he strode forward, white with anger and struck it full in the faithless smiling face till the glass shivered in fine fragments on the white of the marble below and the blood ran down in drops from his hand.

He was beside himself with fury now, and snatching the picture, frame and all, he dashed it to the hearth and ground it beneath his heel.

Then out from behind the heavy curtain, with a wild cry like a young tigress, darted Athalie and flung herself upon him, beating him back with her hands and screaming out:

"Stop! Stop! You shall not! That is Lilla! That is my mother! Ohhh!" and her cries were like the rending heart of an infuriated creature who had never been controlled.

She pushed him off by main force and crouching low with raining tears gathered up the fragments of the picture and clasped them to her breast. Standing thus she faced her father, a glare of hate in her black glittering eyes and looked him down even as he had looked at her and all who witnessed could not but see a resemblance to him in her eyes and attitude.

"You murderer!" she hissed between her painted lips. She ground her teeth audibly, and repeated, "you murderer!" and then she suddenly reached out with one hand and seized a large triangle of glass that still remained on the edge of the marble shelf, and hurled it with all her force straight into the face of the wonderful painting above her, where it cut a deep jagged gash between the lovely eyes, and fell in a thousand pieces below.

As the glass slithered through the canvas Athalie gave a scream like a lost soul and darted from the room, almost knocking over the white and frightened Truesdale in her flight, and tore up the stairway to her room, slamming the door with a thunderous sound behind her and flinging herself with wild weeping upon her bed.

Meantime Blink had arrived at the front door with his offering of worms, and had rung several times before Molly, who thought Joe and Anne were engaged in the drawing room about the fire and lights, had slipped to the door and let him in, bidding him wait in the front hall until the housekeeper came to show him where to go. Blink had stood by the door, his cap in his hand, and been a most unwilling witness to the whole awful scene, with its climax of flying coral gauzes, pink flesh and silver slippers hurled up the distant staircase. He stood for an instant uncertain what to do, and then with innate courtesy stepped to the door of the darkened library where only a dying fire flickered on the hearth, and slipped within. At least in here, they would think he had not heard. He dropped silently into one of the great leather chairs at the farther end of the room, and tried to think what it all might mean and what connection it had with the girl who had climbed out the second story window and telephoned to a man in the city.

It was most silent in the big drawing room after Athalie left. No one dared hardly to breathe. Patterson Greeves stood white and dazed, gazing up at the injured picture, with a stricken look upon his face, as if he had suddenly seen a loved one put to death. For an instant he looked in silence, then uncertainly he put up his hands and rubbed them across his eyes as if he were not seeing aright. It was as if the mutilated eyes of the picture were accusing him. He turned a pleading pitiful look on the group standing about him, and with a moan he suddenly dropped into a chair, burying his face in his hands and relapsing into an awful silence.

"Dontee, dontee, master Pat, dearie!" crooned Anne Truesdale, in her sorrow forgetting the presence of the others and relapsing into his childhood's vernacular, "she's only a naughty child! She didn't mean—she doesn't know—!"

A great shudder passed over the man's body, and the woman gave a frightened look toward the other two and retreated.

Bannard stepped forward.

"Get that washed off the picture, can't you?" he whispered, "and sweep up the glass?" Anne Truesdale vanished, glad to have something tangible to do.

Bannard stepped to his host's side and put a firm hand on his shoulder.

"Come, Greeves, don't lose your nerve. This isn't nearly as bad as it seems—!"

The man groaned and shuddered again.

"It really isn't, you know. The woman was right. She's only a naughty ungoverned child. And besides, you've another little girl to think about—" Greeves raised his eyes to the sorrowful girl in the doorway and Silver crept to her father's side and knelt, slipping her arm within his and putting her face close to his.

"I'm afraid this is all my fault, father," she said with a catch in her voice. "I ought not to have come. I knew as soon as I saw her. It hurt her, you know, to have me here. She wanted your love for herself—"

The man stirred uneasily and lifted his head drawing his arm around her.

"Don't say that again!" he commanded sternly, "she is worse than nothing to me! Never can be or could be!—"

Anne had come in with soft cloths and a basin of warm water followed by Joe with a step ladder, brush, and dust pan. They tiptoed in silently, awesomely, as if to a place where a murder had been committed. They did their work swiftly and well and withdrew. The master of the house remained with his head down resting on one hand, the other arm still encircling his daughter. Bannard stood a little to one side thoughtfully until the servants were gone. Then he raised his eyes to the picture.

"Come, Greeves," he said with relief in his voice, "it's not so bad at all. I'm sure it can be fixed. They mend those things so you'd never know. And it isn't as if the artist were dead. You can have him touch it up himself—"

Patterson Greeves arose shakingly, his arm still about his daughter, who slipped up from his knees and stood beside him. The father gazed agonizedly up at the picture, tears blurring into his eyes.

"The little devil!" he murmured, "that's what she is! A little hell cat!"

"Oh, I wouldn't talk that way, friend!" Bannard's hearty voice was like a breeze from a wind-swept meadow driving the sick miasms away from the room. "Nothing gained by that. Try to go back of her and see what has made her like this."

"Do you mean to say I'm to blame for her devilishness?" Greeves demanded excitedly.

"I wasn't saying who was to blame, my friend, I was merely suggesting that you might look farther into the matter before you feel in utter despair. The mother is responsible for a lot, I should say, but your problem is not who is to blame, but what can you do about it."

"I shall send her away at once, either to some school where she will be made to behave, or else back, back to the mother who made her what she is." The man's tone was hard, unforgiving, uncompromising. "I shall *make* her take her back. Money will do it!"

"Then you *would* be to blame!" flashed Bannard. "What! would you give her no opportunity *ever?* Would you force her to remain what she is?"

"I would get her out of my sight forever."

"Isn't that just where you made your mistake before? Pardon me. I realize that I know nothing about the matter It is only a suggestion."

"You do think I'm responsible for having a child like that!"

"Well, isn't a father responsible? Isn't that what God meant he should be?"

Silver had moved away from her father and was standing by the mantel looking up at the pictured eyes of her mother, her eyes full of wistfulness. Her father began a restless striding up and down the room, answering nothing, now and then tossing back his head in an impatient way he had. At last he wheeled and faced Bannard.

"I cannot think there is any fairness in that," he said harshly and took another turn across the room. Then coming back with more of a grip upon himself he said:

"But I have made scene enough of this day. I had hoped you were to be my friend. If you stand this test you will indeed be a friend. I must thrash this thing out by myself. Let us forget it if you can and endeavor to wrest a little friendship at least from the evening. We came in here to have some music and I have exhibited a family skeleton instead. Let us close the door on it for the night and do something else. My daughter, after all this are you equal to giving us a little music?"

The girl forced a smile and came quickly toward the piano. "Anything that will please you, father," she said with an attempt at brightness.

Bannard opened the old grand piano and drew out the creaking stool with the hair-cloth cushion, and as Silver seated herself it suddenly came over her that here she was in the old ancestral home, sitting at the piano where others who were gone had often sat bringing sweet strains from the old instrument. It thrilled her to realize that she was really here at last in the home she had so long dreamed about. She touched the keys tenderly, and there came forth a sound as if she had caressed them. Her father settled down in the old tapestry chair and shaded his eyes with his hand, watching her graceful outline of head and neck and shoulders, and the sweeping curve of the young body as it swayed gently to the music.

Over the library Barry Lincoln nestled back in the big chair and closed his eyes to let the music sweep over his soul, while the fire burned low and fell in bright sparkles among the ashes, and a long young angle worm from the can in Barry's lap struggled up and out and over draping itself in an arabesque, perhaps in some modern attempt to interpret the music.

Upstairs in the bed in a tumbled heap of coral and silver Athalie clasped the bits of her mother's broken picture to what heart she had and wept and wailed, "Oh, Lilla! Lilla! Lilla! Why did you send me here?"

But not even Anne Truesdale, white and anxious down in the back hall listening for developments, and trembling with weariness, heard.

Chapter XIII

DIAGONALLY across the street, about a furlong from the Silver place, next to the meadow, whose white picket fence bordered, and whose old brindle cow thrived on, the meadow, stood a small brick cottage, somewhat Anne-Hathaway style in architecture, low and thatchy, with moss on the roof and sunk deep in the thick green turf. It had a swing gate with an iron weight on a chain to make it latch, and a lilac bush leaning so low that the visitor had to duck his head to enter.

The household was entirely feminine, and they looked on the cow and the old yellow cats as their protectors. They were called the "Vandemeeter girls" though the mother and the ancient grandmother were still of the company. There were three elderly spinsters, Maria, Cordelia, and Henrietta. There was also a niece, daughter of a fourth sister long since dead, who rejoiced in the name of Pristina Appleby. Pristina was "thirty-five if she was a day" according to Ellen Follinsbee the Silver Sands dressmaker who always wore pins in her mouth and kept the other corner open to pass on pleasant conversation.

Pristina was tall and thin and spent much time studying the fashion magazines and sending for all the articles in the advertising pages. She sang in the choir and her voice was still good though a trifle shrill on the high notes. She held her book with elbows stiffened and always opened her mouth round and wide, and she took care to have plenty of fresh change of garments, and always got a new hat four times a year. She felt it was due to her position as first soprano, although it was not a paying proposition, and frequently required much sacrifice of necessities to compass it. They were a progressive family and took several family magazines besides a church paper and the Silver Sands *Bulletin*. Pristina belonged to a literary club entitled "The Honey Gatherers" and sipped knowledge early and late. She had recently been appointed to write a paper on some modern author and had chosen Patterson Greeves, "Our noted townsman" as the first sentence stated, and waded through quartos of technical works, and thoroughly mastered the terms of bacteriologists in order to do her subject justice. Maria and Henrietta had not approved. They thought the choice of a divorced man, especially as he was reported to be returning to his native town to live, not a delicate thing for a young girl to do. Cordelia maintained that it was a part of the strange times they were living in, and added: "Look at the flappers!"

"Well, I never supposed we'd have a flapper in our family," said grandma sadly. "The Vandemeeters were always respectable. Poor, but always respectable."

"Now, ma, who says Pristina ain't respectable?" bristled mother appearing in the kitchen door with a bread pan in one hand and a lump of lard in the other. "Pristina has her life to live, ain't she? I guess she's got to think of that."

They all looked at Pristina standing tall and straight, her abundant brown locks piled high in a coil on the crown of her head, a little too much of her slim white ears showing, a faint natural flush in the hollows under her high cheek bones, the neck of her brown voile guarding well the hollow of her throat, and her bony arms encased in full length bell sleeves. She wore sensible high buttoned shoes (with the addition of tan spats in winter) and her dresses were never higher than eight inches from the ground, even at the highest water mark of short dresses. Yet she seemed to them most modern. They could not have been more worried if she had taken to chewing gum. She was the kind of woman you would pick out for a good step-mother of eight. Conscientious and willing to take what was left.

"That's all right, Pristina. Write your paper the way

you want. You have to follow your own bent," said mother.

And Pristina wrote her paper.

Grandma and the three girls talked it over once when mother was setting cakes for breakfast.

"You don't suppose Pristina is getting notions about Pat Greeves, do you?" suggested Cordelia.

"Gracious!" said grandma dropping her knitting, "what put that into your head?"

"Oh, nothing—only, she's so anxious to write that paper and all. And it wouldn't be strange. She's young, you know."

"Well, I should hope she'd have sense enough not to think of marrying a divorced man. That wouldn't be respectable! And she a church singer!" This from Maria.

"Patterson Greeves isn't so young any more you'll kindly remember!" said Henrietta pursing her lips. Patterson Greeves had been a senior in high school with Henrietta. They might all remember that he gave her a bouquet of jacqueminot roses when she graduated.

"That's nothing!" said Cordelia, "old men always pick out young girls."

"He's not *old!*" said Henrietta.

"You just said he wasn't *young.* Oh, well! I only suggested it. I shouldn't like to see Pristina get notions. That man has lived *abroad.* And he's lived in *New York.* He's no fit mate for a girl like Pristina. But then, I don't suppose he'd look at her. Only as I say, I hope she doesn't get notions."

"We've always been respectable," said grandma. "It's likely Pristina knows that. She's rather respectable herself. You remember how she wouldn't let that young drug clerk hold her hand. Blood will tell generally. I wouldn't worry.

But after the paper had been read before "The Honey Gatherers," Mrs. Arden Philips, the wife of the postmaster, dropped in with some cross stitch embroidery doilies for her new hardwood table and casually asked:

"Henrietta never kept up her acquaintance with Pat Greeves did she?"

Mrs. Arden Philips used to be Ruby Hathaway of the same class in high school.

"Henrietta?" said Cordelia looking sharply at that sister.

"Henrietta!" exclaimed Maria contemptuously as if Henrietta had somehow endeavored to outclass her sisters.

"Mercy, no!" said Henrietta. "Why, Ruby, he's a married man, very much married. What makes you ask that? It's years since I've heard a word of him."

"Well, I told Julia Ellen so. After Pristina read that paper there was a great to do about it, how she got to know so much about him, and then Julia Ellen and Jane Harris both remembered that he was sweet on Henrietta once and we thought maybe—although Arden said he never noticed any foreign letters coming. Well, Henrietta, how did Pristina come to find out so much about Pat Greeves anyhow? All that about his books on bugs, and how he came to be called to those colleges and everything. I'm sure Miss Lavinia Silver never told anything. She was so close mouthed. She always just smiled and said something pleasant and you came away knowing no more than when you went."

"She got it out of some sort of an encyclopedia," said grandma indignantly, "it began with Bi, I forget the name of it. She took it out of the library. It had a lot of other great men in it. She read it all aloud to us. And then she sent for his book to the city and studied that a lot. It wasn't very interesting. I tried to read it one day but it had a lot of words I never saw before. Pristina said they were names of animals and bugs that lived before the foundation of the world or long about. I'm sure I don't know. But Pristina is real smart. She believes in patronizing home talent. I thought it was a bright idea myself, telling people about him before he came back to live here."

"Why yes, of course!" said Mrs. Arden Philips, looking sharply at grandma, "that's what *I* said; but then people will talk you know. But if I was Pristina I wouldn't mind in the least. It'll all blow over, and Pristina's reputation can stand a little whisper now and then I guess. But say, wouldn't it be interesting, thinking back to how he used to like Henrietta, if he should make up to Pristina sometime? Quite romantic, I say. Aunt and niece, you know. It might be."

"Nonsense! He's too old!" said Henrietta sharply.

"Besides he's divorced!" said Maria with pursed lips.

"Yes, of course," said the visitor, "but they do say in the city, that doesn't count so much, and besides, he's lived in the city so long he probably doesn't know the difference. It isn't as if he'd lived here always and kept Silver Sands's standards. I heard the new school superintendent say in the Home and School the other day it was standards counted. And he can't help his standards can he?"

"We've always been respectable!" said grandma sharply, "and I hope we'll always stay so. Pristina has standards if Standish Silver's nephew *has* lost his! Ruby did your grandmother send you that receipe for strawberry preserve? My daughter was wishing she could get it."

"Yes, I have it. I'll copy it off for you. Well, I must be going. We're having the minister to supper tonight. I only just dropped in to satisfy myself that I had told the truth to Julia Ellen. I never like to sleep on a lie. I was real sure Pristina hadn't been corresponding with him."

There was silence in the room while Maria went to the door with the visitor, and until she had reached the picket gate and the iron weight had swung back and clicked against the chain as it always did when the gate shut after any one. Then grandma's pursed lips relaxed and her needles began to click.

"Cat!" said Henrietta, "she always was jealous about those roses!"

That happened three months before Patterson Greeves came home. Nothing more was said in the Vandemeeter home about the matter, but whenever

Anne Truesdale opened and aired the front rooms, or stuck pillows out of the windows in the sunshine for a few minutes, "the girls" took occasion to glance over and wonder. And when at last the signs of a more thorough housecleaning than had gone on in years became unmistakable, grandma had her padded rocking chair moved to the side window where she could watch the house all day long. She declared the light was poor at the front window where she had been accustomed to sit. When the news of the imminent arrival went forth officially, Pristina went up to town and bought her new spring hat. It would not do to look shabby on the first Sunday of the noted man's arrival. After that the Vandemeeters were in a state of continual twitter, making errands to the front window on the slightest possible excuse, and always glancing out across.

"I declare it looks good to see the house alive again," said mother. "I can almost think I see Miss Lavinia's white hair at the window over there. My! If she were only back!"

"It's a good thing she's not!" said grandma sepulchrally, "it couldn't mean anything else but suffering to have her nephew come home divorced!"

"Well, I don't know about that, mother," said her white haired daughter, "there's some women you're better divorced from. You know even the Bible says that!"

"Well, why did he *marry* her then? That's what I'd like to know. A boy brought up the way he was, why *did he marry her?* Oh, you can't tell me. He just went and got into the nasty ways of the world, the flesh and devil! That's what's the matter. If he'd just come to his home town and taken a good sweet girl he'd known all his life—"

"There now, mother, for mercy's sake don't say that. Somebody might think you meant one of ours!"

The curtains were in requisition at every side window of the Vandemeeter house the night that Patterson Greeves came home. Henrietta at her chamber window high in the peak of the roof noted the gray hair crisply short beneath his soft hat, and the slight stoop in his shoulders, and said to herself quite softly:

"Goodness! do I look as old as that?"

They watched the house quite carefully until the lights from the side windows announced the dinner hour in the house across the way and then they retired to their own belated meal. While they were eating it Henrietta on a visit to the kitchen for hot water for grandma's tea spied the red glow in the sky and called them all to the back kitchen window, else they would have seen their neighbor vault the fence and sprint down the meadow to the fire.

But the next morning they were up betimes and keeping tab from every window spryly.

When the big racing car drew up in front of the house and Athalie got out they were fairly paralyzed with astonishment.

"Perhaps he isn't divorced after all," said mother in a mollified voice.

"Yes, he is," insisted Pristina, "I read it to you from the Biographical Encyclopedia. A book like that, that's in all libraries, wouldn't make a mistake."

"Well, maybe he's married again," said Cordelia. "That's what they do nowadays!"

"I don't believe he *would!* Not with his bringing up!" said mother. "He *couldn't!*"

"Well, the law allows it!" snapped Maria. "That's why I'm glad I can vote. There ought to be laws!"

"Well, who is she then?" asked grandma petulantly.

"She's young," announced Pristina who had the best eyes for far seeing, "and her cheeks are awfully red."

"She's *painted!*" said Maria, "that's the kind! Maybe she's—!"

"Maria!" said her mother, and made eyes toward Pristina, "you shouldn't say such things."

"I didn't say anything, mother, I was going to say maybe she is just some friend of his wife's. Or maybe she is a secretary. Writers have secretaries. I've read about them."

"I should think it would be more proper to have a man!" said grandma. "There's no excuse for a man having a girl always around him. If he does a thing like that I should think it was plain nobody ought to recognize him."

"Well, she's taking an awful while saying good-bye to the man that brought her!" declared Cordelia. "Perhaps he's her father. He looks old enough to be. He's held her hand all this time. Why, she's only a child. Look, she's got short hair!"

"That's bobbed!" said Pristina in disdain, "I should think you'd know that Aunt Cordelia. Plenty of the young girls in Silver Sands have had their hair bobbed."

"Oh, yes, bobbed. Oh, yes, young girls! But not like that!"

"There goes the minister in!" announced Henrietta a little later. "I wonder why? He's not the kind that todies to rich people."

"He would think he owed respect to the relative of so prominent a former member of his church," suggested mother. "The Silver family really gave the money to build that church you know. Gave the lot anyway."

"I hope the minister is not going to countenance divorce," said grandma with a troubled look out the window over her spectacles.

"He preached against it two weeks ago," contributed Pristina, her hands clasped on the window fastening, her chin on her hands.

"Perhaps he doesn't know about Patterson Greeves," said Maria. "Somebody ought to have told him."

"He's coming out again. Perhaps Mr. Greeves wouldn't see him. There's his car. That rowdy Lincoln boy driving it again. What the minister sees in him!" announced Cordelia. "See, he's hurrying. I wonder what's the matter."

"Perhaps he's just found out," suggested grandma.

Speculation ran rife, and the watchers hovered not far from the windows, doing extra dusting in the front sitting room to keep near. It was almost like the time when the circus rented the meadow for a week and they could watch the rhinoceros and giraffe go to bed at night. None of them really admitted they were watching until suddenly the minister's car drew up in front of the Silver house.

"He's back!" said Pristina glued to the window, "and there's another woman—no, girl with him!"

"It looks as if there might be going to be a wedding!" declared Maria primly, "I declare some men are the biggest fools! You'd think after two experiences he'd be satisfied. Oh, Men! Men! Men! I've no patience with them."

"Well, I certainly don't think much of a woman that comes to his house to get married!" said Pristina. "I wonder our minister has anything to do with it."

"A woman that will marry a divorced man, too," sighed grandma.

"Well, I wonder which one it is, the first one or this one?" questioned Pristina. "They both look awfully young. Perhaps they don't know a thing about him."

"And neither do you," said mother, "Pristina why don't you take that cake over that you baked for the sewing circle tomorrow? You've plenty of time to make another before the circle, and anyhow now you've found out Stella Squires has made a chocolate cake it would be better for you to make some other kind, say marble cake or a cocoanut. If they're going to have a wedding it would be nice in the neighbors to help out a little."

"I think I'll find out whether there is a wedding or not first," said Pristina with a toss of her head. "We'll *eat* the chocolate cake ourselves. I'm going to cut a big piece now."

Pristina was like that sometimes. And when she was the aunts looked at her in a hopeless sort of way and kept still. They called it the "Appleby" in her.

All day long they kept their watch upon the house. When Silver and her father came out to walk after lunch, they huddled anxiously at the window, and commented. This was the bride probably, and the other one—who was the other one? Bridesmaid or secretary? It was hard to decide.

While they were still discussing it Athalie's trunks arrived, and brought them all to the window again.

"Upon my word, there must be more coming!" said

Pristina from her window. "Look at the trunks. They surely wouldn't have more than one apiece."

"A bride might have two," suggested mother.

"Yes. You know New York! They're very extravagant livers!" declared Maria who had had the advantage of a week in New York when she was sixteen and had been going on the strength of it ever since and claiming obeisance from her family therefrom.

"Well, even so. Count them. One, two, three, four! Are those others boxes? They must have books in them. They probably belong to Mr. Greeves. But the girl that came first had her baggage with her. She wouldn't be wanting a trunk."

"Well, there's one apiece and one other besides the boxes," said Henrietta. "A man wouldn't want a trunk would he? Not if he carried his books in boxes. What would a man find to put in a trunk?"

"His clothes, of course," said Cordelia sharply.

"But a man has so few clothes. Just a suit or two. It seems as if he could hardly fill a trunk with those. Perhaps he brought home relics from the war. If he did I certainly do hope we get a chance to see them."

"Perhaps, sometime, if they're away Mrs. Truesdale will ask you in quietly to see them," suggested mother.

"Those trunks are enormous! See, grandma, they had to get Hank Lawson to help carry that one in. I think that's scandalous!" This from Maria.

The shades of night settled down and left them still wondering.

"There's a light in Miss Lavinia's room. It's strange they'd let anybody be put in there!"

"Maybe he took that room himself!" suggested grandma.

Arden Philips and his wife ran in on their way to a committee meeting at the town hall, something about a supper to be given in the fire house as soon as the first strawberries were ripe. They settled into the window seats and asked everything that had happened all day. Arden contributed the fact that a great pile of mail had come for Mr. Greeves and among them three from New York City.

"Whatever became of that child of Pat Greeves?" asked Mrs. Philips loosening her silk wrap and throwing it back to adjust a long string of green beads slung around her scrawny neck and looping down below her waist! "Did it live? Boy, wasn't it?"

She was a tiny wiry little woman with bright beads of eyes and the quick restless motions of a bird. She perched on the edge of her chair and looked quickly from one to another as she talked.

"Girl," said grandma pursing her lips and looking over her spectacles. "It was a girl. He gave it to its mother's parents. I heard they didn't have much to do with one another."

"Well, I should think not!" said Ruby Philips. "A man that would marry again!" Mrs. Philips didn't believe in second marriages.

"And then get divorced!" reminded grandma.

"Well poor thing. I hope she hasn't suffered from her father's sins," said Maria righteously.

"Now Maria," reproved mother, "you're going a little fur. You don't really *know* that her father sinned."

"Well, he got divorced, didn't he?"

"Yes, but Maria, he might uv *had* to—you know it isn't *always* the *men's* fault."

"It's pretty generally the men's fault, I guess," declared Maria, tossing her chin. "I thank goodness I never got tied up to one."

"Well, Maria, I don't think you're very polite to Arden," said Mrs. Arden, rising with a flame in each cheek.

"Oh, Arden's Arden, of course. Besides he's my third cousin. And present company is always excepted you know," laughed Maria sharply.

Mrs. Arden drew her cape around her briskly and stepped toward the door. There was still a stiffness in her voice. She pursed her thin lips as if her mouth shut with a drawstring like a bag of marbles.

"Well, I must say I don't like insinuations, even when it's a joke," she said coldly, "come Arden, we'll be late to that meeting. You'd think if there *was* a wedding he'd invite someone from the town, just for old time's sake, wouldn't you? Of course the minister;

but he's a comparative stranger, and he *has* to have him. Well, I suppose we'll know sometime. Good night."

Arden, drab and homely, with blue eyes and light eyelashes followed her obediently out with an air of getting in the way of his own feet. She tripped along down the walk like a sparrow and Arden loped behind, a long limbed, disproportionate man who never seemed to be quite inhabiting all the room in his garments. They crossed the street and passed the Silver house, looking closely and walking slowly. The street lights twinkled over their heads as they passed.

By and by a shadow passed along the street, with something low trailing after, but there was no sound of footsteps though grandma had her window open a trifle. A moment later the front door of the Silver house opened letting out a stream of light and shut again before they could see who had gone in. There seemed to be a dog about. He howled once from the neighborhood of the Silver gate.

At ten o'clock some one came out, perhaps two. It almost seemed like a group. Was one the minister? Was that a dog or only a mote in the eyes that had strained so long through the darkness?

Lights appeared upstairs over the way, went out, and the Silver house remained a white shape against the velvet blue of the night sky. Little stars blinked distantly and the tree toads sang uninterruptedly in the meadow and down by the brook. Grandma was snoring gently in her downstairs bedroom, and Pristina lay in her narrow bed up in the roof bedroom and wondered why life had seemed to pass her by.

Chapter XIV

To the right of the Silver house and almost directly across from Vandemeeter's stood a neat gray house with wide verandas and white trimmings. There were tall trees of great age in front of the place that gave it a retired look, and the fine lace curtains at the front windows were always immaculate. The fence was gray with square fat gate posts, and a row of blue and yellow and white crocuses were picketed on either side of the gravel path. It was one of those places that you always feel you can depend on, and the people who lived in it were like unto it.

Joshua Truman was the Silver Sands banker, and the fact that the whole neighborhood called him Josh and that he had a hearty handshake and a smile for everybody in no wise detracted from his dignity. He seems to have been an honest banker, and beloved by everybody. He had shaggy overhanging gray eyebrows, but they hid a twinkle in the mild blue eyes. Mrs. Truman was plain with sweet eyes, wore her hair in close satin ripples above her ears as she had done ever since she was married, and kept always a neat brown silk with touches of velvet trimmings for her best dress. She was president of the missionary society in the Presbyterian church. There were two children, David, a lump of activity aged ten, and Mary, a tall lank girl of fifteen with a heavy braid of yellow hair down her back and big, dreamy eyes.

"I think Patterson Greeves has come back," Mrs. Truman announced at the breakfast table next morning. "I didn't notice any one coming in, but Hetty says she saw some trunks arrive. I thought perhaps you'd want to run in and see if there is anything we can do—"

"Oh, why, yes of course," said the banker heartily.

121

"I forgot to speak about it, those men coming in and staying so long after supper last night. He did come. I met the minister and he told me. It seems he has brought his two daughters home. One is about Mary's age. I think she had better arrange to run in today sometime, and show a little attention, perhaps offer to take the girl to school or something just to make her feel at home."

"Oh, mother!" said Mary in dismay, "I can't call on a strange girl! *You* go."

"Is his—? Did he—? Well—what about his wife, Joshua, isn't he—*married* now?"

"Oh, well—no—I believe not. That is—" he glanced at the children, "I should think that was all the more reason why we should show some courtesy to those motherless girls."

"Yes, of course," said his wife with a look of relief that the matter was settled. "Certainly, Mary, you run in after school this afternoon and call. You can take some of our strawberries and a bunch of daffodils and just run in without any formality."

"Oh, mother!" said Mary aghast, "I promised Roberta I'd play duets with her this afternoon."

"Well, take Roberta along," said her mother crisply. "The Moffats were always good friends of the Silvers."

"Yes, certainly," spoke up the father. "Get some of the other girls to go too. It will be a pleasant thing for a stranger to feel that she is welcomed into a community the first day. Talk to some of the girls and make it *go*, Mary."

"All right," said Mary reluctantly, with a speculative glance over at the Silver house which she could see from her place at the table. "I might ask her to go to Christian Endeavor," she suggested, "we girls are on the Lookout committee. We all promised to try and get some new members. What's her name?"

"Well, that I didn't discover. I guess it's up to you to find out, daughter," said her father with a pat on her shoulder as he got up and went to kiss her wife good-bye for the morning.

"Do I have to dress up mother?" asked Mary,

still thinking of her prospective call, "I don't mind going if I can wear my school dress but I hate to waste the time dolling up. Besides, I always feel so embarrassed in my best clothes."

"I don't think it will be necessary to dress up," said her mother with a quick inspection of the neat blue gingham with its sheer white ruffles and the crisp dark blue hair ribbon that tied the heavy braid of hair, "little girls don't have to bother about their clothes. She'll probably like you far better if you go just as you come from school. Be sure your hands are clean of course."

Mary brightened and went off to school quite full of her plans for the afternoon. Her grade was in the old brick schoolhouse up beyond the Truman house. She did not pass the Silver place. She would have been surprised to know that the girl she was proposing to call upon was still in bed asleep. Mary had been up for two hours, had practised an hour and a half, and helped her mother get the breakfast on the table because Hetty, the maid of all work, had a lame foot and was being saved. Mary glanced back at the Silver place and felt a warm spot around her heart. It was going to be nice to have a girl friend living there. They could go to school together. Living next door she naturally would be "best friend." The Silver place would be an awfully nice house to have a Christian Endeavor social in sometime. Would Mr. Greeves be willing? She would suggest this to the girls. This would make them eager to go and see her. She could hear the first bell ringing as she hurried along. She started to run to have more time to talk before school began. Her eyes were bright with the new idea when she entered the schoolyard. She decided that she would ask the new girl over to make fudge that evening if all went well.

On the other side of the Silver mansion, the side where Athalie's room faced, there was an old brown wooden house. It hadn't been painted in years and was not likely to be painted in years to come if it lasted so long. It was built in the days of scroll work and rejoiced in a cupola, lofty and square, with alter-

nate lights of red and blue and yellow glass bordering
a large clear one, two on each side. The front gable
was ornamented with a fret work of ancient wood,
faded brown like the rest, which had somehow, either in a storm or in consequence of the mending of the
roof, become detached from the ridgepole on one side
and fallen out of plumb. The result was rakish, like a
woman with her bonnet on cock-eyed. The windows
of the house were gothic and latticed, and the doors
all sagged. The Weldons lived there and they sagged
too. Uri Weldon usually did his sagging down in the
lobby of the one hotel, sunk deep in a worn-out
leather chair with his heels above his head on another,
and a large sagging cigar in one corner of his mouth.
He kept up the hallucination that he was thus con-
ducting business, which consisted in trying to get
someone to patent some of his inventions, but his business sagged too and never came to anything. Lizette
Weldon, his wife, was spare and wore a false front
over little black gimlet eyes. When she walked she
was the shape of rain in a driving storm but nothing
ever escaped her vision whichever way she was
going. The property was theirs for life, entailed so
that they could not sell it, and would pass to a nephew
now residing in China when they no longer had need
for it. They had been there for years, however, and
seemed likely to outlast the nephew in China. Gentle Aunt Lavinia had had her trials with Lizette, and
young Patterson Greeves owed many a sound thrash-
ing to her sharp eyes and ready tongue.

A long stretch of ill-kept wire grass constituted the
lawn in front of the Weldons, ending abruptly in a
row of sombre pine trees behind which the house retired as if aware of its hopeless shabbiness. Had it not
been for these pines the whole place would have been
a sorry contrast to the well-kept Silver estate. There
was something shielding, almost dignifying in the
pines.

But the side windows had no row of pines and
looked across a clear space straight to the side of the
Silver house; and Athalie's window presented a liberal
view for any interested eye.

On the first afternoon of her arrival Lizette was mounting the stairs for her daily nap when she happened to notice a curious figure climbing from the window. Having been occupied in the kitchen during the morning she was as yet unaware of the arrivals, although she had seen a light in the front room the night before, but the shades were drawn almost immediately and the light remained but about five minutes so she thought nothing of it. But this was startling.

Lizette hastened to get an old field glass which she kept handy and wherewith she had often settled uncertainties in the neighborhood in time past, and brought it to bear upon the object of her interest. She applied the binoculars to her eyes and screwed them hastily into focus, then withdrew them and stared with her naked eyes.

"Oh, my!" she said aloud, "ain't that awful!" She lifted the glass once more and gazed. "Pants!" she ejaculated wildly, a kind of triumph in her tone, "well, now I guess they're coming down a peg! What would the old Silvers say to that! A girl in pants! Of course the papers advertise them but the Silvers never were that kind. And look at her hair! My soul! How does she get it to stay out so. Ain't it redickilus! Where's she going? My good fathers! if she isn't going to climb down! Well, that beats everything! Who is she?"

Lizette hurried down the stairs and rushed to the front window to get a closer view between the pines, then noting the stranger's general direction toward the stores she hastened to the telephone; calling up a friend who lived farther down the street.

"That you Miz Hoskins? Well go to your front window and see that girl in pants coming down the street. She just climbed down off the old Silver pergola out the side bedroom window. Hurry and I'll hold the phone."

Mrs. Hoskins had a hot loaf of bread in a pan, holding it with a wet towel in one hand when she took down the receiver, but she hurried to the window, hot pan and all. There succeeded a pause during the passing of Athalie, then steps and a voice.

"My, ain't that scandalous? And all those young boys down around town! Not that I mind the pants so much if everybody wore 'em. It's sensible you know. But the way she walks and all. And her face. Did you see how it was made up? Why those girls that sang at the minstrel show weren't half so coarse looking. And the air of her. You said she came from Silvers? Well I guess there's going to be some doings there from all I hear. My husband took the express over with the trunks. Say, you oughta have seen those trunks. Seven of 'em I think there was, and not one could be lifted without four men. Just to think such goings on in this respectable town!"

"But who is she?"

"Dear knows! John says she might be most anybody. You know Patterson Greeves got a divorce! Maybe she's his typewriter. That's the way they do things nowadays. Isn't it the limit? Say, I smell my other loaf of bread burning. Excuse me a minute please. You hold the wire. I want to ask you about what happened at the sewing circle the other day. I'll be back in a minute."

Mrs. Weldon took no nap that afternoon. She was too excited. She felt it her bounden duty to keep a watch and find out if there were "doings" going on in the old house, and if she ought to do something about it. What else should a good neighbor do when the respectable dwelling of an old neighbor was threatened with modernism?

The hedge was too high for her to see the terrace and the scene in the garden, but later when Athalie, having cried out her brief wrath, attired herself in a gay little suit of pajamas with lace ruffles around the ankles, and having turned on all the lights proceeded to practise a little aesthetic dancing in front of the window, Lizette was there, glass and all, with her fat husband behind her staring over his spectacles and laughing coarsely in her ear. This was a good joke, a good joke to tell down at the hotel. Those religious Silvers come to this!

The next morning when she slipped through the garden and under the back fence across lots to the garden of Aunt Katie Barnes's neat little place on the side street where the minister boarded, to get a cup of sour milk, she paused with her apron over her head and said:

"Oh, have you heard what's happened over at the Silver place? They do say Pat Greeves has come back and brought a *woman* along! I've been told she was his secretary or typewriter or something. But she's very ordinary. I saw her go by myself and I was shocked! Painted and powdered, her hair all kind of wild, the queerest hat, and *pants,* mind you, in the middle of the afternoon! I feel so sorry for poor Miss Lavinia. She set such store by that boy! But it never pays to bring up other people's children does it? I can mind how she used to sit out there in the garden by the hour playing with him and reading to him. A waste of time I say—but aren't you surprised that he should do this? It seems as if he might have managed to stay respectable even if he is divorced."

Aunt Katie looked up from the potatoes she was frying for the minister's breakfast and smiled.

"Oh, didn't you know who that was? It's one of his daughters. He has two, but this must have been the younger one. She's only a child, fourteen I think Mr. Bannard said, and she's been off at boarding school—I suppose you must expect some craziness from little girls nowadays, there is so much more freedom in the world, especially in New York. But isn't it nice Mr. Greeves has two daughters to keep him from being lonely? The other one is a little older. Her name is Silver. Mr. Bannard says she is the perfect picture of her mother's portrait hanging over the mantel in the drawing room. Do you remember it, that lovely Sargent painting?"

"No," said Lizette coldly eyeing her adversary, "I don't go over there. That Mrs. Truesdale doesn't show herself very friendly. I think she takes on airs. *Daughters,* you think then? Are you *quite sure?* Well, I suppose the minister ought to know." She surrendered the bit of scandal reluctantly, "it certainly is strange we never heard of them before. Daughters! Well, he better keep a little control of them then. One

of 'em was having carryings on in her room last night,
I'll tell you! Dancing, that's what she was doing, in her
underwear! A great big girl like a full grown woman,
and all her shades up! I never did approve of those
pajamas for men even. They don't seem, well, Christian you know. And when a woman takes up with
such outlandish fashions it's time she was stopped by
law, I say."

"Well," said Aunt Katie soothingly, "we don't all
have the same taste in dress you know—"

"Dress!" sniffed Mrs. Weldon, "*un*dress I should say!
However, as you say, it takes all kinds to make a
world. Well, I just ran over to see if you could let
me have a cup of sour milk. Mine got too sour and I
had to throw it out."

Aunt Katie always seemed to have whatever was
needed by anyone and the sour milk was immediately forthcoming.

There being no further excuse for lingering, the
neighbor lingered anyway.

"The minister told you! So he's been over to the Silver place *already!* He's a good deal younger than Pat
Greeves. He must be nearer the age of one of the
daughters. Curious he should run after a man like
that right off the first day! I thought he set up not to
be a tody-er, but I suppose they're all alike. They
know which side their bread is buttered when a rich
man comes along."

"Oh, they met at the fire down at Frogtown night
before last. Mr. Greeves ran across the meadow as
soon as he heard the alarm and got into the thick of it
helping with the best of them. Then they came home
together and took to each other right away. It's going
to be grand having the old Silver place open again,
young people in it, and folks going back and forth
visiting." Aunt Katie's face was innocent as a lamb.
The guest eyed her keenly, but could detect no hidden sign that Aunt Katie realized she had ignored
the criticism.

"Oh, well, if you take it that way of course. Some
might feel they wanted to wait and be sure all was
as it should be. But time will tell. Well, I must run

home and stir up my batter cakes. Uri'll be waiting."

Down at the fire house where Uri spent much of his time when he was not sitting in the lobby of the hotel, it was discussed that morning. There was always a knot of conversation around the fire house door even in early morning. It was just across from the blacksmith's shop, and the hotel, and "handy-by" from the market and post office. When any frequenters came down to the business portion of Silver Sands, morning, noon or night, they always dropped around for a minute, or an hour, to wait for whatever errand had brought them to mature, it might be the mail to be distributed, the horseshoe to be set, or the drummer to arrive at the hotel for their appointment with him, and there paused for a bit of gossip. It was a distributing agency for the private affairs of the town and now and then the outlying districts. It was the country club for the so-inclined of the town, and stood in place of golf for the men who did not aspire to athletics. The good old fire engine was athletic enough for them, and between fires they stood around and polished it and worshipped it, and told tales of their own valor.

Uri Weldon hastened early to the rendezvous that morning with an air of myserious importance, and felt gravely the responsibility of so choice a bit of news as he carried.

Back in the dim shadows of a windowless apartment under the stairs where the oiling and polishing rags were kept, a tramp awoke at the first scraping of the first armchair on the cement floor. Awoke to the dismal necessity of another day, and the immediate problem of getting out of his concealment before he was discovered. His hairy, dirty face appeared weirdly in brief relief on the doorway, and leaned up against the door frame, one either as Uri Weldon settled back with his feet on an old soap box, and his pipe tilted at the right angle for conversation. Ted Loundes and Flip Haines lounged up to the doorway, and leaning up against the door frame, one either side of the door like a couple of bronze figures personifying Ease and Relaxation.

Uri Weldon started in on his tale with many an embellishment, interrupted by loud haw haws on the part of the younger men. The tramp frowned and ventured another look, scouting for a back exit and finding none. The tale went on. The tramp was not interested. He could not help hearing, but he took no heed till Ted, helping himself to a long slither from the batten door behind him and cautiously picking his teeth therewith remarked:

"I hear that guy Greeves has a pile of dough."

Uri Weldon nodded, importantly.

"Well, yes, he's got a pile. Them Silvers was always well off. Course they owned the beach and the sand business, and all that ground the fact'ries were built on, and then the right of way where the railroad went, and stocks, and so on. But now you know a lot of land they had somewhere out in Oklahoma has begun to produce oil. They say the money is rolling in from that. And besides all that he writes books! Everybody knows they charge a turrible price for books. It always beat me how they got it. Just a little paper and ink, and words—just *words!* And getting paid for it! They tell me he's written a book about *bugs* that they charge three dollars and seventy-five cents for, and the people in the colleges are buying 'em like hot cakes! It beats me how with all that learning they can be so easily fooled! But so it is, and Pat Greeves is profiting by it. Well, I suppose his pretty little brats of daughters will inherit a coupla millions apiece or more when he kicks off. Seems queer though. You boys don't remember, but Pat Greeves and I used to be in a fight in school pretty near every day when we was kids—Hi, there boys! Look up the street there! I bet that's her coming down this way now!"

Uri's feet and the front legs of his chair came down to the cement pavement with a crash simultaneously, and the two younger men came about face with alertness and looked in the direction of Uri's finger.

"Gosh!" ejaculated Flip, "she's some winner, isn't she?" "Get onto that epidermis, Ted? Some heft to her too."

All three men with casual manner sauntered eagerly nearer the street and the tramp, peered earnestly out, stealing across the open space with catlike celerity, then drifting hastily behind the offset at the side of the fire house, paused to take his own observation. This then was the daughter of the rich oil magnate who wrote books about bugs.

He had once been a city tramp and he flattered himself he knew style when he saw it. The cut of a garment, the hang of a fold that bespoke quality, the deep blue flash of a jewel, the peculiar dash of the whole makeup that spoke of lavish purse. The tramp watched and listened to the comments of his companions unaware of his very existence, and thought within himself how might he turn this accident of knowledge to his own account. But when the three friends returned to their former attitudes in the doorway of the fire house the tramp had melted away like the shadows and was seen no more.

Chapter XV

PATTERSON GREEVES had not slept at all the night before. His mind was wrought to so high a pitch that it seemed as if he never would sleep again.

Silver's music had not soothed him, instead it had wrought his heart to sorrow with the memories which came trooping, flooding, threatening his self control. Her touch was so like her mother's, her selections, many of them Alice's own favorites. It seemed as he sat there with half-closed eyes watching her that it must be Alice. It could be no other.

At last the girl herself had seemed to feel the strain she was putting upon her father, and whirling about on the piano stool she declared she had played enough for the first night.

It was then the minister roused from his delight in the music, realizing that it was time for him to take his departure and leave this father and daughter to settle their own situation by themselves. He expressed his pleasure in the music and his hope that he might hear it again, more and often, and made his adieu.

"Just a moment, Bannard," said Greeves as they neared the front door, "I'll get that book for you I was speaking of. I saw it this morning in its old place on the shelf—if you don't mind taking it with you."

They stepped into the library and turned up the light. There sat Blink, sound asleep, with a draping of angle worms all around the rim of his tomato can, and one bolder than the rest strewn out across his knee.

Roused, he declared he had not been asleep, but had been enjoying the fire and the music, merely waiting till they were through to present his gift.

Trust Blink to be equal to a situation. Nevertheless he grinned at his worms, and gathering them up flashed a joke at them that brought a little breath of mirth into the tense atmosphere of the evening and made everybody feel better.

When Blink and the minister had taken their leave Silver and her father sat before the fire hand in hand, half shyly for a few minutes and talked.

If the music had not helped Patterson Greeves to solve his difficulties, it had at least made the situation clearer to his daughter.

"Father," she said shyly, almost hesitantly, "don't you think perhaps if you will have a quiet talk with Athalie in the morning it might help? I've been thinking about it. She's probably as excited as we all are. It must be hard for her too. I think perhaps if she understood you might be able to make it easier for her. I was trying to think how I would feel if I were in her place—she was terribly excited and hurt—you could see that—".

They talked for sometime and when Silver finally went to her room Patterson Greeves turned out the light and in the dying firelight he paced the room for hours, back and forth.

In the small hours of the night Anne Truesdale from her anxious chamber off the back hall heard him come softly up the stairs to his room, but when she went in the morning to put his room to rights the bed had not been slept in. There was only a deep dent in the coverlet where folded arms and a head must have rested as of one on bended knees. But Patterson Greeves had no one left to pray to, unless it might have been his dead wife Alice, or his sweet departed Aunt Lavinia, for he did not believe in a God. And if there had been a God he was angry with Him for bringing all this horrible thing to pass upon him.

But when morning dawned, even before Anne Truesdale had been down to open the shutters and tidy up the rooms, he was back in the library again, pacing back and forth. And as soon as ever it would have done any good to call, he was after long distance trying to telephone his divorced wife. He had decided that Athalie must go back to Lilla. He would make it worth her while.

He made a pretense of eating some breakfast with Silver—no sound had as yet been heard from Athalie's room, and none in the family were disposed to disturb her—but it was plain that he was nervous and overwrought, and the slightest sound made him start and listen for the telephone.

When the call came at last, he hurried to the library only to be informed that Mrs. Greeves had sailed for Europe the day before to be gone indefinitely.

He hung up the receiver and stared about the room with that dazed expression he had worn the day before when he first knew that Athalie was coming to him. And again there sounded in his ear the ring of that derisive laughter, echoing along the halls of his soul with taunting sweetness. Lilla had won out again. It was as if she had tossed her daughter over into his keeping and put the sea between them, so that he was not able to send her back, not even able to bribe Lilla with money to take her unwelcome child to her heart again.

After a few moments he rose and gravely walked to the window. The stun of the blow was subsiding and he was beginning to take it in for the first time that this impossible child was his irretrievably to keep and to care for from this time forth, and that he could not rid himself of the trust. For the first time he was taking it in, and some of the things he had flung out in his first bitterness of soul in talking with the minister the night before came back upon him as great truths that he had uttered. He was responsible for the child, responsible for what she had become. He could not shirk any longer what he had tried to shirk for life. He must face it now. There was not distance enough in the whole universe to put his responsibility away from him. It would follow him like a shadow wherever he went, whatever he did.

How could he ever write again with this horror hanging over him? Well, what difference did it make to anyone whether he ever wrote again? What difference did anything make to him?

Gradually, however, the business habits of his life settled upon his mind and he began to come at the question more sanely, more seriously, and to really try to think what he could do, and what he should say to this strange, unloving, unlovable girl.

Perhaps the thought of Silver with the Alice-eyes writing some letters up in Aunt Lavinia's room, a sweet strong sane presence, helped to keep him from the insane desperation that had come upon him the day before. At any rate his tortured mind finally thought out a way, made a semblance of a plan, of what he should say to Athalie and how he should say it.

Thinking more coolly now he could see that he had antagonized her. She was like Lilla. That was plain. Strange that both his children should be like their mothers entirely—and yet—no, he could see some things in Athalie exactly like himself. That being the case perhaps he could understand her a little better if he would come at her in the way he would like to be approached himself, reasonably, gently, firmly, but pleasantly. Subconsciously he had known that yesterday, but it had seemed too much like yielding to an outrageous imposition to treat her in any way but imperiously. Well, that was all wrong, of course, from her standpoint. He had simply antagonized her. It would be of no sort of use to try to control her until he had some hold upon her. He had shown his utter disapproval of her, her dress, her appearance, her habits, from the start. Could he possibly retrieve the past and begin again? Well, it was up to him to try. He could not rid himself of her by making her hate him, though he had no real desire to win her love. Still, he must try something. He could easily see now it would be useless to send her to any school against her will in this state of mind. She would only disgrace him and be back upon his hands in a worse condition than before. He must do his duty somehow, whatever a father's duty was. Somehow he had never thought before, till Silver looked at him with Alice's eyes, what a duty of a father might be.

So he rang the bell for Anne and asked her to say to Miss Athalie that he would like to see her in the library as soon as she had finished her breakfast.

Athalie took her time.

She bathed herself leisurely, toying with her perfumes she bathed her face many times in very hot water and only powdered it lightly, giving a becoming touch of shadow under her eyes as of much weeping and no lip stick at all to her full mouth. It took quite a while to get just the right atmosphere, for it was difficult to make the healthy Athalie look as if she were going into a decline.

She really was trying to please her father. She chose a little dashing frock of dark blue wool with a great creamy white wool collar curiously rolled about her shoulders, and a daring scarlet sash of crimson silk with fringe that hung several inches below the hem. She even put on black silk stockings, thin they were and extremely lacy, but black, and completed by little fairy patent leather slippers with straps intricately fastened to look like ancient Greek foot attire. A black velvet band about her forehead completed her costume and she descended slowly, casually, to the dining room and rang the bell imperiously.

It was Molly who brought a tray with ample food, but she rang again and sent for more, and pursued the even tenor of a prolonged breakfast with satisfaction, until Patterson Greeves awaiting her in the library was almost at the limit of his patience and his newly assumed gentleness, and could barely keep his resolves from leaping out the door and escaping him altogether.

But at last, after lingering in the garden a moment to gather a flaunting red tulip and stick it in her dress where it flared against the white of the collar, she sallied into the library without waiting to knock and gave her father a cool good morning, quite as if he might have been the naughty child and she the casual parent, with many, many greater interests than just parenthood.

Following out his resolves with a visible effort he

wheeled a comfortable chair for her to sit down where the light would fall full upon her face and he might study her as they talked. She watched him sharply and then turned and stood with her back to him looking out the window.

"Come here and sit down Athalie," he said, "I want to have a little talk with you."

"Fire ahead, Pat," she said nonchalantly, "I'd rather stand here and look out."

What could a father do under those circumstances? I ask you what *would* a father do? His blood boiled. His temper arose and clamored for satisfaction. He was no father of course, but how could he be? Here was this impish child of his defying him again, making it practically impossible for him to exercise the self-control and gentleness he had intended. It was as if she suspected his scheme and was blocking it. How could he have a heart-to-heart talk with a broad blue and white back, a blurr against the sunshine of the morning. How was he to make her understand that he meant to do his best by her, do all that was best for her whether it was hard for himself or not, if she stood like that and ignored him? He ought to give her a good whipping. That was what she deserved. It was barbarous of course, but she was a little barbarian, and nothing else would probably reach her. Nevertheless—he glanced around and summoned his new resolves that were just sliding out the door, grappled them to his side, and began:

"Athalie, my child," he began, realizing that it was necessary for his own good that he recognize the relation openly. He cleared his throat, "I—ah—"

"Aw, cut the comedy, Pat! What's eating you? Spit it out! I know I'm in for the deuce of a time, but if you're going to preach a sermon you'll have to do it without me. This is too gorgeous a morning to be shut up in the house. Say, Pat, don't you ever play golf? What say if you and I go to some country club around here and have a game and then take lunch? Let's have a ripping old time together and get acquainted, and after that if you haven't got it all out of your system yet I'll agree to listen."

For an instant the astounded father gazed at the face of his cock-sure amazing daughter and wavered, almost considering whether he could accept this high handed proposal. Perhaps if he had this story might have been a different one in many details, who can tell? But Patterson Greeves' sole contact with youth since he passed out of that class himself had been in the class room or on the battle field, in both of which places he had been the dictator, able to put his victim through instant discipline if he did not obey in every particular; where a mere black mark on a report card, or a spoken word to an under officer, meant that the delinquent would be dealt with speedily and thoroughly, and where respect and obedience were the foundation of breath itself and nothing else was to be tolerated.

And now, while his flesh shrank from the encounter before him, and his whole soul cried out for respect and the open air, a relaxed conscience, and a chance to get things into some natural order again, his puritan inheritance and his whole training demanded respect and obedience, and the moment passed. The scene of the night before rose in his mind's eye and his blood boiled. He was again in the position of an outraged parent struggling for self-control while he read the ten commandments to a naughty child.

And perhaps it was as well, for Athalie knew how to take advantage of the least opportunity, and she *had* to learn *sometime* that law was law.

The silence was growing very tense. Athalie, quick to note his every phase of attitude toward her, so sure of him when she finished her wheedling sentence, began to grow uneasy as his gaze continued, staring, stern and displeased.

"Athalie," he spoke at last and his words were like icicles, "I can go nowhere, do nothing, until I have had an understanding with you."

A sullen cloud settled down over the girl's face.

"Sit down." He pointed to the chair. Athalie hesitated a second, then with her sullen eyes like smouldering fires fixed on him, seemed to think best to obey, but she sat down tentatively, with one foot slid slightly behind her in readiness to arise again if he offended her. Her lips were pouted angrily. She shrugged her shoulders with a bored attitude as if she were but humoring him for the moment.

The speech he had framed through the long hours of the night deserted him now when he most needed it. Strangely it did not seem to fit. He struggled to find the phrases, cutting ones, intended to show her her place, and keep her in it, an ultimatum which would put things on a proper basis. But the whole thing was gone, and nothing but his own helplessness was upon him.

Then something Silver had said the night before about talking gently, reasonably, came to him. A sense of the room and its hallowed memories filled him. It was as if those who had loved him and cared for him in his earlier years might be hovering around unseen waiting to help him through this trying time. He dropped his forehead on his hand for a moment almost humbly, and then lifting his eyes he tried to tell the girl what was in his heart. None of the sentences he had planned were there. Many of the words he spoke he would not have wished to say to her, it was condescending too much to one who had treated him and his so lightly.

"Athalie," he said, and his voice sounded now more gentle, with that certain something which always brings attention, "you and I are not in a very pleasant position. Perhaps it may be as hard for you as for me, I do not know. I may not have seemed to you very kind nor sympathetic when you arrived. I certainly did not welcome you. I was utterly unprepared for your arrival, as your mother must have known and intended that I should be. I do not intend to speak of her nor the past any more than is necessary; and there must of course be a great many things that you do not understand about our peculiar situation. We shall just have to put away the past and try to build up a relationship from the beginning. In order to do that there are one or two things that must be clearly understood.

"In the first place we belong to an old and respectable family with many traditions that must be honored, and standards that must be upheld. We owe it to the past."

He studied her blank sullen face for a moment wondering if she understood.

He struggled to make his words plainer.

"There are certain customs and laws of society which we have always maintained. I cannot have my daughter transgressing these things. Our women have always been good and pure, and have never sought to imitate men, nor to flaunt their personalities or their persons. They have always been modest, quiet, sweet women, dressing unobtrusively, becomingly, and in a modest way. I cannot countenance the way you speak, the flippant, pert, rude disrespect, both to me and to the old house servants who have been with us so long that they are an integral part of the family. I cannot countenance your mannish ways, nor your cigarette smoking, nor your decollete dresses. I like sweet, modest girls, and if you and I are to get on at all together you must drop these ways and try to be a good girl."

Athalie's eyes smouldered furiously, and her lips curled in contempt.

"I suppose that other girl just suits you!" she stormed, "little simp!"

"Silver seems a very modest, sweet girl," he assented, wondering what he ought to say about the way she had treated the picture last night.

"Well, I *hate* her!" said Athalie in low hard tones, "I HATE HER!—and you sound to me awfully what they call at school, 'mid-Victorian.'"

Patterson Greeves began to realize that he was not getting on very well. He looked at his hopeless offspring and longed to vanish out of her sight forever, caring not where or how his soul was disposed, so he might finally escape the problem of her. But something in his puritan conscience refused to let him slide away from the issue. He must face and conquer it. He had slid out of his situation with Lilla by letting it take its course—or had he? Was she not even now as poignant and tangible an element in his life as though he were struggling to live his daily life by her side? It passed through his mind that perhaps nothing was quite ever shoved aside or slid out of. Perhaps we always had to reckon with everything we did, sooner or later—sooner *and* later. That was a question of life that might be worth looking into, might make a good subject for an article for a magazine—what strange thoughts form themselves beneath the surface when we are in the midst of a tense and trying time! Patterson Greeves brushed the thoughts away impatiently and sat up. He must get these things said that he had resolved to say.

"It makes no difference what I sound like," crisped the father, "nor by what names your school friends choose to call things. I am telling you certain facts which must be acted upon by you as long as you are under my care. They are the only basis upon which you and I can have any dealings whatever. You cannot carry things with a high hand, ignore everybody else and overturn systems. You are not the ruler here, and you must understand it from the beginning."

He paused and eyed her, but she gave no sign, just let her smouldering eyes rest on him sullenly, unflinchingly, the slow contempt in the upper lip continuing to grow.

"Those things being thoroughly understood and complied with on your part willingly," he went on hurriedly, determined not to give her an opportunity to demur, "I am entirely willing to talk over your future with you, and try to arrange as far as is possible and best for you, to make such plans as will be agreeable to you. As to the school you will attend, I shall be glad to send for catalogues and let you have a part in the selection of your—"

She raised her hand imperiously.

"Stop right there!" she demanded sharply, "if you're banking on me being a good little girl and going to school you might as well understand that I won't! I came here to live with you. The court said I was to be under your care, and here I'm going to stay. If you try to send me away anywhere I'll simply run away and make you more trouble. I'd drown myself before

I'd go to another boarding school. I've lived in boarding schools all my life and I'm *done* with them! You can't shunt me off that way for it can't be done!"

A glance into her eyes showed that she fully meant every word she said and something in her tone reminded her stubborn father that she had inherited his power of sticking to a decision. Remembering last evening it seemed fully likely that she would carry out any threat that she might choose to make. He shuddered inwardly and began to weaken.

"Of course, if I found that you were entirely submissive and obedient it might be possible to arrange a school not far away—"

Athalie arose abruptly.

"Is that all you have to say to me?" she asked in a business like tone, "because I've got some letters to write."

"Athalie, sit down," he thundered, entirely unnerved feeling that his work was all undone again.

"Not when you speak to me in that tone," said the girl shrugging her shoulders and raising her chin. "I suppose you call that kind of talk up to the standards of your respectable family."

The crimson swept over her white sensitive face. Her voice was so perfectly like Lilla's, the reply so entirely what she would have given.

"I beg your pardon, Athalie. It was not. I am very much upset this morning. I will endeavor to control my voice. Will you kindly be seated? Now, I want to ask whether you are going to be willing to be subject to my authority? If not I must begin to take immediate steps to place you where you will be looked after in the right way. I cannot have such scenes recurring. I may as well say I *will* not have them. I am a busy man with important work to do, and this is utterly upsetting. Will you be a good girl and try to do right?"

His offspring regarded him coolly.

"I don't know whether I will or not," she answered calmly, "it depends upon how you behave. If you let me have my own way and have a good time I presume I shall—depends upon what you call good. I don't intend to be goody goody. But if you try to bully me you'll wish you hadn't, that's all. That's what I told Lilla when I left her. I said 'Lilla, he may have bullied you, but he's not going to bully me. It isn't being done.'"

A sudden startled wonder came to him as she spoke of her mother that made him forget to listen to the arrogant ending of her sentence.

"Athalie," he said suddenly changing the subject, "are you aware that your mother has sailed for Europe?"

The girl gave him a look as if he had unexpectedly stabbed her, and her eyes filled up with tears, her lips trembled. She struggled for an instant with a sob, gave a slight nod of assent with her chin and broke down with a heart rending little cry, sinking her head upon her arms, her whole gaudily attired body shaking with suppressed sobs, as if the thought was too deep for sound.

Patterson Greeves stared at her for a moment uncomprehending, unable to meet this amazing phase of his most mysterious daughter, resenting her change of combat as if she had broken some rule of the game. She was not being true to type. How could he meet such an antagonist? Lilla used to cry prettily, pettedly, outrageously, to order, when she found all other weapons useless; but this was grief, genuine, deep, terrible. The grief of an uncontrolled nature. Grief of the kind he always had felt in his own troubles. Was it possible that something in his heart was stirring toward her, yearning—? No. This child of Lilla deserved all she was getting—ah! but child of himself too. Could it be possible that Lilla loved the child? If so why had she sent her away from her? It seemed out of the probable that Lilla could love anything but herself. Could it be possible that the child loved Lilla? She did not seem like a loving child. But those sobs were not angry, they were hurt, stricken cries. Had Lilla been unkind to the girl? His sense of justice roused toward her. He put out a vague hand and touched her shoulder.

"Athalie, haven't you had a—*happy*—life? Hasn't your mother been good to you?" he asked hesitatingly.

She lifted a tear stained face from behind which fires flashed in her eyes, and shook his groping hand off.

"That's none of your business," she said, "you never tried to make it any happier, did you?"

The father sat and saw a few more of his shortcomings marched out before him in the open, and swallowed hard on the sight. He, Patterson Greeves, of a respected family had contrived to do some of the most contemptible things a man can do on earth! It was unbelievable, and yet he was beginning to believe it.

He stared at her a moment with that dazed expression coming again. It dazes most souls to really look in their own eyes and behold how different they are from their fancied selves. Then he drew a deep sigh and arose going to the window to stare out across the meadow.

"No. I don't suppose I ever did," he said reluctantly at last. The sobs ceased as suddenly as they had begun. There ensued a prolonged silence. Then the father added as though to himself:

"I had no intention of overlooking any duty, I simply did not realize."

Finally the girl raised her head and in quite a controlled voice said:

"That's all right, Pat, I'm here now. Forget it! We aren't getting anywhere and I'm going up and wash my face. If you change your mind about that golf just send me word."

She was at the door when he wheeled about and said hesitatingly: "There's one thing, Athalie, I wish you wouldn't call me Pat. I don't like it. It sounds disrespectful. It makes me ashamed. I—"

"All right, dad, since you ask it that way I won't, but I like you a lot more when you're Pat. It seems to make you more homey and understandable. Well, so long! You know where to find me!" and she flashed away like a bright-throated, naughty blue-jay.

The father sat down in a chair and covered his face with his hands. The interview for which he had been all night preparing was over and he had got nowhere.

Nothing had been accomplished, except that perhaps he himself had weakened. A sense of his own forgotten responsibility, and a certain wistful turn of her voice had undone him. How was he ever to do anything with this unmanageable child?

The door suddenly opened without warning and Athalie's head flashed in again.

"I just wanted to say, dad, that if you take that other girl along you needn't count me in. She and I are two people. I hate her. So don't go to bunching us up for it won't work, and don't give me any more of that line about getting advice from her about dress, see? I won't stand for it, that's all. If you want me to live up to your standards you've got to live up to mine! understand?"

She was gone. And if she had suddenly hurled a leaden weight on her father's heart the world could not have turned darker or his heart been more heavy. How was ever such a state of things to work out?

A soft knock on the door broke in upon these thoughts, and Silver stepped within the room dressed in coat and hat and gloves, with her suitcase in her hand.

Chapter XVI

WHENEVER Silver came anew into his vision again she gave her father a start, her appearance was so much like his lost Alice.

There was something exquisite and spiritlike in her face that rested and soothed him. It was curious that the word "blest" flitted through his mind when he thought of how she made him feel. He lifted a troubled face to greet her now and a sick dismay stole over him as he saw the suitcase in her hand.

She put it down and came quickly over to him, her lips smiling although her eyes were grave. Her voice had a lilt of sorrow in it though she tried to make it cheerful.

"Father, I've thought it all out in the night," she said perching on the arm of his chair and putting her arm softly around his neck—just so her mother used to sit and touch his hair lightly with her fingers. He had not thought of it in a long, long time.

"You see, I've sort of promised this man I would take this position, and he has held it for me already for several days while I was getting packed up. I feel that I ought to go back right away and get to work."

She was talking rapidly, trying to stem the tide of emotion she evidently felt, and the stricken look on his face made it no easier.

"I didn't tell you this morning at breakfast because I didn't want you to be disturbed by any other question till you had had your talk with Athalie. It wasn't fair to her. But I saw her just now as she came upstairs and I feel sure you have come to some understanding.

"Now, father dear, please don't try to change me," she took the hand that he put out in protest and held

it close. "Listen to me. It isn't at all what you are
thinking. I'm not being driven away nor anything. I
am simply going away because I feel that it is my
duty. No, you're not to talk, please, till I'm through.
Listen, father, Athalie is younger than I am and she
needs you more. You must get acquainted with her
and teach her to love you. She hasn't ever had anybody real to love her, I am sure, and I have, you know.
And it isn't as though I didn't have you too. It's quite,
quite different from what it was before I came. I
have a father now and I know he loves me. And we
can write to each other, and that will be wonderful!
And I'll have someone to advise me—"

"Stop!" cried Patterson Greeves springing to his feet,
his tortured nerves refusing to hear more. "Stop! don't
speak of it again! I tell you I have borne enough. You
shall not go away, Silver, my Silver-Alice! I need
you! I want you! You remember your grandmother
told you to find out if I needed you. Well, *I do!* God
knows I do! Do you suppose for an instant I would let
the welfare of that other strange child come between
us? She is nothing to me, never can be. Her mother
was a viper, and she is going to be just like her! I will
send her—!"

Suddenly both of them became aware of the opening of the door and there on the threshold stood
Athalie, attired in giddy sports clothes with a golf
club in her hand, but the bright smile with which
she had entered had died on her lips and her face
was white as death, her eyes like two blazing coals.

For an instant she stood there facing her father, her
eyes wide with sorrow, consternation, something terrible and inscrutable. Then she turned with a quick
glance of hate toward Silver and exclaimed:

"Oh, heck!"

The slam wherewith she emphasized her exit from
the door reverberated through the house like thunder
as she stormed upstairs again. Anne Truesdale hurried in from the back hall with her apron wrapped
around her hands and over her heart, and stood like
an old gray squirrel her head on one side perking her

ears, watching, listening. But Athalie's sobs were smothered in the pillow for the hurt had gone deep, deep!

The two left in the library white and shaken looked at one another.

Silver's eyes said sadly: "Father, don't you see I must go?" but the man's lips spoke the answer.

"It would be impossible, Silver. I could not endure her."

It was an hour before they arrived at a compromise. Silver was to remain for a time, was to send for her trunk, and to be allowed to follow her own course about keeping out of Athalie's way, on condition that the father was to make an honest effort to win Athalie to a better way of behavior, and to try to cultivate a little love between them, though that Patterson Greeves declared was an impossibility.

To this end he had agreed to keep his feelings in the background and try to show Athalie a good time, that being the thing which seemed to be uppermost in her mind and the most likely to make her amenable to reason.

When Silver left him to go back to her room it was with the satisfaction of seeing Anne Truesdale precede her up the stairs to tap at Athalie's door with the message that her father was now ready to go with her to the golf links if she would come down at once.

How had the slip of a girl learned to wind one round her finger? Just as her mother used to do. Always able to make one see the sensible sane thing to do, always willing to give up herself and stand in the background while someone else was being helped. Oh, why, why could that mother not have lived? He wondered all these things as he waited for the other daughter to present herself, half hoping she would declare against going.

Athalie came slowly down with a gloomy air. Her eyes looked heavy and her mouth slouched at the corners. She carried her bag of sticks slung over her shoulder and she had taken care to wear a bright skirt in place of the knickers which she would have chosen, obviously trying to please him if he had but known it, trying to respect that vague respectable family standard of which he had spoken.

"Pristina!" called grandma from the sitting room, "come here quick and tell me which one this is."

Pristina hurried from the kitchen where she was making cake, a flour sifter in her hand.

"That's number one," said Pristina assuredly, "she was the fat one with the painted face. I wonder why the other one didn't go too. They are going to play golf."

"Seems to me that's rather frivolous to begin with— golf," said grandma. "Seems as if for a man of his years he ought to be getting settled and getting out his work. If he's really so great as they say, writing books and all, why don't he write 'em? I have no patience with people trying to keep from growing up. Golf! H'mmph!" sniffed grandma.

"All great people do it nowadays, grandma," assured Pristina, "they talk in the magazines about it's keeping you in condition."

"Condition! Fiddlesticks! If he'd get out and do a little digging in his own garden it would keep him in condition enough. What was that Pristina, that your Uncle Ned said the last time he came down from New York? It was something very fitting about this golf."

"Oh, uncle said he had no time for knocking a pill around a ten-acre lot. But grandma, that wasn't original. I've heard it since, and read it in the joke column."

"Very likely they got it from your Uncle Edward," said grandma reprovingly. "You have a way of discounting your relatives that is very disappointing, Pristina. Your own family are as good as any you'll find anywhere. Don't go yet, Pristina. Who is that coming up from the post office? She's met them. Perhaps she'll be coming here. She'll be able to tell us something and then we shall know what to think. I declare it's very embarrassing not knowing what to think, nor how to act."

"That's Lizette Weldon, grandma, and she's bringing back the cup of yeast she borrowed last week. I see a cup in her hand."

Lizette had seen Greeves and his daughter start out.

"My soul!" said Lizette and hastened to grab her brown cape and get the cup of yeast that she might not miss this so great opportunity. She met them as they were passing the gate.

"Yes, that's the one! My, ain't she coarse!" she commented inwardly. "Now, does he think he's going to pretend he don't know me? Well, I rather guess not. Good morning, Mr. Greeves. We're pleased to see the old house lighted up!"

"There, now!" she said to herself, "that'll make that fat thing understand that I saw her last night and perhaps she'll be more careful when she cuts up her antics."

Patterson Greeves startled into recognition lifted a belated hat.

"Oh, yes, good morning. It is a long time since it was lighted. Thank you. I hope you are quite well!"

"He didn't know me from the man in the moon," she told herself as she hastened up the street with the yeast. "What a man! I don't wonder she divorced him. Mercy, but that girl is fat! And her clothes looked like my patchwork quilt with the rising sun pattern. I wonder he lets her go out that way. He knows what's expected in this town, he lived here long enough, goodness knows. But perhaps he doesn't care what we think."

Pristina hastened to the door. Ordinarily Lizette was not overly welcomed, but a common cause does a great deal to bring folks down to a common level.

"Well, what do you think of Patterson Greeves' daughters?" she asked almost before she had her breath from coming up the steps.

"Daughters?" chorused the Vandemeeter girls, all present but Harriet who was hastening down from the third story as fast as possible, having left a pillow in midair as she was making the bed, when she heard Lizette's voice at the front door.

"*Daughters!*" reiterated Lizette sitting down complacently with the cup of yeast still in hand, "sort of startling ain't it. I never heard of them before, did you? Strange that Mrs. Truesdale or someone never let it out, but land! she's as close mouthed as Miss Lavinia Silver was, every bit, and a thousand times more aristocratic. Well, I met one of 'em face to face and I don't think much of her. She's fat and coarse and dresses outlandish. I was just thinking on my way down she looked as if she had on my rising sun bed quilt, all queer stripes and stitches over her skirt and sweater."

"*Daughters!*" echoed the Vandemeeters again and looked at one another. "We must tell Arden's wife!"

"What's her name?" asked Pristina.

"Well, he didn't name her when he introduced her," evaded Lizette. "Perhaps that's the fashion now. But the fact is I don't believe he remembered my name, although he pretended he was awful pleased to see me."

"Well—it's only natural—after all these years—" said mother comfortably.

"No tain't natural, you know tain't. Why, I've spanked him for stealing my cherries!"

"That's probably the reason," said Pristina, "one can't be dignified in the face of a spanking. How old is that girl anyway?"

"Well, I hardly know, Pristeen, she looked older, an younger, 'n she oughtta be. I couldn't quite describe it. Kind of as if she was an old woman that hadn't growed up, or a baby that had lived a hundred years. One thing I know, she had smut under her eyes, and them lips never grew red like that. It ain't natur'."

"Is she the oldest or the youngest?" asked mother, biting off her thread and holding up her needle to the light.

"Well, 'deed I can't really tell you Mis Vandemeeter, but I shud judge she might be the youngest. But then I ain't seen the other so you can't tell. This one wears pants, regular pants like the boys, if that'll tell you anything. But laws! The other one may too for all I know. She keeps herself mighty close."

"She went out with Pat—with her father I mean—yerterday afternoon," contributed Harriet. "She looked to me like a real modest appearing girl. She has pink cheeks, not too pink, and light hair, a real girl. I liked her looks."

"I'm sure I don't see how you could tell at that distance, Aunt Harriet," said Pristina coldly.

"Well, her dress seemed quiet," defended Harriet.

"Well, they may wear dresses that scream for all me," said Pristina crossly, "I'm going back to my angel cake."

Lizette's languidly alert eyes followed her mournfully, and when the click of the flour sifter could be heard she lowered her voice sepulchrally:

"Wasn't Pristina rather interested in Mr. Greeves at one time?"

"Mercy, no!" clamored mother so audibly that her voice could be heard in the kitchen, "Pristina was a babe in arms when he went away from here. Just because she did her duty by honoring a fellow citizen in her essay at the club everybody has jumped to the conclusion that she's in love with him. I wish to pity's sake you'd turn your attention to someone else, Lizette, and not carry gossip around about my child."

"Well, now Lucy, I certainly think you'll have to take that back. I don't know what you mean. I only asked a simple question, didn't I? And I don't originate all the questions in this town do I? If I give you a little hint of what's passing isn't that only kindness?"

Mrs. Vandemeeter pursed her lips around a pin and looked angry.

"Well, all I've got to say," said Lizette rising offendedly, "is, if you don't ever find any worse things said about you than I say you can count yourself well off. There's your yeast. Don't trouble to get up. I've got to run right back. I thought you'd be interested to know, but of course if you're not I'll keep the rest to myself. Good-bye."

She shut the door with a slam and swished down the front walk.

"Cat!" said Pristina from behind the pantry door.

"There, now Lucy, I'm afraid you've done it. She'll tell something a great deal worse. It never does to make an enemy mad, especially if she's got a tongue, let sleeping dogs lie, the saying is, and it's very true," said grandma. "Something about it being better to have even a dog your friend, too, what is it? Don't any of you know? It bothers me so to have something like that I can't remember. Now I shall lie awake all night tonight thinking of that, and it will worry me like anything that you gave her a chance to talk about Pristina, Lucy. She'll talk, I know she will."

"Let her talk!" said mother with her head in the air, "I guess Pristina can stand it. Pristina's a lady."

"Well," said Pristina, "I'd like to know what those girls are named. You can tell a whole lot by names."

"You'll know soon enough," said grandma, "get back to your cake. I wonder if Arden's wife knows about their being daughters! Well, I must say it's a relief to know they're daughters. The neighborhood has always been so respectable."

Athalie was a different creature on the golf course, alert, strong, skillful, full of eagerness, like a boy. She whistled and talked slang and patronized her father till he began to feel like a small boy himself, and all the time as he walked silently from point to point studying his amazing child, he was seeing himself in all her actions, and then seeing Lilla in her waywardness between, and realizing more and more that he was responsible for this queer tantalizing creature. Part of the time also he was wondering why he had been persuaded to come out on the golf course with this child whom he disapproved, whom he did not want to be with, and why he was trying with all his might to control his temper and make her have a good time. It was all Silver's doings, "Silver-Alice!" he said it over and over to himself "Silver-Alice! Silver-Alice! Silver-Alice!" and the name sounded sweet to his soul. Why had he not known what sweetness there was in fatherhood?

On the way home it almost appeared from something Athalie said that she had been trying to make him have a pleasant time. He felt strangely touched and chagrined. Not that he liked to have her put herself out for him. It went against the grain to find her doing such a thing. But the justice in his soul cried out for her due. He found himself promising that the morning should be repeated and then groaning within himself over the interruption to his life this was going to be.

But when they reached the house and Anne told him that the minister had called up to ask if they would like to take a drive that afternoon he found himself entirely willing to be interrupted still further.

There was a struggle in his mind about taking Athalie along on the drive. He felt she would be a disturbing element. But when he asked her finally if she would like to go she asked suspiciously:

"Is *she* going?" and when he answered in the affirmative she shrugged her shoulders and said, "thank you, no. I told you how I felt about that. You can't expect me to come when you take her."

He was relieved. It made things easier. He felt sure Bannard would be better pleased.

Silver too was relieved. He could see that. Yet there was a cloud in her eyes, a weight upon her heart. Her conscience was over active. It troubled her that there should be enmity between her father's daughter and herself.

But the day was gorgeous, one of those caressing days in spring when June seems to have anticipated herself and earth's tuning has begun. Little warm scents flitted about, and tiny melodies of living creatures moving, the whir of a bee's wings, the grumble as he worked, the stir of things growing, budding, blossoming, grass blades like rockets shooting everywhere, sharp emerald sounds broadcasting only to those whose ears attuned to their pitch, a meadow lark's note, high, clear above it all.

And then the three seemed so congenial. There was so much to see and talk about, so much in which all were interested.

Bannard was the guide, Greeves the historian, Silver the audience, eager, questioning.

They started up the road past the schoolhouse

where Greeves had been a student, out the old Pike, across the covered bridge and curving back of the village along the beach of silver beside the sparkling stream, down toward Frogtown. Bannard wanted to show them his mission, and to point out a good location for the proposed building.

They drew up in front of a row of old stone hovels crazily jostling each other facing the road and the creek. Bannard pointed to a vacant lot not far away, and he and Greeves were discussing whether it would be better farther up the hill. Silver sat watching the children playing on the path, dirty little things, yet beautiful beneath the dirt. Wonderful starry black eyes set in faces that might have been the models for some of the angel faces in the paintings of great masters, tumbled curls, and rosy cheeks, tiny earrings glittering sharply under the dirt and tousle, little bodies scantily clad, little savages unaware of their soil and nakedness. Clamoring, fighting, throwing mud, the older girls carrying babies too large sizes for their backs, the younger babies huddled to watch the automobile.

A woman hurried out from one of the houses, a curious three-corner shawl of bright colors thrown over her head and folded back like a head dress. She had an air of excitement. Bannard called to her:

"Good morning, Nuncie, all well at your house?"

"Oh, it's the maister!" cried the woman, her voice full of agitation, her dark lined face working with emotion.

"It's the baby, little Mary, Angelo's Mary. Vary seek. I go for the doctor. He come two times yesterday. I tink she got the pneumonias. She turn all black. Her heart stop—"

Before the account was finished Bannard was out of the car. "Will you excuse me a moment?" he said hurriedly, "I must go in and see. This is the beautiful baby I told you about," he finished, looking at Silver.

"Oh, please let me come too. Perhaps there is something I can do. I have had a course in nursing."

"Come then," said Bannard and hurried into the house without knocking.

Greeves put out his hand to stop her, but Silver was gone before he realized. Pneumonia! Didn't the child know that was contagious. What did Bannard mean by letting her go? Suppose she should take it and die, now when he had just got her, leave him as her mother had done! He shuddered and sprang out of the car, resolved to bring her back again into the clean air and sunshine, away from germs and contamination. What was the use of being a specialist on germs if one couldn't save one's own from danger? So he stumbled up the steps and into a deserted room.

There was no squalor nor dirt. The walls were grimy with age and use, and the bare floor was worn in hollows by many feet, but both were clean as soap and water could make them. He stared about. There was nothing in the room but a cookstove neatly blacked with a pot of stew simmering away, a wooden table covered with oilcloth, two chairs and an old sofa with lumpy springs. A painted dresser held a few cheap dishes, some spoons and forks; and a pair of rude steps shallow almost as a ladder led up through an open door, winding out of sight. He could just see the flash of Silver's gray-blue tweed skirt as she disappeared up those impossible stairs.

"Silver!" he called and then without knowing it, "Alice!" but no one answered him. The sound of the factory near by kept up a monotonous clatter in regular rhythm, and there was subdued voices overhead. He stepped to the door and looked up. Such stairs! He never had seen their like. They were like carvings in a sheer wall. They went winding up in the shallow space like pictured stairs, like the stairs in a nightmare. How did anybody ever climb them? How had Silver and Bannard climbed them? Didn't Bannard know any better than to let a girl go up a place like that? He put a tentative foot on the first step and perceived that it was hollowed out in bowl shape by many feet that had gone before. He groped with his hand to the wall that seemed to advance and slap him in the face. He lifted another foot to another step, and went winding and groping up in the dark and uncertainty. A woman appeared at the head of the stairs weeping. She had wonderful dark hair and her eyes were piteous.

"I have come for my daughter. She ought not to be in here," he shouted at her. The woman chattered some jargon at him that had a tang of French, or was it Italian? But he could understand nothing but the words "doctor" and "little ba—bee" and then more tears. She passed beyond his vision.

He lifted himself another step, and yet another and stood head and shoulders in a room light and clean with whitewash, a large framed picture of the painted Christ on the cross hung on the wall opposite him over the head of a big brass bed made up with white draperies trimmed with hand knit lace, and on the clean pillow lay a little face, the most beautiful baby face Greeves had ever looked upon, short black curls tumbled on the pillow, long curling lashes dark upon the rounded cheek, beautiful baby lips gasping for breath, treacherous blue shadows deepening about the eyes and nose.

"These windows ought to be up if it's pneumonia," Bannard explained in a whisper. He stretched out a strong arm and threw up both windows. Silver was leaning over the baby feeling of her forehead touching the pulse of the little fluttering restless hand.

"She ought to have oxygen, Mr. Bannard. Can't you get some quick?" Silver looked up.

"I'll get it," said the minister. "Can you stay here till I come?"

She nodded. "Quick!" she was down on her knees beside the bed, putting the spoon which the mother handed her to the little tight-shut lips.

"She ought not to be here!" repeated Greeves wildly. but Bannard swept him along down the stairs with a strong arm.

"Greeves, just run over to that grocery and ring up Doctor Carr. Tell him I said to come instantly to Angelo's house. I must go for oxygen. You stand by till I come. I'll be back in five minutes."

Before the dazed professor of bacteriology knew what was happening or could put in a protest Bannard's car had given a lurch and darted down the

road, and Greeves found himself walking across that
squalid street, entering the grimy unsanitary grocery
and asking if he might telephone for the doctor. It
reminded him of France. But it was very different
from sitting in an office and telling other officers where
to go and what to do. He had done reconstruction
work, yes, by proxy. It was not the same. He had
been an executive. But this was close contact. He
hurried back with the idea of carrying Silver bodily
out of the infected air, and found himself once more
standing at the top of those ladderlike stairs in that
white airy room, gazing at the little blackening face,
listening to the gasping of the baby, the mother's tears,
and his daughter's voice praying in low gentle tones:

"Oh, Jesus, you know how this mother loves her
baby. Come and help us if it be your will, save this
little darling's life. For Jesus' sake we ask it," and the
mother bowed and crossed herself, hushing her sobs.

Someone brushed roughly by Greeves on the stairs
almost upsetting his balance. To think these people
lived every day on stairs like this. Incredible! A tall
man, young, splendidly built came quickly to the
bed and knelt on the other side from the mother and
Silver. He took the little fluttering hand in his big
rough one. His face was tender and there were tears
raining down his cheeks but he paid no need to
them.

"Poppie come, Mary, poppie come! You hear poppie, Mary? Poppie come home from his work to stay
with Mary!"

Greeves stood and gazed transfixed at the face of
the rough man before him, transformed by love, tender and sweet with fatherhood! So this was what it
meant to be a father!

This was the way he would have felt if he had
let himself! This was what he threw away carelessly
when he took himself out of the reach of his first little
child, and brought another carelessly into the world
to leave to any Fate that came her way.

"Let poppie hold it Mary. Let poppie hold it!" the
stong hand grasped the weak restless fingers, and the
little hand relaxed. For an instant the great dark eyes

opened wide in recognition of the beloved face, and the dark head that had kept up its restless motion back and forth, from side to side on the pillow rested. The parched lips that had murmured hoarsely—"No! No! No!" were quieted. Then the blessed oxygen in the hands of Silver and Bannard reached her nostrils and she drew a long deep breath. The gasping ceased little by little and another breath came. A sigh of relief. The fluttering lids drooped and the long lashes lay on the white sheets again. A restful natural sleep was coming upon the little one.

The doctor came in quietly, laid a practiced finger on the fluttering pulse. The child started and opened her eyes once more. Her glance rested on the doctor in frightened question, then turned to the father and was content, dropping off to sleep again. The doctor nodded to Silver in answer to some question about the oxygen, opened his case and prepared some drops which he handed to Angelo. The father took it and held it to the little lips with as much skill as one trained to such service could have rendered. Greeves stood there watching him with almost jealous eyes, seeing as in a vista a long line of tender services he might have rendered had his heart been right to his own. Where did this rough untaught man learn such angelic gentleness? Here in this bare little house with an environment of the plainest necessities, the father had fenced in a little piece of the kingdom of heaven for his child. Greeves suddenly realized that he was envying this rough untaught working man. With all his knowledge and culture he had missed the blessedness of living which this other man had found, and even his sorrow was sacred because of the love that was between him and his child.

Bannard had gone out again and now returned bringing with him the district nurse. She quietly took things in her capable hands and the minister's group was no longer needed.

As he stumbled shakily toward the treacherous stair Greeves caught hold of the rude railing and gave one more glance back at the big brass bed with the exquisitely knitted white spread, and the wee white face framed in dark curls on the big pillow. The madonna mother was standing at the head on one side, the tender father kneeling at the other, tears raining unchecked down their sorrowful faces, and the face of the painted Christ overhead looked on with yearning eyes. It was a sight he never would forget.

He felt his way down the dark chute, for it was little else, groping with his feet for the shallow steps, and stumbled out into the sunshine, silent and thoughtful. He forgot how it was that he came to go into that house of sorrow, forgot that he had let his child stay as long as she was needed, forgot the words of criticism he had prepared for Bannard for letting her go into the infectious atmosphere. For the first time in years he had become a part of a great suffering universe. He forgot his own individuality, and his grievances, and his heart was throbbing with sorrow for another.

Meantime, Athalie at home, was preparing an elaborate toilet for her evening with Bobs in the city.

Chapter XVII

Down the street from the direction of the school-house proceeded a merry group of girls, stopping at their various respective houses on the way to leave books, lunch boxes, and tidy up hair and hands and face. Laughing and chattering they came on with a sudden hush of awe as they approached the Silver gate, so long an unopened portal to young people.

Mary Truman and Roberta Moffat went first by reason of Mary's having been the instigator of the function. Mary's heavy braid of bright long hair had needed little tidying. It ended in a massive wave of gold below the crisp dark blue ribbon, and frilled in little golden tendrils about her face. Mary wore no hat to rumple the smoothness of the ripples from the delicate line of parting on her crown. She scorned hats, except for Sunday.

Her neat blue and white checked gingham was just low enough to show the white of her throat, above the sheer collar that matched the rolled back cuffs and pockets banded with the gingham. The whole school thought that Mary Truman was always well dressed. Those little gingham bindings on the organdy pockets for instance marked the line between the banker's daughter and other girls whose mothers had not the time to bother with such details.

Roberta Moffat was short and fat, attired in pink chambray whose hem had visibly been "let down" and whose yoke had faded to a nice dependable flesh tint, but her round pleasant face was always wreathed with smiles. She had a glitter of white even teeth and a pair of nice black eyes above the little pug nose that was covered with freckles. Always copying Mary as far as her limited means allowed, she wore no hat, gathered her scant locks into an attenuated pigtail, and acquired a habit of tossing back the straight locks that would keep falling over her eyes where the hair wasn't quite long enough from a defunct bang to catch into the confining pink ribbon that started the pigtail. The ribbon was washed and dyed, and showed signs of droop, but had been retied and stuck out bravely for the occasion.

"I guess she'll be glad when she sees somebody coming to call on her soon, don't you, Mary?" whispered Roberta with a soft giggle.

"I should think she ought to," said Mary seriously, "I certainly am glad you are all with me, girls. Just think how I'd feel now if I was alone!" and she squeezed Roberta's plump elbow lovingly.

Emily Bragg was tall and her sleek brown hair had been bobbed, not for purposes of style however. The top was longer than the rest and fastened at the side with a celluloid slide that gave her the look of an old-fashioned china doll with painted hair all made up hard. She wore a straight little one-piece frock of brown denim with characters worked around the edges in red worsted. On her head was a boy's brown wool cap, one of her brother Tom's, and the big shell rimmed goggles that sheltered her merry eyes gave her the look of a good natured boy. She climbed trees and fences, could whistle as well as any of her brothers, and everybody liked her, but she wasn't a beauty. She was just behind Mary and Roberta, walking arm in arm with little Carol Hamilton, a slight little fairy with pink cheeks and short golden curls who always dressed in pale blue and was adored because she was so pretty.

Della McBride was much taller than the rest, wore her long brown braids in a coronet around her head and had big dark blue eyes with long lashes. The seriousness of her face was somewhat accentuated by a retreating chin. She was wearing a middy blouse and a dark blue skirt, and her companion Vera Morse, a quiet girl with pale eyes and her hair "done up" and brought in sleek loops over her ears, wore a white shirt waist left over from last year, and a brown wool skirt. She carried a brown straw sailor in her hand, and talked in a low sweet voice.

They were a wholesome group as they fluttered up to the steps and sounded the old brass knocker, their subdued chatter like the chirps of a bunch of sparrows on the garden wall.

Anne Truesdale let them into the house and seated them in the drawing room dubiously. Such a circumstance had not happened since the days of Miss Lavinia, six whole callers at once in the old house! Then with deep reluctance, only goaded thereto by an indubitable conscience, she mounted the stairs and tapped at Athalie's door.

"Oh, come in," drawled that young woman affably, "I'll let you fasten this frock. I can't seem to reach around there any more. I was just about to ring for you. It fastens up the back under that drapery."

Anne paused in dismay and surveyed the young woman, but made no move to investigate the hooks in question.

"There are some young persons down in the drawing room come to call on you," she announced severely as if it were a reward far too good for the girl before her, but must be handed over for honesty's sake.

Athalie swung around and faced her.

"Come to see *me?* What are they? Men?"

"Of course not!" reproved Anne. "They're little girls."

"*Little girls!*" scoffed Athalie taking up a powder puff and giving a touch to her nose, "well, you can tell them to go to thunder! I'm busy. I hate little girls."

Anne gasped and tried to begin again, with fearful vision of what it would be if this strange freak of a girl refused to go down.

"Indeed, Miss Athalie, they're quite grown up little girls. They're some of them older than yourself, and they're the daughters of the best people in this town. Your father'll be quite angry if you don't see them."

Athalie surveyed her coldly. She remembered that she was trying to please her father as far as it was compatible with her own plans.

"Very well," she said coolly, "I'll be down after a while and look them over, but I never had much time for girls, unless they have some pep, and I don't fancy they have in this little old town. Are you going to fasten those hooks for me or not?"

"Oh, Miss Athalie," said Anne disapprovingly, "you'll never be going to wear that frock downstairs at this time of the day! The whole village would be scandalized, and your father would be disgraced. The young ladies would not understand it I am sure. It's not at all the custom to dress in that style of an afternoon."

Athalie was attired in a startling costume of scarlet satin and tulle, set off by long clattering strings of enormous jet beads, and pendant hoops of jet with long fringes dangling from her ears. Her hair stood out in a perfect thistledown fluff, scarlet stockings of sheerest silk, and tiny high heeled red leather slippers with intricate straps adorned her plump feet. Her face and arms and neck, of which there was much in evidence, were powdered to a degree of whiteness that reminded Anne Truesdale of a Bible phrase about whited sepulchres. Indeed she was a startling vision as she stood there imperiously waiting for Anne to fasten her scant shoulder drapery and looked years older than she was. Many items of her toilet which happened to be picked up from Lilla's cast off finery doubtless assisted in this impression. But when Anne finished her protest, and made no move to assist her ladyship, a storm arose on the whited face, and the red kid slippers stamped in rage.

"Thank you," she said grandly, "I'm not in the habit of accepting advice from the servants about what I shall wear. You can go! I'll get along without your assistance. I see I shall have to ask my father for a French maid. Go! I said! *Go!*"

Anne went.

When she reached the door she paused.

"You'll be down at once, Miss Athalie, please—! It's not considered good breeding to keep young ladies waiting."

"Shut that door!" stormed Athalie. "I'll be down when I like and not before."

Then in quite a leisurely manner she dabbed more powder on her nose, struggled with the refractory hooks until she conquered them, tilted a bit of a hat of scarlet straw and ribbon atop her fluff of hair, brought it well down over her eyes, jerked it aslant until the dangling cluster of overgrown cherries wherewith it was adorned hung well over one cheek. She surveyed herself in the glass complacently, posed imperiously, then took up a pair of long black gloves, an evening coat of black satin with a collar of white fur and slowly descended the stairs.

Down in the drawing room the waiting girls were having a grand time. They had been little children when last they remembered coming to that dim shrouded room to call on dear Miss Lavinia whom each one of them had loved. They went quietly about looking at the portraits and whispering at first, giving bits of memoirs that were family traditions in their homes. Gradually they settled down to await their hostess' coming.

"We ought to have told Mrs. Truesdale not to have her dress up," said Mary, "we should have said we're just from school."

"Oh, well, what's the difference. She'll come pretty soon," said Roberta, "I like to sit in this big room and wait. Won't it be a grand place to have the Christian Endeavor social? My! I hope she asks us. We could toast marshmallows at that fire, and there's room for a long line of chairs for Going-to-Jerusalem. The boys always like that so they can rough-house."

"Maybe Mr. Greeves might not like rough-housing," suggested Della. "He's a very great writer my father says."

"Oh we'll get father to invite him over that night so he won't hear it," said Mary happily. "Father can always fix people so they don't mind things."

"Well, I'm sure I don't think it's very polite of her keeping us waiting so long. There won't be any time to take her walking nor show her the schoolhouse before supper if she doesn't hurry."

"Maybe she was taking a bath," suggested practical Emily Bragg. "You know you couldn't come down all soap."

The girls giggled.

"Shh!" said Mary, "I think she's coming."

"I wonder what grade she'll be in," whispered Carol.

"Sshhh!" said Roberta, "there she is! Oooohhh!"

Athalie flashed on their vision between the portières, and stood, one hand holding back the heavy curtain, her evening cloak still on her arm, and looked them over half contemptuously. They arose en masse, in silent, breathless wonder. They had never seen anything like it before not even in the movies. Silver Sands was rather careful what films came to town. Mrs. Truman headed a committee of patrons who assisted the managers in making their selections.

At last Athalie broke the stillness which was growing fairly electric:

"I'm Miss Greeves!" she announced, "did you want to see me?"

The girls might have been said to huddle in a group, feeling suddenly that in numbers was strength. Mary as leader and instigator of the expedition gave a frightened glance behind her, and stepped bravely up as her father would have done if he had been there.

"We've come to call," she said pleasantly, watching the twinkling earrings with curious fascination, "mother thought you might be lonesome—"

"Very kind, I'm sure," responded Athalie insolently, "I was just going out, but it's early. I can spare a few minutes."

She flung her cloak and gloves on a chair and sat down, her scarlet tulle draperies flaming about her. She sat with the pose of a society lady, her body flung rather than seated upon the chair. The girls were deeply impressed, all but Emily Bragg who wanted to laugh.

"We don't have to stay," said Emily, "girls, let's go over to Mary's and make fudge if she's busy."

"We just came in because we thought you might be lonely," repeated Mary again, deeply embarrassed.

"Oh, I'm never lonely," flipped Athalie, "besides I have hosts of friends who'll soon be here to see me from N'York. I'm going to have a house party next week, sixteen in all, eight girls and eight men!"

"Men?" echoed Roberta wonderingly.

"Yes, eight men. Of course it's awfully hard to get them this time of year when it's so near time for exams, but they'll be here for the week ends."

"Oh, you mean examinations," said Della seriously.

"We thought perhaps you'd like to join our Christian Endeavor society," braved Mary. "It's awfully interesting."

"I don't imagine so. What is it? A dancing club?" queried Athalie indifferently.

"Oh, no!" said Mary, two red spots appearing on her pretty cheeks. She felt she wasn't getting on very well somehow, "it's just our young people's society. We have lots of good times. Picnics and socials, and we play games, and then we have our meeting Sundays—"

"What kind of games? Bridge? Five hundred? or do you go in for athletics? I don't suppose you play golf?"

"Bridge? Oh, no, not bridge!" said Vera.

"Nor five hundred," said Della, "just games."

"My father plays golf," said Carol. "I've tried it but I don't care much for it. It's too slow. I like tennis better. We have tennis courts at the school."

"Are you going to start school right away? We've been wondering what grade you'd be in."

"I? School? Oh, I'm done with school! Dad tried to talk school to me when I first arrived, but I let him understand he couldn't make anything on that line. I'm certainly sick of school. Of course we had piles of fun at the last one, pajama parties every night, and screams of times. The boys from the prep weren't far away, and they were always onto us when any of us got a box, so they'd come over under our windows and we'd throw down cake, and they'd tie boxes of candy and cigarettes on the strings we let down, and notes, oh, say! Those boys were the limit! There was always something new. But what bored me was the teachers! They didn't seem to remember that they had ever been young, and they kept at us continually, nagged us about our lessons, and exams, it made me hot! They were getting paid for us being there! I don't see what more they wanted."

Silence, prolonged and heavy ensued. The girls looked at one another awe stricken for the father whose daughter had so little daughterly respect. They all had fathers whom they loved, fathers who were trusted, tried companions. It didn't quite go down. Athalie realized she had struck a wrong note. She liked to shock people but when it came to being looked down upon, she didn't quite like it. Neither did she understand the look of awe and disapproval on their young faces. Emily Bragg began to giggle as if somehow she were some sort of show. The others darted quieting glances of rebuke. Athalie felt she must break this silent disapproval. She hated them for not admiring her. She got up with a swagger and whipped out her cigarette case.

"Oh, excuse me girls, do you smoke? Have a cigarette." She passed the gold trinket to Mary.

Mary seemed to turn pale. She got up and took a step toward the curtained doorway.

"I think we must be going," she said coldly.

"Oh, don't you smoke? Not *any* of you? How tiresome! Then I'll order tea. Truesdale!" she lifted her voice, "tea for the ladies!"

Anne appeared instantaneously, as though she had not been far away, her face white with emotion.

The girls eyed one another uncertainly. They wanted to get away. They did not any of them drink tea. It was not allowed in most of their homes at their age unless they were ill. They didn't like it.

But the tea wagon appeared as if by magic, and behold Anne had provided lemonade as well as tea! And there were heaping plates of angel cake and chocolate cake. No one ever caught the servants in that house napping. They were always on the job and always anticipating every possible contingency. Molly was even then in the pantry concocting another cake to take the place of those for dessert that evening along with the strawberries.

Athalie had lighted a cigarette and taken a few puffs at it delicately as the tea wagon was brought in. Now she poured herself a cup of tea and drank it with several pieces of cake while Anne was serving the girls.

Mary with her plate in her hand looked up to find Athalie's eyes upon her with amused contempt. Her heart cried out to get away and weep on her mother's shoulder. She never had felt so utterly outraged in the whole of her happy protected life. It seemed as if the very foundations of her clean beautiful world had been torn away and flung to the four winds. "I hate her! *I hate her!*" her heart kept saying over to herself.

"I thought you were going to ask her over to your house tonight to make fudge," suggested Roberta in a loud whisper, and Mary, lifting her eyes perceived that Athalie had overheard.

"We were going to make fudge tonight at our house," said Mary thus prodded. "I live next door. Would you like to come? We'll have a lot of fun."

"Any men coming?" asked Athalie speculatively.

"Men?" queried Mary half puzzled, "my father—"

"She means the boys," said Emily Bragg, "my goodness!" and giggled.

"Our high school boys will be there," said Mary truthfully, hoping Athalie couldn't read it in her eyes how much she did not want her.

"Boys?" said Athalie, "awfully young I suppose? Well, I'm sorry but I can't make it tonight. I expect to spend the evening at the roof garden in the city, maybe a cabaret or two afterwards. I sha'n't be home till quite late. Sorry—some other time perhaps. Now, I'll have to ask you to excuse me. It's getting late. So glad you called. Good-bye."

She gathered up cloak and gloves and marched grandly out of the room, down the hall and out the front door just as Anne Truesdale appeared with another plate of cookies to supplement the rapidly disappearing cake. She had intended to leave word with Anne Truesdale that she had gone to bed with a sick headache and did not wish to be disturbed for dinner, and then to descend to the street by way of the pergola, but the temptation to sail grandly out before these girls was too great and she followed her impulse. There would be a way out of it all after she had had her fun, and the momentary vision of Anne, startled, her mouth dropped open as she watched her leave, did not worry her at all as she adjusted her long cloak and sailed jauntily down the street.

Over at Vandemeeter's every eye was watching, as they had been since the school girls entered. It made a pleasant little stir in the monotony of the day to feel that festivity going on. It recalled days when they themselves arrayed in best silks, new hats and fresh gloves had accepted Miss Lavinia's sweetly, friendly invitations and felt above the common lot for a few brief hours. Ever since Arden's wife had run in in the morning to tell them that the girls had planned to go they had gone about their work with a pleasant anticipation. They felt in a way concerned, and thought highly of the Trumans for having suggested the call, for was not this a public recognition? And if departed spirits were permitted a glimpse now and then of their old homes, would not Miss Lavinia be pleased that the town had honored her beloved boy's family? They felt the Trumans had done the proper thing and were glad they belonged to a town that knew what to do in a trying situation. Glad, too, that the question of accepting Patterson Greeves or not into good and regular standing in the town had been settled so satisfactorily by the Trumans. No one ever questioned what the Trumans did.

But when the scarlet lady with her flapping coat of black and white suddenly emerged from the old front door and sallied down the front walk with such an air, they gazed in amazement with bated breath, and no one dared whisper till she was out of sight. Then all with one consent drew back from their several windows and looked at one another as if facing some awful thought.

"*Who* was she?"

It was mother, her rugged face almost white with a

kind of social fright, who broke the silence and voiced the wonder of them all.

Pristina whirled back to the window and in a hard little voice answered:

"It was *her!* The fat one! The one *they went to call on!*"

"Oh, my *soul!*" said mother, stooping to pick up a pin and unable to find it in her excitement. "Oh, my soul and body! Why that's an insult." Maria licked her lips with the tip of her tongue with the motion a man uses to whet a scythe.

"Now I wonder what'll happen!" she said, a hard glitter in her eyes, as if she rather enjoyed the prospect. Maria was one of those who having failed in gaining many of the joys of this life was not content to see others receiving them. Not that she was unkindly when it came right down to actions—only in a little cattish way with her tongue, and the expression of her face.

They were watching the Silver house so hard that they failed to notice the minister's car until it drew up in front of the gate. Mother strained her eyes anxiously.

"Well, anyhow, I'm glad it wasn't that one. She seems to be real sweet."

"Now, mother, you always jump to such hasty conclusions," said Maria. "I'm sure I don't see how you can tell whether she's sweet or not at this distance."

Said Pristina thoughtfully:

"She's sitting in the front seat with the minister!"

"Yes," said Maria caustically, "seems to me it's a little soon to begin that."

"Maybe he began it," said Harriet sympathetically.

"Not he!" said Maria. "He wouldn't have to! It beats me what the girls nowadays have done with their modesty!"

"Well, where did modesty bring us?" laughed Cordelia.

"Cordelia Vandemeeter! I'm surprised!" rebuked Maria.

Then Silver and her father and the minister got out and went up to the house and the front door closed again. And what had become of the high school girls at tea?

Chapter XVIII

BARRY LINCOLN was helping Sam Fitch to build a fence for his chicken run. The Fitch place stood up and back from the street on a slight elevation among a grove of light maples. The chicken run was higher up the hill to one side and commanded a wide view of the road winding round to the bridge, and over into the woods. It was the last house on the street as you went toward Frogtown from the south end of Silver Sands.

Barry had just pounded his thumb trying to straighten a refractory nail, and had thrown down the hammer and stuck the soiled thumb in his mouth when the flash of a scarlet hat, and the flutter of scarlet tulle came into sight down the road. For an instant he stared in astonishment for such a sight was not native to Silver Sands and Barry knew everybody that lived there, by sight at least. Then something familiar in the swagger of the plump figure struck him and he drew his brows in a frown and turned a quick look at Sam.

Sam was down on his hands and knees with his back to the street nailing wire to the base. He would not be likely to see her. Barry stooped and picked up his hammer, and began a tremendous pounding on the corner post, straightening another nail, his weather eye to the road, unheeding the blood which was streaming from his bruised thumb.

At just the right instant as Athalie passed behind the group of tall cedars and was for a few seconds lost to view, he threw down his hammer with an exclamation, and called to Sam in an imperative voice:

"Oh, I say, Sam, run to the house quick and get me a rag to do up this blamed thing. It's bleedin' like the deuce!"

Sam accustomed to obey Barry, his baseball idol, dropped his own hammer instantly and with a sympathetic glance toward his wounded companion steamed toward the house without delay. When he returned with the required rag and a bottle of arnica Athalie was well across the bridge.

A tumult of thoughts was running through Barry's brain, foremost among them the telephone conversation he had overheard the day before. Vaguely in the background the sudden flash of coral and silver draperies and little shiny slippers, the tempest of words he had heard in the Silver hall the evening before, with the stormy sobs, lasting long after the music had begun. How much responsibility had he, Barry Lincoln, for this strange fat specimen of womanhood who wore pants and made appointments over the telephone to meet men from the city agreeing to stay till all hours of the night? Barry Lincoln's code was a simple one, but it had an old-fashioned twist to its ideas of womanhood. His mother was a sweet faced, sad-eyed little widow who wore plain black dresses and did her hair smoothly except for the satiny crinkle of it around the edges of her forehead. She had given him the habit of a clean mind in the midst of a wicked and perverse world, and he somehow patterned his ideas of Girl and what she should be on a picture of his mother taken just before she was married, when the light of joy was in her face and her eyes were like reflections of the kingdom of heaven. Barry knew a whole lot more about the world than his mother had ever told him, but he had kept his clean habit of mind, and any deviation from it on the part of a woman, especially a young woman, gave him always a feeling of nausea. However, this was something no one would ever have guessed. Barry was one who told not his thoughts among men.

So, now, when he saw this poor little daughter of Eve taking her way toward the path of temptation he was not interested. But the memory of a haunted look in her father's eyes the night before and the good comradeship he had offered on the evening of the fire, together with the lingering fragrance of cookies imbibed now laid upon Barry's conscience a duty toward his fellowman. If this girl was really going on an unlawful holiday which might bring pain and shame to his friend, ought he not in all loyalty to that friend to do something about it?

Out of the tail of his eye he watched the scarlet flash as it followed along the line of the road, crossed the bridge, left the road and crept up the hill toward the woods. He sat down on the doorstep and kept Sam's back to the hillside until the scarlet hat and the dark cloak disappeared into the woods, and only glimmered unnoticeably among the young leaves as it went farther and farther away from the road. At last his mind was made up.

"Doggone it, Sam, now that hand's goin' to be no good today. Wha'd I have to pound that for? Clumsy! Say, Sam, les finish this t'morra. What'd'ya say we take a day off and go see if we can find Beazley? He ought to be back home from his aunt's by this time and it isn't much of a run over to the Corners. Say, you go get the roadster and run her over to the Pike, an' I'll skip across to the creek where I was yesterday morning and see if I can find my knife. I'll meet you up by the old camp entrance in about fifteen minutes. But if it's half an hour or longer you stick, for I'll be there! Beat it now, and don't talk, Sam. Remember to keep yer mouth shut!"

Sam hurried away with a light of eagerness in his eyes and Barry arose and took long strides across the fields toward a spot in the landscape a quarter of a mile to the north of where Athalie had entered the woods. As he disappeared among the undergrowth he cast a speculative eye to the distant road, but no one was to be seen as yet.

Now the "roadster" above mentioned was as much a part of Barry Lincoln's existence as his dog or his fishing rod or anything but his mother. It was called the "roadster" by courtesy because it could get over the road so rapidly, but there was nothing about it that would have suggested that name in the modern acceptation of the term. It was ancient and worn and stripped of everything that it could be stripped of and be. It consisted merely of its throbbing loyal heart, its four wheels, and enough timber and metal to keep them from flying apart when they went catapulting through space. However Barry and whom-ever he elected to take with him as a companion managed to stick on and always come home alive was a continual wonder in Silver Sands. People told Mrs. Lincoln that they didn't see how she stood it having her son go off in that awful thing, that it wasn't safe and it wasn't Christian, and he always looked as if he was going to destruction and was glad of it, that they should think it would affect his morality, a boy like that to own an infernal machine. He was in daily danger of becoming a murderer!

And besides, how could they *afford* to keep it!

When they twisted on that prying look and said that about affording—it was usually the people for whom she did plain sewing that said that—Barry's mother always crinkled up her lips into a smile that let little gold lights into her brown eyes and made her look like Barry, and answered always quite pleas-antly:

"Oh, the old roadster is one of the family. We couldn't live without that. Barry never has killed any-body yet. I hope he never will." And she never even reminded them how he had saved a girl's life once with it, running after a machine that had got out of her control, nor how he rushed Tad Moffat to the hos-pital in the city in time to save his hand, the time he got it caught in the reaper.

But if you had asked the boys of the town about the old roadster they would have told you that Barry made it "out of pieces of nothin' off the junk heap behind the garage" and that its chief characteristic was that it could "go like the devil."

It was this same go-devil that Sam climbed into, as it stood waiting under its oilcloth lean-to beside the Lincoln cottage, and presently shot out of the yard and around the Creek road toward the Pike, a proud lad that Barry had selected him to run his car.

Barry himself had rustled across the creek by a route well known to himself, and stolen up to a favorite rendezvous of his own near an old tree under which he often sat by the hour fishing, looking down from his perch on a rock into the limpid stream below, or swinging up in the trusty branches above, from limb to limb till he reached a point where all the woods was an open book and himself enveloped in foliage.

It was to this point of vantage that he now hastened, silently, stealthily, as only such as he knew how to go. The tree was the tallest in all the region round about. Looking east from its height he could see the Flats of Frogtown with the gleaming water and Silver Sands shining in the late afternoon sun. Between him and the Flats wound the smooth white ribbon of a road, and far as he could see a black speck sped like a spider down its thread. He watched it an instant and then his eyes scanned the hillside below him, down through the trees. Yes, there was a gleam of scarlet. Her hat. She had thrown it on the ground and was sitting on the log. Her scarlet frock was spread about her radiantly like a splash of vermilion in the spring newness of green. She seemed like some great scarlet tanager waiting for its mate. Yet when she lifted her face to look up at the strangeness of her surroundings, her bare neck and arms, her painted lips and pencilled brows, the white, white whiteness of her face seemed out of place there in the holy quiet of nature's temple, a parody on a living soul, stark and shameless in a setting of God's things as they are. Something of this thought perhaps entered the boy's mind as he saw her first, half startled to realize how near he was to her trysting place, half tempted to slide quietly down and slip away before she discovered him.

Yet her waiting, listening attitude held him. She was evidently expecting someone. If the guy she had phoned up should turn out to be an all-right fellow, why then he would just make a quiet getaway and join Sam, and no one the wiser. If, on the other hand, he should turn out to be one of these fresh rotters from the city he could let him know where to get off and see that no harm came to that silly little simp

down there, just for the sake of her father who was a
good old scout.

Presently Barry turned his eyes westward and
noted the "roadster" darting along like a small black
bug as if it had the speed of a thousand-legger. He
watched it to the Pike, and knew when it passed
behind the old red barn that Sam would be waiting
there for him should it be ten minutes hence or ten
hours. Then he glanced to the south and saw the other car, coming at full speed down toward the bridge.
Now, if he was right this would be his city man. There
were two other cars coming, Eli Ward's old gray
limousine that he bought for two hundred and fifty
dollars and fixed up himself, and the grocery delivery, speeding recklessly back from the afternoon
rounds. But this was a strange car he saw at a glance,
and presently it came to a halt, just below the group
of chestnut trees, and a head came out and looked
around. The car jerked on a few feet farther and the
man got out, looking around him uncertainly. He
measured the distance from the bridge with his eye
and began an ascent at random, looking this way and
that, furtively. As he came on there were places where
the branches were thin and his face was in full view.
Barry studied him curiously. He was tall and thick set,
with a heavy jowl and a tiny black moustache over
his full red lips. He had taken off his hat and was
mopping his face. The climb seemed to be hard on
him. As he looked up once the boy was astonished to
see that he was not young and that there were bags
under his eyes, puffy places that belonged to a high
liver.

"He's old enough to be her grandfather!" thought
Barry disgustedly, "what a doggone little fool!"

Athalie arose and poised on the log with outspread
arms, and the man cautiously approached, a hungry
bestial glint in his eye that the boy in the tree re-
sented.

"He's rotten!" said the boy to himself. "Gosh!
what'll I do about this? Her father oughtta keep her
in! Gee!"

The man was upbraiding Athalie for coming in such

a noticeable dress. "Are you sure nobody saw you come?" he asked her in a surly tone smoothing the plumpness of her bare arms with his well groomed hand as he talked. "It won't do to have your dad get onto us," he added, "you've got to be careful you know."

Athalie pouted, and the man talked to her in a low rumble. Barry could not hear many words. He wished he were well out of that tree and back making a chicken run. He wished he had never gone to that fire in Frogtown nor met the new Silver man, nor taken his old worms to him. Heck! What a mess! What did folks want to be fools for?

The word "divorce" floated up once, and then something about the state line. He heard Athalie protest that she must go home and get on a white dress, but the man insisted that he could not wait, it was now or never. What on earth did it all mean? The state line was miles to the south. Premonition filled his breast. That man certainly was a rotter. He wished he could get down and punch his head, but it didn't seem to be advisable at the moment. He didn't know enough about things to interfere. Maybe the man was just wanting to take her back to her mother. Her mother was divorced from her father. *Sure*, that was it. Some conspiracy to get her away to her mother again. Well, why worry? Wouldn't that be a good thing for Mr. Greeves? From all he had heard the night before, and all the gossip that had been going around the town that day, he would not expect his new friend to be deeply grieved at his daughter's disappearance. And yet—he didn't like that man's face! Of course he might be her uncle or something come after her. But anyhow, he didn't like the way the man felt of her wrist. It wasn't nice. Gosh, she was just a kid! Just a foolish little kid. She was too fat of course. She'd been eating too much candy and soda water. If she'd only get into condition, and take a little training she'd be all right. Gosh! He'd like to punch that man's head even if he *was* her uncle!

While he was thinking these things the two below him suddenly got up and began to move down toward the road. The man made the girl put on her cloak and turn the white fur inside out of sight. He made her hold up her scarlet dress so it wouldn't show below the black, and tuck her red hat under the cloak, and then he pointed down the road to where a clump of bushes were embowered with wild honeysuckle, close to the roadside making a complete refuge, and the girl hurried off and crept under it. The man waited, hidden in the grove till the bread wagon passed by, and then went down to where he had parked his car.

A few rods up the hill in a shelter of laurel bushes a tramp looked out with greedy eyes like an old bird of prey and watched the girl.

Barry waited only long enough to see the man turn about, drive to the honeysuckle harbor and stop. Then he began quickly to slide down the tree. As he reached the ground he heard the purr of the engine starting again, and his feet hardly touched the sod as he sprang away along the ridge above the creek to where a log spanned the water, across like a bird in flight, and up the opposite bank he ran. Now this field, and the roadster waited for him.

"Over!" he shouted to Sam as he came panting up the hill and vaulted the fence, "we gotta hurry! Took me longer'n I expected."

"Got'cher knife?" queried Sam as he moved over and gave Barry the wheel.

"Yep," said Barry pulling his knife out of his pocket for a brief glimpse and started his engine.

"Say, which way you going, Blink?"

"You don't wantta turn round. I turned here a purpose. You said you were going after Beazley."

"That's all right, Sam. We gotta make the state line now before another guy gets there. You sit tight."

Sam perceived that Blink had had one of his inspirations. This was an expedition! He settled his lank length on the airy structure of his seat and prepared to enjoy himself. Sam had pale blue eyes under golden lashes, carroty straight hair that stuck up like bristles, a gaunt mouth, and was peppered with freckles. He remembered contentedly that his mother was making apple dumplings for supper when he went in for the arnica. He glanced at Blink's hand and noticed that the rag had disappeared. A smudge of blood on the finger was all that remained of the accident.

"Have any trouble findin' yer knife, Blink?"

"Nope."

The roadster was going like a bullet through the air now, its four wheels scarcely seemed to travel the earth. They had rounded the top of the hill and curved down into the lower thoroughfare. Far ahead on the road another car like a speck appeared, and disappeared. Barry eyed it steadily as he shot ahead, the speck in the distance growing visibly larger mile by mile. He let the roadster out a trifle more and watched the distance grimly. Was this his man? He didn't want to waste time.

Sam pulled his hat over his eyes and flipped up his collar with a lank hand. His teeth were chattering.

"Gee! Blink, this is—grrr-reat!" he gulped and held on tight, a trifle pale under the freckles.

Barry shot ahead silently. Was that a glint of scarlet fluttering out the side of the car, or only a budded maple branch by the road?

At last they were within hailing distance and Barry let down his speed a trifle. He didn't want to pass before the crossroad, now half a mile ahead. Strange he saw no sign of anyone on the back seat of that car, and only one head appeared at the front. If that was his man what had he done with the girl? If it wasn't his man it was a pity to waste any more time and lose the trail. He began to cast about in his mind where his quarry could have gone if this was not the right car and to plan for instant action in case he found out his mistake.

The car ahead did not turn off at the crossroads and three minutes later Barry shot ahead. As he passed the other car he was sure he caught a glimpse of something red like a big ball suddenly dropping down out of sight in the back seat.

"Lamp that car, Sam!" he ordered grimly.

Sam fixed his pale eye on a bit of mirror fastened in midair over the engine, but the car seemed to be coming on steadily enough.

"Watch if there's more than one person in it."

Sam shifted the gum between his teeth and gave himself to more concentrated effort.

"Thought I saw something move in the back seat," he said at length. "There it went again. Mightta ben mistaken though."

Barry thought he saw it too. He suddenly ground his brakes on and sprang off to kneel before his engine.

"Nut loose," he explained to the astonished Sam who had been nearly precipitated to the ground by the sudden halt. He wasn't quite sure which car Blink meant "the nut" travelled in.

Barry's car was well into the road. A passing vehicle must turn out if it went by. Barry reclined by a wheel, apparently deeply absorbed. At the very instant however, when the other car was about to curve by him, he was as by a miracle upright on his feet in the middle of the remaining road space, with one arm raised in distress. The on-coming driver had perforce to stop or submit to being a murderer. As the man ground on his brakes and jerked to a violent stop he let out an ugly oath, but Barry unconcerned asked nonchalantly:

"Len' me a wrench?"

"No!" said the man shortly, "mine's lost! Get out of my way!"

Barry lifted his cap from his curls politely and grinned.

"Thank you!" he said with his eye on the tonneau, and stepped out of the way. The car shot ahead, but Barry had seen what he was after, a big black eye peering up over the door of the car, surmounted by a travelling robe that seemed exceedingly alive. A flash of a white arm and a dash of scarlet showed against the darkness of the tonneau as the car swept by, and Barry was satisfied. He was on the right track.

"What's eatin' you, Barry? The wrench's in its place under the cushion." Sam eyed him puzzled. It wasn't like Barry to forget anything.

"Oh, is it?" said Barry innocently, swinging up on his minute cushion, "pile in, boy, we gotta hurry."

Sam scrambled back into place again as the roadster leapt forward. The other car was some distance ahead now. Barry seemed to have lost interest in it. Sam couldn't make him out. Somehow Sam never could quite make out Barry. He said so to the boys once and Ben Holden told him it was because he hadn't any sense of humor, but that troubled Sam still more, because what did a sense of humor have to do with understanding a person who was perfectly grave and serious?

Whenever they came near a crossroad or a village, Barry speeded up. Sam kept hoping he would stop and buy something to eat. He kept remembering those apple dumplings. The sun was getting lower and lower. A dank little breath swept up from the valley, full of sleepy violets and drowsy bees humming. The birds were calling good night. Sam's legs were long for the space allowed on the roadster. He grew uneasy.

"Say, what time do you expect to get home for supper?" he questioned, shifting a leg, and putting his hand under his knee surreptitiously to ease the stiffness.

"Don't expect!" said Barry crisply, "if you do you might get disappointed. Hungry, Sam? Let you out on the road anywhere you say, if you like."

"Oh, no," said Sam detecting displeasure in his idol's voice, "oh, no, no, I'm just enjoying this, havin' the time of my young life. Gee, it's great. Only I was wondering what your plans were?"

"That depends," said Barry, and said no more. With shut lips the two whizzed through the county, watching a little black speck ahead that grew dimmer and dimmer as the light of the sun failed.

Then suddenly it seemed quite dark. The other car was only a place of blackness in the darkness, one could not be sure if it were there or only had been. There were lights ahead. They were nearing a town. The roadster reached the top of a hill leading down into the main street among dwellings. A little trolley like a toy plied to and fro with childish bells and lights. A church bell rang with a sweet wholesome call to prayer. Cottages appeared. A child under a light with a green porcelain shade looking at a book. A family in the dining room eating their supper. Pleasant thought. Dumplings, apple dumplings with plenty of goo! Ummmmm! Sam looked wistfully back.

The other car at the foot of the hill turning into the main street, stopped for an instant by the trolley. Barry made time and arrived in its immediate vicinity as it started on again. Barry slowed up. He let several cars and trucks and foot passengers get between him and the open road. Sam eyed him wonderingly. The other car had gone on. Sam hadn't noticed it particularly.

Barry saw it slow up in front of a drug store, and immediately he ran his car down a side street by the blank side of a real estate office closed for the night, and sprang out.

"Watch me, Sam! keep yer eyes peeled," he said to his astonished vassal. "If I don't come back soon you folla. I gotta get that car and its contents back to Silver Sands t'night! See? But mind you keep yer mouth shut."

He was gone in the darkness, and Sam, whirling dazedly round on his unsteady seat saw him vanishing round the car that was parked in front of the drug store. An instant more and he heard the door on the driving side slam and the engine begin to purr.

"By gosh!" said Sam and unfolded himself to his full height on the curb stone. "He's a nut if there ever was one," said Sam to the roadster aloud.

The other car was moving! It was passing out of sight! Blink was nowhere to be seen. Sam must move too if he were not to lose him. Sam clambered to his task with sudden panic and threw in the clutch.

"By gosh!" he ejaculated, but the roadster was already going so fast that his words fell backward on the real estate curb unheard in the darkness. Sam had already assumed his new importance. Apple dumplings were forgotten for the time. He had to get that roadster home or he'd hear about it all the rest of his mortal days. Besides he knew his mother would keep plenty of dumplings warm for him on the back of the stove against his coming.

He made out to see a dim outline of a car in the darkness ahead and followed, being midlly aware of an excited man on the pavement behind him shouting and waving his arms.

Chapter XIX

ANNE TRUESDALE, bringing another plate of angel cake that had been put aside for "the master" sighted the minister's car through the front window, and urging the plate upon Roberta hastened to the door to meet them.

It was Greeves who was walking ahead, and she put up her hands as if in prayer and almost curtsied in her agony, her words tumbling out in true old country style:

"Oh, master Pat, I'd not be troublin' ye, but the young ladies is in there and ye'll have to tell me what ye want done. I've fed 'em an' fed 'em, everything there is left in the house, tryin' to keep 'em from realizin' they've been insulted, an' now you'll just have to do something about it. It'll be a scandal in the neighborhood in five minutes after I let them be going, for Emily Bragg has an awful tongue in her head an' she lives next door to Arden Philips' wife, her that was Ruby Hamilton ye ken."

"Why, Anne, what's the matter? Try not to be excited. Tell me what has happened? Who is in the house?"

"It's the young ladies, the daughters of yer uncle's old friends, Mary Truman next door, and Roberta Moffat and them, six of them, nice girls as ever was, come to call on your daughters. And Miss Athalie first kept them waitin' an' then she come down all in a red party dress with that bare a neck, and no sleeves at all, and a little red hat like a red hen atop her, and them monstrous cherries a-dangling—"

Anne was almost sobbing as she talked, and was unaware that Bannard and Silver had come up and were standing behind her.

"Never mind, Anne," said Greeves soothingly, "it can't be so very bad. You say they're only little girls."

" 'Igh-school girls, sir, an' comin' on young ladies. Oh, but you don't know sir, it was werry bad, werry bad indeed, sir. She come in an' called herself Miss Greeves, and she offered them her smoking box, an' then she orders tea an' walks out that imperious you'd think she was a queen, sayin' as how 'twas late an' she had a engagement to go to the city an' see a carabay on a roof, sir, whatever that may be, sir. An' she's gone—an' I don' know what to do with 'em. It'll be all over town before the night, master Pat—!"

"Is there somebody in there to call, did you say, Mrs. Truesdale?" interrupted Silver suddenly. "Why I'll go right in!"

Silver ran up the steps and into the hall, flinging off her hat in her transit and dropping it on the hall console, tossing her gloves after it. She entered the drawing room where the embarrassed girls were huddled together, trying to get rid of napkins, eating furtive pieces of cake from the plate on the edge of the tea cart, and planning a hasty exit before any more stupefying and insulting daughters were presented to their indignant gaze.

"Oh, how lovely of you all to run over so soon!" exclaimed Silver ruffling up her hair with a merry attempt at smoothing it, "now tell me who you are. I'm Silver Greeves, I suppose you know—or perhaps you don't. Call me Silver please, I'll feel more at home. And what's your name? Mary Truman? Oh, you live next door don't you? Father was telling me about you this morning at breakfast. We'll be friends, won't we? Now you introduce the rest."

She had them all chattering together in a moment more and they hadn't an idea she was a day older than any of them. She was small and slender, and had a smile like sunshine. They liked her at once and forgot their grievances. They began to tell her as one girl about their school, and their Christian Endeavor, and their fudge party, and she entered into it all eagerly. Christian Endeavor? Of course she would join.

She had been a Christian Endeavorer at home. Fudge? She loved it. Of course she would come!

Bannard stood for a moment in the doorway where he had followed to see if he could help out in the trying situation which he had easily sensed from the few words he had caught of Anne's excited recital, and behold, this wonderful little girl had everything in the hollow of her hand. Then one of the girls looked up, Emily Bragg it was, and giggled.

"Oh, and there's Mr. Bannard! Won't you come to the party too? You like fudge, don't you?"

"Indeed I do, and indeed I will," said Bannard eagerly. "I was wishing you would ask me only I wasn't sure whether the boys were invited or not."

"Oh, yes, the boys are invited," beamed Mary Truman, "they don't know it yet but I'm going to call them up on the phone. Say, Mr. Bannard will you see Barry Lincoln? I'd like to ask him, but they haven't any phone."

"Yes, I'll tell Barry," promised the minister, and then Anne Truesdale with suspiciously red eyes bustled in and began pouring tea for the minister and Greeves. Silver jumped up and taking her father's arm drew him around the group making him acquainted with each one, and the girls marvelled that she remembered their names so well. When they finally broke up and started home to get ready for their fudge party Silver walked with them down to the gate an arm around Mary and Roberta, her head turned backward to smile over her shoulder at the other three who were fairly tied in a knot to get closer to her, and so they took their adoring leave at the front gate to the great edification of the Vandemeeters, who felt that their heads were fairly reeling with the exciting program of the day.

"I declare, if this goes on," said mother mopping her weary brow with her apron, "I sha'n't get half my work done. I do hope things will settle down pretty soon."

Over at the Silver mansion Anne Truesdale was gathering the scattered tea things, and trying to plan for the evening meal which had been robbed of several articles of its menu. Greeves stood in the front hall talking with Bannard, and watching Silver come brightly up the path, both men thinking how wonderfully she had turned the situation.

"You have no cause to worry about *her*," said Bannard with a touch of reverence in his tone.

"I should say not," said Greeves. "She's—she's—like her mother!"

"Didn't I tell you," said Bannard with a twinkle in his eye, "that tomorrow about this time you'd begin to see God's way taking shape?"

Greeves' face turned sharply toward him a heavy shadow crossing his brow.

"Don't talk to me about God's way!" he said harshly, "I've seen too much of that. What about my other girl?" and a spasm of anger went like white lightning over his features.

"That will work out too," said Bannard reverently. "Give God His way and see."

"Don't!" said Greeves sharply.

"What about that man down at the Flats, that father! I can't get him out of my head Bannard. That's cruelty to make that little one suffer so. It's cruelty to take her away from a father and mother like that. She isn't going to live is she?"

"She has a chance, the doctor says. It depends a lot upon the nursing. The father and mother are wonders, but they don't know how."

"Do you know of a trained nurse you can get, Bannard? I'd gladly pay for one! Couldn't we telephone to the city for one? Two if necessary. I'd like to see that child saved. Bannard if there's anything that money can do you'll let me help out? I'd like to make that much amends for the mess I've made of my life."

Bannard cast him a quick appreciative look.

"Thank you," he said, "that means a lot. There'll be plenty of chances for that sort of thing. But in this case it isn't so much a question of money as love. It would be hard to find a regular trained nurse that would fit into that household. You saw how primitive everything was. It would have to be somebody who could love them to make the service possible. I'm

going down now for Mrs. Lincoln. I think she'll spend
the night there. She's done such things before. She
knows how to love."

After Bannard was gone a shadow of care seemed
to drop upon Greeves' face even while he was closing
the front door, as he remembered his younger daughter. Now his was the disagreeable task of finding out
all about what she had done and dealing with her.
How sickening the thought! All the advantage he had
gained, or thought he had gained in the morning
would be gone with the first word. His soul shrank
from the contest. He was angry and disheartened.
How was he to reach her and make her understand,
that at least she must refrain from outward disrespect to him and his family or she could not remain
under his roof? What was the secret of her strange
nature that made her willing to do these astonishing
things? He hurried back to the drawing room where
he could hear Anne's excited voice relating over again
to Silver the chief points of Athalie's offense. He could
see how to Anne, what had been done was almost the
unpardonable sin. To keep the honor and respect of
the village was certainly among the first articles of
Anne's creed. With a deep sigh he pushed back the
curtain and listened.

"I wouldn't bother about it, Anne," Silver was saying, "Athalie probably hasn't an idea how disagreeable
she appeared. She is in a different atmosphere from
any she has ever been in before, and it isn't really her
fault, perhaps, that she acts so. I don't think the girls
will say much about it. We are going over next door
tonight, and we'll just have a good time and make
them forget about the other. After a little when Athalie gets acquainted and gets to know the ways of
Silver Sands she will want to make them like her,
I'm sure she will. Just now she's rather strange and
upset in all her ideas—"

"That's all very well, Silver," put in the father, "but
Athalie can't publicly disgrace us. And she has openly
disobeyed me it seems about the cigarettes. I can't
have that—in this house!"

"She's been brought up to see it I suppose—"

"Oh—yes!" said her father with a look of remembrance sweeping over his face—"of course she's seen it every day. It's her standard. But she's got to learn that it isn't mine!"

"When she learns to love you, father, maybe that will make a difference," suggested Silver shyly.

The father's face was hard.

"I doubt if she knows how to love anyone but herself," he said bitterly, "it was the way with her mother. Anne, will you tell Miss Athalie to come down at once to the library?"

Anne was mopping up her eyes. She seemed to take Athalie's misdeeds as a personal offense. Sacredly all these years she had guarded the honor of the family, and now to have it trampled under foot by an alien in one short afternoon was too much. Anne could not put it easily aside. It was an outrage, like having bad boys tear up the tulip beds after Joe had newly trimmed them, or scarring the family Bible. Anne could not get over it. She came sniffing back from the pantry door with a handful of soiled dishes and her cheeks red and angry looking. When she was excited her cheeks always turned fire red.

"But she's not here!" she affirmed indignantly, "didn't I tell ye she's away down the street like a big red peacock. I would have stopped her if I could but she'll not mind the likes of me."

"She went out?" queried Greeves startled, "I didn't understand you before. I thought you said she went up to her room. Are you quite sure? Perhaps she's returned and slipped up the back way."

"I'm that sure, but I'll go see, master Pat," sniffed Anne, and hurried up the stairs.

In a moment she was back again.

"She's not upstairs, master Pat. And you should see her room! It's like a hurricane. There's frocks and shoes just where she's dropped them, and stockings all over the place. It's scandalous. If there should happen a fire—"

But Greeves was already on his way to the front door.

"I'll go out and find her," he said in a low tone to

Silver, caught up his hat from the rack and was gone.

An hour later he came back with an anxious look upon his face.

"Is she back yet?" he asked Silver who had been hovering from window to window trying to think of a way out of the dilemma for her father, wondering if perhaps Athalie hadn't run away back to her mother, considering once more whether she ought not to go away herself and so remove one stumbling block from this wayward sister's path.

"I met a woman—she lives next door—Weldon, Lizzie Weldon I think her name is. She said she saw Athalie go down the street toward the post office. She was standing at the gate she said and watched her out of sight. She's one of those hawks who knows everybody's business. I used to hate her when I was a boy. She evidently wanted to find out where Athalie had gone. It isn't hell enough to have these things happening but we have to have a lot of vultures around picking at the bones!"

"Well, never mind, father. I wouldn't feel too bad about it. It isn't your fault, and things'll come right after a while—"

"So you believe that too!" he said eyeing her keenly, "well, I must say I don't. They've never come right for me yet. The thing I'm afraid of is they may confuse you with Athalie. I wouldn't have a breath of scandal touch you, my Silver-Alice." He came and touched his lips tenderly to her forehead. She lifted clear eyes to meet his look.

"Why, I wouldn't be afraid of that, father. It isn't possible."

"What makes you so sure?" he asked, "you don't know what old carrion crows inhabit a village like this, till they once get scent of a bit of scandal. Why even really good women, women who live otherwise a right life, will snatch up such a thing and rush about carrying it from house to house till there isn't a tatter left of somebody's reputation."

Silver still looked untroubled, and shook her head. "It can't be," she insisted, "there's a promise, don't you know? Listen! 'No weapon that is formed against thee shall prosper; and every tongue that shall rise against thee in judgment thou shalt condemn. This is the heritage of the servants of the Lord.' "

He looked at her as a man looks at a beloved woman who has just uttered some sweet fallacy concerning which he does not wish to undeceive her. His eyes grew tender with admiration and yearning.

"You are like your mother," he said with a strange embarrassment in his voice. "If only—" and then he stalked to the window and stood looking out for a long, long time.

Dinner was late that night while Molly made short cake for the strawberries, but when they sat down Athalie had not yet arrived.

"It's very strange!" said Greeves looking at his watch anxiously, and he went himself to Athalie's door and switched on the light to make sure she was not hidden somewhere to evade them all.

He made Anne tell over again what she had heard.

"She said it would be that late," insisted Anne, and she was going to the roof garden and a carabay! I'm sure that was what she said, *carabay!*"

Greeves looked thoughtful. What was that Athalie had said about somebody in the city bringing her out the first day? Giving her presents, going to give her a theatre party? Surely the child couldn't have gone in town to meet him without leaving any word. It was absurd. Nevertheless he kept bringing out his watch and looking at it nervously.

Silver too, seemed worried.

"Perhaps we better not go to that little affair tonight, father, unless Athalie comes in before it is time for us to start."

"No, that would be foolish," he said. "Of course you must go. We will both go. Truman was an old friend of mine. I'd like to see him. She will come in before long of course. She is doubtless hiding not far away just for a freak. She is a strange child. I do not understand her."

But at eight o'clock Athalie had not arrived.

"There is no use fretting over it," said her father

as he walked restlessly up and down, realizing that he was more angry with her than worried. Why should he worry about a child whom he neither wanted nor loved? And yet for that very reason something in him rose and prodded his conscience. Why didn't he care? Why hadn't he looked out from her birth that she was the kind of a child for whom he would have to care?

He went to the telephone and called up Bannard.

"That you, Bannard? Say, that strange child of mine is still at large. Have you any way of finding out whether she took a train to town this afternoon, without exciting interest on the part of the whole countryside? Good. I thought you could. I suppose it is foolish to worry. She certainly seems able to look after herself, but somehow I feel responsible. Darned responsible! Thanks. Yes, we're going over. See you in a few minutes."

Greeves and his daughter went to the neighbor's and Bannard went out to find Barry, but Barry was not to be found. His mother was gone to the Flats for the night to care for the Italian baby, and there was no sign that Barry had been home at all. Bannard sauntered down to the station and enquired of the agent who was just closing up, whether he could remember if Mr. Perry went to the city on the four o'clock train, and the agent said no, there hadn't a soul gone on that train. It was late and he had to hang around waiting to give the engineer a message. There never was much travel in the afternoon—only a man and a boy took the six o'clock train and the seven didn't even stop. It only stopped in Silver Sands for flagging anyway unless there was somebody to get off.

He sauntered into the drug store and bought a tooth brush taking plenty of time in the selection, and the soda clerk was relating a tale about the "jane who took two chocolate fizzes and a banana split that afternoon. Some red bird!"

He dropped in at the fire house to ask the chief if the first of the month would suit the fire company to have their annual service in the church, and keeping his ears open, gathered another straw or two more of evidence.

"An ankle like a square piano!" Uri Weldon was saying with his coarse laugh.

"I wonder she didn't scare the birds!" said another. "Some bathin' suit fer a country walk!" Then the front legs of the respective chairs came down reluctantly and the men straightened up to greet Bannard gravely. Everybody liked Bannard. There was nowhere in the town he might not go, nowhere that he would be unwelcome. Young though he was he had that Pauline trait of being all things to all men, though it must be owned that the men at the fire house were all just a trifle afraid every time he came that he was somehow going to save some of them, and take them away from all that life held dear. They had no doubt in their minds but that he could "save" them if he once got them in his clutches.

Slowly progressing up the street, stopping at Mrs. Hoskins to inquire if her nephew in the city had received the letter of introduction he had procured for him he learned incidentally as he had thought he would, that Athalie Greeves had passed there that afternoon about half past four "in a scandalous rig," had gone to the drug store "and it's the second time, Mr. Bannard, the second time in two days, and all those young boys always hanging around the drug store;" had gone on from the drug store down the village street as far as she could see from the gate and passed out of sight without returning.

"And I threw my apern over my head and ran out to look," added the good woman, showing that she always did her duty by whoever passed, that nothing should be missing out of the general report of the day.

"And I think her father ought to look after her better'n that, don't you Mr. Bannard? A young girl like that! And a stranger in the town. Folks might misunderstand her. Don't you think it's queer we never heard that he had any daughters before?"

Bannard finally reached Truman's, but he had little

to tell Greeves about his daughter except that she had not gone on either train to the city, and that she had been seen walking down the village street, and had bought a soda at the drug store.

"I wouldn't be in the least alarmed, though," he added in a low tone, "there really isn't anything much can happen in the town. They're a friendly lot, even the pryingest of them. She'll probably turn up at home before long."

Just at that moment the dining room door opened and in came the next act of the charade that was in progress, led by Silver who seemed to be the prime mover in every feature of the evening. The girls simply surrounded her and adored her from the start. Bannard watched her and his eyes lit up with that strange wonder he had felt when first he saw her the day before. A wonderful girl! A real unspoiled girl in the modern world. He thought of how she had gone into that sorrowing home in the afternoon and entered into the need; and now here she was the centre of all this merriment, and just as much at home, and just as self forgetful.

It was remarkable that part she was taking in the act, playing her delicate features into the contortion of a haughty woman of the world. She was talented! But of course she would be. With such a father! And that spirituelle look must have come from the mother. He remembered the exquisite painted face.

Then eager voices claimed him to come and join the group for the next word and he was drawn away to the other room.

"Oh, have you heard how the baby is?" a low vibrant voice asked as he passed her in the hall.

So she hadn't forgotten! She was in all this, a part of it, but she had thoughts for the anxious home.

"She is holding her own," he said, "I took Barry's mother down there a little while ago. She will stay all night. You don't know Barry's mother yet. She is a strong arm to lean upon, a cool hand on a fevered brow. She knows how to do things without seeming to, and she loves people."

"Oh, that is good!" said Silver, "tomorrow I will go and take her place awhile if I may."

"It will not be necessary," he said looking his thanks, "but—you may if your father does not object."

"Object?" she looked surprised. "Oh, he could not object to that. Of course I will go."

The company clamored for Silver and she was swept laughingly into the other room, but the minister felt that somehow between them a bond had been established that was very good to think upon. Only two days and he felt this way about her! But she was an unusual girl. Then he heard her ringing laugh, smiled into the eyes of the boys who were pummelling him to tell them the best way to act the word "penitentiary," and plunged into the matter before him.

At half past ten they all went home, most of the company being of high school age and not allowed late hours. The half-past was a special dispensation on account of its being Friday night and no lessons tomorrow. The minister walked down the street with Greeves and his daughter and stepped in a moment to learn if the prodigal had returned, or if his further services as detective would be required.

They found Anne Truesdale sitting in the dark drawing room watching the street. She would not have owned to anybody, least of all her master, that she was praying for "that huzzy" but she was. Somehow Anne's sense of justice wouldn't allow her to let even a girl like that be wandering alone in the world in the darkling night without even a prayer to guide her. She deserved all she might get but oh, think of the disgrace of it all in the town. Anne didn't know that she really cared more for the disgrace in the town than she did for the young girl's soul in the dark.

But there! See how all our motives are mixed! Anne was praying for her! That was something gained. Anne had begun to feel her responsibility, and leaven of that kind always works. It may take time on a cold day, but it always works at last.

When the three discovered that the missing one was still absent they stood and looked at one another in dismay, with that helpless air that always says: "What is there that I can do next?"

Then sharply into the silence of their anxiety there rippled out the insistent call of the telephone.

Greeves hurried into the library to answer it, and the others stood breathless, listening, to his voice.

"Hello!"

It was a man's voice that answered:

"I want to speak to Miss Athalie Greeves."

"Who *is* this?" asked Athalie Greeves' father sternly.

"Well, who are *you*?" The voice was insolent.

"I am Athalie's father and I insist upon knowing to whom I am speaking."

"I'm one of her mother's friends. You wouldn't know me. Call Athalie. She'll tell you who I am. I want to speak to her!"

"It will be necessary for you to explain to me first."

"Why? isn't she there?"

"What is your business with her, sir?"

"Is she there or not?" said the ugly voice.

"She is *not*," said the father coldly.

"Oh, well, I'll call up again!" said the voice, and immediately the wire was cut off.

Patterson Greeves turned toward the two who stood in the doorway and looked with a helpless dazed expression for a moment, then hung up his receiver with a troubled air.

"That is very strange!" he said. "Somehow I get the impression that that man knew Athalie was away— or was trying to find out—"

"It is strange," said Bannard. He made no pretense of not having heard. The voice on the telephone had been loud enough to be heard out in the hall. "I wish Barry were here. I'll go out and look for him. If she isn't heard from by the time I get back we'll begin to do something. Don't get frightened. It's probably only some school-girl prank. Barry will very likely be able to find out where she has gone. He's a regular ferret. I never saw a boy like him."

Meantime Barry, out in the night, was having troubles of his own.

Chapter XX

WHEN Barry Lincoln left Sam in the side street with the roadster and darted across the trolley track and around the back of the stranger's car, the big man with the heavy moustache was visible in the brightly lighted drug store talking with the clerk at the back of the store. He was handing out some money and lighting a big black cigar at the taper on the desk.

Barry drew himself up for one glimpse and saw that the girl was now seated in the front, left hand, away from the curb.

He swept the street either way with a quick glance, saw no one coming in his immediate vicinity, gave another glance to the man in the drug store and made a dash for the door of the driver's seat.

Barry had grown up as it were in the garage, that is he had spent every available minute there since he was a small child, hovering over every car that came within its doorway, watching the men at work, as he grew older, helping with the repairs himself, and finally becoming so expert that they were always ready to give him a job on Saturdays and half holidays, and often even sent for him to help them discover what made the trouble in some refractory engine or carburetor. There was no car rolling that Barry didn't know by name and sight, and wasn't able to describe its characteristics and comparative worth. He was a judge of cars as some men are a judge of their fellowmen. Also, he had a way with cars. When he put his hand to a wheel it obeyed him. He was a perfect, natural driver, knowing how to get the best out of every piece of machinery.

And now as he slid into the driver's seat with the owner only a few feet away, a strange unwarned girl beside him, a strange unfriendly town around him, a dark unknown way ahead, it was not a strange unknown mechanism to which he put his hand. He had known that car as a man recognizes his friend even when he was up in the tree some hours before and saw it coming down the road.

The girl was evidently startled, but Barry, his face turned half away from her, threw in the clutch and was off in a whirl.

"Why Bobs! You scared me!" cried Athalie, "I didn't see you come out, I thought I was watching you light a cigar. It must have been another man who looked just like you. Did you get the chocolates? Hand them over quick! I'm simply dying of starvation."

Barry began to fumble in his pocket silently with one hand. He brought out a mobile package, half a cake of milk chocolate and dropped it into her lap. His eye was ahead. He had no time to waste. The owner of the car would be out in a second and raise a rumpus. He whirled the first corner he came to and fled down a dark side street, passed two blocks, a third that went perceptibly down hill, and darted into an old covered wooden bridge.

It was pitch dark in there save for their own lights. The noise of the engine echoed and reverberated like an infernal machine.

The girl was leaning forward looking at the package. An instant more and they roared out of the bridge into the quiet starlight.

"Why, Bobs! I think you're horrid! Was that all you bought for me? And it's not even a whole cake!" She flung it disgustedly on the floor of the car and looked up angrily. "Did you call that a *joke?*" she asked with a curling lip, and then suddenly she saw his face, and was transfixed with horror. For an instant she held her breath, her eyes growing wider and wider with fright, then she let out one of the most blood curdling screams Barry had ever heard.

Just at that second there lumbered into view the lights of a big gasoline truck that was hurrying to the end of its long day's journey. One instant they saw it, the next they were in its very embrace. Barry curled out of the road just in time and back into it again, while Athalie screamed some more.

'They shot into a black road overarched with tall forest trees. The smell of the new earth leaped up to Barry's taut senses with a soothing touch. The road as far as his lights reached ahead was empty. His woodman's sense told him there was no one near. But how far in the night had that scream reached? What straggler might have heard it and sent a warning? There! She was beginning it again! He must stop it somehow. A sudden thought came to him. He groped in the pocket of the door by his side. There ought to be one there, in a car like this! A man of that sort would carry one. Yes, there it was! His fingers grasped the cool metal, found their way with confidence and drew it forth.

"Bobs! Bobs!" screamed Athalie. The echoes rang through the woods on either hand as they raced along. She was leaving the trail behind them for any straggler to report their whereabouts. This must not go on.

Suddenly the dull gleam of the revolver flashed in front of her face.

"Cut that out!" said the boy sternly.

Athalie opened her mouth to scream again and instead dropped her jaw just as the scream was about to be uttered. She turned wide, horrified eyes to her captor and sat white and still in her seat, cringing away from the weapon.

"Now," said Barry, still holding the revolver in one hand, "you might as well understand that you aren't in any danger whatever if you keep your mouth shut, but if you yodel again like that I'll knock you cold. Do you get me?"

Athalie's eyes acknowledged that she understood. She cringed still farther away from the revolver and he lowered it, keeping it still in his hand however. The woods flew by in one long sweet avenue of spring night. Barry settled to his wheel, eyes to the front, with a mind to the back, and a sort of sixth sense keeping tab on the girl by his side. He could see that the revolver had frightened her terribly. Her face was too much powdered to admit of its turning pale, but there was a sagging droop about her lips and eyelids that betokened her whole spirit stricken with fear. She gathered her cloak closer about her and shivered. Her big, dark eyes never left his face except now and then to glance fearfully out as if wondering what were the possibilities of jumping overboard. Barry began to feel sorry for her.

"Nothing but a little kid," he said to himself, "A foolish little kid!"

Two miles farther on they turned into the high road and Barry slowed down a bit. There were two cars ahead, he could see their tail lights, but nothing coming behind. He turned to the right in the general direction of Silver Sands, and then looked at the girl.

"You needn't be afraid," he said half contemptuously, half gently, "I'm not going to hurt you."

"I'm not afraid," said Athalie, some of the old spirit returning.

"Oh!" said the boy. "All right! I thought you were!" They speeded on again in silence. Presently Athalie spoke. Her voice showed returning temper.

"What are you going to do with me?"

"Going to take you home to your father!" said Barry.

The young woman sat up suddenly. This then was no highwayman. This was some meddler in her business. He knew her father. He had somehow trailed her and recognized her. She was furious.

"But I don't choose to go home," she said indignantly.

"That doesn't cut any ice," said Barry crisply. "You're getting there pretty fast all right."

Athalie turned on him angrily.

"Look here," she said fiercely, "I'm not going to stand this another minute. Do you know what a terrible thing you're doing? You'll probably be put in prison for life for it. But if you'll turn right around now and take me back to my friend I'll tell him you just made a mistake. You didn't try to steal the car at all."

"Thank you," said Barry a grim shadow of a smile flickering across his face in the darkness, "I'm not worrying about that just now."

"But you've *got* to take me back," said Athalie, almost on the verge of tears, "I'm on my way to be *married!*"

"Not tonight!" said Barry grimly.

"Well, I guess I'm not going to be stopped by a kid like you!" burst forth Athalie. She suddenly rose with all her might and flung herself upon the wheel, and Athalie had some weight and grip when she chose to use them.

Barry, utterly unprepared for this onslaught, ground on the brakes and put forth all his strength, trying to keep the wavering car from climbing a tree while he was bringing it to a standstill, but he managed to keep his head.

It was a sharp, brief struggle, for Athalie's muscles were untrained, and in a moment more Barry was holding her firmly with both hands and she had ceased to struggle. He had not again brought the revolver into play. He hated dramatic effects when physical force would do as well.

But he could not stay there all night and hold her down. He cast about for some way of making her fast. There was a handkerchief in his pocket. He managed to get hold of it and crossing her hands bind them together.

Her cloak had fallen off disclosing the flimsy dress and the long fringed ends of a satin sash tied about her waist. He pulled at it and found that it came loose. With this he bound her about across the shoulders and down to the waist.

"You're cold!" he remarked as he saw her shiver, "and that flimsy coat is no good. Here, put this sweater on."

He pulled off his own sweater and pulled it down over her head. She started to scream again, but he put his hand over her mouth, and when she was quiet remarked very gently:

"I hate awfully to treat a girl this way, but I'll have to gag you if you try that line again," and she knew by his tone that he meant it.

"I don't think you'd like gagging."

Athalie began to cry.

"I'm sorry," said Barry remorsefully, "but you can't be trusted."

He was down on his knees now fastening her ankles together with a bit of old rope he had found in his pocket.

"But I'm on my way to be *married*," sobbed out the indignant child, "you're spoiling my *life*—" she was weeping uncontrollably now.

"Excuse me," he said quietly, "I guess I'll have to use my necktie for a gag," and he began unconcernedly to take off his necktie. "I can't have all this noise."

Athalie stopped short.

"I won't cry," she said shortly, "but won't you just listen to reason? Would you like it if you were going to get married, to be interfered with this way?"

"Say kid," he said gently, "you talk sense and I'll help you. You know you aren't old enough to get married yet. And I say, did you know what kind of a rotter you were going off with?"

Athalie's eyes fairly blazed.

"He's nothing of the sort!" she retorted, "I've known him for years. He's perfectly darling! He's my mother's friend."

"Is that all?" said Barry witheringly. "I thought you were going to say your grandmother's."

"I think you're perfectly horrid!" said Athalie shrugging what was left of her shoulders, and drawing as far away from him as she could. "You think you're smart!"

"Look here, kid! There's no use you're quarrelling with the only friend you've got just now. I'm telling you facts. Can't you listen to reason? That man's a rotter. I know his kind. If he's your mother's friend so much the worse. He knew he wasn't doing the square thing taking a kid like you off that way at night. What kind of a rep would you have had, will you tell me, when you got back I'd like to know?"

"I wasn't coming back," sobbed Athalie softly, "I told you—I—was ggg-g-oing to be m-m-married!"

"Yes, in a pig's eye you were! If that man ever married you, kid I'd eat my hat. He hadn't any more idea

of marrying you than I have, and that's flat! This isn't
a very nice way to talk to a girl I know, but when you
won't listen to sense why you've gotta be shown."

"He was going to buy me—a—s-s-string of real
pearls!" wept Athalie suddenly remembering, "and
we were going to have a turkey dinner! I'm—ju-s-t—
st-ar-r-r-ved!"

Barry shrugged down behind his wheel disgustedly.

"You look as if you had meat enough on you to stand
it awhile!" he said contemptuously, "I thought you
were a girl, not a baby!"

Athalie held in the sob on a high note and surveyed
him angrily.

"You are the most—*disagreeable* boy!" she vocif-
erated.

"I didn't state my opinion of you yet. But you certainly aren't my idea of agreeable."

"I didn't ask you your opinion."

"Say, look here," said Barry, "let's cut this out. This
isn't getting us anywhere. What I want is for you to
see some sense before I get you home. Your father's a
kind of a friend of mine and I'd hate like the deuce to
have all this get out about you in the town. You see,
whatever you think of this rotter you were going off
with, the little old town would know fast enough
what he was, if any of 'em knew you were off in the
night with him. You can't kid the town!"

"I haven't the slightest desire to bother with your
little old town," said Athalie loftily. "It may go to the
devil for all I care!"

Barry was silent with disgust for a moment.

"Well, if it does," he said slowly, "it will carry you
on a pointed stick ahead of it, and like as not they'll
try out the point of the stick on your father first. You
can't kid the devil!"

There was a long pause. The night was very still.
They had not passed a car for some time. The lights
in the sleeping villages in the valley below them were
nearly all gone out; moist, dank air rushed up in
wreaths and struck them lightly in the face as they
passed. The sudden breath of an apricot tree in bloom
drenched the darkness. Over in the east toward which

they were hastening a silver light was lifting beyond the horizon and in reflection a little thread of a river leaped out from the darkness where it had been sleeping in winding curves among the dark of plumy willows.

"I *hate* you!" said Athalie suddenly. "You called me names! You're a vulgar boy!"

"What names did I call you kid?" Barry's voice was gentle.

"You called me fat in a very coarse way!"

"Well, you're not exactly emaciated, are you?" He gave her a friendly grin in the darkness.

"I hate you!" reiterated Athalie again, "and I want to get out and walk!"

"Anything to please you!" said Barry quickly bringing the car to a full stop and reaching over to throw open the door by her side.

Athalie was surprised to be taken so literally, but she made an instant move to get out, and then realizing that her ankles were tied she subsided again.

"Oh, excuse me," said Barry and stooping unfastened the cord on her ankles, and sat back again.

"Are you going to untie my hands?" she asked imperiously.

"Oh, no, I guess not," said Barry easily, "you don't walk on your hands do you?"

She cast him a furious look and bounced out of the car, walking off very rapidly down the road with her shoulders stiff and indignant.

Barry sat back and watched her. She went on swiftly till she came to the bend of the road, and then she looked back half fearfully. The car was still and dark as if Barry had settled for a nap. The road ahead wound into a dark wood, and the trees were casting weird shadows across the roadway. But no one should call her bluff. She would go on and show him. She stumbled forward on her little high heeled slippers almost falling as she ran fearfully toward the darkness of the wooded road. Then suddenly on her horrified senses came the distant sound of a motor in the opposite direction and a long thin forecasting of light shot out with a blind glare ahead. Another car was coming! And it was away in the nighttime! And she alone on the road with her arms tied! Horrible fear seized upon her and rooted her to the ground. Then with a mighty effort she gathered her ebbing strength and turning fled.

Chapter XXI

IN the first rod her right slipper flew off and lay at the side of the road but she waited not for slippers. Her silken clad foot went over the rough stony highway with the fleetness of a rabbit. She darted to the side of the car and panted:

"Let me get in, quick! Quick! There's another car coming!"

Barry leaned over and pulled her up, cast a quick glance to the oncoming lights, started his motor and dashed along at full speed just in time to pass swiftly as if he had come from a distance, and then when the passing car was out of sight remarked pleasantly:

"Have a nice walk?"

"Don't!" said Athalie shuddering. He looked at her furtively. The tears were coursing down her cheeks but she was not making any sound.

"Look here, kid, I'm sorry!" he said pleasantly, "let's call this off. You're all in! And say! I'm going to untie your hands. I know I can trust you not to make any more trouble. We're almost home now kid. Only a matter of about four miles, and we'll run through the town as still as oil and get you home and nobody any the wiser. But before we get there you've got to make a contract to can that rotter or I'll have to make a clean breast of the whole thing to your father, how you phoned to him, and how you met him in the woods, and what he said to you and all—"

Athalie turned an amazed face toward him now, smeared with powder and tears, and lit by the newly risen moon.

"You know—?"

"Yep! Know it all! Saw you climb out your window and go to the drug store. Was in the next booth and heard every word you phoned. Wasn't ten feet away from you in the woods. I tell you, you can't kid this town."

Athalie looked aghast.

"No, you don't need to worry. Nobody else knows yet, and I don't intend they shall if you agree to can that man. Is it a bargain?"

There was a long pause, during which Athalie sniffed quietly, then she murmured:

"My father—he'll half kill me—"

"No, he won't! He'll be much more likely to kill the man. But perhaps we can fix that up too. You leave it to me. Now, lean over here and let's get those knots untied."

"I didn't say I would yet!" said Athalie with a catch of rebellion in her breath.

"No, but you're going to," said Barry pleasantly, "you're not yella."

Barry worked away with the satin sash talking meanwhile.

"Say, kid, you know you'll forget all this when you get acquainted in town and begin to have good times. What you need is to get into high school and play basket ball. You'd need to train down a little of course, but you'd make a great player. I watched you as you went up the road, and you've got the build all right. Say, some of the girls on our team are peachy players, but you could beat 'em all at it if you'd try. If I was you I'd begin to train down tomorra. Cut out those sundaes and sodas, and chocolates, and don't be everlastingly eating cake and fudge. You'll never make a player unless you reduce—"

It was surprising how their attitudes toward one another had changed. Athalie wiped up her smeary face, and began to take an interest in life. She even smiled once at a joke Barry made about the moon. She was rather quiet and almost humble.

Barry grew almost voluble. He described in detail several notable athletic features of the past that had put their high school in a class with several large prep schools in the state. He opened out on the prospects for the season's baseball games admitting reluctantly on enquiry that he was their nine's captain and coach.

Suddenly the brow of the hill they were climbing was reached and there before them lay the plain of Silver Sands, with the belching chimneys of Frogtown glaring against the night, and off to the left the steeple of the Presbyterian church shining in the moonlight. It was very still down there where the houses slept, and the few drowsy lights kept vigil. Barry cast it a loyal glance and brought the car to a standstill.

"Look, kid," he said with something commanding in his young voice, "that's our town, down there! Doesn't she look great with her feet to the river and her head on the hills? She's a crackerjack little old town if you treat her right, and no mistake. See that white spot over there behind the trees? That's the pillars on the old Silver house. It's a prince of a house, and the people that lived in it have always been princes. My mother says the whole country round has always looked up to the Silvers. They're always been *real!* Do you get me? It's a great thing to belong to a family like that!"

Athalie turned her large eyes on him wonderingly and suddenly some of her father's sentences of the morning came to her, sentences about gentlemen and ladies, and respectable standards, and their meaning went home on the shaft of Barry's simple arrow.

Barry was never one to explain a joke or a sermon. He let it rest and passed to another line of thought.

"We're going around on the beach road," explained Barry, "and come in the lane just below your house. We'll stop at Aunt Katie's where the minister boards and slip through the back hedge. Then there won't be a whole lot for anyone to see and hear. Anybody might drive up to the minister's door any time of night and nobody think anything of it. If Aunt Katie sees us she'll keep her mouth shut. She's a peach, she is. If you ever need a friend, tie up to her, kid. Now, before we go on I'll trouble you for the name and address of that rotter!"

"What are you going to do?" asked Athalie in an alarmed voice.

"Got to return this car haven't I?"

"Oh, why yes, I suppose so. But—he'll be awfully angry! You might get arrested you know!"

"Watch me!" said Barry lightly. "Now I'll trouble you for that address."

"I don't remember the address," said Athalie, "I went there in a taxicab. It's somewhere in a big apartment house. I got it out of the telephone book."

"What's his name then? You haven't forgotten that have you?" asked Barry eyeing her suspiciously. "Is Bobs the first or last part of it?"

Athalie cast a startled glance at him.

"Farrell, Robert Farrell," she answered meekly.

"That's all right," said Barry. "I'll look him up."

Barry started the car again and they were silent as they sped along for some minutes. Then Athalie asked in a scared voice:

"What are you going to tell my father?"

"Nothing much unless I have too," said Barry easily, "if you can that man he doesn't need to know anything about it, but if I find you haven't played square he'll know the whole thing in about three minutes. It's entirely up to you."

Athalie looked frightened.

"I won't phone to him any more—nor write to him!" she said at length, "but I can't be sure what he'll do."

"I don't think he'll bother you any more after I get through with him," said Barry airily.

Athalie cast him another frightened glance.

"You'd better be careful—" she warned. "He's got an awful temper."

"So I should judge," said Barry, "I'm glad you're out of his clutches."

The car slid along the Silver beach quietly as fine machinery can be made to go. Past the belching furnaces with the night shift in sleeveless shirts moving picturesquely past the light in the rosy dusk of the big structures; past the ruins of the pickle factory, and the darkened windows of the rows of little houses; past the house with the lighted upper window where little Mary and Barry's mother struggled with death the long hours through, and the stricken father and mother knelt each side of the bed and prayed; past the darkened cannery and the silk factory, and the buildings of the Sand Company, across the side tracks and the railroad; over the bridge that spanned a small tributary stream; and winding the back way into Silver Sands, down Sweetbriar Lane to Aunt Katie's door.

There was a light in Aunt Katie's upper front window as Barry helped Athalie out of the car. Barry looked up as they passed in the gate and gave a soft, low whistle like the chirp of a bird. But it was Aunt Katie's voice, not the minister's, that spoke in a low tone from an open side window:

"Is that you Barry?"

"Sure," growled Barry cheerfully.

"Oh, you have found her!" said the voice again, "I am *glad!*" and there was something so vibrant and pleased about it that it thrilled Athalie. No one had ever been glad like that about her before. She had always been considered a nuisance, something to be appeased and gotten rid of as quickly as possible. She warmed to a voice like that and looked up wistfully. It almost seemed to her that she ought to say thank you. She had scarcely ever felt that thanking impulse before in all her wild young life.

"Sure I found her!" said Barry. "Mist'r Bannard over t'th'house?"

"Why, yes, he's just gone back again. He said he and Mr. Greeves were going to the city to hunt for her. You better hurry."

"Aw'right. G'night!" and Barry led the way rapidly round the side porch, down through the garden and over the back fence. Athalie was stumbling painfully along the plowed ground with one little high heeled slipper and one silken clad sorry foot. As she struggled up on the fence Barry saw it.

"Say, kid, when did you lose your shoe?" he asked solicitously.

"Up there on the road when I was running," said the girl with a catch in her breath and looking up he saw that she was suffering and that there were tears on her face.

"You poor kid!" he said gently, and stooping, picked her up and carried her all the way up through the garden, to the brick terrace at the back hall door. There he set her down gently, and tapped at the door.

"I wonder what time it is by moonlight," he said glancing down at the sun-dial. "It must be a good piece into tomorrow already. My time piece got kicked across the room the other day by mistake so I have to get along without it."

Athalie stood shivering, a sorry little figure in her tattered scarlet draperies, with her smeary face, her hat jammed over one ear, and one torn silk stocking, but a faint semblance of a wistful smile went over her face as she watched the nice big boy beside her. How strong he had been, and how tender! It gave her that thanking feeling again. How strange! And yet how like a ruffian he had treated her out on the road and made her come home! Her mingled feelings held in check by the very salutary possibility that she was about to meet with a well deserved punishment from the stranger-parent inside the door were overwhelming enough without any addition. But when hurrying footsteps came down the hall, and Anne Truesdale's face red with weeping appeared as she opened the door, Athalie suddenly remembered her exit from the house that afternoon and realized that there were many scores for her to settle, and shrank back behind her protector.

Greeves and Bannard came quickly down the hall, and at the top of the stairs there was a soft stirring and the flutter of a blue bath robe as Silver leaned over the banister by her door to listen.

Barry stepped within and lifted his old cap respectfully. He was in his shirt sleeves and his face looked tired and haggard but with a cheerful grin.

"She got lost, Mr. Greeves and took the wrong road. I happened along and brought her back. Sorry we had to be so late, but it was a good piece away. She's about all in so you better put her to bed. No thanks, I can't stay. I got a borrowed car over in the lane I gotta return. Oh, well, I don't care if I do have some cookies."

They plied him with plates of cake and cups of

coffee and took the attention entirely away from Athalie, and the girl thankfully slipped upstairs. Then she remembered the sweater she was still wearing, and slipped it off quickly, paused to put on another shoe that lay in her way, flung her cloak about her and stole down again.

She had almost a shy look on her face as she brought the sweater over to where Barry stood by the dining room table swallowing down hot coffee and talking to the minister about the baseball prospects.

Both the minister and Greeves looked at her in surprise. Somehow, with the paint washed off, even in dirty streaks she looked more human, and less bold and bizarre.

Barry looked up with one of his brilliant smiles that he gave rarely, and took the sweater.

"I'm afraid you were cold!" said Athalie most unexpectedly to herself. It hadn't occurred to her to think of anyone but herself until that instant.

"Oh, that's all right, kid!" he said setting down his coffee cup and struggling into his sweater with a couple of motions, "glad I had it along. Hope you feel all right in the morning."

Athalie retired feeling for perhaps the first time in her life that she was forgiven and given another chance. Somehow all her escapades up to this time, with nurses, governesses, teachers, and parents, had ended in enmity and a bitter feeling of spite. She went upstairs slowly wondering what it was about this boy that made her feel like a happy little child. She ought to hate him. To be planning some way to get it back on him. He had baffled her and ruled her as no one had ever done before, and he was only a kid like herself, and yet she had a sort of awe for him, an interest in him, a pleasure in his smile. She took off her red tatters pondering this, forgetful entirely of her bridegroom that was to have been.

While Barry was stowing away the sandwiches and cake and coffee that Anne Truesdale seemed always to be able to produce without a moment's warning, Greeves and Bannard withdrew to the hall. The father looked worn and haggard. He cast an anxious eye up the stairs and said in a low voice:

"Bannard I can't thank you enough for sticking by through this. It seems strange but this is getting me worse than anything that has ever come to me. I need some advice. I need some help. How on earth am I ever to teach that unruly child!"

"You need God, Greeves! I mean it! Kneel down, and pray. That will do you more good than any advice that anyone could possibly give you."

"Don't get on your hobby again tonight Bannard. I'm in no mood for trifling. I've got to give that girl some kind of a lesson—"

"She looked to me as if she had learned her lesson pretty thoroughly," said Bannard. "I wonder where Barry found her. I thought he must be out on one of his specials. That boy certainly is a wonder!"

"Yes, I am deeply grateful. What are his circumstances? Can I reward him?"

"Give him your friendship. That's all he would ever take. He's proud as Lucifer, but he's loving as they make 'em."

"Yes, I liked him the first time I met him. I'd like to know more about where he found her."

"Well, perhaps she'll tell you. I doubt if he ever will. He's a man of few words, where it concerns anything he has done. But I wasn't trifling, Greeves, I meant what I said. There is nothing in the wide universe would open up this situation and show you the right way like getting down on your knees and getting back to God, and when you get there that 'tomorrow' I was telling you about will be about to dawn.

"Ready Barry? I'll walk along with you. Good night Greeves. I'm glad your vigil is at an end!"

They went out the terrace door and walked silently down the garden, two dark shadows among the growing things. Even if Lizette Weldon had been wakeful she would not have noticed them for the hedge was tall and they kept close in its shadow.

Silently the two, as those who understand one another, passed over the fence and through Aunt Katie's little garden, around the side of the house to the front gate.

"Anything I need to know, Partner?" asked Bannard affectionately.

Barry considered.

"I guess not tonight, sir." He looked up with a smile.

"Have to go far with that car?"

"Quite a piece."

"Your mother is down at the Flats with a sick child tonight."

"Aw'right! I'll be back before she is. G'night!"

Barry slid into the car noiselessly, and as quietly as a car can go that one backed out of the lane to the beachway, and sped away into the night. He did not immediately take to the city highway however. There was something he had to do first. About an hour later he turned into the highway a mile or so above Silver Sands and made high speed to the city. In his hip pocket under his sweater reposed a muddy little slipper.

The minister had slipped into his door and extinguished the light at once going softly upstairs in the dark. From behind Aunt Katie's door there came a question:

"Was it all right?"

"All right Aunt Katie. Your prayers brought us through!"

About half an hour later Lizette who had fallen asleep on watch woke up and scanned both her windows, but neither Aunt Katie's nor the Silver mansion showed any signs of light, yet she had been sure she heard an automobile somewhere in her dreams. For Anne Truesdale faithful even to a "daring huzzy" prepared a hot bath for Athalie, and a tray of good things for her to eat, but she had been careful to hang a black shawl behind the drawn shade of the window looking toward the Weldon house.

The eastern sky was paling into dawn as Barry drove into the outskirts of the city and began his search for an open telephone station. He found presently an obscure little hotel, and had no trouble in discovering Robert Farrell's name. He purchased a sheet of paper and an envelope and standing by the desk wrote a brief and characteristic letter:

"Mr. Robert Farrell,
     Redwood Apartments,
          Dear sir:—This is to notify you that you are not to have any further communication with Miss Greeves. The police force of Silver County is onto you, and is watching every move you make, and if the investigation of your past that is being made brings any further criminal developments we will make Silver County too hot to hold you. If this warning of the police of Silver Sands is not obeyed, Mr. Greeves will stop at nothing to prosecute you to the limit. Signed, B. Link, member of police force, Silver Sands."

With this letter duly addressed and sealed Barry took his way to the Redwood Apartments and rang up the man in Farrell's apartment. To him, when he finally appeared yawning, Barry handed over the letter and the car and touching his hat politely disappeared, running like a deer to the station as soon as he had passed the corner, and arriving just in time to catch the milk train for Silver Sands.

Chapter XXII

"The only possible condition under which you are free to remain in this town and in my house is that you hereafter conduct yourself as a lady in every way!"

This was the ultimatum which Patterson Greeves after a night of vigil flung out upon his subdued and waiting daughter sometime along in the middle of the morning when she chose to come down to a languid breakfast.

Silver had gone early to the Flats with the minister and Anne Truesdale was out doing marketing. They had the house to themselves. The father girded up his soul and went to the task before him. It had to come sooner or later.

Athalie regarded him composedly for a moment before responding:

"Well," said she, "with Lilla on the high seas, and my money mostly gone I suppose I'll have to make a try. I won't go to school. What is it you want me to do? Go to church and Sunday school?"

Now nothing was farther from Patterson Greeves' intention than to attend divine service of any sort or to make his family do so, but in that instant it flashed across his consciousness that that was the very thing that would have to be done if Athalie was to remain in the town and live as a member of the old Silver family should, in good and regular standing. Athalie could not associate with the young people of the town and expect to be comfortable among them unless she did as they did, unless she did as the traditions of the family laid down. For himself he would probably have ignored what people thought and have shut himself in with his books and his few friends and let the town go hang. But here he was preaching the standard of his old family and insisting upon its being kept high, and in his heart not planning to do so himself. He saw the inconsistency at once, and knew also that the thing she had suggested was the very influence that would readjust her abnormal young soul, if anything could do it. If religion was good for anything it ought to be good for that. In fact, there was somewhere hid away in his own soul the belief not yet extinct that religion did do things to souls when it really got a chance! Also, there was Bannard. He had some sense if he was a minister. She wouldn't likely get much nonsense hearing him. And there was Silver! Of course Silver would want to go to church. Somehow he shrank from letting Silver know how far he had strayed from the religion of her mother, and her mother's people. All this passed through his mind in the lifting of an eye. He was accustomed to control his face and cover it with a mask among men. He scarcely seemed to hesitate as he replied:

"Yes. Certainly. Of course you will go to church and Sunday school."

"Oh, heck!" said Athalie, a kind of hunted look coming into her eyes as she flounced around and stared out of the window.

Greeves watched her painfully trying to adjust his own thoughts to this unexpected turn. He would have to go to church himself probably to enforce this. He felt like reechoing her exclamation. What was he letting himself in for? Well, if it got too strenuous he could always send her away to camp when he found the right place. Then too, he would have to be courteous to Bannard. He had been awfully decent last night, knowing just the thing to be done, and not making a great fuss about it as some would have done, and making every thing public. Yes, of course he would have to go to church occasionally. Tomorrow was the Sabbath. He would have to go then to start things right. Then after that perhaps he could manage to be away a good deal Sundays, run down to the shore or make a visit to New York or Boston—any excuse would do. He would have to go a good deal anyway to consult libraries.

"Well," said Athalie as suddenly whirling back as she had turned away. "What else? I'm game."

Her fixed gaze was rather disconcerting. He couldn't help admiring the way she took it. There was something rather interesting about her in spite of all her devilishness. Where did she get that?

"There are three things that I shall require," he said following out the plan he had evolved during the night. Poor soul, he had gone such a little way in this matter of fatherhood and discipline. He thought it could all be enumerated under three heads.

Athalie watched him attentively.

"Obedience—"

Athalie winced.

"Who do I have to obey? Not that red-faced servant woman! Not that other girl!"

Her father faltered.

"Because I *won't!* That's *flat!*"

"They would come under the next head," temporized Patterson Greeves, "which is courtesy."

"Oh, you mean I've got to be *polite!* All right. I suppose I can. What next?"

"Modesty!" finished the father with a sudden realization that his list was pitifully short and she was dismissing them all and making them shorter.

"Well, what do you mean by that?"

"I mean that I do not like the way you dress nor behave. You constantly call attention to yourself, to your person. It is probably not your fault that you are somewhat stout, although I have understood there are diets that will regulate that sort of thing, but it is your fault when you dress in loud and noticeable colors and strange styles, or when you expose your flesh to view."

Athalie's brow drew down.

She glanced down at her dashing little blouse of orange crochet over a flannel skirt of orange and black stripes. Her plump pink arms showed through the knitted mesh, and the brilliant neckerchief she was wearing jauntily across one shoulder revealed much fat neck. A flush of disappointment rolled up her carefully unpowdered cheek. She had really tried to look pleasing for that interview. According to her standard she looked nice.

"I've worn the only things I had," she said sullenly. "I'm sure I don't know how to please you."

Something in the wistfulness of her tone appealed to him. He cast about how to answer her.

"Suppose you go up and spread out what you have and I'll come and look at your things. If you haven't got the proper clothes we'll have to go and buy some."

A glint of interest shone in Athalie's eyes.

"I'll go up and spread them out," she said eagerly, "it won't take me long. There's really some quite spiffy ones."

He almost groaned aloud as she disappeared like a bright, saucy butterfly. How was he to make her understand that it was their very "spiffiness" that made the trouble.

In a few minutes he heard her calling, and he goaded himself up the stairs trying to prepare to be very diplomatic and gentle and firm.

Athalie stood by the door her face radiant and behind her on the bed lay shining masses of silks and satins and velvets in gaudy array and all around the room were hangers on which hung limp effigies of herself done in all colors of the rainbow, the vintage of Lilla's cast off frocks, made over for her neglected daughter.

Athalie led him around the room beginning with what she considered the sober ones, and going on to the more dressy affairs. He went from one to the other with growing bewilderment and pain, and when he had finished he stood back in dismay and began at the beginning again. He could not find one thing that filled his idea of what a young girl should wear. Once he thought he had discovered it in a simple looking brown affair with a gleam of brilliant green which Athalie had hung behind the door as if she had forgotten it or did not want it inspected because it was too dull. He took the hanger down and began to examine it.

"Now this," he said with a tone of growing satisfaction, and picking up a corner of the long tunic that was bound in tailored fashion, "this seems—why, what is this? Trousers?"

"Yes, those are the knickerbockers," said Athalie, "I used to like that a lot but I'm sort of tired of it. However, if you like it I'll put it on. I thought maybe—but I'll put it on!"

She seized the hanger and slipped into the bathroom, returning in a brief space with the garment on. Patterson Greeves drew a long breath. She seemed to be clothed properly for the first time. The lines were straight, the color was dark, her form did not appear so sensuous.

"Now that—" he began, "step out from behind the bed and let me see."

Athalie stepped out and walked.

"Why, what is that? Is it torn? Is it ripped? Why how short it is!"

"No, those are open all the way up to the waist. That is the knickerbockers underneath. Haven't you been used to the knickerbocker suits? They're all the craze at school. I had one of the first that came out. I just made Lilla get it, or rather I bought it myself and sent the bill to her and told her I'd tell a friend of hers something she didn't want told if she didn't pay it—"

Athalie's tongue was rattling on eagerly, but Athalie's father was sick at heart. As she strode about the room, whirling in front of the long mirror on the old-fashioned bureau, her stout legs were revealed clad in green trousers which finished in a tailored cuff below the knee and fully eight inches above this brown tunic flopped and flared, making her a grotesque figure, neither man nor maid. A fashion that might have been tolerated or even fancied on a slender little child, but was revolting on a girl of Athalie's age and build.

"Take it off," ordered the discouraged parent. "Haven't you anything decent at all?"

Athalie stopped dismayed and retreated half frightened into the other room. When she came out again she was wearing the little yellow dress and she looked lonesome and unhappy.

Her father wheeled about from the window where he had been looking unseeingly into the garden—it was strange how the only relief from things sometimes is to look out of the window and get a wider vision—and eyed her perplexedly.

"We'll have to go to town and do some shopping. I think it would be best to take your sister along—"

"She's *not* my sister! And I won't go if you take her! I thought you understood that!"

"That's not obedience, Athalie!"

The girl looked down stormily.

"Well, then if you force her on me I won't obey. I don't see why you want her along. She can't pick out my clothes! I wouldn't wear a rag she selected. You ask her if she would like what I chose for her."

The father reflected that that was probably true. Silver would certainly not look right in any of Athalie's clothes.

"Well, then we'll take the housekeeper," he temporized.

"That frumpy thing!" said Athalie.

"Well, who would you suggest?" He looked desperately at his daughter and wondered why a creature of so young an age should be able to perpetrate so much trouble and get away with it.

Athalie dimpled into a charming smile.

"I don't see why you and I couldn't go just together. It's you that's to be suited, isn't it? And me that's to do the wearing? Well, then, what has anybody else to do with it."

"I'm not at all certain that I—"

"Oh, if you don't know what you want—" began Athalie with a toss of her head.

"Very well," said her father, with swift decision, "get ready at once. I'll phone for a car. Can you be ready in half an hour?" he looked at his watch.

"Yes," she said brightly, casting a selective eye around her wardrobe.

"But what will you wear?" he asked uneasily looking around also trying to find something that would do. "I don't see anything here that is suitable."

Athalie pouted.

"Perhaps we'd better wait and I'll telephone for something to be sent out on approval, a blue serge suit or something," he suggested helplessly.

Athalie darkened.

"I've got an old tweed thing in the trunk. I hate it but maybe you'd like it."

"Let me see it."

She pawed in her trunk a moment and fished out a brown tweed coat and skirt. He took it up and examined it, his face clearing.

"Now, that's what I call a nice neat, sensible dress for a girl," he said. "Is it all whole? There aren't any slits or anything in it? Well, put that on, and some kind of a hat that doesn't look too fast, and dark stockings and gloves. And—Athalie, wash your face! *Wash* it I mean!"

Athalie waited until he had closed the door and then she looked her thought of him behind his back in a very forceful expression. Having thus unburdened her soul she set about making a hasty toilet and when she came downstairs seemed to him quite presentable in her trim brown coat and skirt. The skirt was more abbreviated both horizontally and perpendicularly than he would have desired, but it would have to do for the present, and she wore a small, neat hat of brown straw from which she had just extracted some kind of an ornament in feathers that resembled a burning bush. It was drawn down over her forehead till she looked quite demure, and her feet were quietly encased in brown stockings and tan oxfords with low heels and rubber soles. She wore gloves and her whole aspect seemed to have changed. Looking on her now her father wondered perhaps if it might not be possible sometime to even—well—rather like her.

That morning's shopping was an experience Patterson Greeves will never be likely to forget. He felt as if he were leading a wild young coyote by a chain, which might at any moment give way in his hand and let chaos loose in the stores. The number of things that Athalie picked out and her father disapproved were too numerous to mention. Sometimes they found a saleswoman who sided with the girl and took it upon herself to advise the father, and then Greeves went to another store. Again they fell to the hands of a prim, sharp woman with a false front who called Athalie "dearie" and patronized her, and the girl simply refused to try on or look at a thing under her guidance.

In his pocket Patterson Greeves carried a brief memorandum the result of a secret interview with Anne Truesdale, which he from time to time consulted anxiously as if it were a talisman that would somehow guide him through the mazes of this expedition. It read:

"Four or five stout gingham dresses for school.

Two sprigged muslins for afternoons.

A nice white dress for evening socials.

A dark blue silk for best.

Two serviceable blue serges made sailor style."

Athalie had two methods. One was to go into ecstasies over something she liked, talk about its simplicity, and its classic lines, and how sweet and quiet it was. The other was to walk off out of the department entirely and be found looking drearily out of a window when she saw her father's eye on something that did not interest her.

On the whole she worked things pretty well, and came off with four wash silks, which by the aid of the saleswoman she had persuaded her father were now taking the place of ginghams; several crêpe de chines, a couple of handkerchief linens, and a one-piece serge that cost twice as much as any dress she had ever owned before. If she was going to have to be severe and plain, by all means let it be the severity of elegant simplicity. After a sumptuous repast at an irreproachable tea room at which she ordered everything on the menu that took her fancy—from lobster salad to café frappe she carried her exhausted parent home triumphantly and spent the afternoon making little alterations in her purchases. He had selected them himself, hadn't he? Well, then he couldn't possibly find fault with anything about them. He would never know what she had done to them.

Life settled down quietly. Patterson Greeves got

out some of his notes and began to put his papers
away in the desk. Silver had sent word that she was
spending the day at the Flats. There was nothing
to hurt or annoy. He reflected that both Lizette Weldon and several of the Vandemeeters had been in evidence at their front windows or gates when he and
Athalie had driven away and again when they returned. Surely Athalie's escapade would be forgotten
if all went on in the conventional manner. Surely he
might relax a little now.

From the region of the kitchen there floated from
time to time spicy suggestive odors.

And the next day was the Sabbath.

Chapter XXIII

MARY TRUMAN called for Athalie Greeves to take her to Sunday school.

She did not want to go. She had told all the girls at the school picnic the day before that she didn't intend to do it. She had cried for two hours and begged both father and mother to let her off, but they had insisted, and so with her neat blue serge suit and her blue straw sailor, her hair tied with a fresh ribbon, and her hands and feet encased in simple girlish fittings, she reluctantly swung the Greeves' gate open and slowly made her way up the path.

It was early. The first bell had only begun to ring. Mrs. Truman had insisted that she must give the stranger plenty of time to get ready. She had also, unknown to her daughter, telephoned Mr. Greeves that Mary was coming.

Patterson Greeves, having come down to breakfast in much better frame of mind than since he had returned to Silver Sands, had forgotten entirely that it was the Sabbath day or that there was such a thing as Sabbath school to be dealt with. Indeed, left to himself he might have been persuaded to forget it altogether for this time, but when Mrs. Truman offered an escort he jumped at it eagerly, and Athalie heard herself promised as a new scholar in the class with "that frumpy little Truman girl."

However, Athalie was going to be a good sport. When her father turned from the telephone and informed her that she must get ready for Sunday school she looked up with just a flicker of a gasp and stared, but that was all. Quite like a lady she arose from the table and went to her room. When she came down dressed in her brown tweed suit, gloves, hat, and shoes as she had dressed the day before for her trip to the city her father looked her over almost with approval and when he saw her go down the path beside Mary Truman he sighed with relief. Perhaps she was going to be amenable to reason after all.

Mindful of her triple promise to her father Athalie was quite polite, but in a lofty way, like a lion condescending to walk with a lamb.

"So kind of you to come for me," she said haughtily, "I never went to Sunday school before in my life. What do they do?"

"You—never went—to *Sunday school!*" Mary paused in horrified astonishment. "Why! Where have you lived? Ddin't they *have* any Sunday school?"

"Why, I really don't know. I never enquired. Perhaps they had, but nobody said anything about it. I'm curious to see it! Is it as dull as day school?"

"Oh, day school isn't dull! We have lovely times. Silver Sands is said to have the best school in Silver County. We have the darlingest teachers! And debating society! And contests, and athletics! Oh, it's great! I feel dreadfully when I'm sick and have to miss a day. I haven't missed a day now in two years, not since I had the measles."

"Dear me!" said Athalie. "I should think you'd be bored to death! Do all those girls you brought to see me go to Sunday school?"

"Oh, yes, of course. Everybody goes to Sunday school in Silver Sands. Most of them go to our church. Only Emily Bragg, she's a Methodist, but they have a nice Sunday school too, only not so large. I was allowed to go with her once when she was going to speak on Children's Day. We have a lovely teacher. Her name's Pristina Appleby. She lives right across the street from you. She tells us very interesting things about the pyramids and the tablets they've dug up and things like that you know. Sometimes she brings us pictures to help understand the lesson."

"Lesson? Do you have lessons? Mercy! I hate lessons."

"Oh, you won't hate this," laughed Mary, "she just talks. We call her Miss Prissie!"

"Oh! And this Miss Pussy! Is she an old maid?"

"Miss *Prissie* I said. No, oh no, she isn't an old maid. Her aunts are that. She has three aunts and a grandmother and a great grandmother and they all live together in that brick house across the street from you."

"Oh! I hadn't noticed. Then she's a young girl."

"Well, not exactly young. She's not as young as your sister. I think *she's* lovely. We girls are all crazy about her. I'm so sorry you couldn't have come to the fudge party the other night. We had such fun. Your sister was wonderful! She started all the games—"

Athalie's face darkened but she kept her stiffly polite manner, a trifle more haughty perhaps.

"Yes, it was a pity!" she drawled. "Is this your church? What are they ringing that bell for?"

"Why for Sunday school."

"Oh! I thought somebody might be dead! I've read of that! You never can tell what curious thing they may do in a strange place you know."

Mary started to giggle and then looked at her questioningly and grew red instead. Was this rude girl trying to make fun of her again?

"Especially in the country," added Athalie.

Mary said no more. Other girls and boys were standing around the entrance as they went up the path. Athalie stared at everyone as if she had come to a show and that was what was expected of her. Bannard came down the street from the other direction and lifted his hat gravely to Athalie. She dimpled and smiled.

"So he goes to Sunday school too!" she remarked complacently.

"Why, yes of course," said Mary somewhat shortly. "He's the minister. Why shouldn't he come!" She was getting tired of the publicity of escorting this strange girl. She wished Sunday school were well over.

Athalie was much entertained all through Sunday school. She stared at everybody's clothes, kept her eyes wide open during prayer watching the contortion of the superintendent's lips as he prayed. The other girls, duly devout, stole curious glances at her between their fingers. Her conduct of the day before

had been carefully discussed at the dinner tables and
a general taboo placed upon her as far as an associate
for daughters was concerned. To find her in Sunday
school was therefore a surprise. The more so as a
rumor had been started by Pristina Appleby's essay
at the club that Patterson Greeves was one of the new
thinkers and had left the faith of his fathers to wan-
der in dangerous speculations.

But when Sunday school was out there was Patterson Greeves coming up the walk with Silver by his
side, her sweet face smiling to every one, her smile
almost like a part of the sunshine, her eyes as blue as
the dress she wore and the little hat with its black
wing.

Athalie stood by the door with Mary Truman and
watched them approach, noted her father's fine presence with pride, heard the whispered remarks about
him, then heard: "Isn't she sweet!" and saw that all
eyes were directed toward Silver. Tht sullen fires came
back to her eyes. She looked around like a hunted
thing and for an instant thought of bolting straight
through the graveyard. Then her father's grave glance
was upon her pleasantly and her face lighted up. He
was not displeased with her then. She experienced a
sudden surprised pleasure in it. Fiercely did she desire to belong to someone, to have someone care for
her, to be able to please. All her life she had met
with impatience and curbing. This father she had
come determined to win to herself or die in the attempt. Deeply had she longed for a home and parents like other girls and had not had them. Perhaps
she had, down deep in her heart, the thought that
maybe somehow she might draw hers together. All
her young life she had showered upon her selfish
mother a degree of devotion, one might almost say
adoration such as few real mothers get, and it had
only returned upon itself in bitterness. The mother
had regarded her lightly, tolerantly, gaily, yet if that
mother had asked of her any sacrifice, no matter how
great, the fierce young soul would have given it,
gladly, freely. So now Athalie regarded her father
with eyes of pride and of possession.

Another face just then picked itself out from the throng of churchgoers, a young face, strong and manly, vaguely familiar. He was standing under the willow tree near the gravestones, bare headed, cleanly shaven, neat and trim in a much brushed suit, talking to a group of other boys. Presently they sauntered over toward the steps nodding to the girls who came by, calling out a pleasant word. Mary Truman stepped down below Athalie and spoke:

"Why, hello, Barry. Where were you Friday night? Didn't Mr. Bannard give you my invitation to the fudge party?"

Barry turned quickly and pleasantly.

"Sorry Mary, I didn't get home till late. Had an errand that kept me. Hear you had a great time. Save some fudge for me?"

Then he lifted his eyes and recognized Athalie. He did not speak. It was rather a lighting of the eyes, a pleasant understanding that gave her heart that warm glow and she knew him for her captor of the midnight ride. After that Athalie was satisfied to stay and see this thing called church through to the finish.

Oh, she had been to church before of course. At school those things were compulsory. But there was something about this church, like a big family gathering of people who all liked each other and enjoyed being there that was new to the girl. She stared about and wondered at it. Funny old women in queer bonnets, coats that were antique of cut; a few of recognized culture and education, though that counted very little as yet with Athalie; one or two with stylish clothes. She watched the Vandemeeter tribe file into the pew, grandma, first, slowly with a cane, mother just behind, Henrietta helping grandma, Maria in the same black broadcloth coat and black felt hat with the coque feather band she had worn for the last seven years. Maria was never one to put on summer clothes until summer was really there. Harriet and Cordelia with pink velvet roses wreathed around their last year's dyed straws. She eyed them curiously. Each a replica of the other in a different stage of life.

What tiresome people. How did they endure life? She
noted grandma's bent head, mother's closed eyes, the
squarely folded handkerchiefs, the little tremble of
the feathered bonnet when Henrietta handed grandma the hymn book. Everything was strange and unusual to Athalie. She wondered why such common
people wanted to *be*, why they seemed to take an
interest in being? Why did her father stay in a place
like this when there were cities where things were
going on, wild, gay life for which she thirsted?

She was surprised to see Barry sitting in the back
row of the choir. How queer for a boy like that to be
willing to waste his time this way!

Suddenly Bannard's voice arrested her attention.
He was telling a story, though he seemed to have a
small leather book open in his hand as if he were
about to read. He painted a picture with his words.
She forgot the sunny church with its bright carpet
and unfashionable congregation. She was seeing a
walled city in a strange land, under a blazing sky with
hungry faces looking out from little slits of windows in
towers and turrets, and an army camped around on
every hand. They had been there days and days and
had starved out the stronghold. The people were reduced to eating loathsome things. An ass's head, something that would not be thought of as food at another
time, sold for about forty dollars, coarse chick peas
were selling at a prohibitive price. Even the king and
his court were starving.

The king was walking on the wall, visiting his sen-
tries. You could see his face, lined with anxiety, as he
shaded his eyes and looked out across the sea of ene-
mies' tents. There was no sign of discouragement on
the part of that enemy. They had come to stay until
the city surrendered. They knew it would not be long.
They had spies who had discovered its state. They
were well supplied with food themselves and had
nothing to do but eat and drink and make merry until
they had worn out the resources of the people and
there was nothing left for them but to surrender. The
king sighed and passed on, as he went someone
reached out and caught his robe with claw like hands,

a woman from the doorstep of one of the little hovels on the wall. There were deep hollows under her eyes and in her cheeks. She looked more like a skeleton than a woman. "Help!" she cried, "help, my lord, O king!"

The king drew away impatiently. So many cried for help and what could he do. "Curse you!" he said impatiently, "with every barn floor bare and every wine press empty, what can I do?" and he turned as if to pass on. But the woman continued her strange weird cry, and began a terrible story. Another woman appeared crouching frightened against the doorway.

"This woman promised if I would kill my baby boy yesterday and cook and eat him that she would kill hers today, but we ate my son yesterday and now she has hid hers today. I pray you O king, speak to her. Make her give up her son that she has hid."

Athalie's eyes were wide with horror. She had never heard a story like that.

The speaker depicted the horror on the face of the king as he listened to the tale, and watched the faces of the hunger-crazed women, realized that he was powerless to aid, that things could only grow worse rather than better, that the Lord in whom he had put at least a little of his trust had apparently deserted him, and then he laid hold on his kingly robe and tore it.

Like a company of children the listening congregation attended, not an eye looked dreamy, not a brain was planning out tomorrow's work, nor calculating the sum of yesterday's mistakes. The Bible lived and breathed before them as Bannard spoke. They saw that king reach down and tear his robe as he passed on, they were among those who looked beneath and saw the sackcloth next his skin, oriental symbol of humiliation, of repentance, of prayer. They caught a glimpse of King Jehoram's past, his mother the wicked queen Jezebel, his father of whom it was written, "there was none like unto Ahab, which did sell himself to work wickedness in the sight of the Lord."

One saw that Jehoram was not quite so bad as his father and mother. He put away the image of Baal which his father had set up for worship to please his mother, but he wrought evil in the sight of the Lord.

The king on the wall in the torn robe, with the sackcloth showing beneath suddenly turned and swore a terrible oath that he would have the head of God's prophet that day, the prophet who had been promising day after day that God would deliver them from the enemy; and now they were come to the great extremity and God was not helping. Why should he wait for God any longer?

The king walked to his palace and sent a messenger to the little house where Elisha lived. One saw the soldier from the palace hurry along with sword in hand down the narrow streets of queer flat-topped oriental houses, and Elisha sitting quietly in his door talking to some of the old men, and suddenly lifting his eye to his servant and saying in a quiet voice "The king is sending a soldier to behead me. Shut the door and lock it. The king will be here presently. Keep the soldier out till he comes."

The hurrying feet, the hastily shut door, the altercation. Athalie sat breathless with glowing eyes of wonder. The impudent air of the king as he came, the parley: "Behold, this evil is of the Lord; why should I wait any longer for Him to help me?" and Elisha's quiet voice answering: "Hear ye the word of the Lord. The time is up! Tomorrow about this time shall a measure of fine white flour be sold at less than pre-war prices."

"Ha!" the laugh of the servant on whom the king leans, "if God were opening windows in heaven just now this might be!"

The quiet rebuke: "You shall see it but not eat thereof."

Night drops quickly, suddenly in that eastern land. Twilight on the white parched city where skulking shadows pass on the wall and huddled human beings sleep and forget for a little while their sufferings. The king in his palace asleep. No faith whatever in what Elisha promised. Twilight outside the wall in the little leper village, four lepers waiting at the gate, starving, talking it over. Shall they throw themselves on the mercy of the enemy, and beg something to eat? "If they kill us we shall but die anyway!" The hesitant approach, peering like white ghosts into the first tent, the pause, the eager going forward. No one there! The table spread. They snatch the food and devour it, and move on to the next, and suddenly are struck with the silence throughout the great camp. The hurrying investigation, then the hastening back to the city to tell, the waking of the unbelieving king, the five men sent to verify the story, the garments strewn in the way as the enemy fled, the rejoicing, the crowding out of the city to spoil the tents of the enemy, crushing out the life of the astonished servant who had laughed the day before! The wonderful reason of the enemy's flight, that the Lord had caused a sound of horses to be heard by them!

Athalie looked around the church to see if anybody was really believing it. Where did they get a strange story like that? The Lord! *The Lord!* How strange that sounded as if the Lord was a real person! Did her father believe that? She glanced at him as he sat with stern listening attitude, his gloved hands on his knee. She could not tell whether he were astonished at it or not. She listened again. The minister was talking now about world problems. He said the world was waiting today as then for the Lord to deliver them from a state of siege into which their own sin and folly had placed them, and blaming God that He did not come. They were tired of wearing sackcloth and ready to do murder. When all the time God's wonderful tomorrow was waiting, just over the way, waiting for them to reach the limit of their own possibilities that God might show His power and grace. He said that the troubles of the world would never be solved and peace never come until Christ came into human hearts, and that all these things pointed to a time close at hand when some tomorrow about this time Christ Himself was coming back to relieve His own forever from a state of siege.

Athalie never took her eyes from the face of the speaker during this closing talk. She had never heard anything like it in her life before. It made realities

out of what had been vague mythical stories, like
fairy tales, before. Was there really a Jesus Christ
then? He died, didn't He, long ago? On a cross? What
did they mean, *coming again?*

She was silent and thoughtful all that day. Her father looked at her relieved. She wandered around
the house, played a few little jazzy tunes on the
piano which scandalized the Vandemeeters and Lizette who both made it a point to listen intently for
any sign of a hymn tune, then drifted away to her
room and her fast disappearing stock of chocolates
and literature.

Silver had gone to the Mission school at the Flats.
The house was silent all the afternoon, with a Sabbath stillness Athalie had never known before. Sabbath meant nothing to her but a gayer day than
usual, the focus of the gaiety of the week.

Mary Truman, still under parental pressure called
for her to go to Christian Endeavor that evening, and
because Athalie saw nothing else to do, and her father and Silver were talking in the library before
the fire, she went. She wondered if the strange boy
would be there. Barry. What a nice name!

He was there. He passed her a hymn book and
looked pleased when she came into the bright little
chapel room where they met. He sang in a quartette,
growling a nice low bass. She watched him wonderingly, remembering how he had held her like a vice
when she tried to get the wheel away from him. Remembering how gently he had lifted her and carried
her.

It seemed a queer meeting. The girls and boys
spoke, just like a frat-meeting at school, only they
said queer things. They referred to the sermon of
that morning as if they were altogether familiar with
the story of that siege. They spoke of Mr. Bannard
as if he were a brother and comrade. Mr. Bannard was
there among them, just like one of them. It was rather
interesting, only it was embarrassing when they
prayed. She didn't know what to do with her eyes so
she watched them all.

That boy Barry gave a notice about a committee

meeting after service. Two others jumped up and
spoke about socials that were being planned. They
all seemed so eager and friendly. Athalie felt lonely
and outside everything.

When they went in the church again there was
Silver sitting with her father. Mary asked her politely to come in their seat and she went. She did not
want to sit beside Silver again.

Mr. Bannard spoke about the coming of Christ
again. He made it plain that He was really coming,
and that some people, good people presumably for
Athalie didn't understand that language about "be-
lievers" were to be taken away and the world would
wonder where they had gone. Athalie looked over at
Silver. She thought Silver would be one that would
be taken away. Well, that would be good. She hated
good people and she would be left with her father.
It was reasonably sure a noted man of the world like
her father wouldn't be taken away from earth like
that. He didn't have that spirit-look that Silver wore
as a garment. It frightened her a little this talk about
the Son of God coming back to earth. She hoped on
second thought that it wouldn't come till she was old,
very old and didn't care about living any more. It
stayed with her after she got home, and when she
went to bed and thought of Lilla in a little boat on
the great ocean she cried a few tears sorrowfully.
Lilla was the only god she had ever had.

On the whole she was rather docile about going to
school the next morning when her father suggested
that she enter high school and finish out the spring
term. She remembered what Barry had said about
athletics and resolved not to eat any more chocolates
for a week after this last box was gone.

So she polished her nails to a delicate point and be-
took herself languidly to school to see how she liked
it. She was astonished to see how little impression
she made on the wholesome atmosphere of high
school. The teacher, a placid faced elderly woman
with a firm chin, said to be the finest school principal in the county, smiled at her pleasantly and put
her in the front seat directly before the desk. None of

the boys gave her a glance, save Barry who showed
mere recognition. The girls she had met smiled politely and went on with study. Whenever she looked
up she was met with that pleasant challenge of a
smile. There was absolutely no opportunity to get
away with anything unless one first crossed that
friendly smile, and Athalie wasn't just exactly ready
to do that yet until she had tried things out. There
had not been any too many smiles in her life. She
took the book that was handed her to read until the
principal should have time to examine her and place
her in the classes where she fitted, and was surprised
to find it was an interesting novel. The teacher explained it was the book the English class were
reading for review and conversation that week.

Her father glanced into the study-hall half an hour
later, after an inspection of the building led by an
old friend who was the Latin teacher, and saw her absorbed in the book. He went home with a sigh of relief, comforted.

But that very night Athalie wrote eleven invitations to six boys and five girls for a house party that
week end, and mailed them early in the morning
before she went to school. But that no one in her
family knew.

Chapter XXIV

THE tramp had found work as a laborer in the glass factory through the efforts of some of the good Presbyterian women whose wood piles had been supplying his breakfasts and dinners for some time. He worked feebly and with great effort and managed to maintain his role of semi-elderly invalid who was doing his best.

He was working with a gang of other men shovelling sand into a cart when Silver Greeves came by with a basket of broth and oranges and a lovely dolly for the little Mary who was now on the high road to recovery.

The tramp paused in the monotony of his service. He put in regularly one shovelful to the other men's two. He always paused longest for interruptions and rested his weary back. The other men paused also and watched the progress of the lithe girl as she stepped down the roughly cobbled path and entered the cottage.

"That's that girl from the Silver family," said one of the man. "Take notice of her? She's been comin' down to that wop's house every day. She's been takin' care of the sick kid."

"Well, they'd oughtta do things like that. They got aplenty ain't they? Don't we keep 'em in cash with our labor? They couldn't sell this sand if we didn't shovel it, could they? She'd make a pretty hand shovellin' sand, now, wouldn't she? How would she live if we didn't shovel her sand fer her? I ask you."

"Oh, they got aplenty else 'thout sand anymore. They got stacks and stacks of money. I heard they got sompin like a million fer the railroad right of way. She'd oughtta take notice of the poor folks. I guess that family wasn't named Silver fer nothin'."

The tramp gazed steadily at the door where Silver had disappeared and began to turn around what he heard in his cunning old brain. He let his companions heave five shovelfuls before he started in again at a rapidly diminishing sand pile, and his face wore a thoughtful look. Whenever he stopped to rest he eyed the house where Silver had entered. When she finally came out, lingering on the doorstep to talk with the smiling dark-eyed mother he took another siesta and studied the scene carefully, taking in details of dress and height and coloring. Then his cunning eyes dropped to his task again and lifted for an instant to meet hers only when Silver passed opposite to him, as she smiled and greeted them all in a friendly way.

"Some gurrul!" remarked a short burly man with red curls and a brogue, "the master must be proud o'her. I guess he'd not take all his millions for the likes of her!"

"Yes, she's a fine lady! But it'll take a plenty of millions to keep her in all she'll want," grouched the other man.

"Well, what's a lady!" said the tramp as he lifted another shovelful of sand.

Down by the bridge Silver met Bannard and lingered there to watch the little fishes darting in the stream. She had much to tell him of the condition of some of the families she had visited. Sam was bringing his wife over from Italy, and Carmen was having trouble getting his citizen's papers. Something about his questionnaire during the war. He had not understood enough English to make out what they were asking him, and he couldn't write it himself, so some absurd mistake had been made. Could he see the County Judge and straighten it out?

Bannard finally turned and walked back with her through Sweetbriar Lane, into Aunt Katie's for a moment to get a taste of the honey cakes she was baking, and so on through the hedge into the sweet old Silver garden. They lingered talking beside the sundial, tracing the quaint figures on its face, watching the slow, sure march of the sun from point to point. There was powdered gold in the air and sunshine,

owdered fire shimmering over the tulip bed. The
irds sang with joyous abandon as though they would
.plit their throats. Greeves looked out of his window
rom his work, and his heart was at rest. That was a
iice fellow. A bit wrong in his head knowledge, and
iis beliefs, but all right in his heart and living. And
after all if one could believe in the old legends they
were a wonderful safeguard. Far be it from him to
disturb such saintly faith. He would be careful what
he said about unbelief. It almost seemed as if what
the minister had said had been true. Things had settled down into a pleasanter way. The siege was lifting, but of course God had nothing to do with it. It
was merely the adjusting of all elements to environment. It was sound philosophy anyway, to be patient
and wait for things to adjust themselves. Then he
went back to his preface which he was writing with
great care.

"If the present advance of science—" How was it
he had meant to phrase that sentence?

And down in the garden the two had sauntered into the summer house and were telling each other
about their early life. It is a beautiful stage of friendship when two who admire one another reach that
point. It is the building of a foundation for something
deeper and truer.

Well for them that the garden was located behind the house, with tall hedges surrounding, and that
neither the Weldons nor Vandemeeters could pene-
trate therein, and only the kindly eye of Aunt Katie
knew where they were, or the whole town would have
been agog. They found so much to talk about that the
minister forgot to go back to the Flats until the lunch
bell rang in the Silver house, and then he made his
sudden apologies and departed hastily over the fence.
Silver went in with flushed cheeks and bright eyes
thinking how wonderfully life was opening out for
her who had been but such a short time before bereft
and alone.

Athalie came home from school quite pleasant and
tractable. She had an armful of books and she seemed
interested in them. Her father looked the books over

and talked with her a little about them, gave her a few hints how to concentrate in studying, and went away to his library again entirely satisfied that he was doing the father-part as well as could be expected. Perhaps after he got used to it it wouldn't be so bad after all.

Meantime Athalie up in her room was working with needle and thread and scissors to transform several of her new frocks against the coming of Friday evening, while her books lay in a heap on the floor not to be touched until the next morning, and her thoughts were wandering a woolgathering.

About half a mile below the bridge at the lower end of Silver Sands, to the left of the road where it curves around to go to Frogtown there rises a little hill. On its top, set in a thick grove of maples, birches and oaks with plenty of undergrowth, there stands a little one-roomed hut. It had been built of field stones a long time ago, when the grove was a big woods of sugar maples, perhaps for a shelter at sugaring off time. There was a fireplace at one end, a little prison-like window and a sagging wooden door. The window was boarded up and the door had stood ajar for years. The boys of the town used to use it for a rendezvous but had long since deserted it for newer quarters below the bridge where some enterprising seniors in high school had built a camp among the pines.

The tramp had sighted this empty dwelling, and after watching it for several days and sampling its hospitality at night, he took up his abode therein, repaired the door, unnoticeably, left the window boarded up, and built his meagre fires at night when no one would see the smoke. There was plenty of wood around for the rustling.

The floor was the bare earth, and in one corner a pile of leaves and moss made a bed, with an old blanket he had taken from somebody's clothes line down in the village. In a big packing box that he had found behind the cannery quite early one morning, he kept his frugal stores: eggs, butter, bread, tobacco, half a ham, and a big black bottle. The top of the box served as his table. Here he crept at evening when his shovelling was done, taking care to arrive by a circuitous route, and to close the door before lighting his bit of a candle. Here at evening he sat with his pipe and pondered many a scheme, or went over and over the various mistakes and failures of his life which had landed him in confinement within stone walls for a time, and searched how he might carry something through yet again.

That same night he crept to his lair and sat on the sheltered side looking away toward the village thinking. Through its nest of trees he could see the white pillars of the Silver house standing as it did at the eminence of the street, lifting its head just a trifle above all the other houses. As the twilight deepened and darkness gave opportunity for Sin to walk abroad unrecognized, he loitered down the hill and crept by unused paths into the town where he had a few patrons who kept their little odd jobs for him at night. They talked about him in their sewing circle and said he was a self-respecting man, and one had given him a shirt, and one some pairs of much darned socks and they talked about helping him to find a place to board where he could look after the furnace for his keep when winter came on. Drab he was as he walked along in the shadow side of the moonlit street, and drab he faded into space when he came to a high hedge. Carefully he stole around the old Silver place, and felt out the garden paths, rubber tired he surrounded the spot and peered in cautiously at all the windows. He studied the lines of Patterson Greeves' thoughtful face as he sat at his desk working on that preface, and judged it cannily with the eye of a specialist. He put his ugly mask to the very pane of glass beside Silver's head as she sat reading in the big easy chair at the other end of the library. He cautiously searched the darkened drawing room with a pocket flash, and he took in the dining room, especially the silver on the sideboard while Anne and

Molly were setting the table for breakfast. The kitchen en was not so easy, but he managed it while Joe and Molly and Anne sat eating their dinner.

"I thought I saw a face at the window, Joe, go out and see if someone is looking for you," said Anne in her calm voice, and Joe shoved back his chair noisily and went out, but came back presently and reported that Anne was "seein' things."

"It must be the young huzzy upstairs is gettin' on yer nerves, Anne."

"The young lady's all right the last two days," said Anne complacently, Athalie's church going and willingness to go to school had done much toward mollifying Anne. "And *I saw* a face at the window. It was likely Jock Miller brought back that sickle you lent him. I'm not so old that I can't tell a face at the window when I see it."

Back in the lilac bushes among the lilies-of-the-valley a drab shape huddled, listened, and presently shrunk away, puzzling. That wasn't the young lady he saw pass the fire house that day. Were there two?

For the rest of that week life settled down into the grooves of what a well regulated family life should be and Patterson Greeves took heart of hope and plunged into his book. Athalie had been regular at school, late only once, and seemed to be giving actual attention to her studies. She professed to be deeply interested in education for the first time in her life, and took her books upstairs to her room immediately after dinner at night. Her father began to hope that perhaps she had inherited his love of study. Several times she came to him with some question about her lessons. Usually some unusual question. She was sharp as a needle. Would he ever learn to be proud of her? If she only weren't so fat, so sort of fleshy.

Friday morning as Athalie was about to start for school she stepped into the dining room where Anne was crumbing the table preparatory to taking off the breakfast cloth and said loftily:

"Oh, Truesdale! Have plenty of cake ready this afternoon. I'm bringing guests."

"There's always plenty of cake in the house," said

Anne stiffly. She wasn't sure she cared for being called Truesdale. Of course it was English, but she had an inkling that in this case it was intended for patronage.

"I mean—*lots!*" said Athalie. "There'll be about twelve of us altogether."

"There's always cake enough in the house for twenty if need be!" Anne froze.

"They'll all be here for dinner I think," added Athalie as she closed the door and ran down the steps, "I told dad about it."

Now it happened that "dad" had gone to the city on the seven o'clock train to consult a book in the library.

"It's strange he said nothing to me about it. He's always that particular about making trouble," said Anne as she reported the invasion to Molly.

"Aw, that's all right, Anne," said Molly cheerfully, "you'd oughtta be glad she's going to be friendly with the townspeople. We'll just get up a real dinner Anne, and let her have a good time. The master'll like it. He seems real satisfied with the way she's took to school."

"Yes," agreed Anne grudgingly, "but I'd a been better satisfied if the master had a spoke to me hisself. Howsomever!"

The house was always spick and span. Anne saw to it that there were flowers in the vases, and the best doilies as if for a company of ladies.

"Because them childer has eyes and tongues in their heads," she explained to Molly who came in to consult her as to whether she should make hard sauce or boiled sauce for the bread pudding that was destined for lunch.

Athalie telephoned at noon that she was not coming home to lunch.

"She'll be taking it with some of the girls!" she said happily, "it's nice to think of her gettin' in and bein' like other girls. Mebbe she'll get rid of her queer hair and eyebrows some day. I think she might be passable lookin' if she didn't dress so queer! Now them dresses he bought her. They looked real simple, but when she gets um on they somehow look diffrunt.

But I'm sorry she didn't come home, I wanted to ask her more about who's coming? How'll we know to set table?"

"Oh, there'll be time when she comes! Half past three is aplenty." So they set about the delightful task of getting up a young dinner party again in the old house which had not happened since master Pat's twenty-first birthday.

It was nearing three o'clock when a taxi from the city drew up at the door causing great sensation over at the Vandemeeter's. They had seen Mr. Greeves go away early in the morning. They could not figure out who this might be.

A young woman got out and paid the driver, preceding him up the walk to the house as he carried two armfuls of luggage.

"She's all tails around her feet," said grandma Vandemeeter, "and I can see myself without any glasses that she's got a painted face even if she has got a mosquito netting over her hat."

"This is Marcella Mason," announced the stranger as Anne opened the door. "I suppose you're expecting me. I'll just have my bags carried up to my room at once. I'm frightfully dusty. Hot water please. I suppose you have plenty of it here in the country? If not please heat it at once. I'm accustomed to a hot bath."

A silver dollar skillfully manipulated slid into Anne's astonished hand and out again to the floor quicker than it went in. She stepped back indignantly, with blazing cheeks and snapping eyes.

"Is that your money, Miss? You dropped it!" she said crisply.

"Why, that's your tip!" laughed the girl, "don't you want it?"

"Tip?" repeated Anne with her chin aloft. "tip? I don't understand you. You'd best pick it up, Miss or it'll get lost. You can step this way." She led the way up the wide stair, thinking rapidly. It was not in the possibility that this upstart should occupy one of the best rooms. Anne led her down the back hall to a little bedroom off the sewing room where a seamstress sometimes stayed. Neat and trim it was with a single iron bed, a bit of a bureau and a stationary wash-stand. Silver house was not behind the times in the matter of conveniences.

"You can put your things down on the chair," said Anne indifferently.

The stranger advanced and surveyed the room.

"Oh, I'm afraid this room won't do for me!" she looked around. "No pier glass. And don't you have private baths? What other rooms have you? I came first to make my choice. This seems to be a large house."

"This is the only one, Miss. You can take it or leave it as you like. I'm busy just now. You'll have to excuse me. Miss Athalie will be home from school in a short while."

"School! You don't mean to tell me she goes to school! That's rich! She swore she'd never enter a school room again!"

Anne gave her a withering glance and departed in high dudgeon.

"You should see the huzzy now!" she told Molly. "Rings on her fingers and jewels on her toes. And the impertinence of her! Offering me money like a porter in a hotel. Well, I wonder what the master'll be saying now!"

"The master just called up whilst you was upstairs. He says he may miss the first train and not to wait for him, to go right on and have dinner. I guess he thought he'd like to get out of the fuss of it."

"Well, I shouldn't wonder! I wish Miss Athalie was here. Miss Silver hasn't got back from the Flats yet, has she? She's a good girl. She would go see to that thing upstairs. Keep watch for her comin' and tell me. I'll warn her afore she goes up the stair."

But Silver was helping an Italian woman to make a little dress for her baby and did not come home until five o'clock. Before that time many things had happened.

Before Athalie arrived the three o'clock train had come in and a troop of young people, shouting, laughing, hooting at every person they passed, criticizing the houses, jeering at the stores, came pouring down

the street. Their baggage followed in Hoskin's express
wagon, with two men on behind to help and observe.
The girls were attired in most striking costumes, and
lolled on the boys' arms, pulled off each other's hats
and threw them into the street, and in general conducted themselves with great indiscretion. The vil-
lagers came to their front windows in astonishment
and deep disapproval and one woman even telephoned for the police who happened to be away
from his headquarters at that moment.

They stormed up on the Silver front veranda like a
hurricane, having enquired of everyone they met
where "Greeveses" lived, and while they awaited the
answer to their continuous and imperious knocking,
two girls and a young man had a skirmish in the yard
incidentally breaking off three of Joe's most cherished
hyacinth blooms.

Then down the stairs with boisterious laughter
tripped the young woman who had arrived in a taxi;
and opened the door before the scandalized Anne
could get farther than the pantry.

"Oh, boy! I guess I put one over on you this time!"
screamed the girl.

The horde swarmed in, flinging caps and handbags
in every direction.

"Here's Marcy! I say that isn't fair, Marcy! You got
the best room! You always do."

"Come on up and take your choice. There's not
so awful many as I thought there'd be. The old prune
that showed me up gave me a sort of servant's room,
but I got rid of her and went around till I found what
I wanted. I take the left hand front, and I've got my
door locked so you needn't try to get in. I'll take
Maebeth with me and nobody else. There's plenty of
room. I've been everywhere. You two girls better take
that other front room. There's somebody's things in
there, but you should worry. Possession is how many
points? I forget. Violet better go with Ath. Her things
are in that second door. Say, boys, did you bring
the booze? Plenty of it? Isn't that great. We'll have a
real time! You boys better go up to the third story.
There's five big rooms up there! Come on Beth, let's

hurry and get dressed before Ath comes. She goes to school! Isn't that the limit? She must have some old grouch of a governor! Don't say anything. His clothes must be in this closet and I'm going down to dinner in *his dress suit—!*"

"Oh Marcy! Do you *dare*, Marcy?"

"My soul!" said Anne Truesdale, "what'll we do? Do you think maybe I better send for the minister? Oh, I wish you had told me master Pat was on the phone."

"But you didn't know it then."

"Well, no, but I coulda told him about there being company."

"Well, you didn't. I guess that harum scarum'll be home pretty soon. There she comes now, running! I'd give her a piece of my mind, I certainly would!"

Chapter XXV

But before Anne could get into the hall Athalie had stormed up the stairs and there ensued such greetings as made the old house sound like a vaudeville show behind the scenes. The girls in various stages of disarray opened doors to call to her, the boys issued from a cloud of cigarette smoke on the third floor by way of the old mahogany stair rail and came shooting into their midst amid howls and screams and pretended running to cover. Anne hurried up to do something about it and resembled an old hen running from the person who was trying to catch it while she clucked at her young to get out of the way but she made no impression whatever on the young people until suddenly a great stalwart youth discovered her in his way and stooping over said:

"Here, auntie, what are you doing here!" and picking her up like a child ran fleetly down the stairs with her in his arms, depositing her on the console in the hall and vanishing up again in three strides.

Anne, when she recovered her breath crept fearsomely into the pantry white and spent, her dignity drooping like a broken feather, and while she stood panting, her hand on her heart, her back against the swing door, a gentle hand pushed it, and Silver's voice said:

"It's only me, Anne. What is the matter upstairs."

"It's a 'ouse party!" sobbed Anne, and buried her face in Silver's neck. "They've took the master's room, and Miss Lavinia's. I don't know what the master'll say when he comes. And your things! They maul everything they lay their hands on, Miss Silver. Oh, I oughtta have prevented this! I oughtta! I oughtta! I'm no housekeeper at all to let this come behind his back. I'm getting old! I'm no good any more—"

250

"There, there, Anne, don't feel so badly. There isn't any harm done. They are only a parcel of kids out having a good time, and it's gone to their heads. Don't worry. Father won't blame you. It's Athalie, I suppose. Let's try to see what we can do to make everything move off quietly. How long are they going to stay? Just for dinner?"

"I don't know. I don't know! She said a 'ouse party, that first one that come. How long does that last? As long as the 'ouse stays together I'm thinking, and that'll not be long if they carry on as they have been goin'. They've slid down my nice polished stair rails, and there'll be scratches on everything. And I've kept it all so nice all the years! Oh dear, oh dear!"

"Never mind, Anne, it won't be half so bad as it seems. Cheer up and get dinner ready. Are you going to try to have tea?"

"Deary knows! Miss Athalie ordered cake made before she left this morning. And me athinkin' she was that good a girl to please her father an' invite the neighbors' children home from school to have a good time an' make 'em forget how she treated 'em Saturday afternoon!"

"Well, never mind. I'll go upstairs and see if I can't stop that noise."

Silver went, but her arrival proved no more than if she had been a fly on the wall. The girls and boys were having a scuffle in the hall, and one girl's dress was half pulled off of her. They did not even glance at Silver as she hurried by them to take refuge in her room and think what she ought to do. But two other girls were in there attired in lacy lingerie and one was smoking a cigarette.

"I beg your pardon," she said pleasantly, "I think someone has made a mistake. This room is occupied. If you will let me help you gather up your things I will show you to another room."

Silver did this, not because she was so disturbed at having her room taken as because Anne had felt so strongly about Miss Lavinia's sacred chamber being desecrated.

The girls simply stared.

"Who are you?" asked the girl who was powdering her face at the glass.

"I am Miss Greeves. Athalie's sister. You must be her school friends."

"Oh, I know who you are. You're that baby that was given away. Your name isn't Greeves at all. It's Jarvis. Ath told us all about you. You needn't bother about us, she put us here and we'd rather stay. You can take your own things out if you want to." The girl turned back to the mirror with an air of having dismissed her. Silver reflected for an instant. What chance had she to maintain her rights against such insolence? She would frustrate her desire of quieting the company and getting control of things if she was not a perfect lady. She was amazed that girls could say such things. There must be a whole school of them, bred in the same atmosphere.

The color had fluttered into her face at the insulting words, but her sense of humor came to her assistance and as once before she had foiled insolence by her silvery laugh, so now she let it forth again, until the visiting girls turned and stared. They even grew a little red. They had intended to make her angry, and lo she laughed!

With a quick turn Silver went out of the room and closed the door.

"Boys!" she said placing a firm hand on the arm of the scuffling gentlemen nearest her, "I know where there's some awfully good cake. If you'll follow me and be perfectly quiet about it I'll get it for you!"

Instantly every boy of the six was surrounding her and clamoring with all his might, even attempting to lift her off her feet and bear her down the stairs.

But there was something about Silver when she chose to be so that awed every boy in the vicinity. Her spirit face suddenly could become grave and stern, with a power of command that arrested the attention and demanded respect.

"No, you've got to be perfectly quiet!" she said smilingly, "the spell won't work unless you do! No quiet, no cake!"

Athalie had forgotten when she summoned all

these gorgeous young hoodlums to dissipate her gloom, and informed them well about her unbeloved sister, that Silver was a girl and that a boy will "fall for anything" sometimes, as she said with a shrug that very evening. To the amazement of the other girls the boys became tame at once and Silver led them all off quietly down the stairs and to the drawing room where she rang the bell and said in low tone:

"Anne, dear, would you bring that cake now?"

The "Anne dear" got it. Anne brought the cake in bountiful supply, and Silver improving the brief and shining hour got all their names and made quite a little ceremony learning them so she would remember.

The boys were quite pleased with her, and she held them there with talk about things boys like. Dogs and athletics, and national games. She had seen some big ones. She talked familiarly about some of the fraternities they longed to be bid to join, she spoke of college, and with just that rare flattery of smile and comraderie that touches a boy of seventeen and brings him to her feet, she sat on a low divan and chatted with them bringing burst after burst of gruff laughter, and winning them thoroughly as her friends.

In the midst of an exciting recital of how a famous baseball nine got ahead of an opposing team that was employing unfair means to win the game, they all became aware of a hostile presence standing on the stairs.

Athalie had come down in gorgeous array in a brief frock of gold tissue strapped over the shoulders and down the skirt in floating panels with peacock feathers. Around her forehead was bound a frontlet of green and blue sequins, and the gold tissue of which her stockings were composed was so exceedingly sheer as to give the effect of bare skin above the tiny jeweled gold slippers. Nobody would have bought such a rig for a young girl, but Lilla had been regal in it once upon a time, and the long pendulum earrings that dangled from the ears of her daughter and gave her such an Egyptian-princess effect had been especially designed in jewels to match the costume for some great occasion. It might be possible that

Lilla on the high seas knew nothing of the where-abouts of some of her most valued possessions. Athalie had helped herself as she chose before her departure.

But Athalie's face was marked with disdain, jeal-ousy, hate in startling lines. Silver arose quickly with a smile that faded as she saw the girl's fixed look as if she were not there at all. Athalie was determined to ignore her among these her friends. How could she put up any kind of a front against that? And yet she must for her father's sake, and keep things within bounds if possible until his return. It occurred to her that she might telephone Bannard and ask him to dinner. He would help her and know what to do, but supposing anything unforeseen should occur, any-thing out of the conventional order, that should get aboard, it might not be well that the minister should be known to have been there. She had been brought up to think of those things. She had not been a min-ister's granddaughter for nothing. Therefore she shut her firm young lips and determined to fight it out alone.

She was wearing a crêpe de chine dress of soft gray the right tint to bring out the pink in her cheeks, and the gold in her hair and lashes. It was simple of line and girded with a sash of itself heavily fringed and knotted at one side hanging a little below the deep hem of her skirt. She wore no ornaments and the elbow sleeves and round neck were without dec-oration. It was scarcely a dinner gown for a formal affair, yet she could not have changed if she wished since the invasion of her room, and she would not if she could. There were more important affairs on hand.

Her sister's attitude plainly dismissed her, but she rose and deliberately turned her conversation to one of the boys nearest her, ignoring the look, and finally Athalie spoke, as one speaks to an inferior:

"You don't need to eat with us Alice Jarvis. It will make an uneven number. We have just men enough to go round."

"Oh, that's all right," said Silver with a careless smile, "father'll be here pretty soon you know," and went on talking to the admiring boy, although her heart was beating wildly and she wished herself far away from this scene of dissension and frivolity.

"Oh, very well. Suit yourself!" said Athalie with her haughtiest voice, and began to devote herself to the entire group, and attract them all from Silver.

Silver slipped out of the room and went back upstairs. If she could keep the bunches of girls and boys apart till dinner was ready it might help. She went from room to room offering help. Had they all the towels they needed? Could she help them with their dresses, or play ladies' maid in any way? Would they like ice water? Her insistent, pleasant serviceableness met with no response except silence. They whispered behind her back and exchanged glances. She saw that the way ahead was to be most unpleasant, but she went steadily on ignoring the meaning of their attitude. She was the pleasant elder sister waiting on her younger sister's guests.

But she had committed what was to them an unpardonable sin. She had taken their devoted admirers away from them and interested them herself. That could never be forgiven.

Silver was very tired when at last the scene changed to the dinner table. She had placed herself at the head and was there as they came into the room, acting the part of hostess. Athalie stopped and looked furiously at her, but finally decided to get her revenge some other way and leaving the other end seat unoccupied proceeded to seat her guests to suit her own purposes.

The chairs were all filled but one.

"Marcy! Where are you? You sit at the corner next to dad's seat. Hurry. I'm starved."

Marcella Mason who had just tripped downstairs and was entering from the hall paused a moment lifting up a monocle on a long silk cord.

"Good evening, gents and women!" she saluted elegantly, "so glad you all could come!"

Every eye turned toward the doorway and then a shout arouse gradually growing into a roar.

"Marcy! Marcy! Look at Marcy!"

For Marcella Mason was attired in Patterson

Greeves' full dress suit, broad white shirt front, patent leather shoes and all, and looked the very personification of impudence and daring.

Silver and Anne Truesdale had agreed before dinner was served that whatever happened they would keep their composure and not look shocked nor horrified. Poor Anne Truesdale scuttled hurriedly into the pantry. This was too much for her. Silver struggled with her irritation and mastered a grave little smile. It was rude of course, impudent, but only a prank after all. It was not for her to deal with a thing like this. Her father would be here pretty soon. Oh, that he might arrive at once!

From the start the hilarity was uproarious. Several times bits of bread went whizzing back and forth across the board that had for years seen gathered around it grave and dignified and honored men and women. Anne trembled for the delicate long stemmed glasses in which the delicious fruit nectar was served.

The dinner progressed through a rich cream soup, roast chicken, with vegetables, home-made ice cream with crushed strawberries, and great plates of delectable cake.

The little cups of black coffee were being served when Athalie reached under her chair and brought forth a lacquered box which she passed around. Cigarettes! Strange Silver had not thought that might happen! And the guests were all taking them, girls too, and lighting them. Little curls of smoke rose delicately in the stately dining room, and six little flappers pursed their painted lips and blew six more wreaths of smoke into the air.

Silver took her coffee cup and toyed with it thoughtfully. What would her father say to this? She was not quite sure whether the time had come for her to take a stand or not. But when at a signal from Athalie one of the boys arose and stepping out of the room brought back two tall bottles of dark liquid, then she knew her time had come. He had pulled out the cork and was filling an empty glass by one of the girl's plates. The fumes of the liquor arose hotly to her sensitive nostrils. What chance had she against so many? Her face was white and stern like a spirit as she rose from her chair and faced them. "Stop!" she commanded to the astonished boy who held the bottle, "Joe, will you remove these bottles at once? And Anne, will you kindly take that tray and gather up the cigarettes and throw them out? My father does not allow such things to go on in his house nor around his table!" she said addressing the company in a clear ringing voice. "If you want to smoke and drink you must go elsewhere!"

Then Athalie arose suddenly with her glass of water in her hand and flung its contents at her sister.

"Shut up!" she said roughly. "It's none of your business what we do. This is my party and I'm the *daughter* in this house?"

"*Athalie!* What does all this mean?"

Patterson Greeves was standing in the doorway his hat still on his head, his hands still cluttered with packages of books as he had come in, his face stern with anger.

Chapter XXVI

THE entire company turned in startled surprise and Anne and Joe scuttled furtively over to stand by him. They had been plainly frightened by a situation that they knew they could not control.

"Oh, dad, is that you? I didn't hear you come in. I'm glad you've arrived. It was naughty of you to be late the first night of my house party," broke forth Athalie nonchalantly. "Come and let me introduce you to my guests."

Patterson Greeves made no move to go forward. He handed his packages to the attendant Joe, and took off his hat and gloves, still standing where he had first appeared, still looking the company over, person by person, his eyes growing sterner, his mouth more displeased.

"I do not understand," he said coming forward enquiringly, giving a searching glance into each impudent countenance, guest by guest.

"Let me have that bottle please!" He took the big bottle from the unresisting hand of the once arrogant youth and lifted it near to his nose.

"Where did you get this liquor may I ask? I'm afraid somebody has been breaking the laws of the land. I shall have to put you all under arrest until we investigate. Joe, will you kindly call up the chief of police?" The entire company of would-be revellers arose in consternation and looked to right and left for a place of exit, but Anne Truesdale, her cheeks flaming an angry crimson, her eyes like two sword points barred the way of the pantry, and the angry householder and his ancient servitor stood in the wide doorway leading to the hall. They began to steal furtively behind one another and sidle toward the pantry fancying Anne less redoubtable than their inhospitable host.

"Why dad! I think you're horrid!" broke forth Athalie, her lips trembling. "Why, *dad!*"

"Be still Athalie! You may go to your room! You have broken all three of your promises. I have nothing more to say to you at present. You know what the consequence was to be."

"But dad—"

"Leave the room!"

And Athalie actually left it.

The moment was awful. Even Silver felt sorry for them.

"Now, ladies and gentlemen, while we are waiting for the officer let me get your names and addresses," said Patterson Greeves his class room tone upon him, as he brought out pencil and note book. "Your name sir?" He turned to the first white-faced boy, the one who had held the bottle as he entered.

The boy lifted a face from which the fun had fled and tried to brazen it out.

"Oh, cert., my name's Brett Hanwood. Hamilton Prep pitcher you know."

Straight around the table he went writing down carefully the addresses, asking a searching question now and again. When he reached Marcella Mason he eyed her curiously for an instant, felt of the sleeve of her coat, a flicker of amusement passing over his otherwise grave face and said:

"And this—ah—gentleman?"

Marcella winced.

"This completes the list I think."

Patterson Greeves lifted his pencil and counted, "four ladies and six—" his eye was on Marcella, "men! The ladies of course we will not hold accountable. And now as it is not convenient for me to entertain guests tonight they will be returned to their homes or their schools as the case may be. The men—" again he glanced at Marcella, "will await the officer's verdict. Doubtless they will be held till the trial, or possibly let out on bail if they can furnish sufficient.

The state is laying stress on this matter of prohibition just now and—"

"Oh!" gasped Marcella and collapsed in sobs.

"Now," said Greeves, "if you four young ladies will just go into the library I will call up your school and arrange for your return."

"Oh—h-h-h!" murmured the girls in a panic.

Just then the officer was brought in by Joe, and Greeves explained to him in a low tone. Then he turned back to his frightened victims. "You four girls may come into the library now."

The girls huddled in a mass and followed him. The sound of hasty feet scuttling after and Marcella arrived red and teary.

"I—I—I'm a girl too!"

"Oh," said Greeves surveying her through his glasses, "curious specimen I must say. Man and girl! Well, well! Which school do you attend?"

Marcella bore the sarcasm meekly and tried to hide her borrowed plumage behind the other girls. They made a curious group in their wild young flapper frocks with their plump, bare shoulders shivering in the shadows of the big old room while they waited for Patterson Greeves to get long distance. They glanced mutely into one another's eyes and thought of the school records already against them.

"Is this Briardale school for girls? Is this the principal? Let me speak to the principal please. I have four young ladies here in my house who claim to belong to your school. They have been attempting to have a hooch party during my absence. Can you tell me where they are supposed to be tonight? Shall I return them to you? Their names are—"

He consulted his paper and read off the names. The girls stood and shivered as if he were striking them.

"I beg your pardon. Did you say Miss Mason was at home at the bedside of her sick mother? Yes? And this Violet? Her sister is being married? Oh! I see!" His eyes dwelt mercilessly on the trembling Violet. "Having her eyes examined? I see. And the other one? Oh, she was taken sick and was sent home? I see. Then you would prefer that I return these young ladies to their various homes—"

"Oh, no, no!" broke in Marcella, "my father would half kill me! I'd rather go back to school."

"Mine would take my next month's allowance away and it's spent already," wept Violet. Then hushed to hear what was being said on the telephone.

"You say this Violet lives in our neighboring city? And Miss Mason in a suburb? Where? Oh, Hazelbrook. Yes, I know it quite well. I'm not sure but her father is an old friend of mine. Walter Mason? That's the one. Very well, then. I quite agree with you that these two should go to their homes. I will personally escort them there at once. The other two you would prefer to have return to the school tonight? Just how far is that from the Junction? I see. No, there is no train out of here until ten o'clock. That would miss connection. I think it would be better to get an automobile. Yes, I have a reliable man and his wife, old trusted servants. I can send them in their care. Oh, that's all right. I'm only glad to get it all so easily arranged. They will be there tonight. It may be late. I may be delayed in finding a car, but they will arrive, don't worry. Thank you! Good night!"

The girls were trembling and furious, but looking in his determined face they saw they had no way of escape. Especially did Marcella quail as she looked down at her borrowed garments and thought of her father's face when he should hear the report of his old friend.

Patterson Greeves hung up the receiver, rang for Anne Truesdale, and said:

"Now, young ladies, you will go upstairs in charge of Mrs. Truesdale and find your belongings. We shall be ready to start in twenty minutes."

He herded them to the stairs, and went into the dining room to consult with the chief of police who had the bottle of liquor in his hand and was asking keen questions with eyes that were used to reading human countenances and penetrating human masks.

After a brief consultation between the two men, the

uncomfortable boys were called into the library and subjected to a telephone conversation much like that which the girls had passed through, except that it was decided by the headmaster of the school that the boys should be returned in a body under police escort, and that their fathers should be at once summoned from their various homes. The boys looked even more hunted than the girls had done. They perhaps had more reason to fear both parental and scholastic discipline.

The boys were marched out of the house at once with hastily packed suit cases and sober looks on their faces. A grocery truck was requistioned, the boys piled in, and six men, two of them regular police aides, the other four pressed into service from the fire house with hastily improvised uniforms, climbed in after them, a man to a boy. There was no escape.

The guards hugely enjoyed the occasion. They were getting a night's excitement and a long ride free. It would be something to talk about at the fire house for many a day. Uri Weldon had been the first one to volunteer. He had no time even to telephone to Lizette before leaving. But then Lizette was not one to worry about him.

In a quarter of an hour an automobile arrived and two unhappy maidens with handkerchiefs to their eyes stole out and crept into the back seat. Molly in a flannel petticoat and an extra sweater under her long winter coat, climbed fearfully in between them, and Joe took the front seat beside the driver. They moved off hurriedly through the night and presently Patterson Greeves and two silent, angry, frightened girls emerged from the house and walked down the street to the ten o'clock train for the city.

"Well, they're all getting away early!" sighed mother Vandemeeter. "Now we can go to bed in peace. I was afraid they were going to have a dance and that would have been so out of place in the old Silver house. I just couldn't have gone to sleep for thinking."

"I don't know as they could have gone much later!" said grandma, getting stiffly up from her padded rocking chair and tottering toward her downstairs bedroom door. "This is the last train, isn't it?"

Said Pristina up at her top bedroom window:

"Now! I wonder which one he is taking to the train!"

Silver and Anne Truesdale busied themselves in putting the house to rights and gathering up the debris of the brief onslaught of the enemy.

"Them old stemmed fruit cups was one of Miss Lavinia's best prized set," Anne mourned. "To think one shoulda got broke tonight fer them little fools. I almost just used the old sauce dishes and then I thought the master might not like it!"

"Never mind, Anne, what difference does a glass or two less make? They're gone. They might have broken more if they had stayed longer. It looked to me as if they were out to break more than fruit glasses."

"Yes!" said Anne. "My soul! So that's that!"

Five hours later, Patterson Greeves, dismissing the car that had brought him back from the city, walked up from the post office corner where he had got out, and let himself silently into the house. Anne, released from her vigil, turned over and murmured drowsily to herself again:

"So that's *that!*"

In the wee small hours of the morning, with the east paling into pink, the only two who had got any enjoyment out of the affair, Molly and Joe on their way home from their long pilgrimage, sitting in the back seat holding hands, and never saying a word, were having a second honeymoon. Their first automobile ride! An all night affair. They were sore and stiff with the long ride, next day. But what mattered it? They had something to remember to their dying day. They might have other rides, doubtless would when Patterson Greeves got time from parenting to buy a car of his own, but never would any be like that first one, where the moonlight lay like thin sheets of silver over the springtime world.

Chapter XXVII

SOMETIMES a storm will settle the atmosphere, for a time, and it seemed as though Patterson Greeves' summary dismissal of the house party had really subdued Athalie and made life bearable, and even almost pleasant at times in Silver house.

There had been a stormy scene the next morning between Athalie and her father, but his brief experience in dealing with the young hoodlums the night before had seemed to give him confidence. He laid down the law in no uncertain manner to the young woman, who went through various stages of rebellion, to argument, then pleading and finally surrender.

"But I told you about that house party when I first arrived and you never said a word. You had no right to come in and raise a row afterwards," had been her opening sentence of the interview, spoken with stormy eyes.

She left the library with downcast countenance and a promise to apologize to Silver for her insolence of the night before, a condition of her further remaining in the house.

"Although I hate her just as much as ever and always shall!" she added as she was about to close the door behind her.

Her father thought it as well to let this sentiment go unanswered, and Athalie went up to Silver's door, walked in without knocking and announced:

"My father sent me to apologize." Having said it she slammed the door after her and departed, leaving Silver no opportunity to reply.

Thus matters had settled into a semblance of amity between them. The conversation at the table consisted in animated talk between Silver and her father, and absolute silence on the part of Athalie whenever her sister was present. The two girls walked their separate ways as much as if they were in separate spheres. Silver made one or two unsuccessful attempts to bridge over this chasm between them and finally settled down to forget it and be happy.

Silver was living a rich and beautiful life, entering into the church work of the new community with zest and rare tact, already beloved by everyone, and spoken of often as being like her great aunt Lavinia.

The minister was a frequent visitor at the house, going often on hikes and fishing trips with Greeves, and spending long hours in discussions on political, scientific, and on rare occasions, religious subjects; and often Silver was a third member of the party on these occasions. But the minister was a busy man and did not make his visits to Silver house too noticeable. It was fortunate for him that Aunt Katie's back fence joined the Silver garden, and that the high hedge made passing possible without calling the attention of the neighbors, for Silver Sands was very jealous of their minister, and would never let him pay more attention to one family or individual without an equal amount somewhere else. Much of his friendship with Silver and her father was carried on in the evening, or morning when they had taken a tramp to the woods and come on the minister, also sometimes when there was no school, with the addition of Blink and his dog.

Athalie had begun to take a real if rather puzzled interest in high school. At first she had attempted to become a leader, had even offered to furnish cigarettes and teach the girls to smoke, telling them they were far behind the times, but this resulted in an instant aloofness on the part of the girls of the better class, Emily Bragg being the only one who really accepted the offer and attached herself to Athalie like a leech.

This was no part of Athalie's plan. She retired from the field as leader and studied the situation for a few days. She began slowly to perceive that she would never be accepted nor welcomed as long as she lifted her own standards. She must accept the standards of

Silver Sands or count herself as an outsider forever.

Experimentally she made an attack on the boys, and found to her amazement that they too had standards. They might not be exactly the same as their sisters', and there were some few among them who were ready surreptitiously to meet her half way and laugh with her, yet on the whole, she was losing rather than gaining in influence, because for some unaccountable reason even the boys seemed to feel that she was unclassing herself. She sat down to ponder and decided that it was the old-fashioned town and that it was hopeless. Whereupon she brushed her hair a long time one day and began to curl the ends under and teach it to be "put up." She ceased even the surreptitious application of cosmetics applied on the way to school since her father's distinct command had put an end to a careful make up before her own mirror. Her eyebrows began to grow in their legitimate place, with a strange likeness to Patterson Greeves' and altogether she took on a more wholesome look in every way.

Saturday mornings, at Silver's suggestion, Patterson Greeves made it a point to be at home and to take Athalie to the country club for a round of golf. Even when she grew more intimate with her school mates and found some of her amusement in their Saturday picnics and little round of simple parties she never failed to accept his invitations for golf with alacrity. At such times there were flashes of something like real affection in her eyes, although he was usually too preoccupied to notice her. Indeed he would often have forgotten the engagement if Silver had not reminded him.

Greeves had sought to induce Athalie to eat more wholesome food. He had hunted out a diet menu and urged it upon her, and in some degree she had acquiesced, though he found her often with surreptitious boxes of candy, or taking more cake at tea than the law allowed. It was not until Barry again wielded his influence that she really got at it and began to show a loss in weight.

It was one Saturday morning that she had at last decided to try her father on the subject of knickers. She came down nonchalantly arrayed in them, and announced herself ready for the country club. Her father looked up from a page he was correcting with an annoyed frown upon his brow. He had forgotten that it was Saturday and was exceedingly anxious to finish the theme he was at work upon. He took her in, knickers and all, and laid down his papers with a stern look on his face.

"You'll have to go by yourself in you're going to wear those things!" he said sharply. "It's strange you don't know what a figure you cut in them. You're too stout for any such rig!"

Athalie cut to the heart as she always was when her figure was criticized, turned with a shrug and a flip and an "oh, very well!" and flung out of the room.

Her father settled back to his writing again, thinking that probably she had gone to change, but as she did not return he became absorbed once more and forgot all about it.

Athalie meantime, had stamped out of the front door, down the street, and was making her way swiftly to the old log in the woods, the only refuge she knew outside the house where she would probably meet no one and would be free to cry her heart out and wonder what had become of Lilla. She had not had word from Lilla since they parted.

She was sitting on the log weeping with long quivering sobs when suddenly she felt a hand upon her shoulder and looking up she saw that Barry was sitting beside her.

"What's the matter kid, has anything happened? Anyone been treating you mean?"

She lifted eyes that were brimming with tears, and there was something childish and almost sweet about her helpless young despair.

"You poor kid," he said again, "what's the matter?"

He fished a moment in all his pockets, then brought out from the breast pocket of his brown flannel shirt a neatly folded clean handkerchief.

"I thought I had a blotter," he remarked, and moving up gently proceeded to wipe the tears from her eyes.

In a moment he had her smiling through her tears with his bright remarks.

"Oh, there's nothing much the matter," said the girl relapsing into her despondency. "I guess I'm only mad. Dad called me fat, and I hate it! He said he wouldn't go with me in my knickers. He said I looked awful!"

Barry surveyed the garments in question.

"Does make you look sort of wide," he admitted. "Must be a lot easier to walk in than skirts though. I like 'em. Why don't you get thinner, kid? It's easy. I can tell you what to eat. We tried it one year when we wanted to run. Listen. I'll write it down for you."

"I hate spinach!" remarked Athalie coldly.

"Oh, well, that doesn't cut any ice kid! When you get skinny you'll be glad. Try a month and get weighed and see what a difference it makes."

They talked for sometime and Athalie finally agreed to try it. Then they drifted into more personal talk and Barry said he wished she'd come and see his mother sometime.

Athalie told him about her mother being off in Europe somewhere. She spoke drearily and the boy read much between the lines that she did not dream she was telling. He was quick to read the heart-hunger and yearning in her voice. There was much that was comforting in his cheery tone and the way he talked of common things. Athalie soon sat up and began to smile. Somehow the world looked brighter and life more possible even without chocolates. Barry said again he wished she would come and see his mother, and this time she said she would, and almost thought perhaps she meant it. It would be interesting to see what kind of a mother Barry had.

Then suddenly the boy stood up quite sharply as if he had but just thought about it.

"But I oughtn't to let you stay here," he said. "Your father might not like it. Why don't you go home and put on the togs he likes. It won't take long. Wait till you get skinny and then wear these again."

"They won't fit me," giggled Athalie. She was growing quite light hearted.

"Come on over this way. I'll show you a short cut home, and you won't need to pass the fire house. There's always a lot of crows there waiting to pick the flesh off your bones."

"Maybe that would be quicker than dieting," laughed Athalie brightly.

"You bet it would!" said Barry, "we won't try that way this time. They'd make remarks if an angel flew by. Now come on down by the creek. It's pretty there. Have you ever seen the rapids? Not very rapid, but it takes some strength to get a canoe up 'em. Some day we'll get your sister and take a canoe jaunt."

But at that Athalie's brow darkened and her chin went up. "I don't think she'd care to go," she said, stiffly. "She's all taken up with doing things down in that Frogtown place."

"Oh, wouldn't she?" Barry's voice was disappointed. Athalie looked at him jealously. The sun seemed to have grown gray. Her loneliness had settled down anew.

Barry was tactful for one so young. He saw that for some reason she did not want the sister. He turned the subject immediately to the day and the beauties about them.

"There's a squirrel up in that tree that throws nuts down on me when I'm fishing sometimes," he said. "Do you like to fish? Why don't you come along with your father? He and the minister often come up here. Your sister was along last time."

Ah! It was the sister! Athalie stiffened perceptibly.

"There he goes now, look!"

Athalie looked up while the boy talked, pointing out the squirrel harbor, telling how the squirrels stored their nuts, how they often ran up the tree with a mouthful of leaves to stuff in their harbor for a bed.

"See that branch of scarlet leaves up there!" exclaimed the boy suddenly. "It's early for them to turn

red, but aren't they peachy? Shall I get them for
you?"

He was off up the tree in no time, nimble as a
squirrel himself up, up, and up, till the girl watching
felt dizzy for him, then out on a hazardous limb,
and whipping his knife from his pocket. Presently
down came the splendid branch, fluttering like thousands of scarlet blossoms, and fell at her feet.

She stooped and picked it up wonderingly. It was
almost the first time in her life she had gathered
trophies from the woods, the first time any boy had
presented her with anything so glorious and so wild.

Barry was down again in a trice as if it had been
nothing to climb like that, and was walking beside her
telling her about the scarlet maples in the fall. Then
all at once he turned and pointed.

"Now, you go across that meadow. When you get
to the corner of the board fence turn to the right
next the pasture and go straight ahead. You'll find
your house just ahead of you, and nobody will get a
chance to see who you are before you are at home. I
won't go with you. It will be better not. Those
Vandemeeters have eyes all over the house. Here!
Do you want this junk?"

Athalie with her arms full of the gorgeous leaves
made her way slowly across the sod of the pasture,
and around the corner of the fence thinking over all
that had happened, wondering why the boy didn't
come all the way with her, why he minded those old
Vandemeeters, getting a thought of his reasons into
her soul, comparing them with all her father had said,
resolving to try again, and saying over as she entered
her own gate, "Spinach! Spinach! How I hate it!"

The spring deepened into summer and school had
closed. Athalie felt lost. Her father was immersed in
his book and had little time for golf. Mary Truman
and her mother and brother had gone away to the
mountains for a month, several of the other girls were
visiting relatives in the country or at the seashore, or
taking little trips. She had to stay around the house
and garden. Always there was Silver everywhere in
the way. She did not get any nearer to Silver.

Barry came one day and took Silver away in the minister's car to see a sick child two miles out of town. The minister had sent for her to come and bring some broth. They all came home together with a sheaf of golden rod and got out with much laughter and chatter. Athalie from the upper window watched them. There was a look in Bannard's eyes as he helped Silver from a car that made her suddenly feel all alone in the world. Barry too! He came in after them carrying flowers. Silver had a heap of velvet moss in her hands dotted with scarlet berries. She was carrying it carefully. The minister put out his hand to catch a falling spray of the vine whereon the berries grew. Barry was close, with deep admiration in his face. He answered something Silver said and flashed his beautiful smile. Silver on the step above him broke a tiny spray of golden rod from the armful he had just handed her and stooping fastened it in his buttonhole. She could not hear the byplay of words that went with the act, she could only see the flush of pleasure on Barry's face, the tender smile on Bannard's, Silver's look of utter joy and content. A pang of jealousy like to none she had ever felt before shot through her undisciplined heart. Her face was almost distorted with hate, and the red hot tears went coursing down her face so that she could not see Barry and the minister as they went back to the car. They had not asked for her. They had not either of them suggested that she go along. If Barry had done so when he came for Silver she would have gone. This once she would have gone, if just to keep Silver from riding in the front seat with Barry. But Barry had not asked it. Barry had not cared about anything except just to make her safe for her father's sake, and to make her get thin, so her father would be pleased. Nobody cared for her!

Her young lonely soul raged fiercely within, going over and over the doleful situation, until she scarcely knew what she was doing, and suddenly a gentle hand touched her on the shoulder.

"Athalie, dear! You are crying! Is there anything I can do to help you?"

It was Silver in her white dress with her arms full of golden rod, come softly up the stairs on her rubber shod feet, and finding Athalie still at the hall window.

Athalie turned in a fury of anger to be caught this way, and shook off the gentle hand.

"Don't you dare to touch me!" she hissed. "I *hate* you!"

"Athalie!"

"Yes, *Athalie!*" mocked the angry girl. "You mealy-mouthed hypocrite! You liar! You thief! That's it! You are a *thief!*"

"Athalie, what has got into you?" asked Silver in dismay. "What on earth can you mean? What have I done to annoy you?"

Athalie had not been in such a fury since the night she spoiled the painting. She was simply blind with rage.

"Done! done!" she screamed, "it isn't enough that you stole my father away. Stole him! Stole him! You had no right to him! He gave you away, and you had your home, and you had people that loved you! You had a grandfather and grandmother. I never had any grandfather or grandmother or anybody. My mother never loved me!" Her tone was growing higher and more excited. The pent up anguish of the weeks was breaking forth in a flood. Silver lifted up a hand and tried to make her listen, but she rushed on in a torrent of words.

"She went away and left me to come here alone. She hasn't written to me. She doesn't love me. And I came here to find a father. I would have made him love me. Yes, I could, if you hadn't poked your nose in and got ahead of me. You had no right. He had given you up. You thought just because you had that old Silver name—"

"Athalie!" said Silver compassionately, but Athalie was beyond hearing.

"Don't speak to me. *I hate you!*" she raved on. "It wasn't enough that you stole my father, and the house, and are trying to get the money and Mr. Bannard, but you have to steal my only friend!"

Her head went down on the window frame and she sobbed aloud.

"What do you mean, Athalie? I haven't stolen any friend away from you!" said Silver in a puzzled indignant voice.

"Yes, you have. You've stolen Barry. He was nice to me. He brought me back when I was going to run away and get married!"

"Athalie!"

"Oh, you needn't Athalie me! I guess I could have done it if I wanted to, and now I wish I had. I would have got out of this old hole anyway. Isn't Mr. Bannard enough for you? Why can't you let Barry alone? You pretend to be so loving and all, calling me *dear*, and all that mush, and yet you spoil every nice time I try to have. It was you spoiled my house party! You can't deny that! And you're at the bottom of my having to wear frumpy old-fashioned clothes. If you hadn't come here dressed like a mouse my father wouldn't have known the difference. He just wants me to dress like you, and I won't! So there! But I won't stand your making eyes at everybody that likes me either. Look how you did when I had the house party! Carried all the boys off downstairs and flirted with them. Got everyone of them crazy about you. Oh, but the girls were furious about that."

Under the torrent of words which she could not stay Silver suddenly collapsed into a chair and dropped her face into her hands.

"Oh, yes! That makes you ashamed doesn't it? You don't like it put like that. Well, why can't you marry somebody and get away? I've been waiting and waiting for you and Mr. Bannard to get things fixed up so you would get out of the house and let me have a real home for once in my life."

Silver lifted a white face and listened sternly.

"Athalie! Stop! You mustn't say such things. They are disgraceful. The neighbors will hear!"

"I don't care if they do! I hope they will!"

"Athalie, if you will stop I will go away!"

"Well, go, go! Why don't you go then? You don't mean it at all, you know you don't. You intend to stay right here and spoil my life. I came here to try and get my father to marry my mother over again. She didn't know it, but I've always wanted to do that. I've always wanted a home like other girls and a real father and mother! And then when I got here I found you! What good do you suppose it would do me to get my father to see my mother again while you were here? She wouldn't come here with you! She would hate you too, worse than I do. She would smile and do something terrible to you. That's Lilla! But she would never come here with you here! Oh I shall never have a real home nor anybody that loves me!" She suddenly broke away from the window with a wild sob and darted toward the door of her own room.

Silver turned putting out her arms to try and stop her.

"Athalie! Let me speak! I will go! I did not understand before."

But Athalie broke away fiercely.

"Well, *go* then!" she shouted and slammed her door so that it reverberated through the house like thunder.

Down in the kitchen Anne Truesdale and Molly stopped working and looked at one another anxiously.

"It's Miss Athalie got one of her tantrums again!" said Molly in an awed whisper.

"Well, the master's coming home early tonight, praise be!" said Anne, and tiptoed to the door to listen. But all was still upstairs.

Silver was in her room with the door shut, kneeling beside her bed.

Chapter XXVIII

THE tramp was not working that afternoon. He was recovering from a three days' vacation he had taken in the city following the weekly pay day. He sat in the door a long time looking down toward the village and hating the world. He always took it out in hating the world when he was out of condition. He had a settled conviction that the world owed him a living.

He looked as usual toward the Silver house with jealous eyes and began to calculate as he had often done before, how many millions they must have and what he could do if he had only a small portion of their wealth. And as before he began to work at a plan that had for a long time been maturing in his brain. He had worked it out link by link till he had all the details perfect up to a certain point. There he always had to stop. He never could quite get beyond that missing link. He always thought if he could just think a little harder it would come to him, that missing link, but as yet it had not come.

And now he felt sick and sore from the three days' debauch and the fire was out and there wasn't a bit of food in his lair, neither was there wood to cook any food if he had any.

He stirred his stiffened limbs and got himself to his feet shivering from sheer revolt against life. He knew that the afternoon was waning and that he must go soon to get wood or there would be no way to get supper, and supper he must have if he was to go work in the morning. And to work he must go if he were to live longer, because his last cent was spent and bacon cost money. They were not trusting tramps for bacon and tea in Silver Sands.

So down the mountain he trudged, gathering wood slowly in little heaps by the way to be gathered up on his return trip. He must go trim that hedge of Truman's and that would bring him enough for sugar and butter and all that he needed that night. Then on his return he would gather up the wood and have a little comfort out of life. Strange that with such a life he could still gather comfort from it. And Athalie Greeves in the fine Silver house wept because there was nothing left for her in life!

It was ten minutes to five when he returned with his sugar and bacon and cheese. He hadn't cut the hedge very well, but Mrs. Truman had been having a missionary meeting and hadn't come out to see. She had sent the money out to him before he had quite finished and he lost no time in getting down to the store. His inner man required immediate refreshment.

So he sat down in a sheltered spot not far from the road to eat a snack to stay him before he should gather up his wood. And suddenly his slow jaws lagged and moved slower, and his little eyes peered cunningly between the bushes, and his ears pricked up and listened, for down the road in the distance he saw the missing link in the well forged chain of his plans, approaching, and with eager caution and much peering he stowed away his bundles under the leaves and moved down to a more convenient station nearer the road where he could watch and be ready for the right moment.

Silver had risen from her knees with a face in which sorrow and purpose were having their way. She went straight to her desk and drawing pen and paper toward her began to write rapidly.

"Dear Athalie:—

"I have been praying ever since I came that you and I might learn to love one another and be real sisters. I have always wanted a sister. But I see that I was mistaken and that cannot be. So I am going away at once to show you that I really wanted to love you. I haven't wanted to hurt you in any way, nor to steal father or anybody or anything away from you. You said a good many things in your excitement that hurt me, but perhaps you won't remember them when you get calmer. I want you to know that I forgive you, and want you to be happy. As you say, I have had a happy home and you haven't. Besides I am the older and ought to go if one of us must, so it is all right. Only if I go, Athalie, please make father happy. He is lonely too. And I shall always pray that God will give you joy.

Sincerely, Silver."

She folded it and wrote "Athalie" across the back then drew more paper toward her and began again. This one was harder to write. It began:

"Dear Father:—

"Something has happened since you went to the city this morning that has made me know that it is not right for me to stay with you any longer. Not now, anyway. You know how sorry I am about it, but I feel this is the only thing to do, so I am going to do it quickly before you return. That will be easier for us both. I have not time to tell you all it has meant to be with you, to know I have a father, and to be sure I have your love. I shall be rich in that knowledge always now wherever I am, but I feel that Athalie needs you more than I do, and that you never can be everything to each other while I stay. You will see it this way too after a little and know that I did right. Perhaps some day it will be right for me to come back, and then I shall return with joy. Now I am going away and I am not going to tell you where just yet for I am not quite sure of my plans, but as soon as I am located I will send for my trunk which I will leave packed and ready, and then perhaps you will write and tell me you forgive me for going away without seeing you. I just felt that I could not quite bear the good-bye, precious father! I love you. Don't feel bad. Love Athalie.

Silver-Alice."

Silver paused a moment to wipe away the tears that would gather in her eyes as she wrote the words that meant so much to her, then she began another note.

"My dear Mr. Bannard:—

"I am writing in great haste and dismay to let you know that I cannot fulfill my promise to go with you to the orchestra concert in the city tomorrow because I find that I must suddenly go away. It is a deep disappointment to me for I had looked forward to the pleasure eagerly. I cannot tell you what pleasure I have found in our work among the little children on the Flats, nor how disappointed I am that I shall not be able to carry out our plans for this winter. I am not sure how long I shall have to stay. It may be quite a while. It is hard for me to have to go, and go thus suddenly without bidding my new friends good-bye, but I know I am right in going at once.

"I thank you for what your friendship and your sermons have meant to me while I was here, and I hope that some day I may have the pleasure of seeing you again.

Very Sincerely, Silver Greeves."

This letter she sealed, addressed and stamped and put in her pocket. Then she arose and quickly folded her garments from the closet, laying them in her trunk, opened drawers and boxes and stowed everything away with expedition. There was not very much for she had not brought a great deal when she came. In her little suitcase she put the few things of immediate necessity, locking her trunk, put on her hat, and a long silk wrap over her simple dark china silk frock and taking her suitcase slipped across the hall with her letters. Her father's she laid on his chiffonier where he would be sure to see it as soon as he came in, and Athalie's she slipped softly under her door. It was all still in the hall when she went down. She longed to speak to Anne and Molly before she left but knew she might upset all her plans if she did, so she went swiftly out the door.

"Well, now, where's she going?" announced grandma from her window, "a suitcase in her hand too! And this time of day!"

"Maybe she's taking her suit down to the cleaners," suggested Pristina.

"They would send for it if she phoned," said Harriet.

"Well, she's pretty independent. She doesn't take any rich folks airs on herself," said Cornelia. "I wonder why they never go together. They're not so far apart in age."

When Silver reached the station she found that the next train to the city did not stop at Silver Sands, being an express, its only stop was at the Junction two miles below.

Looking at her watch she found that there was plenty of time to walk it. She knew the way well for she had driven there several times with Mr. Bannard. She mailed her letter to Bannard at the station and took the back street for several blocks to avoid the centre of the town as she did not care to be noticed in this sudden flight.

When she came to the last cross street she turned into the main road again and crossed the bridge. She hoped with all her heart that Bannard would not happen to be out in his car and come across her. She felt she could not bear that. But if he did she would just have to tell him how things were. She somehow felt sure she could make him understand.

But nobody came along to disturb the afternoon peace. The white road stretched like a ribbon ahead under arching trees, the crickets sang under the browning golden rod, a cicada grated out his raucous voice, the wild asters, white and pink and blue and yellow nodded in the soft breeze with their first opening clusters of stars, and yellow butterflies whirled dreamily, lighting in the dusty grass by the roadside. It was beautiful and still. It looked so dear. She could not believe she was going away from it all, out into the world alone. Her soul cried out to return, to destroy her notes and unlock her trunk and try to make some other finish to this day that had begun so gorgeously and was ending so sorrowfully. But something drove her feet forward in the way, and she passed on around the curve of the road till Silver Sands and the way to the Flats were out of sight and the tears were blinding her eyes so that she could not see ahead.

"Good-bye, dear home!" she whispered softly to herself. And then just ahead of her, an old man hurried hobbling into the road and waved his hand.

"Oh, lady, lady! I'm so glad you come by. There's a little child up there in that shanty dying I'm feered. It fell over the rocks an' broke its leg, an' done somepin to its insides I guess, an' I'm runnin' to get the doctor. Won't you just go up there lady and stay with the baby till I git back? I sha'n't be five minutes. I just cantta bear to leave it all alone."

Silver looked at her watch and glanced up the hill. There was plenty of time if the man hurried, even if it took him ten minutes, for the train did not leave the Junction till ten minutes of five and it was just as well that she should not get there till train time, lest someone might see her.

"Yes," she said, "but hurry! I must make my train." Then she turned and began swiftly to climb the hill while the old man began to run stiffly down the road.

The hill was steeper than she thought and the suitcase heavy but she managed to reach the little hovel in very good time, and stepping inside, rubbed her eyes to get the sunshine out for the room seemed very dark. She put down her suitcase and began groping across to find the child, pausing a moment to get used to the dark, when suddenly she felt the door shut behind her with a slam and something like a key turning in a lock.

In horror she rushed back, almost falling over her suitcase, and groped for the knob, but there was none. The door was fast, and when she pounded on it there were only hollow reverberations. It was so still in the little place that it did not seem possible that there could be anyone else in the room, even a dying child. Perhaps it was dead already. She felt so alone. Her heart was beating wildly. She tried to tell herself that of course the door had blown shut and a night latch had fastened it, but a night latch usually opened from the inside. It must be she would be able to find a knob when she grew calmer and could see better. She groped back to the door and tried once more, but with no better success. The door seemed smooth all over and fitted close. There was no crack for light to come in. Was that a step outside? No, she must have been mistaken. And yet—how strange! She had seen the man run down the road! But the child! She ought to be attending to it! Could it be that she had got into the wrong place? Were there two buildings on the hill? Should she cry out for assistance? It was not far from the road. Someone would be passing soon. Surely there was no need for her to be frightened. The old man would soon return with the doctor and then she would be set free.

She remembered her little pocket flash that she always carried in her handbag. She tried to find it and at last located it and touched the spring. The ray of light revealed the bare stone walls, the rude box, and huddled leaves, the empty fireplace, the frying pan, and cup, and a crust of dry bread. There was no child anywhere.

She examined the window carefully and found it firmly sealed. There seemed to be no implement with which she might attempt to break it open. She swept the room with the light and saw no possible way to get out. Her heart was fluttering so that her breath was labored.

"Help me, O Christ! Steady me! Show me a way to get out of here before it is too late!" she prayed. Then she advanced to the fireplace and turned the flash upward. The rough sooty stones loomed above her in irregular knobs, jogging out here and there, and above them, in the brilliancy of the speck of light, a branch of a tree, thick with leaves, waved backward and forward.

"There is always a way up," came the words in

memory from some famous story or sermon, she could
not tell which, but it thrilled her soul. It was not far
to the branch. Could she make it, up the slippery,
cobbled way? Was the space big enough? Could she
get her suitcase out too? She measured the distance
with her eye, noted the stones that stuck out. Would
they bear her? But how could she climb with a suitcase? Yet she must have it if possible. There was a
bolt of blue ribbon in her suitcase, a whole ten yards.
Was it strong enough to hold the suitcase if she tied
the other end around her waist and then pulled it up
after her? And supposing she made the top of the
chimney, could she climb down without breaking her
neck? Well, it would be better there out in God's open
than shut in this dark place where no one could see
her or hear her and perhaps she could climb the tree.
As for the suitcase she would do her best and then let
it go if she had to. But she must get out of here before
that man returned if he was the instigator of some
intention against her. If it was only some mistake of
a dead-latch she must find the child. It even now
might be crying with fear. She must work fast in any
case.

She hurried back to her suitcase, searched out the
ribbon, tied one end firmly to the handle, the other
round her waist. Put her purse inside the neck of her
dress, turned her wrap inside out and tied it firmly
over her head and shoulders to protect hat and dress
as much as possible, and flash in hand began her
perilous climb. It was a narrow place to squeeze
through. She put her suitcase up a couple of feet and
rested it on a ledge, supporting it with one hand as
she climbed, setting a foot here on a projecting stone,
putting a hand there in a crevice where the crumbling
plaster gave way before her touch. Slowly, painfully,
stopping for breath, cautious because one wrong move
might undo all, she crept on. Once she missed her
footing and the stone rolled down leaving her with
only one foot on a loose stone, and once the suitcase
slipped off suddenly jerking the ribbon around her
waist and almost bringing her down with it, but she
caught herself in time, and clinging to the wall prayed,

"help me! Help me! O Christ, give me strength! Give me steadiness!"

It was like those dreams that come sometimes, where we find ourselves crawling through an endless tunnel that grows smaller and smaller, and finally our strength gives out, we collapse and are stuck fast. Two or three times she thought she could not go on, and closed her eyes to rest. She could not look up because the dust and soot filled her eyes, so on and on she crept, coming to one place so small she could just get her head through, and was sure she could not go further, but finally managed to wriggle through, with the dead weight of the suitcase dangling after, hitting against the wall and bumping, impeding her upward way. Perhaps after all she would have to cut the ribbon and let it drop.

"Help! Help! O Christ—" and the blessed breath of air struck her face, and light. Real sunlight blinded her eyes. She was out! She caught a firmer hold, and just then the little flash light slipped away! She caught at it and almost lost her own hold, but could not get it. She heard it knock its way to the bottom of the hearth. Well, what matter! She would not need it now. Then she pulled herself free from the encasing wall and was out, head and shoulders above the little hut.

She paused to rest and look about. No, there was no sign of any other building. No sound of crying child. What did it mean? Down below she could see the road and there was no pedestrian on it. An automobile swept by going very fast, but it was not the doctor's car. Fear clutched her by the throat. She must get away at once.

She writhed herself up out of the chimney. It proved to be a mere knob above the low sloping roof. She had a struggle with her suitcase and almost gave it up once, but finally brought it forth, crushed at one side and badly scratched, but still intact, and then it was a comparatively easy thing to slide cautiously down the roof and drop carefully to the ground.

She was free! But she was trembling so that for a moment she could not move. Her hands and face were scratched and sooty, and her arms were bruised and sore. She looked up at the blue sky and her heart said quickly in a burst of joy, "Oh, thank you Christ!"

Then new strength seemed to come, and breath, and she flew away down the hill on the side where the undergrowth was comparatively light, got into the highway, and the sunshine, and saw that she was not pursued, gradually grew steadier, and began to straighten her garments, wipe off the soot and give more thanks to God. There was a long strip torn out of her crêpe de chine dress from hem to waist, an inch or two wide and left somewhere behind in that chimney, but what did that matter? She was free. Her shoes were scratched and dusty and not fit for a lady to take a journey anywhere in, but that was a small matter. One glove was split from wrist to finger and the other entirely gone, but what were gloves in a lifetime! She was on the road, some road. It did not look familiar and perhaps coming down this side of the hill she had missed her way, but there would be a train sometime, somewhere, and she would find it. God had set her free, and now she knew she had done right in coming away. God had helped her on and not let her be hindered to make a lot of trouble for everybody. She would be able to get to her destination and write back in due time to set her father's mind at rest. Then all would be well.

Half an hour's walk brought her to a small hamlet, but it was not the Junction. She had missed her way and missed her train, but they told her that a trolley line passed half a mile below and the cars ran every half hour. They would take her to her destination in less than two hours, and what did it matter? She lifted up her tired head, and went forward.

Chapter XXIX

GREEVES came home an hour earlier than he had planned, with it in mind to take the young people all into town to a concert that he had unexpectedly discovered. He stepped into the pantry and told Anne to have dinner ready by quarter to six if possible, and then up to his room to wash his hands and make one or two changes in his toilet.

No one seemed to be about though the doors of both the girls' rooms were closed. They were probably dressing for dinner or resting. There was time enough. He would not disturb them for another half hour. He stepped to his chiffonier and there lay Silver's letter. He read it quickly with a fear at his heart, and then again. Then tearing down to the library wildly he took up the telephone and called up the station. No, Miss Greeves had not taken a train from there. She had come in and asked about the train but when she found the next one only stopped at the Junction she had gone out again. No, they hadn't noticed which way she went. They were busy with some freight and they couldn't stop to watch every female that came into that station anyhow, they were busy men, they were.

Patterson Greeves slammed the receiver on, and stared at the wall. What was he to do next? She had taken a car to the city probably. He called up the garage. No, they had not even seen her. Bannard? Perhaps Bannard had taken her. He would find out if Aunt Katie knew.

But as he took up the receiver to phone, Bannard himself walked into the room having been let in by Anne, an open letter in his hand, his face white and questioning.

"Has something happened Greeves? I just found

this in the post office. Has Sil—has Miss Greeves gone back to her former home? What's the matter?"

Patterson Greeves turned a white, anxious face to the minister. "Upon my soul, Bannard, I don't know what's the matter! I just got this myself," and he handed over his letter. "I suppose it's another outbreak of that other devilish child of mine!"

"Perhaps Anne will know."

He rang and Anne appeared.

"Did Silver say anything about going out, Anne?"

"No, master Pat. I think she's in her room! I heard her there a little while back."

"She's not in her room, Anne. She's gone!"

"Gone, master Pat! Gone! Oh, that can't be! Why, it's not over an hour since she called to me something about a package she'd left in my room, a collar she promised to give me."

"Well, she's gone. Did anything happen, Anne? Anything especially out of the way."

"Miss Athalie," Anne had her hand over her heart, "I heard her crying and carrying on in one of her tantrums," she said anxiously.

"That's it! I thought so! Silver has gone because she thinks Athalie would be happier with her out of the house. She wanted to go once before and I wouldn't let her. Oh, my God!"

"Oh, master Pat, don't be a swearin' now, please. She was that sweet a Christian. Surely she'll come back."

"Why certainly," said Bannard eagerly, "we must find her and bring her back. *I* will find her. Let me phone for Barry to bring my car. He can take his car too. It can't surely take long to find her. She can't have gone far in this short time. What time did you say she spoke to you Anne?"

Suddenly they all became aware of Athalie standing in the door, her face stained with tears and white with recent emotion. A letter in her hand, a frightened look in her eyes.

"Is—Silver—here?" she asked in a scared little voice, as she looked around the room.

Athalie had been growing taller lately, and had

really lost a good deal of flesh. And now as she stood and watched them all as if she had heard what had been going on she looked fairly fragile. Her father turned on her with fury in his eyes.

"No, your sister is not here. You have driven her away, you little devil! Get out of my sight. I never want to look on your face again!"

With an awful cry like the rending of soul from body, a continued cry that screeched through the house as the scream of a moving locomotive through the night, Athalie regarded her father for an instant and then turning tore up the stairs screaming as she went. She flung herself with a mighty thud upon her bed and went into raving hysterics, but nobody paid the slightest attention to her. Bannard and Greeves had gone out of the house to meet the car, and Anne Truesdale was doing some telephoning for which the master had left orders, a message to Silver's lawyer, another to the city station where she was to be paged, a discreet word to the chief of police.

Barry met the two men half a block from the house and waiting only for a brief explanation of what he was wanted to do, went down the street on a dead run after his own car. The Silver house grew silent as the dead everywhere except in Athalie's room where loud cries and sobs continued to ring out, until grandma called:

"Come here Pristina, don't you hear something queer? It sounds like some animal in distress."

Lizette Weldon hurried up the five stairs to her bay window landing and turned her head from side to side to try each ear and identify the voice. An hour later, Aunt Katie, unable to stand it any longer quietly slipped through the hedge with her smelling salts and asked Anne Truesdale who was slamming things around in the dining room with pursed angry lips and streaming eyes, if she might go up.

"Please yerself!" said Anne, jerking a chair into place. "She's not worth it, the nasty little tyke! Let her cry herself sick if she wants. She and I are two people!"

So Aunt Katie went up with her smelling salts and

talked kindly in a low, soothing tone, but Athalie knocked the bottle across the room and took on more wildly than ever, and finally Aunt Katie departed with a sigh, saying to Anne in the kitchen as she went out:

"The poor thing! The poor wilful thing!"

The weeping kept steadily on for an hour longer. Then Anne's patience gave out and she went up with a glass of ice water and threw it in Athalie's face, but the girl only strangled and choked and cried on the harder, so Anne went down, half frightened and wondered if she ought not to call the doctor.

But at last the sounds died away, and Lizette and the Vandemeeters were able to get a little rest. It was growing very late but Greeves and Bannard had not returned. Anne sent Molly and Joe to bed, with instructions not to undress, but be ready for any call, and herself put out the lights and took up her watch by the front drawing room window. Once she thought she saw a face peering round the lilac bush, but she knew it must be her eyes after all the excitement so she put the thought away. By and by she dozed off and the town slept.

When the morning dawned and the sun finally penetrated the lilacs and shot into the drawing room window Anne Truesdale sat up and blinked.

"I must have dozed off," she said shamedly to herself, "I wonder if the master has come. I'll just slip up and see if that tyke is asleep."

But when she reached Athalie's room there was nobody on the bed. With a growing fear she hurried from room to room, thinking perhaps she had changed her bed as once before, but found no sign of her and on the pillow in her father's room was a little blistered note dramatically left open written large.

"Dear Dad: I've gone to find my sister. I won't come back without her. I'm sorry. Athalie."

When Greeves read that, a few minutes later, having come in with Bannard after an all night fruitless search, he sank his haggard face in his hands and dropped into the nearest chair.

"My God! What have I done to deserve this?"

"Dearie, dearie," said Anne to Molly, "he's swearin' again. I guess mebbe there's a pair of 'em. Mebbe she mightn't to be so much to blame after all, takin' after him as she does."

In the library the tray of breakfast that Anne had brought stood untouched.

"What shall I do, Bannard? What shall I do? I have lost them both—!"

"I tell you, man, you must pray! If you ever prayed you must pray now. Get down on your knees quick and tell the Lord you're a sinner. He's the only one can straighten this out."

And Patterson Greeves dropped down on his knees and prayed:

"Lord I have sinned! I have sinned against Thee and against both my children. It is right I should be punished but don't let them suffer. O Lord, forgive and help and save—!"

And while he prayed, the telephone rang. Bannard answered it.

"Is that you, father?" a sweet voice called that thrilled him with its familiarity.

"Oh, Silver is that you? Are you all right?" said Bannard his whole soul in his voice, and knew not that he had called her by her dear name.

"Yes, your father is here. We have searched all night for you. Your father is quite broken by anxiety. Is Athalie with you? Yes, she's gone. She apparently went sometime in the night. She left a note saying she had gone to find you and would not come home without you."

"Oh, the dear child! I'll come right home. I just got the message father phoned to the lawyer. I'm sorry I've caused so much trouble."

"Where are you now? The city? Good. There's a train in a few minutes that doesn't come through. You take it and I'll meet you at the Junction with the car."

Barry had come in while the conversation was going on and he turned a startled face to Anne in the doorway.

"Athalie gone?" he asked. "Aw, *gee!*"

Anne handed him the note that Greeves had

dropped on the floor. He read it with softening eyes, then turned to Anne and said in a low tone:

"Say, you get me a shoe or something of hers. I've got the dog here. He's good on following a scent. I'll see what I can do."

Anne obeyed and Barry departed with instructions for Anne to tell Bannard when he had finished telephoning.

Greeves was still upon his knees, his face buried in his hands. Bannard stepped over and put his hand upon the man's shoulder.

"Silver is found," he said gently, "she's coming right home on the next train. I'm to meet her at the Junction. Will you go with me?"

He had forgotten for the moment that Athalie was gone.

Greeves roused and stood up, his face white and deeply marked. There were tears upon his cheeks.

"I must go and find my other girl," he said hurriedly, "my poor wronged child!"

Chapter XXX

IT was growing light enough to see the way around her room when Athalie Greeves, making a queer, nasty little toilet of any garments she found lying around the room, and not stopping to even wash her poor swollen face, climbed softly from her window and swung herself down the pergola trellis, and to the ground.

She hadn't an idea of where she was going or what she was going to do. Her one thought was to find her sister. It had come to her in the long sobbing hours of the night that that was one thing she could do before she died to atone for all her misdeeds. She could find and give Silver back to her father and so show him that she had really loved him. For she did not doubt that she was going to die.

This strange, wild emptiness that filled her being, this utter weakness and collapse was unlike anything she ever remembered before except once when she was a very little child with the measles and had cried herself to sleep because Lilla was afraid to kiss her good night. Lilla had gone to a party and left her with the nurse. Lilla was afraid of catching the measles.

She stumbled down the gray morning street like a wraith in her rubber soled shoes. There was only one way to go, the way she had always gone on her pilgrimages, out through the town, the long sleeping silent street, and down the empty road to the bridge. She was a little afraid of the sound of the water under the bridge in the dark that way but what did it matter? She would be dead pretty soon and there would be plenty of things down there to be afraid of. This one thing she must do. Perhaps if she could get to the city she might find Silver somehow. She hadn't an

291

idea what a walk to the city would mean. And there were no trains so early.

So she walked on though the lifting night into the gray of the morning hardly able to see out of her swollen eyes, drawing each breath like a sob, stumbling and hurting her feet, crying out with the pain without knowing it.

She did not notice two shadowy figures a little way up the hill in the bushes nor hear a suddenly hushed whisper. She was walking as in a dream with only one thought in mind, to find Silver.

Suddenly as she swerved unsteadily around the curve of the road something large and solid and soft like a bag of sand seemed to come from somewhere up in the air and struck her on the side of the head. She crumpled like a lily and went down in the road, with everything growing suddenly dark again about her.

When she roused again she was lying on a hard place like the ground, only with stone walls all about her and a match was flaring in her face. She saw two ugly faces above her, one old and lined, with grayish hair and sagging features, the other round and hairy and wicked looking, and she heard the old one say:

"It ain't her at all. It's the other one!"

"I've come to find my sister," she piped up feebly, and then was gone again.

A long time after she seemed to see the two men sitting by a box with about an inch of flaring candle between them, and one was writing with a stump of pencil.

"Say they must put the money under the stone and go away back up to town and stay there or the girl won't ever turn up. Say thot, Jerry, and better make it twelve, it's no use havin' all the trouble without some returns. Seein' we missed out on the other gal make it twelve thousand. Not a cent less."

Later they stumbled out together and a rush of air brought a breath to her lips. She heard one say to the other as they went out:

"It beats me, Jerry, where the other one went. She must a ben a spirit fer I had her shut in an' padlocked and not a stone is touched. Nobody couldn't a come an' let her out fer the lock wasn't hurt. I don't know what to make of it."

Far off a dog was barking. It made her think of cool water with little darting fins, and a bank with mosses on it. Nuts falling down and red branches. A dog barking, coming nearer. Rushing feet, a heavy body falling. The dog barking wildly. Sounds of a struggling down the hillside, and then a wild piercing whistle sweet as thrushes. Where had she heard that whistle before? Ah! Now she knew. The day they went to the baseball game and Barry—it was Barry! If she only could call perhaps Barry would help her find Silver, but the sound stuck in her throat and came out a sob. There it was again, that sweet whistle, and the sound of an automobile horn down on the road. Voices. Someone coming on. Voices again!

"Mr. Bannard, come and help me tie up this guy. It's the old tramp that's been going around for several weeks. Got a handkerchief. Sure that'll do. Here you hold his hands. Buddie's got the other fellow by the seat of his pants. I guess he'll keep all right. They were sneaking round here looking mighty suspicious. I wantta see what they've got in that hut. Chief has been looking for a hooch still round these parts. It might be in there!"

Oh, why couldn't she cry out! They would go away pretty soon. There. The dog was coming nearer. He seemed to be just outside the wall. "Buddie, Buddie!"

Ah! The air again! The door had been broken open! She opened her eyes, gave a long shuddering sob, and closed them again. It didn't seem to matter now they had come. She hadn't found Silver, and she heard her father's voice! She had failed!

And then she heard Silver's voice. Was she maybe in heaven? No, heaven was not built of stone walls she was sure. She struggled with her eyelids once more and looked. It was Silver, looking down with that sweet smile. With all the power that was left in her body she summoned her will and crept to her sister's feet. It seemed a long way, though it really was only an inch or two, and she laid her tired hands around Silver's feet and pressed her hot lips to Silver's little dusty slippers. Then she slipped off again, this time she thought for good.

Till she suddenly heard Barry's voice. He was down on his knees beside her with an old tin cup of water.

"Say, kid, drink this, it'll do you good. And say, kid, brace up, you'll make it yet!" Then she looked up and they were all smiling, just as if they loved her, and her father took her hand and smoothed it. Why, he didn't hate her any more! The hate was all gone everywhere, just love left, and she was happy.

They left the tramp and his friend in the hut with the padlock securely fastened, and carried Athalie down to the car. She wasn't sure but that she was dead and they were taking her to her funeral, but she was happy, so happy. Barry and the minister had made a chair and were carrying her down the hillside, while her father held her hand and Silver carried her feet gently, under her arm. It all seemed so wonderful.

They put her in the car and drove her home, and laid her on a couch in the library while they all stood around talking, asking her questions that she couldn't answer. Barry was telephoning to the chief of police and the minister talking to Silver with that light in his eyes. Her father holding her hand and looking at her and saying: "Dear little girl!" Just like that! "Dear little girl!"

It was all just what she had dreamed a home would be.

Then Bannard:

"Well, I guess we'll go home now. You all need to get a good sleep, and then, well, 'tomorrow about this time,' let's celebrate."

Greeves looked up and smiled.

"That's all right Bannard, we'll do it, but I'd just like to begin now by saying that after this I belong to the Lord, soul and body. I have been a poor miserable sinner living for myself and railing out that there wasn't any God, but He answered my prayer when I was in distress, and now I mean to live for Him and for my children the rest of my days, so help me the God that I have blasphemed!"

Anne Truesdale, listening in the offing, said aloud to her soul:

"It's come, it's come, it's come! Th' verra windows of heaven is open. Praise be!"

Novels of Enduring Romance and Inspiration by

GRACE LIVINGSTON HILL

☐ 11506	THROUGH THESE FIRES	$1.50
☐ 10859	BEAUTY FOR ASHES	$1.50
☐ 10891	THE ENCHANTED BARN	$1.50
☐ 10947	THE FINDING OF JASPER HOLT	$1.50
☐ 2916	AMORELLE	$1.50
☐ 2985	THE STREET OF THE CITY	$1.50
☐ 6949	KERRY	$1.25
☐ 10766	THE BELOVED STRANGER	$1.50
☐ 10792	WHERE TWO WAYS MET	$1.50
☐ 10826	THE BEST MAN	$1.50
☐ 10909	DAPHNE DEANE	$1.50
☐ 11005	STRANGER WITHIN THE GATES	$1.50
☐ 11020	SPICE BOX	$1.50
☐ 11028	A NEW NAME	$1.50
☐ 11329	DAWN OF THE MORNING	$1.50
☐ 11167	THE RED SIGNAL	$1.50

Buy them at your local bookstore or use this handy coupon for ordering:

Catherine Cookson

For years a best selling author in England, Catherine Cookson's readership today is worldwide. Now one of the most popular and best-loved writers of romantic fiction, her spellbinding novels are memorable stories of love, tragedy and courage.

☐	11015	**LIFE AND MARY ANN**	$1.50
☐	2686	**FANNY McBRIDE**	$1.50
☐	2855	**ROONEY**	$1.50
☐	8174	**THE FIFTEEN STREETS**	$1.25
☐	10869	**LOVE AND MARY ANN**	$1.50
☐	10078	**KATIE MULHOLLAND**	$1.50
☐	10318	**THE MENAGERIE**	$1.50
☐	10355	**THE DWELLING PLACE**	$1.50
☐	10358	**THE GLASS VIRGIN**	$1.50
☐	10516	**THE TIDE OF LIFE**	$1.75
☐	10918	**FEATHERS IN THE FIRE**	$1.50
☐	10999	**PURE AS THE LILY**	$1.75

Buy them at your local bookstore or use this handy coupon for ordering:

Barbara Cartland's Library of Love

The World's Great Stories of Romance Specially Abridged by Barbara Cartland For Today's Readers.

☐	11487	**THE SEQUENCE** by Elinor Glyn	$1.50
☐	11468	**THE BROAD HIGHWAY** by Jeffrey Farnol	$1.50
☐	10927	**THE WAY OF AN EAGLE** by Ethel M. Dell	$1.50
☐	10926	**THE REASON WHY** by Elinor Glyn	$1.50
☐	10925	**THE HUNDREDTH CHANCE** by Ethel M. Dell	$1.50
☐	10527	**THE KNAVE OF DIAMONDS** by Ethel M. Dell	$1.50
☐	10506	**A SAFETY MATCH** by Ian Hay	$1.50
☐	10498	**HIS HOUR** by Elinor Glyn	$1.50
☐	11465	**GREATHEART** by Ethel M. Dell	$1.50
☐	11048	**THE VICISSITUDES OF EVANGELINE** by Elinor Glyn	$1.50
☐	11369	**THE BARS OF IRON** by Ethel M. Dell	$1.50
☐	11370	**MAN AND MAID** by Elinor Glyn	$1.50
☐	11391	**THE SONS OF THE SHEIK** by E. M. Hull	$1.50
☐	11376	**SIX DAYS** by Elinor Glyn	$1.50
☐	11466	**RAINBOW IN THE SPRAY** by Pamela Wayne	$1.50
☐	11467	**THE GREAT MOMENT** by Elinor Glyn	$1.50
☐	11560	**CHARLES REX** by Ethel M. Dell	$1.50
☐	11816	**THE PRICE OF THINGS** by Elinor Glyn	$1.50

Buy them at your local bookstore or use this handy coupon:

Bantam Book Catalog

Here's your up-to-the-minute listing of every book currently available from Bantam.

This easy-to-use catalog is divided into categories and contains over 1400 titles by your favorite authors.

So don't delay—take advantage of this special opportunity to increase your reading pleasure.

Just send us your name and address and 25¢ (to help defray postage and handling costs).